350

"WATCH MY BACK."

"Sure thing," Raphael whispered in a puff of fog.

Raphael crouched down next to Gideon so he could cover the garage as his bother slipped under the door. Raphael rolled in after him, standing up and covering what was visible of the garage with his automatic. Gideon started inching along the left wall, down the corridor toward the main room. Raphael followed. Each step brought more of the garage into view as Gideon swept his flashlight beam back and forth. Gideon felt his breath catch the moment the Daedalus came into view.

The thing was actually here!

He could hear Raphael saying something, and from the tone, his brother was more surprised than he was. Raphael had taken a few steps away from the wall, toward the machine. Gideon took a half step to follow him—

A spotlight blasted from the left side of the garage. Raphael's shadow stretched all the way to the Daedalus. Raphael was past the corner, near the center of the floor. Raphael, washed in white light, spun around, bringing his automatic to bear. He yelled at the people behind the light, "FBI, free—"

A dull thudding sound filled the room, the noise like an air hammer striking mud. Gideon's instincts took over and he hugged the corner, reaching around and firing at the spotlight. . . .

ZIMMERMAN'S ALGORITHM

S. Andrew Swann

DAW BOOKS, INC.

DONALD A. WOLLHEIM, FOUNDER

375 Hudson Street, New York, NY 10014

ELIZABETH R. WOLLHEIM
SHEILA E. GILBERT
PUBLISHERS

First Printing, January 2000
1 2 3 4 5 6 7 8 9

For Truffles

ZIMMERMAN'S ALGORITHM

$\aleph_0$

0.00
Thur. Jan. 15

LYAKSANDRO Volynskji stood in the parking lot of an abandoned Howard Johnson's, facing the nearby Interstate, watching the passing headlights slice out cones of swirling snow. His breath fogged as he wrapped a heavy leather coat around himself. The fleece-lined coat was the only example of Western decadence he'd allowed himself since coming into the U.S. back in November. Tonight he was glad he had bought it. After all the years he had spent in Tunis, he was not prepared for American winters, especially in upstate New York.

He leaned against a new Dodge pickup, the only vehicle in the parking lot. With the exception of the tracks left by the truck, the lot was a virgin field of snow.

Volynskji was on his third cigarette when the minivan he was waiting for pulled off the interstate, headlights illuminating Volynskji and his pickup. It drove into the abandoned lot, tires tossing up sheets of snow. It stopped facing him.

Volynskji tossed his cigarette aside.

The door slid open on the side of the van and a trio of

silhouettes walked in front of the headlights. "Mr. Smith?" asked the one in the middle.

Volynskji nodded and said, "Colonel Ramon."

Ramon gestured to the van and the headlights dimmed.

The three men Volynskji faced were all middle-aged, and all wore overcoats over dark suits. They dressed as if they wore some sort of uniform—unlike Volynskji who wore jeans, flannel shirt, and leather bomber jacket and generally tried to blend into the rustic setting he found himself in. These men looked out of place here, and Volynskji wondered if it was the best course of action to utilze them.

"I understand you require consultants in a security matter," Colonel Ramon spoke with a flat Midwestern accent despite the fact—Volynskji knew—that he had lived his entire life in El Salvador, until a few years ago when the Salvadoran government became a little too serious about investigating the excesses of the eighties.

Volynskji reached into his breast pocket and pulled out a brown envelope and handed it to Colonel Ramon. "A bank draft for an account in Costa Rica."

Colonel Ramon took the envelope and opened it. He tried to hide his reaction, but Volynskji saw his eyes widen slightly.

"That is half," Volynskji said. "The balance will be on delivery."

"What do you want delivered?"

"A mainframe computer, a special one."

"The catch is?"

Volynskji smiled. "The current owners may not want to part with it."

Sun. Jan. 18

The truck from Infinity Microsystems rode the Interstate alone and unhurried. It sliced through the Virginia night, rarely putting more than five miles per hour between itself and the speed limit. It was a customized Peterbilt eighteen-wheeler, painted the black and cobalt blue of the IMS logo. The trailer's roof was stainless steel, and had a few more vents than was usual.

Colonel Ramon knew that the truck was unique, and its cargo nearly so.

The Colonel sat in the cab of a more conventional Mack truck parked in the on-ramp's breakdown lane. It had been idling there for about ten minutes with its lights off before the Peterbilt passed.

Fifteen seconds after the Peterbilt passed by in front of them, the driver pulled it out onto the Interstate, following.

The Colonel looked ahead, at the brake lights of the Peterbilt's trailer. He watched the mile markers by the side of the road and after the third one passed, he picked up a walkie-talkie that sat on the seat next to him and said, "Now!"

About half a mile ahead of the Peterbilt, another Mack truck pulled out, angled across all four lanes, and screeched to a halt on the icy pavement. The Colonel could hear the Peterbilt braking even though they were a hundred yards back. For a moment he worried that they might collide—like the Peterbilt's driver, he wanted no harm to come to the contents of the trailer. Fortunately, the driver kept control of his vehicle.

When the Peterbilt reached a complete stop, Colonel Ramon's Mack angled in behind it to prevent it from backing away.

Colonel Ramon pulled a ski mask down over his face while the rear door of the other Mack flew open to disgorge a half-dozen men with similar masks, black military fatigues, and M-16 rifles.

The Colonel calmly stepped out of the cab, ignoring the Peterbilt's revving engine, the sound of breaking glass, and the short burst of gunfire as the team secured the cab of the Peterbilt.

There was one security guard on duty with the driver, and he was never really an issue. The Colonel briskly walked through a cloud of diesel fumes toward the trailer on his own truck.

Back down the road, beyond the rear of the trailer, two more of his men, dressed in reflective orange and wearing hard hats, were setting up flares and sawhorses across all four lanes of the Interstate, one car had already been stopped and was making an awkward turn for the exit.

When the Colonel reached the rear of his truck, the doors were open and the ramp down. Inside, three men were backing a Bobcat forklift out of the otherwise empty trailer.

He clapped his hands and his voice fogged as he yelled, "Get moving. That should be unloaded already."

The Colonel checked his watch and looked back toward the Peterbilt. The other team from his truck was on time. Two men handled a pair of bolt cutters and an acetylene torch, busily removing the barriers to the rear of the Peterbilt's trailer. The area between the two trucks was awash with the orange light and the twisted shadows cast by the torch. The Colonel could already smell the acrid smell of burnt paint and molten metal. It was harder to open than a standard semitrailer, both because of the heavy insulation, and the fact that there was some nominal security on it. Its cargo *was* worth fifty million dollars.

Not that Infinity Microsystems had ever expected anyone to steal it.

By the cab of the Peterbilt, the Colonel saw the IMS driver and security guard, facedown on the road, handcuffed and shivering. The guard looked to have taken a slug in the shoulder; there was a steaming black puddle under him.

Colonel Ramon thought things were going better than expected.

Behind him, the Bobcat rolled out of the trailer as the doors to the Peterbilt's trailer popped open. The men who had broken open the door rolled their tools away and set up a portable ramp.

The Colonel walked up behind the Bobcat as it maneuvered itself to drive into the trailer. As the little forklift mounted the ramp, Colonel Ramon looked past it to get his first view of their objective.

He stood next to the swung-open door of the trailer, and could feel hot, dry air blowing past him. Some of the heat radiated from the sputtering remains of the trailer's lock, but most came from vents in the sides of the customized trailer.

Past the Bobcat he could see the Daedalus, the only cargo. It sat braced in the center of the rear half of the trailer. Cables led from it to a wall that blocked off the forward half of the trailer, and a series of ducts emerged from the upper portion of the Daedalus to merge with the vents in the ceiling of the trailer.

The Daedalus resembled an industrial refrigeration unit. With the exception of the processing unit, which was a small box the size of four briefcases, that's what it was. From the exterior, all that was visible was the stainless-steel skin of the state-of-the-art refrigeration units which were needed to keep the core processor at twenty degrees below freezing.

Colonel Ramon could hear the Daedalus humming from where he stood.

Inside the trailer, two men carefully disconnected the vents from the Daedalus, and the sound of the refrigeration unit briefly intensified, accompanied by a dry, transformerlike smell. Then the noise died as the cables were detached from the unit.

The Daedalus was silent.

They were now in a race against time. Once the refrigeration units were cut from the power supply, the core temperature of the Daedalus would start rising, despite the near-impenetrable insulation around the superconducting core of the machine. When it reached five degrees below freezing, the ceramic processors in the machine would cease to function; if the core ever reached a temperature above twelve degrees Fahrenheit, the million-dollar chips that formed the heart of the computer would be irreparably damaged. That would take about twelve hours.

Colonel Ramon watched as the Bobcat rolled up to the Daedalus. The forklift strained to get the machine a half-foot above the floor of the trailer. The vents above didn't allow a greater clearance. It took about ten minutes for the Bobcat to move the Daedalus from the IMS trailer to the refrigerated trailer attached to Colonel Ramon's Mack. It was the longest part of the operation, and the time they were most vulnerable.

The computer was halfway home when Colonel Ramon heard a sound he'd been dreading. The whoop of a siren, back beyond the barricades his men had set up.

Ramon turned and started walking back in that direction. The blue flashers of a Virginia Highway Patrol car were drowning out the red glow of the flares. The officer had already gotten out of the car. He had the radio microphone in his hand and was trying to yell at his dispatcher and Colonel Ramon's men at the same time.

". . . Accident, the *first* thing you do is call emergency services, the *second* thing you do is report it—"

"Just happened, Officer." One of the men in the hard hats was saying. "We have a call in—"

Ramon rolled up his ski mask. As he approached, he smiled and asked, "What's the problem, Officer?"

The patrolman looked in his direction and said, "The problem is you have an Interstate blocked off, and no one reported the accident."

Ramon nodded, as if he understood exactly the officer's problem. "Things have been chaotic here—one hell of a mess. I guess everyone's been concentrating on the cleanup . . ." Ramon stepped past the barriers and held his left hand out to the officer. "Henry Anderson, Great Lakes Trucking."

The officer looked at him increduously for a moment, still holding the microphone in his right hand. After a moment he took Ramon's hand with his left. "Your men here said that they'd already reported it."

"They probably assumed that someone else had called it in." Ramon talked calmly, looking directly into the patrolman's eyes. He tightened his grip on the patrolman's hand as he spoke, and the moment before the man realized something was wrong, Ramon's fist slammed into his throat.

The patrolman let out a shuddering gasp, dropped the microphone, and collapsed to his knees. His right hand reached for the holster at his belt, but Ramon brought his boot down on the man's wrist, shattering the bone. The officer tried to pull his arm away, but Ramon still held him.

Ramon yelled at one of the men behind him, "Don't just stand there, grab his gun."

One of the men stepped forward and pulled the weapon out of the patrolman's holster.

The patrolman's struggles were becoming weaker. His breath was little more than a hollow wheeze.

Ramon called the other man forward and the two of them manhandled the near-unconscious and barely-struggling officer into the patrol car. The dispatcher was calling, trying to talk to the man, the voice was just starting to sound concerned. Ramon shut off the radio.

He drove the patrol car over to the breakdown lane just

on the other side of the barriers. Once it was parked, Ramon looked at the unconscious cop and felt for a pulse. "Give me his gun," he said quietly.

"What are you doing?" asked one of his men.

"What do you think?" Ramon said as he took the gun. "He can identify me."

Ramon put a single shot through the patrolman's left eye.

By the time the officer was dealt with, the Daedalus had been transferred and the IMS truck had been pulled over to the side of the road about a hundred yards ahead of the highway patrol car. The driver and the guard were both handcuffed in the back of the trailer.

The two Mack trucks pulled away from the scene, headed for Washington D.C., while behind them a half-dozen flares slowly guttered out. The theft had taken less than twelve minutes.

1:00
Thur. Feb. 12

DETECTIVE Gideon Malcolm sat at his desk, looking over the details of a search warrant when he heard Raphael's voice from behind him.

"Someone here call for an FBI agent?"

Gideon turned around. Before he was quite aware of what he was saying, he said, "What are you doing here?"

Raphael frowned. "So, Bro, the reason you called me on the phone rather than the District Liaison is because you *didn't* want me involved."

Gideon shook his head and stood up. "Come on, you know that's not what I meant."

"You know, if you don't want me here, I can just pack up and—"

Gideon grabbed Raphael's arm. "Come here, you bastard."

Gideon pulled him forward, and the two joined in an embrace that was half hug and half wrestling match. After they broke apart, Gideon said, "You could have warned me you were coming. I thought you were assigned to New York."

"I was—am. But your call gave me an excuse to come down and visit. I mean I haven't seen you since . . ."

"I know," Gideon said, the smile slipping on his face. *Not since Dad died.* He stood there for a few moments, unsure exactly what to say. For some reason, his older brother's presence here, now, made him uneasy. "So where are the rest?" Gideon asked.

"Ahh . . ." Now it was Raphael's turn to look uneasy.

"Come on, I told you what I needed on the phone. I called you because I thought I'd get a hearing and less interagency bullshit."

Raphael motioned to Gideon's chair and said, "Well, there's good news and bad news."

Gideon felt his heart sinking as he settled back into the chair.

Raphael perched on the edge of the desk. "Here's the bad news. There *is* no one else. The lead you have is not enough for the Agency to commit any resources. There aren't enough agents to go around, and there are already fifty or so working other angles of this Daedalus case."

Gideon shook his head. "I didn't know why I bothered thinking they might be more help than my own department. Sorry I wasted your time—"

"You're forgetting the good news."

"Yeah, what?"

"You got me." Raphael smiled at him. "I couldn't pull you a team, like you wanted, but I did get permission come down here myself as an official Bureau observer."

"Observing what?"

"What you got?"

Gideon picked up the warrant. "Like I told you over the phone, what I have is an informant named Lionel, and an address."

Raphael nodded. "And you're wondering why the Bureau is reluctant to spend manpower on the word of a two-bit crackhead?"

Gideon chuckled and shook his head, "No, Rafe, I already went through this with my Captain. Why did you think I called you and not the District Liaison? I am sort of curious why you came down—everyone else seems convinced that this isn't going anywhere."

"You have to admit, the Daedalus theft seems out of your guy's league."

Gideon nodded. "In Captain Davis' words, 'He probably saw the damn thing on *Nightline.*' So why *are* you here?"

"You seem convinced the lead's genuine."

Gideon picked up the warrant and grabbed his overcoat. "I know this much. Lionel might be a small-time street-level dealer, but so much illegal shit happens around him that he's never had to make up tips before. He's getting the same consideration from me if he's telling me about a fifty-million dollar computer or if he's telling me who jacked a car last week."

Raphael slapped him on the back as he slipped on his coat. "The *same* consideration?"

Gideon looked at his brother and gave him an embarrassed half grin. "Okay, I gave the boy an extra fifty."

Raphael laughed, "Bro, you been conned."

"So they tell me." He started walking past the other

desks and said, "Come on, let's get some dinner. I want to get on this stakeout by nine."

As midnight approached, Gideon and Raphael sat in a ten-year-old Dodge sedan about half a block away from an empty office building just the District side of the Maryland border. Most major city police departments had newer cars for their detectives, but most major cities weren't in the constant financial crisis D.C. was.

Gideon sat in the driver's seat, pointing a pair of binoculars at the building. They'd kept a low profile by shutting the car off, so the only heat came from the open thermos of stale coffee that sat on the seat between them. It didn't do much, because they'd opened the windows to keep the windshield from fogging up.

"It's five past midnight," Raphael said. "When do we give up on this thing?"

"Give it time."

"We've given it five hours already."

For just a moment, Gideon felt an irrational surge of resentment toward Rafe. It was as if he, along with everyone else he'd contacted, just couldn't believe that good ol' Gideon Malcolm would ever get close to something this big. It wasn't just that they believed—Rafe believed—that his contacts were small time. They were convinced that Gideon was small time.

It seemed that he was permanently a step behind his brother. His brother could hack it as a Fed where Gideon washed out during training. The ghost of that failure seemed to follow him everywhere.

Damn it, Gideon thought, *stay focused.* If something

happened and he missed it, that would be much worse than nothing happening at all. He sighed and resumed looking for some sign of *anything* unusual.

A gentle drifting of snow didn't do much to change the basic character of the neighborhood. The street was lined with empty storefronts, and the offices stared down at them with blind glassless windows. Even the liquor store next to them was boarded up. Gideon's Dodge might have been as beat up as any D.C. cop car, but here it was exceptional—one of the few cars parked on the street that looked like it ran.

Gideon tried to understand why Raphael wanted to give up the stakeout. If he thought logically about it, he had to admit that he himself had trouble imagining what anybody would be doing stashing fifty million worth of computer hardware in *this* neighborhood.

Raphael seemed to read his mind. "I told you, you've been conned."

Yeah, your little brother was had by a "two-bit crack-head." It was easy enough to believe that. But this had gone far enough that he didn't want to admit it. "Lionel hasn't steered me wrong in five years."

"Even drugged-out scumbags are mistaken occasionally."

More likely, perhaps, than your little brother being right about something? "Maybe these guys made us," Gideon said, staring at the building which remained as silent and unremarkable as ever.

"You're still convinced that there's something to the story from this Lionel guy?"

"There's supposed to be a pickup. The guy Lionel

heard this from someone who's supposed to hijack a refrigerated semi and meet the guys with Daedalus. Here. Maybe something queered the deal."

Outside, the wind whistled through the empty streets, carrying the smell of urine and spilled beer. A single car drove by them, the bass from the stereo shaking the shocks on the Dodge.

"Today's the day for it," Raphael said. "It just became Friday the thirteenth."

Gideon turned to him, lowering his binoculars. He felt a small chill, almost an evil premonition. "You're not becoming superstitious on me, are you?"

"Who, me? Never?" Raphael reached out and knocked twice on the dashboard.

Gideon returned to looking through his binoculars. The uneasy feeling didn't recede. He hadn't realized it was the thirteenth until Raphael had mentioned it. For all he thought that Lionel had fed him a real lead, he had a strong urge to give in and abandon the stakeout.

After all, he did have to admit that Rafe was right. What they were watching for was *way* out of Lionel's sphere of operation. Lionel was a street-level punk, the kind of guy who could tell you who sold junk to some OD in the morgue, or who was fencing TVs from the Holiday Inn. Raphael wasn't the first one to question why Gideon believed Lionel knew what he was talking about.

"He's not creative enough to make something like this up," Gideon whispered to himself.

"What's that?" Raphael asked.

"I said, let's wait a little while and see if the guy with the truck shows up. It was supposed to be Thursday night.

If he doesn't, we can serve the warrant and see if there's anything in there after all."

"Be great if there was something in there, wouldn't it?"

Gideon looked at Rafe. If there was any sarcasm there, it didn't show. But that wouldn't have been like Rafe anyway. The irritating thing was, Rafe was proud of him. Proud he'd made the force, even prouder when he'd made detective—even if D.C. robbery was not a glamorous assignment.

Never once was Rafe intentionally condescending to him. He was probably genuinely excited about the possibility of Lionel's tip actually panning out. The theft of the Daedalus was big news—the high-tech robbery of the century. Any cops—and any Feds—involved in its recovery would get an immediate boost to their careers.

Gideon wondered if it might all be wishful thinking on his part. Maybe Rafe was right and he had let himself be conned. The Daedalus theft had gotten enough airtime that Lionel—or the driver he was friends with—probably had seen enough of it to invent the story. Gideon wondered if, right now, Lionel was drinking, smoking, or shooting up the hundred bucks that he'd given him, having a good stoned laugh at his expense.

"Have you ever seen one?" Raphael asked.

"A Daedalus?"

"Uh-huh."

Gideon shrugged. And kept watching through the binoculars. "Just the pictures in the news, like everyone else. Oversize filing cabinet mated with an air-conditioning unit."

"Can't be disconnected from external power for more than twenty hours, or the chips fry—right?"

"Something like that. Lionel said that the guy was bringing a refrigerated trailer."

"That's how they hijacked it in the first place."

Gideon knew that Rafe was saying that Lionel would have known to add that detail. Everyone with a TV would know that the Daedalus couldn't last long without its massive cooling unit.

Nightline had gone into depth explaining the peculiarities of the Daedalus. The processors in the thing were made from a high-grade ceramic superconductor, as near room temperature as anyone had been able to get them— but they still needed to be kept at an unhumanly low temperature—minus twenty Fahrenheit. The computer itself was about the size of a stack of four briefcases. The rest of the thousand-pound machine consisted of refrigeration units and a backup power supply.

Twenty-five of the things had been built to date. They were the most powerful supercomputers ever created. They made a Sun Workstation or a Cray look like a pocket calculator.

And if anyone let the cooling system go, it would become a fifty-million-dollar paperweight.

"When you got the warrant for this stakeout, did you get one for Con Ed?" Raphael asked.

Obviously, if the computer was here, the thieves had to have it plugged in somewhere. Gideon had known that and had checked it out as soon as he heard from Lionel. "It didn't amount to anything. All they have is the meter reading from about six months ago."

"Six months?"

Gideon nodded. "The building's empty. They cut off the power back in August."

"What's that, then?" Raphael said. Gideon lowered his binoculars and looked at him. Raphael pointed toward the front of the building.

"What's what?" Gideon asked.

"By the front," he said.

Gideon raised his binoculars again, and turned away from the parking area where he had been concentrating most of his attention. The place was an old brick structure, and the window and front doors were boarded over with graffiti-clad plywood. The streetlights washed the stairs to the front, so it was hard to make out the small light that hung in the alcove just above the boarded-up entrance. Knowing where to look, though, Gideon could see a small cage set in the upper part of the doorway's arch. Inside it, a dim yellow light glowed. The bulb was almost lost in the sodium shine of the streetlight, but it was obviously lit.

"Good eyes."

"Power's supposed to be cut?" Raphael asked.

"*Supposed* to be." Gideon nodded. "Now do you believe we've got something here?"

"Something," Raphael said. "Though your informant probably handed you a meth lab."

Gideon hated to admit it, but his brother was probably right. He usually *was* about things like this. Irritating, but that was one of the reasons Rafe was the FBI agent and Gideon was just a District cop. The more Gideon looked at this old building, the more he wondered why someone would stash a supercomputer here.

But *something* was going on here.

Gideon set down his binoculars. "Okay, let's forget the truck. It probably isn't coming." He picked up the radio and called in his location, telling the dispatcher that he was going to serve a warrant on an abandoned building.

When he put the microphone down, Raphael asked, "Aren't you going to call in some backup?"

"As everyone points out, this is probably nothing. I haven't seen any sign of activity in there for the past three hours. I call for backup now, I'll get my ass reamed for wasting city resources."

"Uh-huh," Raphael got out and drew his gun.

Gideon got out on his side and looked at Raphael, "Observer, huh?"

He grinned and said, "Haven't been in the field in three years. Nice to get the blood pumping again."

Gideon shook his head and pulled out a Mag-lite from under his seat and drew his own weapon.

They walked slowly up to the building, Gideon watched the dead windows for any sign of movement, but nothing stirred, and no other lights showed inside the structure.

Raphael actually took the lead by a few steps. "I wonder if that light out front is on a different meter."

Gideon shrugged. "Drug dealers hijack power all the time. Someone could have wired a single room in this place, and didn't realize the front light was on the same circuit."

"So you do think we've got a meth lab now?"

"I don't know what we have." Gideon grinned at Raphael. "But we do have a warrant."

The building loomed over them as they approached. It was a five-story structure of red brick, the windows set into pointed arches. On the first two stories, the windows were boarded over with plywood. From there on down, the building was almost solid graffiti.

They reached one corner of the building and one spray-paint logo stood out. Gideon noted it in passing. It was a red Hebrew character, "א₀." *Since when do we have Jewish street gangs tagging walls?*

"We've been here for hours," Raphael whispered, his breath fogging in the cold air. "Maybe your truck pulled up around back."

Gideon followed Raphael as he ducked into an alley next to the building. The narrow passage was piled with trash and smelled like overripe sewage. They had to step over broken bottles, empty six-packs, used condoms, and someone's old spare tire.

They emerged where the parking lot's weed-shot asphalt wrapped around the building. Gideon noticed that most of the debris was pushed off to the side of the building back here. There wasn't any truck, but there was a crumbling concrete ramp down into the side of the building. It ended in a rolling garage door.

Gideon looked at the garage door, and glanced at Raphael. "Could we have missed a truck?"

Raphael looked down to where the lot curved around the building. "I thought you had the entrance covered?"

Gideon nodded. He had. There was no way they could've missed a truck showing up.

The lot behind the building was bordered on two sides by neighbor buildings. The fourth side, opposite their building, was a vacant lot hiding behind a rusty chainlink fence. A streetlight on a utility pole cast an artificial glow over the whole back lot, making it look like a stage set.

"There's only the one way back here," Gideon said. "Maybe it was already here when we arrived. It's got to be a bitch moving that thing."

"Would it take more than five hours?"

Raphael was right about that point. Reportedly, the thieves who hijacked the Daedalus had taken less than fifteen minutes to move the computer into their truck. Upon reflection, Gideon doubted that the transaction Lionel had told him about would take much longer.

"Come on," Raphael said, slipping down the ramp toward the garage door. Gideon followed, feeling the press of claustrophobia as they walked down the ramp, deeper into the trench it made in the ground.

When they reached the point where the bottom flattened out before the garage door, the ground to either side was above eye level. They couldn't see anyone approaching from the street now.

Raphael was kneeling near the bottom of the garage door. There was about a two-foot-tall gap because the door hadn't rolled all the way to the ground. Probably from someone forcing the old mechanism. The place was probably a haven to homeless squatters or junkies who'd jammed the door open.

"After you," Raphael said, "You have the flashlight."

Gideon knelt next to the gap and whispered, "Seems

quiet enough." Gideon crouched down, preparing to slip under the door. "Watch my back."

"Sure thing," Raphael whispered in a puff of fog.

Raphael crouched down next to him so he could cover the interior of the garage as Gideon slipped under the door. Gideon turned on his flashlight, rolled across the oil-stained concrete under the garage door, and stood up.

The place was cavernous, and what Gideon saw of it was empty. Unfortunately, the door was at the end of a short hall, and the walls managed to cut off the view of more than a third of the garage to either side. There could very well be a truck parked down here, out of sight.

Raphael rolled in after him, standing up and covering what was visible of the garage with his automatic. They both stayed still as Gideon moved the Mag-lite to illuminate the space in front of them.

The floor was at basement level, and the ceiling must have reached above the first floor. Steetlights filtered in from an unseen window, so everything outside the flashlight beam was illuminated in a pale yellow the color of urine. It was diffuse enough to reach the ceiling, and the far walls.

Directly opposite them was a gaping maw that was apparently for a freight elevator. He could see dangling cables caught in the flashlight beam.

Gideon started inching along the left wall, down the corridor toward the main room. Raphael followed. Each step brought more of the garage into view as he swept the flashlight beam back and forth.

The first thing Gideon noticed was a catwalk hugging the wall at about first-floor height. Windows were set into the wall just above the catwalk, streetlights shining through gaps in the wood boarding them over. A small forklift, a Bobcat, was parked by the wall, under the catwalk. Unlike the rest of the place, it looked new and in working order.

Even after seeing the forklift, Gideon felt his breath catch the moment the Daedalus came into view.

It sat a few feet away from the forklift, resting on a heavy-duty pallet. It was stainless steel, built like a tall five-drawer filing cabinet, with cooling vents coming out of the sides. One of the bottom "drawers" had been pulled out, revealing it as just a thin metal panel. Cables led out of the exposed interior of the machine and snaked around the pallet up to a few gray electrical boxes on the wall. Gideon could feel the hot dry exhaust from the machine on his face as he looked at it. He could hear the thing's cooling system humming to itself.

It was actually here.

He could hear Raphael saying something, and from the tone, his brother was more surprised than he was. Raphael had taken a few steps away from the wall, toward the machine. Gideon took a half step to follow him—

A spotlight blasted from the left side of the garage. Raphael's shadow stretched all the way to the Daedalus. Raphael was past the corner, near the center of the floor. Raphael, washed in white light, spun around, bringing his automatic to bear. He yelled at the people behind the light, "FBI, free—"

A dull thudding sound filled the room, the noise like an air hammer striking mud. Raphael fell backward, his head a bloody mess. Gideon's instincts took over and he hugged the corner, reaching around and firing at the spotlight.

The cover the wall provided wasn't enough. He heard several more of the dull hammer blows. The corner of the wall blew apart, spraying Gideon with concrete shrapnel. A shot slammed into his shoulder, and his hand spasmed, letting his gun fly into the garage. He tried to duck away, but another shot, or a piece of shrapnel, sliced into his leg. It suddenly couldn't support him, and he fell to the ground. He couldn't get his arms down to protect himself, and his head struck the concrete with the full force of his fall.

He blacked out for a few moments.

As he came to, he could see the garage was fully lit and filled with men in black jumpsuits and body armor. They ringed him and Raphael. One was staring at Gideon's belt. Gideon's badge was visible where his overcoat had fallen open. One of the men in black said, "Fuck, they're cops."

Gideon's vision was blurred and half focused. He might have blacked out again. When he opened his eyes once more, one of the men was looking closely at him, and Gideon could feel fingers on his neck. "This one's still alive."

Gideon heard the sound of a walkie-talkie from somewhere else in the room. A muffled radio voice said, "The operation is compromised. Move to our fall-back position. All unexposed units are being extracted."

Someone responded, "We copy that."

Past the man leaning over him, he could see the others

removing silencers from the compact submachine guns they carried.

Before he blacked out again, he heard the tearing sound of Velcro. He could just see someone peeling a piece of black fabric from the back of his neighbor's jacket. It revealed bright yellow letters, "U.S. TREASURY."

The last thing Gideon was conscious of was the sound of approaching sirens.

1.01
Sun. Feb. 15

GIDEON awoke to the sounds of two uniformed officers pulling a man with a video camera out of his room. Gideon had just opened his eyes, and for a few moments all he could focus on was the fish-eye lens of the camera, and his own reflection in it. He looked like hell.

Then one of the officers reached a hand over the lens, pushing the camera back. The cameraman didn't move quite as fast as the officer was pushing and the camera tilted back over his shoulder. The camera fell with a crash to the floor. "That's private property," the cameraman yelled as the two officers pulled him out of the door.

"And this is a private room," said a familiar voice from the opposite side of the room. Gideon turned his head, and felt the pull of tubes that went up his nose and down his throat. He wanted to spit up the foreign object, but he could only manage a hacking wheeze. He tried to raise his hand to his throat, but it was immobilized in a heavy cast.

Gideon managed to turn enough to confirm that the speaker was who he thought it was. It was Chief Conroy, which explained the cameraman. Every step Conroy took was controversial, if only because everyone thought of him as the token white on the force. Whatever he did, someone would accuse him of being racially motivated. The man had a lot more respect from inside the force than he had outside it. Very few D.C. residents, most of whom thought of the police as the enemy in the first place, understood why Mayor Harris dragged in some white guy from California to run the police department.

Gideon had to close his eyes. Waking up here, with chaos swirling around him, was disorienting enough to make his head ache. He felt light-headed, drugged, a sensation as if his body was tumbling through space with only the most tenuous connection to his head.

Outside, the reporter shouted, "This is suppression of the media!"

Gideon forced his eyes open to see Conroy shake his head and turn to one of the three staffers who'd accompanied him. Conroy waved at where the camera had fallen. "Get that camera—and an appropriately-worded letter of explanation—to that man's employer."

The staffer walked toward the door.

"And *empty* it first," Conroy added. The staffer nodded as he left.

Gideon tried to say something, but he found it too hard to talk. His throat was raspy, and there was a tube down it.

"Detective Malcolm?" Conroy approached Gideon.

Gideon shook his head. It was beginning to sink in, what had happened, why he was here. The memory was painful enough that Gideon tried to recapture the sense of floating disorientation he'd had before.

He had seen Raphael die.

He remembered his brother's death, and his mind wouldn't let go of the image.

Conroy shook his head, attempting to be sympathetic, and the sight only made Gideon angry. He tried to yell at him to get out, to leave him alone, but all he managed was a painful cough. All the anger and frustration balled up in Gideon's gut with no way out. He couldn't move, couldn't speak, and it felt as if the acid in his stomach would burn a hole in him all the way to the floor.

His vision blurred, and he closed his eyes.

Gideon felt Conroy's hand on his good shoulder. Gideon wanted to pull away, roll over, but he didn't even have the strength to flinch.

"I know," Conroy said. "It's an awful mess."

Gideon shook his head. He felt a wave of resentment for Conroy. Who the fuck was he to sympathize? Conroy must have sensed Gideon's sentiment, because he withdrew his hand.

Mess? Gideon thought. *It was a disaster. What happened?* He stared at Conroy, trying to will an answer from the man. *What the hell happened?*

Conroy took out a business card, and placed it on the nightstand next to Gideon's bed. "You can call my office if you need anything."

Gideon stared up at Conroy's face and felt a burning, unreasoning hatred. He wanted Conroy to feel just a little of what he felt right now.

Conroy turned and walked around the front of the bed and spoke. Gideon felt as if Conroy was talking through him, rehearsing a speech. It intensified Gideon's feeling that he wasn't completely here with Conroy, that he was watching everything from a great distance.

"What happened to you and your brother was a disastrous case of mistaken identity." Conroy looked up, past Gideon. The loss of eye contact made everything seem even more far away. "Apparently the Justice Department had custody of the Daedalus thieves about twenty-four hours after the computer was stolen. They kept their capture, and the recovery of the supercomputer, under wraps because the Secret Service wanted to run a sting operation to nab the 'terrorists' who contracted the theft." He shook his head. "I'm not surprised nobody informed our department about it, but I don't have any idea why no one apprised the Bureau."

Gideon felt his gut tighten in a knot. It was one thing to get taken down by the bad guys. That was a risk that he, and Rafe, accepted as going with the territory. The idea that this had happened because of some interdepartmental screwup was worse than infuriating.

"The papers are already talking about this in the same breath as Waco and Ruby Ridge. The Secret Service has promised me its own internal investigation, and there's talk on the Hill of a Congressional hearing."

Gideon closed his eyes. He wanted Conroy to leave. He didn't want to hear anymore. All he wanted to do was find that little corner of unconsciousness he had before these men had awakened him.

He heard Conroy say, after a moment, "We better leave him to rest."

Gideon was gratified to hear the Police Chief and his entourage leave the room. He was left mired in his own thoughts about himself, and Rafe, and the Secret Service, and what the hell went wrong.

After that, his only other visitor was a uniformed cop stationed outside his door to keep out reporters. He came in and ate what passed for dinner and told Gideon what a raw deal the Feds had given him.

Gideon just shut his eyes until the man went away.

There was no one else. Rafe was his only real family since his dad had died. There was his sister-in-law, Monica, but Gideon hardly knew her. They'd married after Raphael had moved to New York. Now she was burying her husband because he'd come down to "visit." Gideon suspected that she would blame him for Raphael's death.

Gideon found it pretty easy to blame himself. It had been his call, his tip. It should have been him taking the fatal shot. Rafe was the one with a decent career, a wife, a family. . . . Who the hell would miss the fuckup, Gideon Malcolm?

He couldn't sleep. He spent most of the time drifting through a haze of semiconsciousness. During one particularly lucid moment, when his self-loathing had reached a momentary nadir, he could hear a television from beyond the open door to his room.

". . . from the Treasury Department. While there was a federal warrant issued, there was no notification of local authorities. Beyond those basic facts, neither the Treasury Department nor the Justice Department have issued any comment. Attorney General Alexander Lloyd told the media in a press conference today, quote, 'This entire episode is a tragic accident, and I take full responsibility for it.'

"Elsewhere in the Capital, there is growing sentiment in Congress for a full investigation of the shooting."

The sound changed, and Gideon heard a different voice giving a sound bite. "It's clear here that some segments of federal law enforcement have gotten out of control. We have a federal culture that is completely without accountability. Congress abdicated its task of overseeing the executive branch when President Rayburn was elected . . ."

Gideon closed his eyes and tried to tune out the news broadcast.

Not only had he gotten Rafe killed, he had done it before a national audience. It was ridiculous, *Congressional hearings?* Christ, every problem D.C. *had* was because Congress was directly involved in the city government. Congress was why the city couldn't afford new police cars, or more and better-trained police officers. It was why the city government was constantly on the edge of bankruptcy—so much so that the city offices didn't have basic things like paper clips or staplers.

The haggard D.C. police department was a direct consequence of federal control of the District budget, and Chief Conroy—the white knight from the West Coast—couldn't do much about it.

Gideon wasn't one of the blacks who thought Conroy was part of some racial conspiracy, but he also wasn't one who believed that Conroy was turning the force around single-handed. As far as Gideon was concerned, as long as Congress was involved in city finances, *nobody* could.

The idea of a Congressional investigation of what happened came across as some kind of sick joke. What they would probably find was that Rafe had died because some bureaucrat in the city government couldn't afford toner for his fax machine, and never received the warrant from the Treasury Department.

But even as his consciousness slipped away again, he couldn't help thinking about the silencers.

1.02
Sun. Feb. 20

LYAKSANDRO Volynskji sprawled on the bed in his hotel room, remote in hand, flipping through channels on the television. He flipped through half a dozen before he settled on the local public television station to watch the *News Hour*. The Daedalus was still one of the leading news stories, along with calls for a Congressional inquiry.

Volynskji frowned when he saw that one of the feature stories would be about Colonel Ramon and the other men who had stolen the computer. He didn't like being reminded of that. Ramon didn't know his name, or the people he worked for, but he had seen Volynskji's face, and that was bad enough.

Fifteen minutes into the news, the phone rang. Volynskji picked it up, saying, "Are our friends listening?"

Volynskji was asking the caller how secure the phone lines were.

"As they always are," came the reply. If there was a possibility of a live tap on either of them, the caller would have simply said "yes" and hung up. Fortunately, the response meant that they were secure from everything but the government computers that filtered almost all electronic communications in this country. They were safe as long as they avoided certain keywords. Volynskji put down the remote and picked up a dog-eared computer printout. It was a highly classified list of words, ten pages long, three columns to a page. On that list were words like "Daedalus," "Volynskji," "bomb," and the name of the organization Volynskji worked for, the IUF, the International Unification Front.

As long as Volynskji and the caller avoided the words on this week's list, their conversation wouldn't be flagged by any government computers.

"This is a mess," Volynskji said. "You insisted on using the Colonel rather than have me bring my own people into the country. It is unlikely that we'll ever get another opportunity."

"I understand your frustration. Their capture wasn't anticipated."

"You, of all people, *should* have anticipated it."

"You know bringing any more of your people into the country would bring unwelcome attention to our operation, and the Doctor."

"Have you seen the news lately? I think there's more than enough unwelcome attention to go around."

"It's a screwup, but because it was the Colonel and not your people, your organization has remained out of the spotlight."

"If my people were involved, they wouldn't have been captured, and this travesty with your Secret Service never would have happened." Volynskji thought for a moment about the man on the other end of the phone. Volynskji knew he was a twisted and dangerous individual with many reasons to want the IUF to stay out of the spotlight in this country. "This was by your design, was it, friend?"

"No."

The flat denial only made Volynskji more suspicious, but he didn't press the point. "What about our equipment? The Doctor can't proceed without it, and we cannot go out and acquire another one now that everyone in this country is aware that we want one. Security on the existing items will become impenetrable."

"I know. The equipment is my problem now. I have a better chance the way the situation has developed."

"Okay. Should I return to the project now?"

"No, there're still a few things that need doing down here. First, you need to find the leak that led those two cops there. It didn't come from my end, so it must have been from yours."

"Thanks for your confidence."

"Word of the pickup got out somehow, before you were called off. The cops didn't know it was a setup, so the leak didn't come from inside the government."

"I've got you. What do you want me to do with any leaks I find?"

"Plug them, permanently."

"The cop?"

"Forget him for now. He's not a problem."

"What about the Colonel and his people?"

"Nothing. They aren't a threat to us and we need a distraction right now. Take care of the leaks."

"I'll do that."

"I'll be in contact." The phone hung up and Volynskji lay for a moment listening to dead air. He didn't like that man. He didn't like working with an official of the U.S. Government, even if this man had brought his people Doctor Zimmerman and the potential of her work. The fact that his people were beholden galled Volynskji. Now they would be beholden for the Daedalus as well.

On the TV, the show had changed to a program called *The McLaughlin Group.*

"Issue one," said the TV. "Gunfight at the D.C. Corral."

Volynskji watched as the host gave a synopsis of the shooting incident over the Daedalus. It was unnerving to think that it could have been him and his people in there, rather than a D.C. cop and an FBI agent. Volynskji had been warned off shortly after Colonel Ramon had been captured, but he could still picture himself walking into that trap. If it was his call, he would have called off the whole project by now.

"What is the political fallout from this shoot-out? I ask you, Pat."

"John, this is another Waco. We have another federal law enforcement agency going where it shouldn't go, doing things it is not qualified to do—and this time it isn't even the alleged 'bad guys' who are the victims. This just gives more ammunition to people who believe that the federal government has no business in criminal law enf—"

"Are you saying that Attorney General Lloyd should resign—"

The one woman on the panel interrupted. "From all accounts he's already abdicated. The Secret Service was out of control here. They should stick to guarding the President."

Volynskji tossed aside the remote and walked over to the bar. Digging around in the little refrigerator, he came out with a can of ginger ale. He stood by the small sink and thought about possible leaks. Not his people, but maybe Doctor Zimmerman's. He'd had a few of the technical types set up the transportation of the Daedalus, since they had the expertise in the computer. That was most likely the weak link.

"Issue two; Y2K Mark Two," called the TV host, interrupting Volynskji's thoughts. He watched the TV with some renewed interest.

"Everyone who owns a computer has been aware of the much ballyhooed millennium bug, known to the digital intelligentsia simply as 'Y2K.' However the attempted theft of a Daedalus supercomputer has brought to light what may be the true threat of the 21st century—digital terror."

The scene on the television was replaced by stock footage of people surfing the Internet. It showed scenes in typical offices, a library, and one of the popular Internet coffee houses. The host continued in a voice-over. "Item—A Tangled Web. The Internet, especially the World Wide Web, has undergone phenomenal growth. Internet connectivity is now a standard part of all computer operating systems and estimates are that nearly 90% of *all* computers in the U.S. spend some time connected to this data superhighway. But this information superhighway is a two-way street, while these computers are searching for data elsewhere, other parties—possibly with nefarious motives—can access those same computers. According to experts, the security on *most* computers is inadequate to deal with an intentionally malicious attack."

Volynskji nodded and wondered if this blustering Washington pundit had any idea what the words "digital terror" might actually mean.

"Item—Wall Street Meltdown," the TV continued. The voice-over talked over scenes of the trading floor in New York City. "Two months ago there was a panic as the Dow plummeted five hundred points in a single afternoon. Economists were quick to blame a crisis mentality on Wall Street that reflected no true economic factors. In the past few weeks, investigators at the Securities and Exchange Commission placed the blame for the downfall at the feet of an old demon—program trading. Despite safeguards placed in the eighties to stop an automatic sell-off if the market suffered a too-steep decline, *this* drop was the result of computers—not people—engaged in a flurry of selling. This was a repeat of the last program sell-off disaster, but this time with a new, underreported, and sinister twist. Several pension funds, along with two major brokerages, were infected with a computer virus. A virus that seemed otherwise benign, but whose presence prevented the programmed brakes from taking hold during the five-hundred-point drop." The scene returned to the roundtable and the host turned to his left. "Mort, I ask you, shades of things to come, or—"

Volynskji turned off the television.

1.03
Mon. Feb. 23

THE days Gideon spent at the hospital blended into a single, painful blur. Long stretches of second-guessing his walk into the Secret Service's trap, broken only by the physical discomfort of the nurses changing dressings on his leg, and draining the wound in his shoulder. Antibiotics and painkillers kept him semiconscious.

After the first few days they moved him into a room with a television, but most of the time he was too groggy to follow what was happening on it.

His memory of the news was a disjointed series of reports on his progress. Watching reporters talk about him was an alien sensation, like thinking of himself in the third person.

On the news, Gideon graduated from critical to guarded to stable. Though he, himself, couldn't identify any changes.

The one image that penetrated the haze of antibiotics was his brother's televised funeral. The broadcast caught him completely unaware. He was too out of it to realize what day it was, and it was several minutes in before he realized what he was watching.

On the TV he saw the flag-draped casket; officers in dress blues; Chief Conroy and Mayor Harris alongside the Director of the FBI; a series of speakers talking about heroic sacrifices . . .

No one said the words "screw up."

The first time he saw the funeral, televised live on CNN, all he could think of was that no one had bothered to tell him that they were burying his brother, and that he wasn't there. Halfway in, the nurses realized what was on TV and came in and shut it off. He protested, yelling until he was sedated. . . .

However, the following week gave him ample opportunity to see the images of the funeral again and again. By the day of his release he had seen his sister-in-law take the flag from Raphael's coffin about twenty-five times on seven different networks.

The last day, he watched it again, as part of a special on the whole Daedalus disaster. The tube was out of his nose, he had a fresh cast on his arm, and he was more lucid than he had been through most of his stay. Which meant that there was little reprieve from the numb sense of loss he felt, staring at the screen, at a funeral they didn't let him attend.

He watched the camera pan across the first row of the mourners. Next to Monica, Raphael's widow, stood Alexander Lloyd, the Attorney General of the United States. He was one of a half-dozen white faces in the crowd other than Conroy, and he looked very uncomfortable. Gideon thought he *should* look uncomfortable. He was probably there to offer some gesture of apology, but Gideon thought his presence there was in horrid taste. It gave the appearance of being some cynical attempt to re-claim the political capital Lloyd had lost when his agents shot up Rafe.

Gideon was glad that Lloyd never got up to speak. He could tell Lloyd's presence was a strain on most of the attendees. Gideon noticed that the Director of the Bureau stood far away from Lloyd, and carefully avoided refer-ring to him, or the Secret Service, during his short eulogy.

"*Damn.*" Gideon whispered.

As he watched the funeral, the door to his room opened.

Gideon turned, expecting to see an orderly with a wheelchair ready to take him down to a waiting taxi.

Instead, he saw Monica, his sister-in-law. He felt his breath catch and his hand shook the remote as he tried to shut off the TV. The remote tumbled out of his hand and clattered to the wall, dangling on its cord.

Monica stood there looking at him, her expression set into a hard mask as the TV continued with Mayor Harris' speech, "—a man who paid the ultimate sacrifice in the service of his fellow man—"

"Oh, God," Gideon said after a moment, trying to gather his wits about him. "I'm sorry." The words sounded so weak and lame as they fell out of his mouth. He wanted to say that he felt the loss, too, that he mourned for his brother as she did for her husband, but he couldn't bring himself to say it—

"You're sorry?" she said. She almost spit the words. "Is that it, Gideon? You're *sorry?*"

Gideon was at a loss. He felt himself tied up in a knot

of guilt and grief that kept his voice from working right. "I wish I could do something."

"Like what?" Monica asked softly. She looked around the room. Her face was angry, ready to tear into him, but her eyes were shiny with grief. She walked to a pile of cards and flowers that the staff had been piling on a dresser opposite the door.

Gideon watched her, and felt a need to justify himself. "From people on the force, the rest is just from people who saw me on the news."

Monica stood with her back to him. Her shoulders started shaking.

"Are you all right?" Gideon asked her.

"How *dare* you," Monica whispered.

Gideon sat up, but couldn't move any closer because of the cast on his leg.

"How dare you survive." She spoke so low that Gideon didn't know if he was meant to hear the words. Even so, he could feel them rip a hole inside him. What could he do? She was right. It was his fault. He was the one who should have died.

Monica turned around, and the hardness was back in her face, and her eyes were drier. "I came here because I knew Rafe loved you, and I know he would want—more than anything in the world—for me to forgive you—"

"You don't have to—"

"Let me get through this," she spoke through clenched teeth, harshly enough that Gideon winced. "I came here because it's what Rafe would want. It was a mistake. I'm not that strong." Her hands balled up into fists, and she pounded them at her sides as she paced in front of the bed.

"I look at you, and I don't see Rafe's little brother. I see the man who took my husband away."

Gideon looked down. He could feel the pulse in his neck, and acid burned in his stomach.

"Rafe would have hated this—that I can't forgive you—but I can't help but see that as your fault too."

"Maybe we should talk about—"

"*Talk?* Talk about what? How you lured Rafe here from a safe desk job, and led him in front of a firing squad?" Monica shook her head. "If you want to talk, talk to the vultures outside. It was a mistake for me to come here."

She forced her way past a cop pushing an empty wheelchair into the room. The guy looked over his shoulder at Monica leaving, then rolled the chair into the room. "Your ride home's here, Detective Malcolm."

Vultures? Gideon thought.

They wheeled him out to a waiting patrol car. He was wearing sweats the hospital provided, and he had a pair of crutches propped between his knees.

They had barely gotten him out of the door, when he was confronted with a sea of faces. Microphones and lenses aimed at Gideon as an officer forced a path through the throng. An orderly pushed his wheelchair after the cop, toward the patrol car.

The journey between the doors and the waiting car was only a matter of yards, but with the reporters in their way, the passage seemed interminable. All of them shouted

questions, talking over each other, not even leaving space
for breath between them, much less an answer.

"Can you confirm that there's a wrongful death suit
being filed against the Treasury Department?"

"Are you going to testify that the Secret Service fired
first?"

"The President has promised 'a full investigation,' do
you have any comments?"

"Do you intend to continue working for the D.C. Police Department?"

"Do you think there should be a criminal investigation
of the agents involved?"

It was worse when they actually reached the car, and
Gideon had to maneuver out of the chair and into the passenger seat. He felt vulnerable and under attack. He held
his head down and tried not to listen. He stared at the
progress of his feet across the asphalt. He pushed himself
along with the crutches, the reporters just barely staying
out of his way.

"How do you feel about your brother's death?"

Did someone actually ask that?

He managed to get both legs inside, and the orderly
slammed the door shut. Gideon watched out the window
and saw the orderly disappear in the onrush of people.

Microphones knocked on the windows as the driver
tried to pull away. He was forced to use his siren and rev
the engine threateningly to move reporters out of the way.
Even so, he had to drive out of the parking lot at a crawl
to avoid bowling over the press.

Gideon looked out the window and stared at the reporters as they passed. Some were still shouting ques-

tions, as if they somehow expected an answer. Gideon felt a pit inside himself and whispered, "I didn't know it was this bad." He wasn't referring to just the reporters.

The driver shrugged and blew the siren agin.

The police car went to Dupont Circle and took P Street northwest, toward the fringes of Georgetown. To his father's house. The place Gideon lived was better than most detectives—especially D.C. detectives. When his father had died, he had left Gideon and Raphael the house and some money. He and Rafe had come to an agreement; Gideon had bought Rafe's share of the house with Gideon's share of the money.

As the police car rolled up to his house, Gideon realized that he felt guilty about that.

The scene outside his father's brownstone was no better than the one outside the hospital. He didn't know if the reporters from the hospital had beat them here, or if there had been a press encampment lying in wait for him to come home.

The driver got out first, to help him out of the car. As soon as the door opened, the questions started again.

He tried to ignore the questions, and the press of people close to him. The cop next to him said something, but he couldn't hear him over the din.

Gideon concentrated on climbing up the steps on his crutches, one, two . . .

On the top step he bumped one of the reporters and one of his crutches slipped out from under him. He tumbled forward and his escort managed to catch him by his broken arm. The impact jerked him up short, slamming his teeth shut firmly enough to make his jaw ache—

"God*damn*." He choked the curse out through clenched teeth.

He spun around on the reporters. The patrolman started to say something. "Detective Malcolm—" The uncertainty in his voice showed he suspected what was coming.

Gideon swayed a bit on his remaining crutch. And the patrolman held out a steadying hand. "You bastards won't be satisfied until you have another dead cop on your hands!"

The reporters didn't seem at all taken aback by the sudden confrontation. One shouted, louder than the rest, "Do you have a statement about what happened?"

The question was a fist slamming into his stomach, the shamelessness of these people made him gasp, wordless for a few moments as they shouted questions about his brother.

The patrolman tried to pull him back toward his doorway, away from the confrontation.

"You want a statement—" Gideon sucked in a breath, "Here's your statement—"

"Detective," the patrolman whispered into his ear, "we're not supposed to comment about—"

Gideon wasn't listening. "You're a collection of shameless parasites drooling over my dead brother, and you're going into rating orgasms because it might be someone's fuckup. I don't want anything to do with any of you. I might be on disability leave, but I'm still a cop, and anyone standing on my property after the next five

seconds is going to be arrested for trespassing, harass-
ment, and anything else I can think of."

The bastards didn't seem to miss a beat. Someone even
called out, "What problems do you see in the coverage of
your brother's death?"

Gideon turned around, shaking. The cop handed him
his fallen crutch and helped him get his keys out of the
fanny-pack the hospital had given him to carry his pos-
sessions.

The cop helped him into the house and they slammed
the door on the reporters, whose only reaction to Gideon's statement was a slight retreat down the steps to the
sidewalk.

"Was that a good idea?" the cop asked him.

"I don't really give a shit."

The cop tried to stay and help him out, but Gideon was
in no mood for company. After a few minutes, the patrolman left.

Once he was alone, Gideon hobbled around the first
floor, pulling shades, closing drapes, trying to complete
some sense of privacy. The phone rang three times while
he was wandering around. After each time proved to be a
reporter, he took the phone off the hook.

He wanted to go upstairs to change, but he didn't feel
up to it. He collapsed on a threadbare couch that had been
in the same spot since he was six years old and closed his
eyes. In ten minutes he had fallen into an exhausted sleep.

Franklin Alexander Jones, Davy to his friends, sat in
his apartment sipping a beer and watching a woman
named Amber Waves ride some lucky motherfucker to

orgasm on his giant 29-inch television screen. This was the tenth day of him feeling sorry for himself. A hundred grand up in smoke. Christ, what a life.

Davy kept telling himself that it was a damn good thing that the Doctor had called off his end of the job. Otherwise, he might be as dead as that FBI agent. But the whole thing left a bad taste in his mouth.

Davy thought of that phrase, looked at what Amber Waves was doing on the screen, and started giggling. His beer dropped empty next to seven others on the floor by his end of the couch. He didn't stop laughing until a sour belch gripped him and tore the laugh apart.

"Oh, fuck." Davy raised his palms to his eyes and rubbed. He felt a wave of vertigo telling him that he was far more drunk than he'd given himself credit for. He shook his head, felt the woozy sensation of blood sloshing from one side of his brain to the other, and decided he needed to get out another six-pack to take the edge off.

He got up and staggered to the kitchen.

He should have known it was too good to be true. A hundred grand just to move this Daedalus computer thing out of the office building, north. Of course, that meant hijacking a refrigerated semitrailer, but that was Davy's specialty—semis and heavy construction equipment. He'd boosted everything from backhoes to garbage trucks. He had already picked out his transportation when they called off the job.

If it hadn't been over the phone, he probably would have slit the throat of the guy who told him. He'd like to cap the bastard, even though it was now all over the news that the Daedalus pickup was some goddamn Fed ambush—one he could have ended up in.

Davy leaned against the side of the refrigerator and opened it.

The thing was completely empty except for a single Chinese takeout container laying on its side, leaking sauce that had turned black and smelled like a dead rat he'd found once in a prison john. He needed to go on a beer run.

He opened the freezer door. Inside, sitting on a six-inch-thick layer of ice, were two ice trays and an old frozen orange juice carton. Davy took out the cardboard cylinder, flipped off the metal lid with his thumb, and shook out a roll of bills on the counter in front of him.

He stared at the wad of twenties for a few minutes, trying to get his eyes to focus. *Need to do a job soon. Running out of cash.*

He decided that he probably should go turn his cell phone and his beeper back on. He'd been out of it a little too long. He needed his regular customers to be able to reach him, or he was going to have go back to boosting cars—which didn't pay nearly enough to support him.

Back in the living room, Amber was moaning to a rhythmic soundtrack as Davy made his way to the end table where he had tossed his phone and his beeper.

He turned the beeper's sound back on, and looked at it to see what messages he'd missed.

Fifteen times, someone had left the number for *The Zodiac*. He knew the number, he'd taken calls there himself. Somehow, he knew it was Lionel calling. The little shit was in some sort of trouble. He couldn't think of anyone else who'd be calling his beeper twice a day from a strip club.

Oh, fuck, Davy thought. *What's gotten up his ass?*

He fumbled out the cell phone and walked back toward the center of the room. He swayed a little as he waited for someone to pick up. On the television, Amber Waves undulated under a scrolling list of computer-generated credits.

"*Zodiac,* Renny speaking—"

"It's Davy, Lionel there?"

"Wait a mo, man—" In the background Davy could hear seventies disco music blaring, and people shouting. He heard Renny shouting Lionel's name.

After a few minutes, he heard Lionel's voice. "Where the fuck you been?"

"Me? What's gotten into you, my man? You living at *The Zodiac* now?"

"Damn close. I need to hit you up for some cash—"

Davy shook his head and stumbled back toward the couch. He half sat, half fell, back into his seat. "Shit. You think I'm made of money? I ain't your momma, I'm not here to bail you out of every tight spot you get into."

"Look, the cops are looking for me, I haven't been able to get to my apartment since I saw you last. I've been crashing at—"

Davy rubbed his head, the blood was sloshing around again. "Don't give me your goddamn life story. Fuck, you know that job fell through on me. I'm strapped myself. If I don't pull a job out of my ass soon, I'm going to be living at *The Zodiac* myself."

"I need to get out of town, Davy."

"Yeah, so's everyone. D.C. sucks."

"I'm serious. They want me because of the fucking computer."

Davy sat up. "What you talking about?"

"The cops are looking for me 'cause of that goddamn shoot-out where you were going to pick up that thing."

Davy's vertigo was getting worse. "What do you mean they're looking for *you?* How the fuck do they know you have anything to do with it—fuck you *don't* have anything to do with it—"

"I don't know, man, but I need, like, three hundred dollars to get out of town."

"Why they looking for you?" Davy had an evil thought. "You didn't tell anyone about my little job, did you?"

"Fuck no! What kind of scum you think I am? I didn't tell the cops anything."

Davy's half-drunken mind had already figured out that Lionel was lying.

At first Davy'd thought maybe Lionel had let what he'd known about the job slip to someone else who was feeding cops information. Davy would like to believe that. After all, Lionel was supposed to be his *friend* from the joint. Lionel was supposed to be solid, if not very bright.

But now his asshole friend had pretty much accused himself of selling Davy over to the cops. Lionel had probably tipped off the cops that had gotten themselves shot up. No wonder the police were looking for him, and no wonder the shithead was panicking.

Davy did his best to sound calm and reassuring. "Yeah,

I know. Guess we better get together and talk." Davy felt
a burning anger, but he managed to smile as he said. "I
think I might be able to spare a couple hundred. Neither
of us want you being leaned on by the cops— You come
down here, okay?"

"Sure." There was the sound of relief in Lionel's voice.
"I knew you'd come through."

Davy nodded and shut off the phone. "Yeah, I'm going
to come though all over your ass, motherfucker."

Davy fantasized about how he was going to stomp Lionel, until the paranoia kicked in. What if Lionel was
completely in bed with the cops? What if Lionel was
coming here with a wire? Or worse?

Davy stood up, starting to wonder if he should get his
gun, or split town himself, when he heard someone
knocking on the door.

*Shit. No way he could have gotten here that fast. No
fucking way.*

Davy stood up and headed toward the entertainment
center. He tripped and fell on his face. He lay there a moment, stunned, head throbbing. In front of him the tape
had stopped and the television cast a blank blue glow
across the room.

As he pushed himself upright, he heard his front door
rattling.

The bastards were jimmying his lock. He crawled forward on his hands and knees and pulled a shelf of pornographic videos down so he could reach the Smith and
Wesson .44 Magnum that he kept hidden behind them.
His hands had just reached the gun, grabbing the barrel

instead of the butt, when an unfamiliar voice said, "I suggest you put that down."

Davy turned and looked up into the barrel of a silenced
automatic that looked much bigger than his chrome-plated
Smith and Wesson—probably because it was pointed at
him. He knew instantly that this guy wasn't a cop.

His fingers slipped from around the barrel of his gun,
and he backed off slightly, still on his hands and knees.
"What do you want?"

Two other men came into the living room, and stationed themselves to either side of him. They grabbed his
arms, hoisted him up, and dragged him back to the couch.
"You were contracted to do a job," said the man with the
gun. "Move a computer from one place to another."

While the gunman spoke, the man on his left pulled out
a small zippered case and opened it, setting the contents
out on the coffee table in front of them. The items included
a spoon, a hypodermic needle, a rubber hose, a Zippo
lighter, and several bags of crystalline white powder.

The man on his right pulled his arm out straight and
rolled up his sleeve. Davy tried to pull away, but the man
with the gun stepped up and pressed the silencer to
Davy's forehead.

"Who else knows about your mission?"

Davy stared at the kit the man to his left was prepping.
He had already spilled some powder into the spoon and
was melting it with the lighter. A sharp, slightly tinny
odor started to fill the air.

The man holding his arm took the hose and pulled it
taut around Davy's upper arm. Then, when it was
painfully tight, he grabbed Davy's hand in both of his and

forced him to make a fist. Davy noticed that all three men
wore latex gloves.

"Who else knows?"

Davy spilled his guts. He had no problem giving up Lionel after the bastard had given *him* up. The only thing he
didn't mention was that Lionel was on his way there.

Davy had some hope of the bastard showing up—now
he was hoping Lionel wore a wire, or was leading a
SWAT team. That might surprise these guys enough to
get them off of him. . . .

But as far as Davy ever knew, Lionel never came.

Lyaksandro Volynskji waited outside of Franklin
Alexander "Davy" Jones' apartment in his Dodge Ram
quad-cab. It took twenty minutes for his men to enter, do
their business, and withdraw. When the last of them got
in the truck and closed the door, Volynskji asked, "Are
we safe now?"

The man stripped off a pair of latex gloves and said,
"There's another man he called 'Lionel,' real name Kareem Rashad Williams. The police are looking for him."

"Who is he to us?"

"Drug dealer, apparently a friend of Mr. Jones. Mr.
Jones confided in him about the Daedalus, and Mr. Jones
believed that it was Lionel who informed the police."

Volynskji sighed. "Then we must find him, before the
police do."

The Dodge Ram pulled away from the apartment
building. On the side of the building facing the street, the
window to Davy's apartment was lit only by the blue
phosphor glow of a television watching a dead channel.

1.04
Wed. Feb. 25

GIDEON was sitting on the couch, watching the third episode of *General Hospital* he'd ever seen, when the doorbell rang.

He made no move to answer it, he had no desire to see any reporters, and he fully intended to remain sequestered in his house as long as his food held out. By then he hoped that the press would've backed off a little.

He turned the volume up on the remote, but too late to miss hearing a familiar voice call out, "Detective Malcolm."

"Damn it," Gideon whispered to himself. He turned off the television and grabbed the crutches that leaned on the couch next to him. The doorbell chimed again and Gideon called out, "Hold on!" as he levered himself up and began hobbling to the door.

The meeting was inevitable, but he had hoped that it might wait until he was off of disability leave.

It took a bit of maneuvering to open the front door one-handed while balancing on a crutch with his busted arm, but he managed to swing the door open on Captain Davis, who was accompanied by a dour-looking plainclothes de-

tective. Davis was a large man with thick hands who
looked more like a steelworker than a cop, the detective
with him was thin and about a head shorter than he was.

"Detective Malcolm," Davis said, "I would have called
first, but your phone seems to be busy. May we come in?"

Gideon nodded and lurched back a few steps.

Outside, past the Captain and his companion, Gideon
could see the mass of reporters—somewhat thinner now,
but still camped on his doorstep.

Gideon led them to the living room and let them have
the couch while he collapsed into a recliner facing them.
He didn't offer them anything, he didn't feel up to hobbling around to fetch drinks when this wasn't a social
call.

"What can I do for you?" Gideon asked.

"I hope you're feeling better," Davis said. "If you
aren't up to talking, we can come at a better time."

"I doubt there'll be a better time."

"My condolences about your brother," said the man
with Davis.

Gideon looked at him. "You are?"

"This is Detective Charles Magness, Internal Affairs."

Gideon looked back at Davis, and felt as if he was
being shot at again. "Why are you bringing him here?"

"Calm down," Magness said. "IA investigates every
incident where there's a weapon discharged. It's SOP."

*Yeah, standard operating procedure. Otherwise known
as "bend over, you're fucked."*

"There are a few things we want to go over—" Davis
began.

"Like this 'Lionel' who tipped you to the location of the Daedalus."

"Bastard," Gideon muttered. "Have you picked him up yet?" Gideon would've liked a few hours with Mister Kareem Rashad "Lionel" Williams alone in an interrogation room, preferably with a baseball bat. Not that he'd mention that to Mr. Internal Affairs here.

Magness shook his head. "No. Apparently Lionel went on the lam shortly after news of the shoot-out was made public. We were hoping you might provide some leads to his location. . . ."

The moment Magness said that, Gideon knew he was in for a very long afternoon.

He went over the whole shooting in excruciating detail for Magness. Not just the event—reliving Raphael's death—but the events leading up to it as well. The tip from Lionel, his attempt to get backup in place from the District's excuse for a SWAT team—which was refused—and his attempt to call in the FBI through his brother.

Magness made a few comments about the irregularity of the situation, but Gideon knew that they couldn't fault him for procedure. He'd jumped through all the right hoops and had done the right paperwork. Somehow, Magness' demeanor made Gideon feel as if he were still the one to blame for everything that had gone wrong.

After it had gone on for an interminable hour, Davis said, "I think that's enough. Why don't you go wait in the car. I have a few more things to discuss with Detective Malcolm."

Magness nodded and looked at Gideon as if watching
for telltale signs of guilt. "I'll probably have a few more
questions once you file your official statement."

I bet you will.

When Magness left, Gideon tried to suppress a smile
as he heard the reporters descend on him outside.

"Gideon," Davis said, once Magness had left. "The administration has some issues with your handling of the
media."

Whatever amusement Gideon had in Magness' plight
evaporated. The memory of his homecoming was fresh in
his mind. *What were the words I used? "Shameless parasites?"* He cringed inwardly at the memory. "I suppose
so." He'd hoped that his tirade would've faded from the
spotlight by now. Apparently, he had underestimated the
press' interest in a completely irrelevant temper tantrum,
and the District administration's interest in the Press' interest.

"Have you seen the papers?" Davis asked.

"No." Gideon's stomach sank.

"Yesterday's headline in the *Post,* 'Wounded Cop says
someone "screwed up," ' apparently they decided to clean
up your language. The *Times* has a picture of you waving
a crutch captioned, 'shameless parasites—' Did you actually club a reporter with a crutch?"

"He tripped me," Gideon said. "I lost my temper."

"Did you actually use the words, 'rating orgasms?' "

Gideon wasn't able to come up with an appropriate explanation. He tapped his cast against his crutch, shaking
his head. He felt the anger burning again, at the reporters,

at the bastard who set them up, at the men who shot them, and most of all, at himself.

"Gideon?"

Gideon closed his eyes and nodded. Through clenched teeth he said, "Yes."

"You threatened to arrest them?"

"Can you blame me?"

Davis sighed. "No. Not after what happened. But do the words, 'public relations disaster' mean anything to you? The only thing that mitigates your little tirade is that you went off on the media, which lies in the public affection somewhere between politicians and lawyers."

It felt as if Gideon had to physically swallow his anger to speak. Slowly, he started to say, "I apologize for—"

"*I* don't need your apology. I agree with you."

"Captain?"

"*But* . . . Look at the big picture. This is a damn delicate situation. Right now we have the public—the *national* public—on our side. This can mean a lot for our department."

Gideon stopped rapping his cast on his crutch. "I don't follow you."

"The administration has a chance to take its case directly to Congress with these hearings—"

"What hearings?"

"—we could finally get some decent funding for this department."

"What hearings?"

"There are going to be Congressional hearings investigating the incident. It's an opportunity for us to gain some sympathetic ears on the Hill."

That was the last thing anyone needed. Congress. Gideon couldn't believe that the body responsible for the crippling of the D.C. civic government would do anything but mangle a criminal investigation. They would probably end up giving immunity to the people responsible for the screwup that led to the shooting, all in the name of getting at the "truth." A "truth" that would be little more than a bludgeon tailored to club someone's political enemies.

"What do you mean, 'opportunity'?"

"First off—and this is coming down straight from the Mayor—you aren't to talk to any more reporters, period. You aren't to say anything to anyone that might lose us sympathy on the Hill."

"Oh, God," Gideon whispered.

"I don't like it either," Davis' voice softened. "But I'm not the one with the ultimate decision about what happens to you after you come off of disability leave."

Gideon's jaw was clenched so hard it ached. It was an effort to speak. "Is that some sort of threat?"

"That's just how things are. It's not worth it to fight the administration on this. You know that Congressional hearings are just a sideshow anyway, right?"

Gideon lowered his head. "Okay. I won't go around bad-mouthing the department."

"There's more."

"God help us. What?"

"Harris had his speechwriter prepare a couple of statements—"

There was a long pause before Gideon realized what Davis meant. He whispered, "Oh shit."

Davis reached into his breast pocket and removed two folded sheets of paper and set them down on the coffee table. "Look them over. First is a draft apology for that tirade yesterday. Second is an opening statement for when you're called before the hearings."

Gideon stared at the papers on the table. "I don't believe this."

Davis stood up. "Take some time to consider it. All we need is your approval, and they'll release the first one to the press. Call me sometime today or tomorrow to okay it."

Gideon nodded. He felt numb. He looked at the second statement, laying on the table, and asked, "Have they even scheduled these hearings yet?"

"There's going to be a press conference next Friday. That's when we expect the hearings to be announced."

"Wonderful. Nice to know the administration is a step ahead of Congress." It was hard to keep the irony out of his voice.

Davis sounded relieved. He stepped over and held out his hand. "Thanks for cooperating with this."

Gideon didn't take the offered hand. "Good-bye, sir."

Davis was quiet for a moment and finally said, "You're a good cop, Malcolm. I'm sorry this had to happen."

"Yeah, thanks. You know where the door is."

Davis stood a moment, apparently having run out of things to say. He walked off, leaving Gideon alone with the two statements. In the distance, he heard the front door close, and the sounds of massing reporters.

Gideon wondered if Davis knew how demeaning this all was. Asking him to mouth someone else's predigested political bullshit. He bent over and picked up the first statement. Glanced at it without really reading it, and decided that it didn't really matter what it said. They had his job in their hands, he pretty much had to call Davis back and okay the thing.

He balled up the statement and tossed it aside.

It landed on a short table next to his chair. On the table were the personal effects that he'd carried back from the hospital—his keys, a scattering of loose change, his wallet, and his badge.

Gideon picked up his badge. It had been clipped to his belt above his wounded leg. It was splattered with his blood. Maybe also with Rafe's.

In the dim daylight filtering through the curtains, the blood gave the appearance of being tarnish. Gideon slowly clenched a fist around the badge, until the tension made his hand shake.

He threw the badge against the wall.

1.05
Mon. Mar. 2

GIDEON held his cast awkwardly upright as his left hand rested on the Bible.

"Do you swear to tell the truth, the whole truth, and nothing but the truth, so help you God?"

Gideon nodded to the grand jury foreman and said, "I do."

He sat down and faced a panel of twenty jurors. It was a familiar position, part of being a cop, testifying before grand juries and criminal courts. Gideon had long ago lost count of the number of times he had been subpoenaed to testify. It was always a somewhat nerve-racking experience, whether it was a grand jury or a trial.

This time was worse than usual. He kept going through the shooting in his mind, racking his brain thinking of the hundreds of things that he should have done, or shouldn't have done, anything so it would have ended with a result different than the one that had actually happened.

The more he had thought about it—after the shock of Rafe's death had withdrawn enough for him to consider the details of the event—the more it seemed that there was something wrong with what had happened. The news kept reporting fewer Secret Servicemen involved than he remembered. The men in the building were in contact with teams outside, Gideon remembered the radio traffic. Then there was the fact that they'd been armed with silenced weapons. Most bizarre to him was the memory of the men pulling black Velcro covers off of their jackets to reveal the yellow letters "U.S. TREASURY."

Gideon would've thought that the men weren't Secret Servicemen at all, if it wasn't for the Attorney General taking the heat for the fiasco.

Gideon kept thinking of Monica, her grief, her all but accusing him of shooting Raphael himself. Could he trust his own suspicions, or was he only trying, somehow, to find someone to blame other than himself?

He felt sweat rolling down the back of his shirt as he sat down. Here, with the grand jury, at least there wouldn't be a defense lawyer calling him a liar. All he would have to do was answer the prosecutor's questions. . . .

That would be bad enough.

The prosecutor shuffled a few papers and said, "I'll try to make this brief."

Gideon nodded. *Thank God for small favors.*

"I want to ask you about what happened in the early morning on February thirteenth of this year. Do you remember what you were doing then?"

Gideon swallowed and tried not to think of the jurors staring at him. "Yes, I was on a stakeout."

"With Agent Raphael Malcolm of the FBI?"

"Yes."

"Why was he there?"

"I felt the Bureau would be interested in a lead I was following up."

"A lead on the possible location of a stolen Daedalus supercomputer, correct?"

"Yes."

"You then had no knowledge that there were already suspects in custody and the computer had been recovered."

"As far as I knew, no one did."

"Agent Malcolm was related to you, wasn't he?"

"Yes, he is—" Gideon sucked in a breath. "Was my brother."

The prosecutor nodded. "Why was he with you, and not some other FBI Agent? There is a liaison that the DC Police Department normally works with, isn't there?"

"Yes." Gideon felt cold, the sweat under his shirt had become like ice on his skin. Were they going to accuse him of causing Rafe's death, here? What could he say if they did? Could he deny it? He couldn't even deny it to himself. "I went through my brother because I thought I'd have a better chance of getting an expedited hearing. I had a specific date, after which the Daedalus was going to be gone, who knows where. I couldn't wait for the liaison to sift through his priorities and kick it upstairs when he felt like it."

"What was the Bureau's reaction?"

"There wasn't one. They felt the same as the department. The tip I was working off of wasn't credible enough to assign the manpower I requested."

"But they assigned you Agent Malcolm?"

Gideon nodded.

"Why did they do that?"

"He—" Gideon's voice caught a bit. "He requested the assignment."

"So it was you and Agent Malcolm, your brother, alone on this stakeout?"

"Yes."

"You *had* managed to get a warrant to do this?"

"Yes, Judge Bachman, based on an informant's tip."

The prosecutor nodded again, as if he was making some sort of point. "Who was this informant?"

"His name is Kareem Rashad Williams, his street name is I ionel. A small-time drug dealer."

" 'Small-time drug dealer?' But you believed him when he gave you information on a theft worth fifty million dollars?"

"Based on my prior experience with him, I thought he was credible. He had no reason to make up something like that."

"No one else seems to have shared your view."

"That was why we were alone—"

"Why didn't you call for backup when you decided to go into the building?"

"By then I suspect we didn't believe Lionel either. It was after midnight and since no pickup had shown for the computer, we didn't expect to find anything."

"Now let me see if you can walk us through what happened, step by step—"

That was what they did, in excruciating detail. Gideon felt as if every step he took had half a dozen questions attached— Why did he do this? Why didn't he do that?

It seemed to be hours before they reached the ambush that had taken Rafe's life.

"Now," the prosecutor asked Gideon, "what were Agent Malcolm's words as he turned toward the light?"

"He said, 'FBI, freeze.' "

"He was holding his gun at the time?"

"Yes."

"It was then that the shooting began?"

"Yes."

"As he spoke?"

"Maybe during, things were going fast—"

"During?"

Gideon nodded.

"Did you both return fire?"

"I did, I'm not sure about Raphael. I think the first shot hit him before he could do anything."

The prosecutor shuffled his papers and looked back up at Gideon, "I think that's about it."

"But—"

"Thank you," said the prosecutor.

Gideon didn't have a chance to object; they were already bringing in the next witness. He stood up, and seemed to feel the world lurch underneath him. The prosecutor hadn't asked him anything about the men who'd shot at them. Gideon had no chance to mention silenced weapons. . . .

As he walked out of the room, he couldn't help thinking that there was something *very* wrong going on.

A gentle snow was drifting down on Washington as Senator Daniel Tenroyan was taking his regular lunchtime stroll around the Mall. It had been three years since a triple bypass, and he had become religious about his exercise. Every day that Congress was in session, he made two complete circuits around the Mall during his lunch hour.

He was passing the baroque pile of stone that housed part of the Smithsonian when he noticed someone sitting on a bench about thirty feet away, watching him intently. At first Tenroyan thought it was one of the homeless people that dotted the landscape in D.C. But as Tenroyan approached, and the man stood, Tenroyan recognized him.

"D'Arcy?" Tenroyan said.

Another step and he was certain. He was facing Emmit D'Arcy, President Rayburn's national security advisor. The last time he had seen D'Arcy, it had been from across the table at a Senate Intelligence Committee briefing.

The short man pushed his glasses back on his nose and said, "Let's walk for a while."

Tenroyan felt uncomfortable next to D'Arcy. The man had the reputation of being the most active proponent of black covert operations since William Casey. Tenroyan had gained a deep distrust of such things back when he was a Congressman and had served on the House-Senate Committees for Iran-Contra. That had left a bad taste in his mouth ever since. He felt that it was that bungled intelligence operation that kept Ronald Reagan's presidency from achieving what it might have.

Tenroyan walked next to D'Arcy, but he refused to start a conversation with the man.

"I understand that you're having a press conference this Friday."

"Yep," Tenroyan said. He looked up to watch the flags snapping around the base of the Washington Monument. Tenroyan had a Coolidge-like reputation for being laconic, and it came in handy when dealing with hostile reporters, and anyone else he didn't trust. He had a motto, *don't engage the devil in conversation.*

"I understand you're going to chair this committee on the Secret Service incident."

"Yep."

"The Administration wishes to cooperate with the investigation."

Then what are you doing here? Tenroyan thought.

D'Arcy continued as if he heard Tenroyan's thought. "I just wanted you to know that there are some sensitive issues tied up in this. If the hearings turn into a fishing expedition, some uncomfortable things could be made public."

Tenroyan stopped walking and turned to face D'Arcy.

D'Arcy kept going. "I don't know if you remember Operation Firewall—"

Tenroyan nodded. He did. It was just a few years ago, when the Internet was a big new thing, and people on the Hill were running around terrified of it, passing blatantly unconstitutional legislation like the Communications Decency Act. That atmosphere bred the largest "sting" on the Hill since Abscam.

The little-reported "Operation Firewall" was a Secret Service project to test the security of the computer networks run by Congress and a half-dozen other civilian agencies. Their forays broke into most of those systems, revealing gaping security holes, as well as nearly fifty

Congressional aides who were using government computers for illegal purposes from credit-card fraud to child pornography.

"I'm breaking security by telling you this," D'Arcy said, "but the NSA had a hand in the operation—"

Tenroyan snorted and shook his head. That news ranked up there with the fact that Bill Clinton had improper sexual relations in the White House—ugly, somewhat disgusting, but no real surprise.

Tenroyan didn't like the idea, but as a member of the Intelligence Committee he knew that the ubiquitous nature of the net made it nearly impossible to impose restraints on domestic espionage when it came to computer traffic. The Internet was a giant web spanning the globe, and the NSA was the giant spider straddling the network. Legend had it that every signal on the net passed through the NSA's computers at least once.

"I'm telling you," D'Arcy continued. "Because I have access to all the Firewall data that wasn't made public."

"Get to your point." Tenroyan was losing patience with the man.

"I just wanted you to know that there are thousands of gigabytes of data that would be embarrassing to many people still sitting on the Hill, especially those in the leadership."

Tenroyan took a step back, feeling anger building. "Son, are you threatening me?"

D'Arcy was an incredible actor. He actually looked shocked at the accusation. "No, no—I just want you to know that there are probably areas that would be better left unquestioned, or you might inadvertently open all of

Firewall to public scrutiny. It would be as much of an embarrassment to the Administration and the NSA as it would be to Congress."

"I see," Tenroyan said.

"I'm glad you do," D'Arcy slipped off his glasses and Tenroyan was struck by the thought of how much the man resembled Peter Lorre. "I want you to know that I'll always be available to help steer you away from any embarrassing revelations." D'Arcy wiped off his glasses and replaced them. "It's been a pleasure talking to you, Senator."

"I wish I could say the same."

D'Arcy left the Mall, walking down Fourteenth, where Tenroyan saw a black Ford Taurus idling behind the concrete traffic barriers. He watched as D'Arcy got into the car and it drove off.

What do they have on me? Tenroyan thought. *Pornography, certainly.* At one point or another Tenroyan had downloaded smut off the net. It wasn't all that much, and it was all normal and heterosexual—but anything pornographic related to the net was the kiss of death. In the public's mind, it was all child pornography or bestiality. . . .

Worse than that was the possibility that they had his e-mail. He had, years ago when e-mail was still a new thing, carried on a torrid written relationship with a woman who wasn't his wife. It was all virtual, he had never even met the woman. But he knew that if any of those letters were made public, his personal life would disintegrate, and his political life would become impossible.

He had ambition, but he wasn't a Bill Clinton. He couldn't see himself pressing forward inexorably, not caring what scandals turned up in his personal life.

For the first time since his triple bypass, Tenroyan didn't complete his circuit around the mall. He turned his back on the Washington Monument and walked back past the Smithsonian, toward the Capitol Building.

1.06
Tue. Mar. 3

AT eight in the morning, Kareem Rashad Williams, aka Lionel, walked down Twelfth Street in Brookland. He walked with an exaggerated swagger, staring at each passerby, as if daring anyone to make something of him. He looked at everyone as if he wanted them to start trouble, trouble he'd enjoy finishing. It was Lionel's crazy look, and he always used it when he was scared shitless.

He hadn't slept more than six hours in the past week. He hadn't gone home—hadn't even gone back to *The Zodiac*. He'd been walking the streets of Washington since he'd found Davy.

Now Davy's cash was almost gone. What the fuck was he going to do?

It was one thing knowing that he'd tipped a cop—a cop and a Fed—into a world of shit. He could care less about what happened to Detective Gideon Malcolm and his brother, that was the cop's own lookout.

But *Davy*, that was too fucking close to home.

Davy had been a little guy who'd boosted cars for a living. He and Lionel had been buddies since they'd shared a six-month stretch together. They'd been released the same day with fifty other small-timers that the District couldn't afford to house. The two of them had been tight since then.

Davy had been the ambitious one. While Lionel had been nickel and diming as a street-level dealer, turning to the cops for extra scratch, Davy had been moving up and out. He'd gone from boosting cars and chopping them, to boosting heavy equipment and truck hijacking. Davy had been talking lately about becoming a regular wiseguy. He had talked about taking down loads of everything from cigarettes to VCRs. He had talked about the special job that was going to land him a hundred grand all for himself.

Lionel thought Davy just talked too damn much.

But Lionel was beginning to think that God was getting him back for ratting on Davy. Christ, why did Davy have to tell him about that one job? Why'd he have to keep repeating the fact that he was going to make a hundred grand just for delivering a refrigerated truck—

Lionel had felt all too justified in giving the whole deal over to Detective Malcolm. Davy hadn't needed to rub his face in the hundred grand, more money than Lionel was going to see in his entire street-peddling life. The one concession that Lionel had made for friendship's sake was he'd held out for an extra fifty bucks before he gave over the address.

Then things had gone to shit.

First, Davy had come over the night before the job and gotten drunk on Lionel's couch telling him how the Doctor with the hundred grand had pulled out of the deal thinking there was some sort of setup. Lionel had spent the entire evening in a panic thinking that he'd blown the job and not only was Davy going to find out—and maybe have his mob friends put a hit out on his good friend Lionel—but Detective Malcolm was going to show up for his fifty bucks because nothing'd been going on at the address Lionel had sold him.

Then the next day, he'd heard about the mother of all setups. He had heard about the whole damn thing on the news, Davy there with him hungover and staring at the TV screen. For fifteen minutes, all Davy could do was shake his head. Lionel had gotten the gut feeling that Davy had known, that he was going to draw down on him right there while Lionel's gun was on his bed under a pile of underwear. But all Davy had said was, "Guess it was a good thing they canceled the job, huh?" Then he had turned to Lionel and grinned at him. It was such a fucking irritating grin that Lionel'd wanted to cap him right there.

But he hadn't.

It wasn't long before Lionel's little tip-off began haunting him. For a while he was crashing at friends and at *The Zodiac* trying to keep a step ahead of them. It lasted a while. Then his money dried up, and with it, most of his friends. It was in desperation that he tried to lean on Davy for some cash, maybe enough to get out from under this heat he was feeling.

When he'd gone to Davy's to see him about the money, he'd almost turned around and left before he entered the building. There was something about the whole setup he didn't like. The more he had thought about it, the more he didn't like the way Davy had sounded on the phone. He'd stood out on the street, paranoia gripping him for the better part of an hour.

Lionel knew then that Davy knew. He could feel it in his gut that Davy had seen through him and was waiting up there with his chromed Magnum to blow his old friend Lionel away.

For half that hour, Lionel was going to leave, find a way to split town broke. The second half, the hard ass in him took over and he decided he wasn't going to let any assholes, Davy and cops included, put the fear on him.

When the street had cleared of the last occupied car, an idling Dodge pickup, Lionel raced into Davy's building, his hand on the butt of his nine millimeter.

Lionel had decided that Davy was not going to get the drop on him.

Davy hadn't.

Lionel had his gun out before he'd reached Davy's floor. He took the steps slow, expecting an ambush at every landing. He made it fine to Davy's door . . .

The first sign that something had happened to Davy—the door hung open, spilling dead-blue light into the hallway.

Lionel pushed the door open with his gun, still worried that Davy might be waiting to whack him.

"Davy?" he called, pointing his gun into the apartment. "You all right in there?"

No answer.

Lionel stepped slowly into Davy's apartment until he could see the whole living room—the TV on, showing a blank digital-blue screen. Across from it—the couch. On the couch—Davy.

Lionel knew what had happened the moment he saw

Davy's rolled eyes and the rubber hose around his right bicep. The smack was rank in the room, the kit strewn across the table in front of Davy.

Davy had shot himself up a bit farther than he'd been ready to go.

Lionel stood in the center of the living room, pointing a gun at Davy as if it was all a trick, as if his old friend was about to jump up and whack him for selling him out.

Davy didn't move, didn't breathe.

The fucker was stone dead.

It took a few minutes to register.

Afterward, after Lionel lowered his gun and took a step or two into the apartment, the real nasty part of it had begun to sink in.

Davy'd never done heroin before. Something Lionel *knew*. Lionel would've been selling the shit to him otherwise. Just looking at Davy lying there, Lionel could see that there weren't any tracks on the arm with the hose. The kit on the table was brand-fucking new. The spoon didn't even have soot marks.

Two words in Lionel's mind, *"Set up."*

Someone else shot Davy up. Not Davy's wiseguy friends. Phony ODs were too fucking elaborate for the mob. It began coming down on him. Detective Malcolm shot down, Davy dead with a needle in his arm—

Took no genius to figure who was on the short list to be next. Lionel stayed around only long enough to liberate what cash was immediately obvious, then he got the hell out of there, making sure the door was closed and locked behind him.

Afterward, he'd hit the streets and tried to think.

His thinking had involved at least three liquor stores. Lionel's memory was a little fuzzy on that point right now. He was close to the end of his rope.

What the fuck was he going to do?

The words kept running through his mind. He couldn't get rid of them. He thought of leaving town, but Davy's money was just about gone now. There was a grand or two back in Lionel's apartment, but he knew if he stepped near the place, he'd end up with a needle in his arm like Davy. He thought of going to the cops, but, Christ, the cops might want to whack him for what happened to Malcolm.

He passed a news vending machine. In it was a copy of the *Post* with the headline, " Wounded Detective Testifies Before Grand Jury." Lionel caught sight of a picture of Detective Malcolm.

He stopped and thought, *Maybe this shit's still worth something.*

Enough to get out of town.

Gideon was doing one of a set of half-dozen exercises that were supposed to help rehabilitate his injured leg. The flesh had healed into a mass of tissue that left a long concave scar where a large strip of the calf muscle had been chewed by shrapnel.

The muscles in that leg were weak, barely strong enough to support his weight more than a few minutes at a time.

He was lying on the floor, his bad leg angled above him and shaking with fatigue as he counted to ten. On five he was about to give up.

The phone rang.

Gideon let the phone ring as sweat poured down his forehead and stung his eyes. There weren't many people he wanted to talk to. Chances were, it was another reporter. The calls weren't nonstop anymore, but there were still one or two a day.

He didn't move to get it. Even if it wasn't a reporter, there wasn't anyone he wanted to talk to this early in the morning.

When he got to seven, his answering machine got the call. He heard the beep, then a strung out voice.

"Yeah, yeah. Malcolm? This you?"

Gideon cursed and let his leg drop. With the notoriety of the shoot-out, it was only a matter of time before he started hearing from his share of cranks. The only surprise was that they hadn't joined with the reporters earlier.

He needed to change his phone to an unlisted number.

"It's Lionel " the voice continued.

Lionel? He suddenly recognized the voice that was hiding under the stressed-out breathlessness. Gideon tried too fast to scramble to his feet. His bad leg gave way, and he fell on his ass.

Lionel kept talking, breathless and sounding as if he was in a daze. "You interested in some info, man? Better deal than last time—"

Gideon pulled himself across the floor, toward the corner table with the phone.

"You want to know something about the fuckup with the goddamn computer, be down at Metro Center, noon. Bring at least tw—three hundred bucks with you."

Gideon grabbed the phone cord and pulled the whole

thing off the table. The answering machine fell, springing the tape loose to scuttle across the floor.

"Hello, *hello?*" He was too late, he was talking to a dial tone.

"Fuck!" He slammed the receiver down on the cradle.

Everyone and their brother in the department had been looking for Lionel since the whole fiasco went down. The guy was a minor street-level dealer who occasionally heard shit that was good enough to make a bust out of—which meant the fucker had no ties to *anyone* and could vanish into the D.C. underbelly like a rat into a garbage dump. No one knew anything about Lionel, what he was doing, where he was—

Now the fucker who had gotten Rafe killed was calling him, trying to cash in on whatever it was he knew. . . .

For all that he wanted to cap the bastard himself, Gideon knew that he wanted to know what it was that Lionel was trying to sell. What he might know about the Secret Service sting that had killed his brother.

However much he hated the fucker right now, he knew that the information would be worth three hundred bucks to him.

He looked across at the clock on his VCR. It was nine o'clock.

He pushed himself up onto the couch and called Captain Davis.

"Captain? I think I've got Lionel. No—I have to be there. . . ."

*   *   *

An aide carrying a handful of papers burst into Colonel Gregory Mecham's office shouting, "Sir, Mother has dropped us a flag on a hot target."

Colonel Mecham looked up from his desk. He didn't wear a uniform; in that he wasn't much different than the other twenty percent of the National Security Agency that were on active military duty. The aide bursting in to his office was one of the people monitoring SIGINT, the NSA's primary, and most overt, mission.

Mecham pushed aside the file he was looking at and waved the man in while he fumbled to remember the fellow's name. "What've we got?" The man had to be new, otherwise he would have just forwarded the data to him. As far as the vast majority of the NSA staff was concerned, all the fax and data lines at Fort Meade were ironclad secure. Mecham was one of about half a dozen people who knew that Mother might be compromised. That was such a sensitive bit of information that command had made the explicit decision not to alter any internal procedures for fear that such a change might inadvertently reveal that the systems might have a security breach.

"It came in on a routine keyword search of telephone traffic—"

"Let me see," Mecham said, holding out his hand for the papers. The man—Gerhard, his name was, Mecham finally remembered—handed over the printouts. The paper was slightly greasy, an effect of a coating that prevented copy machines, faxes, or optical scanners from reading anything more than a fuzzy black image from the pages. Even with that security precaution, the printouts were prestamped with the legend, "Destroy after use."

The printout was from a voice recognition program, and it bore the transcript of a call from a pay phone in Brookland to a Georgetown residence at 8:17 this morning. It had taken Mother about twenty minutes to parse the call through its decision tree and flag it for attention.

The message was ranked about as high priority as Mother could assign, "Vital, immediate attention." Mecham studied the papers letting his eyes scan the highlighted keywords. "Malcolm . . . Lionel . . . Computer . . ." Something about those words, combined with the destination of the call—the address in Georgetown was highlighted as well. Then Mecham saw who lived at that address.

"Gideon Malcolm . . ." he whispered, beginning to see what this intercept was.

"Sir?"

Mecham waved at his visitor. "Thanks for bringing this to my attention."

Gerhard walked out. Mecham didn't explain the significance of the intercept to him. Instead, he reread the transcript two times, committing the words to memory. Then, without the pages leaving his sight, he picked up a phone that was firmly bolted to his desk—one of the few outside lines that he knew was confirmed secure.

The line didn't even ring once as he put the call through.

"Sir?" Mecham asked.

"What is it?" asked Emmit D'Arcy.

"We have a situation with regard to Zimmerman—"

"Yes?" Mecham heard the breathless anticipation in D'Arcy's voice. Mecham knew that D'Arcy was hoping that someone had finally turned up Dr. Zimmerman. Even so, Mecham knew enough about the missing Doctor—and more importantly, the Doctor knew enough about them—to doubt that any lead on Zimmerman's location would ever come from Mother.

"Mother identified someone as associated with Zimmerman. Name's Lionel. We have a transcript of him setting up a meeting with Detective Gideon Malcolm."

"*That* Detective?"

"Apparently he has some information to sell."

"Where's the meeting?"

Mecham told him.

"Anything more to the transcript?"

"No, sir."

"Do you have any notes about this, any memos, other records?"

"No, sir."

"That's good. Keep me apprised of the situation—but take no action yourself."

Mecham nodded and hung up the phone. Then he slowly fed the transcript into his shredder.

1.07
Tue. Mar. 3

LIONEL sat on the Metro, passing stop after stop, waiting for the shit to hit the fan. He had been on the trains almost constantly since getting on in Brookland. Half the time he had a plan in his head, get the money from the cop, get back on the train, and make for the airport.

The other half of the time he was feeling his gun bite him in the gut where he'd shoved it in his waistband, and watching the people who got on and off the train. He studied each face as if it belonged to someone who might want to kill him. It was nuts, but he felt like he was being watched. He had that feeling every time he got on the Metro. It had to do with the cameras at every stop. Today, it was worse. Every time he looked up, he saw Davy's glassy eyes staring at him from behind the lenses.

He had changed trains a few times, and had gone as far as Arlington, just to avoid someone following him. But those damn cameras were everywhere, making him nervous.

The people on the train made him nervous, too. Fortunately, none of them chose to sit by him. His psycho stare was giving him some space.

When they reached Metro Center, he raced to the door and bumped into a lawyer type—three-piece suit and all. Lionel might never have noticed the guy if it wasn't for something the guy carried—keys, pens, Lionel couldn't tell—stabbing him in the hand.

"Pardon," the man said, without even looking at him. Lionel wanted to tear into the bastard, but the crowd leaving the train had already separated them.

"Fuck out of my face," Lionel yelled at the guy, through the closing doors of the train. Frustration was thick enough to make him sweat. He pushed aside a woman who was just a little too close to him and muttered, "Lucky shit. Don't know how lucky . . ."

The train was pulling away, and the motion ignited a wave of vertigo that sent the inside of his head spinning. The walls were about to close in on him.

Lionel stumbled out onto the platform. Cradling his hand, which was burning like a motherfucker, he looked at it, and all he saw was a red welt where something had scraped across the skin. Just a scratch, but it hurt like the asshole had driven a spike through his hand.

The cameras *were* watching him.

Him specifically. He saw them pan after him as he moved. The concrete ceiling seemed incredibly far away.

Lionel began to sweat, and felt real terror. His heart seemed to race, trying to smash through his rib cage. . . .

His hand, the one that didn't burn, began to drift toward the gun.

They were here, he could feel it, knew it with a certainty. The sharpness of the knowledge matched the razor clarity with which he saw the platform. Everything, the benches, the poster ads, the train pulling away, was torn out with a bold relief and colors bright enough for his eyes to ache.

And the people, everyone on the platform, stared at him with Davy's dead gray eyes.

Someone called his name, and Lionel knew it was death, come for him.

Gidion called out, "Lionel," again.

Lionel was normally nervous and shaky, but Gideon had never seen the guy looking this strung out. Gideon approached on his crutches, and made it a half-dozen steps before Lionel reacted.

When he did, he surprised the hell out of Gideon.

Lionel looked dead at him and shook his head, "No, no, man, you ain't taking me. Not like Davy."

After halving the distance between them, Gideon could see just how bad off Lionel was. Lionel was soaking with his own sweat, staring through pupils dilated enough to swallow the iris in a dead, black hole.

"I have your money—" Gideon started, hoping to calm him down.

Lionel scrambled backward and someone shouted, "Gun."

Gideon didn't know if it was one of the undercover cops on the platform, or one of the transit boys manning the cameras shouting over the PA system. But the crowd reacted, a sudden panicked rush of people running past Gideon, toward the exit.

Gideon fell backward, seeing Lionel waving an automatic, not seeming to know where to point it. As the civilians rushed for the exit, Lionel pointed it at Gideon, at the escaping people, and at the cameras.

One of the undercover boys had Lionel covered, pointing his weapon at him from behind a bench. In the chaos of moving people, Gideon heard a single gunshot. In response, a dozen other shots reverberated through the giant concrete chamber.

Lionel was cut to pieces as every undercover cop on the platform fired into him. He was probably dead before he slumped to the ground. Gideon watched, sickened, as Lionel spun, blood spraying from wounds in his chest, his throat, and his legs. It was like watching a replay of what had happened to Raphael.

The firing stopped when Lionel was motionless, face-down on the concrete. In the few moments of gunfire, the platform had emptied of everyone but cops.

"Fuck . . ." Gideon gasped as he grabbed his crutches and struggled to lever himself upright.

Eight plainclothes cops closed on the corpse, ringing Lionel with their guns drawn, as if he might still make a threatening move. Gideon, moving slowly, was one of the last to join the ring.

Gideon had nurtured a faint hope that Lionel might still be alive, but once he stood next to the body, he could see it was hopeless. The shot to the neck was final.

One of the detectives turned to Gideon. "You all right?"

"Yeah, damn it. He wasn't even aiming at me."

Someone else said, "Bastard didn't give us a choice."

Gideon nodded. Once they heard a shot, the only duty

that remained was protecting the civilians on the platform. There was no way around it.

Gideon crutched around to the other side of Lionel and looked at the other cops. The transit boys would have the ambulance call in already. All they had to do was wait.

"Any of you have some gloves?" he asked the others.

One nodded, holstered his weapon, and pulled on a pair of latex gloves. He looked at the body and asked, "What do you see?"

"Pick up the gun," Gideon asked. "See how many shots he fired."

The cop with the gloves bent over and retrieved Lionel's gun from the pool of his blood. He looked at the gun, shook his head, frowned. Then he pulled the clip and stared at it for a few moments.

Gideon didn't like his expression. "What is it?"

"This weapon hasn't been fired at all." He turned it around so the circle of cops could see the side of the gun. "He never even took the safety off."

1.08
Fri. Mar. 6

AT eight-thirty Friday morning, Gideon hobbled into Captain Davis' office. He had spent the last day sorting out the paperwork on Lionel's shooting and giving interviews to Internal Affairs.

His captain looked worse, as if he'd hadn't slept in the past week. His desk was piled high, as if he was trying to barricade himself in his office with paperwork

Gideon leaned on his crutch and waited for Davis to notice him.

Eventually Davis looked up. He frowned and said, "So what are you doing here?"

"I want to know what was happening with Lionel—"

Davis looked at him, and Gideon could hear him sigh. "You're off duty, Gideon."

Gideon crutched up to the desk. "I have a right to know what's going on with that case."

Davis shook his head. "What the hell gives you that idea?"

"My brother—"

"This is a police department—not some freelance detective agency. Go home. Rest."

"All I want is—"

"All *I* want is a double-digit drop in the homicide rate and an adequately funded department. Who gets what they want? Get some rest and let this be."

Gideon stood there, debating whether to push the issue or not. He looked at Davis and decided not. The phrase "public relations disaster" went through his mind as he thought of the incident on the Metro. Shooting someone to ribbons on the platform of what was supposed to be the safest subway system in the nation could not be helping the PR situation.

He hobbled back out of the Captain's office and crutched over to one of the desks. Behind it sat Tamon Gardener, a homicide detective he knew from the academy.

Gardener was doing his best not to look directly at Gideon. He managed to avoid eye contact until Gideon had crutched up to directly in front of his desk.

"I'm sorry, man," he said. "We aren't supposed to talk to you about any police business."

"Christ, why—" Gideon was about to repeat himself, he *had* a right to know what was going on. He had a right because it was *his* case, *his* brother. He wasn't about to let some political bureaucracy in the department shut him out of the investigation.

However, it was obvious from Gardener's expression that word had come down from on high in the department. It would be pointless to voice his frustration.

Instead, he decided to try a little finesse. "Look, all I need is one thing for my report—"

"Look, I shouldn't even be talking to you."

"I just need the case number for the Metro shoot-out."

Gardener looked up at him as if trying to decide if he'd be breaking any standing orders by giving Gideon that information.

This has got the whole damn department tied up in knots, Gideon thought.

Gardener scribbled on a pad. "Look, steer clear of this until things calm down. IA's breathing down the neck of anyone who touches this case."

"I'll put in a good word for you with Magness," Gideon said. He pocketed the slip of paper while balancing on his crutches.

"Don't do me any favors."

When Gideon got home, he crutched his way upstairs and turned on his computer. The old machine took a while to warm up. It gave Gideon a chance to find himself a comfortable position in his chair. It took him a little longer to get oriented, moving the mouse with the wrong hand.

Eventually he called up the department. The computer dialed, and soon he was hearing the whine of a carrier.

He hadn't used his account in the DCPD database since he'd been gunned down. He'd spent all his time on his own private account. He was hoping that all the folks who wanted him on vacation had overlooked his mainframe account. He logged in and waited.

In a few seconds the screen flashed a prompt at him. He was in.

He fished out his copy of the Case ID for Lionel's shooting. It took him about ten minutes, typing with the wrong hand, to enter the fifteen digit ID number and get Lionel's file up. The computer thought about it for a few minutes, then the screen showed the first page of Lionel's file.

Kareem Rashad Williams had quite a rap sheet tagged onto his ass. Gideon didn't care much about that, he knew most of it anyway. He paged into the active case file on the Metro shoot-out.

The autopsy records were on file. The cause of death was no surprise; what did surprise Gideon was the fact that the toxicology scan showed enough PCP in Lionel's system to send the Mormon Tabernacle Choir into orbit. That was enough of a surprise for Gideon to back up to the guy's rap sheet.

Dealing heroin, dealing coke, dealing speed. No Angel Dust. Not much in itself, but that combined with the odd fact that Lionel had decided to go flying right before he was supposed to meet with a cop that had no reason to like him made the whole thing seem somewhat fishy.

Back to the autopsy.

The cause of death was no big surprise. A bullet had severed his spinal column. The neck wound had finished him off.

It was the ballistics that really made Gideon wonder. The police, collectively, had fired twelve shots. Lionel was hit by five shots. Seven bullets were dug out of the walls of the Metro station. That meant that at least one bullet had passed through Lionel and had lodged in the wall. That was possible, only two slugs were dug out of Lionel's body.

What bothered Gideon was the fact that all the bullets,

except the fatal shot, could be tied to a specific police gun. The one in Lionel's neck had fragmented explosively, as if someone was firing hollow points. More disturbing, the neck shot had hit him in the front, in his throat. From Gideon's memory, that meant that the shot had come from in front of Lionel, from behind where Gideon had been standing.

But the only thing behind Gideon at that point was a mass of panicked civilians.

But someone had shot first, starting that firefight, and it wasn't Lionel. There had been another shooter on the platform. There was little sign that anyone was investigating that, and—at this point—Gideon doubted he would be welcomed if he brought it to the department's attention.

Shit.

He spent the rest of the evening getting himself acquainted with Lionel, the guy who was responsible for Rafe's death.

Gideon only stopped his computer research to hobble downstairs and watch the televison. He had been waiting for this moment for a long time. Three-thirty PM, the press conference announcing the Senate investigation into the Daedalus incident.

By three he was sitting on his couch in the living room, his foot propped up on the table in front of him. On his lap was a copy of the opening statement that Mayor Harris' speechwriter had drafted for him.

On the screen, Senator Daniel Tenroyan, Republican from Maine, was talking to reporters. He looked like an

English professor, standing in front of a podium as if giving a lecture to a bored classroom. ". . . the first hearings will be held on April second, and should last for two weeks. Because of some sensitive testimony we'll be hearing about the Daedalus computer, these hearings will be in closed session—"

Gideon sat up, spilling Mayor Harris' statement from his lap. He wasn't the only one that Tenroyan had caught by surprise. The entire press corps had erupted in a flurry of overlapping questions. For a moment Tenroyan was stuck, unable to be heard over the reporters' questions, his stillness highlighted by camera flashes.

The anchorman cut in, saying, "There you have it. There will be a House-Senate investigation of the shooting of two law enforcement officers by the Secret Service, but the hearings will be in closed session. That means that there'll be no press coverage of the hearings themselves. There's no word yet on whether there'll be any offers of immunity in exchange for testimony . . ."

"I don't believe it," Gideon muttered. He looked down at the canned speech—an emotional plea for the financial salvation of the D.C. police department.

The statement was pretty much irrelevant now. It was one thing when an opening statement was in public view on CNN, it was another when only a few Congressmen and Senators would hear it—the people responsible for perpetuating the problem in the first place.

They had to know something was wrong here. There was something more than a simple fuckup that had gotten his brother killed. But the people who were supposedly investigating were turning away from it. First the DA and the grand jury avoiding the subject, and now Congress wanting to hide the whole process from prying eyes—bargaining with immunity at the same time.

"Fucking politics," Gideon muttered.

Gideon knew what it was. Some bastard stood to be embarrassed, someone powerful enough to put the brakes on the investigation. It infuriated Gideon.

He reached over and picked up the phone. With the Administration bearing down on this, there was no one left on the force he could turn to. But there was at least one ex-cop he knew who might be able to help him.

Gideon called the number for the man who had been his first partner as a detective. He muted the television as a deep voice answered, "Kendal Associates Consulting."

"You still answer your own phone, Morris?"

"That who I think it is?"

"Yes, it is," Gideon said. "You up for meeting me for dinner?"

"Five to one they never even return an indictment," Gideon said, stabbing a piece of lamb stir-fry with his fork. His aim was a little off; he was still wasn't completely used to eating with his left hand.

Morris Kendal looked across the table at him and shook his head. "You're being pessimistic." Kendal was a large man, nearly three hundred pounds. He was bald, black, and built like a pro wrestler.

They were sitting in a Mongolian barbecue restaurant a block east of the garish Chinatown Friendship Arch spanning H Street. They sat a few tables away from a circular dais where a quartet of chefs were grilling the patrons' meals.

Kendal had been a ten-year veteran of the detective bureau when they paired Gideon with him. Kendal had spent two years as his partner, teaching him, keeping him from screwing up too badly. Gideon had had no idea how lucky he had been to have been assigned to Kendal, not until Kendal announced that he was retiring and going into business for himself.

At the time, his mentor's decision had surprised him. Kendal had seemed every inch a cop and it was impossible to envision him as anything else. Now Kendal was making about six times as much as a private security consultant as he'd ever made as a detective. He drove a Mercedes and wore thousand-dollar suits. Now the only thing that surprised Gideon about Kendal's move was the fact that he hadn't made it a lot sooner.

Somehow, Kendal's skepticism about what was happening with the investigation seemed too reminiscent of Rafe's skepticism about Lionel. "Look," Gideon said, "this kind of crap worries me. It's not like he didn't know what he wasn't asking." Gideon finally speared the strip of lamb.

"So what does this have to do with you asking me to dinner?"

"I need someone to get to the bottom of this thing."

Kendal grinned. "There isn't anything here to get to the bottom of—"

"I know you've got contacts in the CIA—"

"—and even if there was, you couldn't afford me."

"I'm asking this as a favor."

Kendal laughed. "*A favor?* I'll say this, they didn't shoot off your balls."

"Come on. This isn't just cop pride—they killed Rafe, Morris. I saw the top of his skull peel away, and his wife just about believes I shot him myself." Gideon shook his head. "I've spent hours with IA. If someone big's behind it, who you think will get tagged with the blame?"

"You're being paranoid."

"Am I?" Gideon shook his head. "The Attorney General of the United States might have to resign over this, and *he's* probably taking the fall for somebody—"

"Taking the fall?"

"I told you what I saw. Silencers? Black ninja suits with 'Treasury' hidden until the last minute? I doubt those were Lloyd's boys."

"So, what, you think you stumbled on some black op? Who by? The CIA?"

Gideon shrugged. "I don't know. An agency with the clout to stonewall a grand jury and convince Congress to close the investigation to public scrutiny."

The air was filled with the smell of roasting pork as the chefs emptied someone's bowl onto the grill.

"Free suggestion," Kendal said.

"Yes?"

"Walk away."

Gideon shook his head. "You think I could if I wanted to?"

Kendal attacked his bowl of chicken, pineapple, and rice. He took a few bites, shaking his head all the while. "You know the odds of you just stumbling in on someone's clandestine operation? And if you're right, you know what you're getting into? You're my friend, don't get mixed up in this."

Gideon leaned over and said, "I'm mixed up in it *now*. This is the nation's number one screwup and they need someone to hang the blame on."

"You think you're being prepped for that duty?"

"IA has been glued to me. This guy, Magness, eyes me like he's already scripting the trial."

"You *need* to get into this?" Kendal took another slow bite of his chicken. "You have a story, and you have the triggermen, right?"

"How long before they turn the screwup into the work of one reckless cop?"

"Was it?"

Gideon's throat clenched shut and his fork clattered to his plate. "*How can you—*"

"You're too close to this. Can you tell me that it wasn't?"

Gideon lowered his eyes and whispered. "He was my brother."

He heard the scrape as Kendal pushed his chair away. Gideon looked up at the man, who towered over him like an impending avalanche. "You aren't going to help me."

Kendal shook his head. "I've always been willing to back you up. You know that. I will look into this for you," he walked up and squeezed Gideon's shoulder. "But I just want you to know that there isn't necessarily a conspiracy here just because you happen to *need* one."

1.09
Sat. Mar. 7

PRESIDENT John Rayburn sat behind his desk in the Oval Office, his chair half-turned toward the window, away from the other men in the room. He was possibly the most physically imposing man to occupy that seat since L.B.J. He loomed over everyone, even when he was seated and only half paying attention.

The two other men in the office with him were his National Security Adviser, Emmit D'Arcy, a short man with thick glasses that he kept adjusting on his nose; and the director of the CIA, Lawrence Fitzsimmons, a man with sandy brown hair and a dead gray beard.

Outside the windows, dawn was drawing a dull gray light across the rose garden.

"This is where we are right now," Fitzsimmons said. "There's no sign of any connection between Kareem Rashad Williams and Zimmerman, despite what the NSA's computers might have said. There's some chance that it might have been deliberate misinformation.

"We've coordinated efforts with the DISA to follow up every breach and near-breach of computer security in about twelve hundred secure intelligence and defense systems looking for any attacks that might have been engineered by Zimmerman. We have every regional office monitoring Internet activity overseas—"

Rayburn turned the pages on a file in front of him. Eventually he said in a slow Texas drawl, "Hellfire."

"It's only a matter of time before Zimmerman makes a slip—" Fitzsimmons started to say.

Rayburn shook his head. "God*damn*—I'm starting to think that the damage from the search is going to be worse than anything Zimmerman could engineer. This is the second shoot-out across the evening news. Things like this have sunk more popular administrations than this one."

"We are dealing with a severe threat to the National Security—"

"Don't patronize me, Larry. I was Army Intelligence when we self-destructed in Vietnam. I know exactly what kind of threat Zimmerman poses. I also know what kind of threat your own Agency poses."

Rayburn stood up. "You still can't even tell me who Zimmerman defected *to*."

"As soon as we can trace some computer activity . . ."

"That's what you were saying a week ago." Rayburn shook his head. "Larry, you aren't getting anywhere. The Daedalus theft was as close as you've managed to get, and all that's gotten us is two corpses, a wounded D.C. cop, and a half-dozen Central Americans who only know about some 'Deep Throat' in a Howard Johnson's parking lot. Meanwhile, I'm feeding my Attorney General to the dogs to cover this operation, and Zimmerman's trail is as cold as the chips in that damn computer."

Fitzsimmons seemed to wince slightly.

"It is unfortunate," D'Arcy said.

"*Unfortunate?*" Rayburn replied. "You have a gift for understatement, Emmit." He turned to Fitzsimmons and said, "At the moment, Emmit is the only thing standing between Congress and your balls-up operation."

Fitzsimmons looked across at D'Arcy.

"I'm giving D'Arcy overall control of the effort to recover Zimmerman."

"But," Fitzsimmons protested, "this was the Agency's—"

Rayburn stared at Fitzsimmons. "If you want to split hairs, this is counterespionage and should be the FBI's bailiwick. Especially since it looks like Zimmerman hasn't left the country."

Rayburn turned to the National Security Advisor. The man was small, but unlike Fitzsimmons, he didn't seem to shrink from under Rayburn's gaze.

D'Arcy took a handkerchief, removed his glasses, and began cleaning them. "We can't let rivalries or past mistakes cloud the issue." D'Arcy replaced his glasses, and his eyes enlarged behind the lenses. "Zimmerman's a serious threat. We cannot dwell on this one 'cluster-fuck.' We're dealing with a time bomb here. We have to recover her before she irreparably damages the security of every computer system in this country. From what I know of the CIA's investigation, we only have one tenuous assumption—that Zimmerman is still in the country."

D'Arcy shook his head. "And whatever damage has been done, Zimmerman's retrieval needs to be covert. More covert than the Daedalus incident. If it became publicly known that she's out there, it would be nearly as damaging to our security as her defection."

Rayburn walked back to his desk and picked up the file he'd been leafing through. "Back at square one."

D'Arcy shook his head. "No, we've lost ground. The Daedalus might have lured her in, but this 'accident' will have made her more wary. She's unquestionably a genius, and while she may be naive about covert operations, she won't make the same mistake twice."

Rayburn closed the file. "I hope I can say the same about the CIA." The President glared at the two men. "No more cowboy shit on CNN, understand? You have to take this woman, but god*damn* you can be subtle about it. Get out of here."

D'Arcy and Fitzsimmons left together, and as they walked down the hall out of earshot of the Oval Office, Fitzsimmons asked, "Emmit?"

"Larry?"

"Think I should start looking for a job in the private sector?"

Morris Kendal sat in a booth in the rear of a diner. The diner was on the fringes of Arlington, toward Largely. The booth was a little too small for him, the table pressed against his three-hundred-pound gut. He whiled away the time wondering if there could be anything to Gideon's paranoia. Even though he was here on Gideon's behalf, he still felt that his friend was engaging in an elaborate self-justification because his brother was the one who got killed in the shoot-out.

Kendal understood. If he was in Gideon's place, he'd

want to believe that there was some great conspiracy behind what happened.

However, even if he thought that the thing was a generic Washington law-enforcement screwup, he was still treating his friend's fears seriously. That was why he was here in an anonymous diner with dirty windows and flyspecked lamp shades.

Kendal was on his third cup of coffee when Christoffel walked in. He walked up to Kendal's booth and asked, "Is this seat taken?"

Christoffel knew it wasn't, but he always asked anyway.

"Go ahead," Kendal said. He had cultivated Christoffel for a few years now. Always with these informal chats. What Christoffel got out of it was the information Kendal gathered as a security consultant for a half-dozen embassies and foreign officials. What Kendal got out of it was the opportunity to pump Christoffel for information.

Kendal nodded slightly to the seat next to Christoffel. "You're sitting next to Saudi Arabia."

Christoffel slid down the seat, and though Kendal didn't see him do it, Kendal knew he palmed the CD that'd rested on the seat next to him. On the CD was a catalog of security measures of a Saudi diplomatic attaché, including a list of the procedures used against electronic surveillance.

"So how're things at the Agency?" Kendal asked.

"Same old, same old."

Kendal gave his disarming smile and commented, "Not what I hear." It was the usual banter, but Kendal noticed something wrong. Christoffel looked nervous. He never looked nervous. It was as if his offhand comment had struck a nerve. Maybe Gideon *was* on to something here.

"Do you need anything?" Christoffel asked. "I'm late for an appointment."

Then why aren't you looking at your watch?

"Yeah," Kendal asked. "I want to talk to you about a certain Secret Service operation." Kendal swore the guy actually paled when he said that. This was a guy who had once told him of covert operations to topple three different third-world governments in a single conversation without showing a twinge of discomfort.

"I can't help you," Christoffel said, and stood up.

"Wait a minute," Kendal said. "You've got to give me something."

Christoffel looked at Kendal, and did something he'd never done before. He took the CD out of his pocket and laid it on the table in front of Kendal. "No, I don't, Morris."

Kendal looked at the CD, then back up at Christoffel.

Christoffel shook his head. "As much as I know, which isn't much, I shouldn't know. Leave it alone." He walked out of the diner, leaving Kendal with his CD full of Saudi intelligence secrets.

Morris Kendal met Chaviv Tischler in the Georgetown Mall. Tischler was a minor diplomat at the Israeli Embassy. He was also Kendal's contact with the Mossad. Not that Tischler ever identified himself as anything other than a secretary.

Kendal wasn't in the habit of dealing with governments other than the U.S. However, since he worked for so many Middle Eastern states, it was only natural that he'd develop some sort of relationship with the Israelis.

If anything, his relationship with Tischler was even more informal than the one he had with Christoffel.

Tischler was a white-haired old man with a humorous glint in his eyes that were otherwise as hard as steel. He was as tall as Kendal, but much less massive, so it still seemed as if Kendal loomed over him.

Tischler was leaning on the railing, looking down a level at the people going from shop to shop on the ground floor. Kendal walked up to the railing and put a hand on it.

"You wanted to see me?" Tischler asked.

"I have some data you might find useful." Kendal's hand was on the Saudi disk in his pocket.

Tischler nodded. There never was any question about Kendal's intelligence. If he brought it to Tischler's attention, Tischler knew he could use it. Tischler also knew that there was a quid pro quo involved.

Tischler pushed away from the rail and waved him along. "Come, let's walk."

Kendal followed the old Israeli diplomat as Tischler asked, "Now what is it you want?"

"I'm looking into a certain Secret Service fiasco—"

"Ah. That is a U.S. matter. I don't think you expect us to spy on our allies?"

And tell me about it? No. "I was just hoping that you may have heard something . . ."

"Through the grapevine, so to speak?"

Kendal nodded.

"Keep your data, my friend. This is not something I wish to be involved in."

Christ, what is it about this that has everyone running scared?

Tischler turned to face Kendal. "Some advice, leave this be. All I could give you would be rumors."

"What's going on, Chaviv? What the hell has got you spooked?"

Tischler chuckled and looked at the ceiling. "What does everyone on the planet fear? What binds me to a Ukrainian, a Slav, a Thai?"

"What are you talking about?"

"The United States." Tischler shook his head and turned to walk away.

Kendal grabbed his shoulder. "What the hell do you mean?"

"I mean that I can't even appear to be interested in this matter. If you would please let me go."

Kendal released his hand, and Tischler walked away from him, not looking back.

What does everyone on the planet fear?

The United States . . .

What was Tischler talking about? It was obvious that he knew more than he admitted. Kendal doubted the Israelis shied away from any information—but Tischler's comment about "appearing to be interested," that was chilling. The intelligence relationship between the U.S. and Israel was close enough that they often—not a lot, but often—shared intelligence with each other.

But Tischler had just about said that what was going on was sensitive enough that it would cause an incident if the Israelis were involved, or expressed interest in it. The *way* he'd said it made Kendal think that Tischler believed that that kind of incident might lead to war.

Kendal fingered the Saudi disk in his pocket and wondered what could've scared Tischler that bad.

1.10
Sat. Mar. 7

GIDEON drove his Nissan through Brookland. He hoped he was driving toward one of the men responsible for his brother's death.

After calling on Kendal for help, he had spent all night nonstop on the computer, paging through the department's computer records. Somehow, there was some concrete connection between Lionel and the Daedalus. Gideon was obsessed with finding that connection.

How did he know that the Daedalus was there? And what was it that he wanted to sell to Gideon for three hundred dollars?

Gideon had spent most of the night pulling the sheets for Lionel's known associates. He felt that Lionel must have gotten his information from one of the creeps he hung out with.

On the seat next to him a printout from his computer was weighted down by his crutch. It was the results of that search. He had found one possibility that made sense—Franklin Alexander "Davy" Jones. The man started out in assault and car theft and had graduated all the way to truck hijacking. He had spent a stretch of time in the same prison as Lionel, and they had been released together. Of all the names Gideon looked into, Davy seemed the most likely candidate for involvement in the Daedalus theft and Gideon could see him as the driver of the truck that never showed.

And one of the last things that Lionel had ever said was the guy's name.

Gideon pulled to a shuddering stop on the street in front of Davy's apartment building. The lurching stop was due to his bad leg and arm. He probably shouldn't have been driving. The only thing that made it possible was the fact he drove an automatic. A manual would be near impossible with his cast.

As the Nissan's engine ticked into dormancy, Gideon looked up at Davy's building. It wasn't the most inviting of places, a pile of sooty brick with a dozen plywood-covered windows. An old man sat on the stoop eyeing him suspiciously.

He spent about five minutes maneuvering out of the car and getting himself positioned on his crutch. Outside, in the cold air, he could smell the rubber of his own car, and the fainter smell of an old fire hanging in the air.

Gideon psyched himself for the ascent. The bastard lived on the third floor.

For a few moments, he forgot Raphael and considered leaving the whole thing alone. Let the rest of the department deal with it. He was supposed to be on leave. He was too caught up in this, and he probably wasn't thinking clearly.

But if he didn't go, who was going to keep the whole thing from being buried?

He had drawn his brother into this, and he was the only person who cared enough to make certain that the people responsible were held accountable.

Gideon looked up the steps and remembered an event from years ago, something he hadn't thought about, or even remembered, in nearly twenty years. It had happened back in grade school. He had come home from school—run home was more like it—with a black eye and a busted lip. He didn't remember now who had beat him up, or why, but he did remember his older brother, Rafe, carefully explaining how he couldn't run, or forget about it, because if he let them get away with it, they would do it again. He could fight back or call the cops, but he couldn't run away or ignore it.

Eventually, Gideon had fought back.

He felt as if Rafe was talking to him here now.

"You can fight back, or call the cops, but you can't run away or ignore it. . . ."

If he left this alone, there wasn't going to be a prosecution, or any public hearings. Right now, there was only him and Kendal. And Kendal doubted that there was anything more to what happened than what the papers said.

Even if there wasn't a conspiracy to bury the investigation, why would his department deal with it? They were understaffed, and already had the shooters. The computer's theft wasn't their jurisdiction, and any new information would be making a tied-up case more complicated— A case the Administration wanted to turn into a political asset.

If he passed the buck on it, he doubted anyone would even follow up on Davy.

"You can't run away or ignore it. . . ."

And, damn it, he *was* the cops.

Gideon sighed and made his way up to the apartment. As he levered himself across the stoop, one step at a time, the old guy looked up at him and said, "I know you, Chief."

Gideon shook his head and said, "I don't think so." He didn't look down at the man. It took all his concentration to pull himself up the steps. At one point the crutch landed on a plastic bag and nearly slipped out from under him, but he managed to recover and reach the front door.

"Yeah, Chief. You that cop they shot up."

Gideon had no choice but to nod. He looked at the intercom. It was painted over and looked as if it hadn't worked in ages.

The old man kept talking at him. "You should get another job, Chief. Cop in this town ain't no job for nobody. No folks deserve that kind of shit."

"When you're right, you're right," Gideon muttered. He tried the door to the stairs. It was unlocked. It didn't even have a doorknob. He had to grab hold of the hole where the knob should be and pull the door open. The smell of piss and mildew slapped him in the face like a wet, moldy towel.

He started up the steps.

It seemed to take an hour to climb all the way up to Davy's apartment, though it probably wasn't more than ten minutes. He had to stop next to Davy's door for nearly as long just to catch his breath.

When he had collected himself, he pounded on Davy's door with his cast.

"Mr. Jones," Gideon called. "Police. I need to talk to you."

There was no response.

Gideon pounded a few more times. As he did, the copper taste of his exertion left his mouth, and he became aware of a smell.

There's nothing quite like the odor of a dead human body that's been allowed to sit a few days. A slightly wet, greasy smell—something close to rancid bacon fat. It hadn't reached full flower, and the neighbors might not have noticed it yet, but standing this close to the door, the hint of death was unmistakable.

"Fuck," Gideon said as he instinctively raised his good hand to his mouth.

Well if that ain't probable cause, I don't know what is.

Gideon tried the door, and found it locked. He turned and pushed his good shoulder into the door. He felt it give a little even with his weak attempt. The deadbolt wasn't set. Gideon tried twice more, resting between each attempt.

On the third try, the door gave. Gideon lost his balance and fell all the way through as the door swung open in front of him.

Here, sprawled facedown in the living room, the smell was just beginning to reach gagging levels. Gideon turned his head and saw an entertainment system, the rectangular TV screen casting a blind blue glow over everything.

He turned the other way and saw Davy, eyes rolled, kit laid out on the coffee table in front of him.

Gideon grabbed his crutch and made it to his feet. The fall, combined with the exertion of climbing the stairs, had ignited a throbbing ache in his injured leg. He tried to ignore it as he looked at Davy.

It was an obvious OD. Though Gideon had trouble believing in the coincidence. Finding Davy dead only convinced Gideon that he had found the right guy.

He walked over to where a phone sat on a table, pulled a tissue from his pocket, and picked up the receiver. There wasn't any way he could avoid calling this in. And the way his leg felt, Davy might not be the only one who needed to be carried out of this apartment.

Before he called it in, he had an idea. He looked at the receiver on the wireless phone, pulled out a pen, and used the dull end to press redial.

After a short series of beeps—a local number—someone picked up.

"*The Zodiac*, Renny speaking." Behind the voice were the sounds of people talking and dishes clattering.

"I'm calling for Davy."

"Davy ain't here, hasn't been in for near a week."

"How about Lionel?"

"What? Didn't hear about what happened?"

"No."

"Got hisself shot up on the Metro. He ain't taking no calls here no more."

"Okay, thanks."

He hung up with the pen. *The Zodiac*, a bar, club, or restaurant—somewhere Lionel and Davy both hung out at. It was the last place Davy had called. For Lionel maybe? For the person who had hired him?

Gideon put in the call to the department, wondering exactly how he was going to explain to IA what he was doing here.

In the hour he waited for someone to get there, Gideon went through Davy's apartment looking for anything that might give him a lead on who had hired him to move the Daedalus—or just some concrete evidence that he had found the right guy.

In Davy's bedroom he found something. Davy's wallet rested on the nightstand next to an unmade bed. He didn't need to go through it. Someone had already pulled it open and had spilled its contents all over the bed.

No cash. But there was a business card.

It was just a blank white rectangle bearing a symbol Gideon recognized.

"א₀," the same mark he had seen on the side of the warehouse.

What the fuck is this?

This was it, the connection. The pulse throbbed in Gideon's neck, and he felt a copper taste in his mouth. He could leave the thing here, have it bagged in the department, and watch as the case sank. Gideon knew that Davy was murdered, he *knew* it. He also knew that the path of least resistance would have the corpse tagged as an OD with nothing to do with Raphael's death.

Gideon knew that the card was important.

Gideon wrapped the card in a tissue and put it in his

own wallet. He could feel the line he crossed as he did so, but he kept telling himself . . .

"You can't run away, and you can't ignore it. . ."

It took another three hours to get away, between waiting for them to come and haul away Davy's body, and explaining how the hell he came upon the corpse to the uniformed officers who showed up. A pale imitation of what would happen when that IA guy, Magness, caught wind of this.

He would have to worry about that later. If he was lucky, it would be a while before news of this filtered through the department. At the moment, he had more pressing concerns.

"You know what you're asking me to do?" Dominic Mallory was looking at the business card that Gideon had taken from Davy's wallet. Gideon had since moved it into a small plastic evidence bag.

Mallory was an employee of the District forensic lab. One of the fingerprint crew that went over the crime scenes that seemed to merit the attention. Davy, as an OD, didn't merit that kind of attention.

Gideon had come down to Mallory's workplace to ask him a favor. He leaned over the black laminated counter and said, "I'm asking you to do your job."

Mallory snorted. "As if it was that easy. There's not enough resources, time, or money to do the stuff I'm *supposed* to be doing. I have a month-long backlog . . ." He picked up the bag and shook it. "I can't be doing work that isn't part of an official case."

"This *is* an official case."

"What're you talking about? You're on disability leave."

"That card belonged to a DOA overdose named Franklin Alexander Jones, a pal of Kareem Rashad Williams—"

"So?" Mallory looked up from the card.

"The guy who set me up. That card might have the prints of the guy behind that whole fiasco."

"And why isn't this coming down to me through the normal channels?"

"You've seen the news." Gideon shook his head. "The whole disaster has become some sort of political play by the Administration. They don't want an investigation. They *want* a fiasco. If someone discovered who set us up, it might dilute their play for money out of Congress."

"Gideon, you're thinking too hard."

"Will you do it?"

Mallory shook his head. "Of course I will." He sighed. "This'll take a while. Even with the computerized files, it might take weeks to find a match, assuming we even find a print to compare. I can put it on the list."

"That's all I ask."

Mallory took the baggie and looked at the card inside. "Hebrew?"

Gideon shrugged. "I don't know. Does it mean anything to you?"

Mallory shook his head. "Go on, I'll get hold of you if anything turns up from this."

When Gideon came home, he hobbled up to his computer and connected to the Internet. The symbol "א‎ ‎°,"

kept running through his head. It had something to do
with what was going on, he just didn't know what. It
could be the symbol of some terrorist group, or it could
be a word in some language he didn't understand.

He was hoping that he would find something out there
that might tell him what it meant.

Gideon loaded his own netsearch software into
Netscape and told it to fetch him information on the Hebrew alphabet. The symbol was Hebrew, that was about
all Gideon knew about it.

The number of pages he found were in the thousands,
but the most basic information he needed was in the first
two documents. He looked at a page that simply named
the characters in the Hebrew alphabet and showed their
cursive form. The symbol, at least the first part without
the little circle, "א," was called "aleph." The first letter.

The letter had no inherent sound, according to what
Gideon read. In transliterating a Hebrew word it would
disappear. In trying to find some sort of meaning for the
little subscript, he kept hunting. The closest to some sort
of meaning he found was the discovery that the original
Hebrew alphabet contained no vowels—the fact that
something named "aleph" was not a vowel seemed odd to
him—and the only way the written language had of
showing vowel pronunciation was as a pattern of dots and
dashes above or below the written text.

That kind of text was called "pointed" text, and when
he first read about it, he thought that might be what the
circle was. But when he saw an example of what pointed
Hebrew text actually looked like, he saw that it wasn't
anything like what he was searching for.

He discovered that the Hebrew letters doubled as numbers, with the first ten representing the numbers from one to ten, aleph being the number one . . .

Some sort of deeper meaning had to be there. Using the first letter as a trademark meant something. Somehow Gideon felt that it was something beyond an initial.

Gideon's search for meaning in the symbol began to take him further afield than just an alphabet. He found a site that used the *Sefer Yetzirah,* an ancient Hebrew occult text that explained how The Creator used the twenty-two letters of the Hebrew alphabet to create the Universe and all the living things in it. The site assigned Hebrew letters to various amino acids. It was strange, and Gideon didn't quite understand it, but it started him thinking toward the occult.

On the *Sefer Yetzirah* page he found references to Kabbalah, apparently an old form of Hebrew numerology that used the number-letter equivalence of the Hebrew alphabet extensively. He redid his search for the word "Kabbalah." He read how, to Jewish mystics, every letter was connected to the life force of God and possessed of sacred meaning.

He found a New Age page that ascribed relationships between the Kabbalistic letters and tarot cards. Aleph seemed associated with the tarot card "The Fool."

Gideon searched until he found a picture of "The Fool," and found an image of a young man carrying a pack over his shoulder, a dog nipping at his heels. He seemed caught just before he took his last step over a precipice. Gideon felt as if he were going in the wrong direction, but there was something about the Fool that seemed prophetic.

After a while of finding esoteric things like the "tree of life" that didn't help him in his current questions, he started over again with a search simply for "aleph."

He found that a lot of agencies, corporations, and software companies used the word in their name or in the names of their products. He also found some more New Age mysticism, a meditation on "aleph," which repeated the association with the Fool.

Gideon ended his search on the "Aleph Homepage," which told him that it was the first letter of the first alphabet—Phoenician, Hebrew, or even Protosinaitic—and the origin of the alphabet went back as far as the eighteenth century BC. According to the page, "Aleph" represented the origin of all written material.

It was after midnight when he pushed himself away from his computer, feeling unenlightened.

1.11
Sun. Mar 8

THE Zodiac was a dark strip club north of New York Avenue, in one of the dozens of depressed areas in the District. It would have been in sight of the capital if it was above ground. Its decor resembled a condemned building. The walls were spray-painted fluorescent colors, and if Gideon stared up through the gloom, he could see pipes hugging the rafters above. It was one of those places that made him feel sick and alone.

The strippers matched the environment, dancing to old Deborah Harry with a passionless fatigue.

The mood of this place, and lack of sleep, made it a little too easy for him to imagine his own future. Old, alone, no family— The fears caught him in the same ache that had been inside him since Raphael was shot.

He had just stepped inside, leaning on his crutches. A minute later, Morris Kendal walked into *The Zodiac*.

Kendal was bigger than either of the bouncers. He snorted at the place, turning so that every part of it got a good look at his sneer. Gideon might have passed for a regular at this kind of place, but Kendal was dressed at least a grand better than *The Zodiac* rated.

He walked up and placed a hand on Gideon's shoulder and said, "This place smells like shit."

He wasn't exaggerating. The air was rank with the smell of cigarette smoke, mildewed plaster, and beer both new and used. Gideon shrugged out from Kendal's grip and started moving deeper into the place. "This shouldn't take long."

Kendal followed Gideon into the room as he walked along the shadowed wall that was farthest from the stage. The darkness was only highlighted where the black lights turned the cuffs of Kendal's shirt a fluorescing sky blue where they poked from the sleeves of his jacket.

The patrons paid no attention to them, but they were under the watchful eyes of the bouncers and of the bartender. Kendal didn't look tense, but Gideon could hear a hard urgency in his whispered voice. "I think you need to slow down this little investigation of yours."

"I'm in this up to my neck." Especially after his visit to Davy's apartment. IA was already leaving him messages. Magness could smell blood in the water. "Even if Rafe wasn't my brother—"

"You need to reconsider."

"Why?" This wasn't going the way he had planned. Kendal was supposed to be his backup, but while he had driven Gideon here, he had spent the entire drive trying to talk Gideon out of this. Kendal seemed nervous. It didn't fit. Kendal was built like a rock, immobile and impervious to that kind of emotion. But the way he looked around the bar, the way he moved his hands, it betrayed an unease that was alien to the man. Gideon had been maneuvering toward the bar, but he stopped and lowered his voice. "What *have* you found out?"

Up to now, he hadn't been forthcoming, but he finally gave him an answer of sorts.

"Very little," Kendal finally said. "But everyone acts as if I have the plague as soon as I bring up the subject. Even those who say they don't know anything about what's going on. You name the Agency, and they don't want to touch it."

"I told you" Gideon whispered. *"There* is *something dirty going on here."* Gideon moved toward the bar, and Kendal grabbed his cast.

"This is *why* I didn't tell you," Kendal said. "You want to dive into this crap headfirst."

Gideon shook his head. "Are you here to help me?"

Kendal didn't let go. "The one thing I have is a rumor that D'Arcy is interested in the investigation into the Secret Service."

Gideon tried to pull away.

"D'Arcy, Gideon." Kendal repeated the name as if it was a mantra that might make Gideon return to his senses.

D'Arcy was a name to conjure with, and Gideon was a D.C. native who was quite aware of who the National Security Advisor to President Rayburn was. Supposedly the Kissinger of the twenty-first century.

However, if anything, Kendal's attitude just made Gideon angry. He yanked his cast away from him. *"Back me up or get the fuck out of my way."* Anger had flattened his voice until his whisper was barely audible under the sounds of "Heart of Glass."

Kendal let him go, but he followed him toward the bar, still talking. "It's possible. D'Arcy has a reputation for black-bag ops as far back as the Reagan Administration. Cut his teeth on Central American psych-ops and end runs around Congress. You really don't want to mess with this." When Gideon didn't respond, he asked, "What do you think you're going to do?"

"Some police work," Gideon said quietly as he reached the bar.

The man behind it was very dark and had dreadlocks down to his shoulders. Gideon leaned his cast on the bar and said, "I'd like to ask you a few questions."

The man kept cleaning the glasses behind the bar. He didn't even look up at him. "Ain't got nothing to talk to you about, man."

Gideon fished out his badge and laid it on the bar. "I think you do."

The man shook his head. "Ain't got nothing to say to no cop." He looked up at Gideon. "And you ain't on duty, I seen you on the TV. Less reason to talk to you."

"Look, I'm not here to fuck with your business. I don't care what you sell with the drinks, or what your dancers might do for an extra fifty—"

"Hey. This is a clean place. Nothing like that going on here, man."

Yeah, right. "Look, you just tell me about a couple of regulars and we won't have Vice down here to experiment with the forfeiture laws."

The bartender put down his glass and leaned toward Gideon. "And if you just walk your gimp ass out of here, my boys won't bust your fucking cop head."

Gideon felt a presence next to him and looked to the side. Bouncer number one was staring down at him from a height of six-six. As he was looking at one, he felt a large hand on his good shoulder. The other guy was, if anything, taller than the first. They both wore black T-shirts with astrological symbols. Gemini and Virgo. Virgo was tugging on his shoulder, saying "I think you better go."

"None of us want any trouble here," Gideon grabbed his badge and put it back in his pocket. He didn't have his gun, because with his right arm in a cast it would've been too dangerous. Right now he wished he'd brought it.

"You making the trouble, man," the bartender said. "I asked you to go."

Virgo pulled him away from the bar, and Gideon stumbled on his bad leg, and the crutch slipped out from under him. Gemini grabbed his other shoulder, and Gideon felt a pain in his old bullet wound.

"I don't think you want to do that." Gideon recognized Kendal's voice coming from somewhere behind him.

"This isn't your business," Gemini said, turning away from Gideon.

"I think you should let the man go."

Gideon dangled from the bouncer's grip. The two of them had stopped moving him when Kendal spoke. Gideon used the moment's respite to shift his feet under him so that he could put his weight on his good leg.

"We don't want things to get nasty," Virgo called toward Kendal. Gideon saw Gemini go for his belt with his free hand. He pulled an object out of a small black holster behind him. Gideon couldn't see if it was mace, a stun gun, or a pistol—it was enough of a threat for him to do something about.

He tensed, balanced himself on his good leg, and as soon as Gemini loosened his grip to take a step toward Kendal, Gideon slammed his cast into the man's kidney. Even as his partner was doubling over, Virgo yanked Gideon so he fell to his knees, his good arm twisted up behind his back. "Bad move," Virgo said as he pushed him forward, into the floor.

Gideon heard the bartender's Jamaican-accented voice calling, "What the fuck you doing?"

Gideon turned his head just in time to see Kendal slam his fist into the side of Gemini's head. Gemini's weapon, a collapsible baton, flew from his hand, toward the stage. As Virgo ground Gideon's face into the floor, Kendal landed another blow on Gemini. Gemini dropped as if someone had swung a cinder block into his face.

The Jamaican cursed, and Gideon heard him dive behind the bar, going for something.

Kendal stepped back from Gemini and pulled a sleek black gun from inside his trench coat. "I'd appreciate it if no one moved." He said it in a calm, level voice that somehow managed to silence everything but the music. The only sounds were distorted Blondie and the scuffle of a half-dozen people backing away from Kendal and the bar.

Virgo backed off, and Gideon pushed himself up off of the floor.

"You, behind the bar. I want to see both hands."

Gideon reached over and grabbed his crutch from where it had fallen on the ground. As he pushed himself up, he saw the Jamaican slowly rising from behind the bar. The patrons had backed up to the walls, forming a half circle around the bar, watching the four of them. Gemini was still flat on the ground, and Virgo was staring at Kendal, seemingly caught between conflicting desires—either make a grab for Kendal, or fade into the background with the rest of the bar's patrons.

Gideon made his way around to the other side of the bar with the Jamaican. The guy was staring at Kendal, his hands spread. Something lay on the floor at his feet, half-pulled from a shelf under a small refrigerator. Gideon knelt carefully on his good leg, leaning the crutch against the bar and reaching out with his left hand to pull it the rest of the way out.

It was a double-barreled single-action shotgun. The barrels were sawed off about as far as they could be and still fire. The stock was sawed down to a pistol grip.

"Well, this isn't legal." Gideon broke open the shotgun and dumped out the shells. He put the empty gun on the counter and opened up the refrigerator. There were some bottles of beer, a roll of twenties, a box of shotgun shells, and about six ice trays. Gideon pulled out an ice tray and put in on the counter. It didn't hold ice. Each little compartment held two or three tiny baggies. Each baggie held a crystalline powder.

Gideon pulled himself back upright with the crutch.

"And that *really* isn't legal."

"Fuck you," the Jamaican said. "You don't have a warrant—"

Gideon shook his head. "You look like a smart guy. Do I really need to explain probable cause to you?"

"You ain't on duty, Cop." He was looking back and forth between Gideon and Kendal.

"Like the Vice boys give two shits. The forfeiture laws are what keep those boys financed. You know that. Even if you walk, with conspiracy to distribute you can kiss this bar gone." Gideon looked around and said, "How understanding is the owner?"

"Fuck," the Jamaican said.

"So what's this?" Gideon picked up a tiny baggie. "Crystal meth? Heroin—"

"Man, you going to arrest me or what?"

"Don't be a pessimist. Talk to me, and the two of us walk out of here like nothing happened."

"What you want to know?"

"You're going to tell me about two regulars. Lionel and Davy."

They took the bartender into the men's room for a private chat. They sat him on the throne while Kendal watched out the front door for more of the horoscope brothers.

The Jamaican had a lot to say. He spoke fast, apparently trying to get Gideon and Kendal out of his dreadlocked hair as quickly as possible.

Lionel and Davy both had hung out at *The Zodiac* a lot. Gideon figured that, since they apparently took calls here. The two were fairly tight, though they didn't seem to work together. Lionel was a small-time dealer and Davy was into much bigger scores hijacking semis and stealing construction equipment. The last time the bartender saw Davy, he was bitching about some score going sour.

About the score the Jamaican claimed to not know any details, beyond the fact that it was a hundred grand for a single truck—an empty truck. Davy began bitching about the score going south about two days before the Daedalus was supposed to have been picked up by a refrigerated truck.

Gideon was certain now that Davy, Franklin Alexander Jones, had to have been the driver who was supposed to move the Daedalus. The hundred grand clinched it. That kind of money would be out of line for just about anything else Davy could've been working on.

The last time the Jamaican saw Lionel, Lionel had just gotten a phone call from Davy—the bartender thought they were going to meet somewhere.

The call was timed right to be the last thing Davy did before he OD'd. As if Gideon needed another reason for Davy's death to look suspicious, he—like Lionel—seemed to have chosen an odd time to go tripping out of his skull, right before he was going to meet with the buddy who had sold him out.

Gideon wondered if Davy had figured that out before he died.

He pressed the point, getting all the details he could out of the Jamaican. The person who hired Davy—all the bartender knew was that Davy called the guy, "the Doctor." This Doctor had never shown in *The Zodiac*. That didn't surprise Gideon. Folks who'd go around shipping multimillion-dollar computers—stolen or not—probably didn't frequent places like *The Zodiac*.

However, the Jamaican said there was this one guy Davy had talked to here, a guy who didn't fit. This white guy with a buzz cut—he'd looked like a college student according to the Jamaican—had met with Davy twice. The first time was right before Davy had started talking about the hundred-grand job. The last time was the day Davy lost the score.

This was what Gideon was looking for, some connection with the people who'd set up the job at the warehouse. Unfortunately, the Jamaican didn't know much of anything about the guy. He thought the guy's name might have been Mike. He'd worn a khaki army jacket over an MIT college sweatshirt.

The last thing Gideon asked him was about the symbol Davy had carried in his wallet. He pulled a wrinkled piece of paper out of his pocket and laid it on the Jamaican's lap. It had a "א₀" written on it.

"This mean anything to you?"

The Jamaican looked down at the paper and said, "Ho? Xo? You got handwriting problems, man."

Gideon took back the paper and looked up at Kendal. "Let's go."

Back in Kendal's BMW Gideon said, "I owe you for helping me out back there."

"You owe me a *lot*. I get two hundred an hour for that kind of bodyguard duty." He looked at his watch. "I say you owe me at least fifty bucks."

"What the hell was it you pulled on them."

"Heckler & Koch MP55D—your basic police-slash-antiterrorist weapon."

"Can you legally carry that thing around?"

"Now that's a disingenuous question." Kendal accelerated out down New York Avenue.

"MIT . . ." Gideon said to himself.

"What?" Kendal asked as he jerked to a stop at a red light.

"Someone trying to get their hands on a supercomputer? A lot of tech-heads around that kind of operation."

"Uh-huh," Kendal said. "You're basing this all on a Rastafarian's description of a *sweatshirt*. You don't know for sure even if this Mike guy ever went to college—"

"It's a lead."

"No talking you out of this, is there?"

"I really don't give a shit if it's D'Arcy or the Pope behind this. Someone's responsible for Rafe's death, and I'm not going to let Magness hang me for it."

Kendal sighed. "Okay, I'll back you up on this thing. You can't do this alone."

"Thanks."

"So what was it you showed the bartender?"

Gideon took the paper out of his pocket. While he was doing it, the light changed and cars started honking. Kendal pulled up, through the intersection.

Kendal glanced over at the paper and the symbol Gideon had copied. "What is it?"

"I don't know. A symbol associated with the people who hired Davy. It was on a card in his wallet."

Kendal kept glancing from the road to the handwritten "ℵ₀."

"It's an aleph," Gideon said. "The first letter of the Hebrew alphabet. But I haven't figured out what it means with that circle attached. It isn't a word—it might be some sort of occult symbol, but if so I don't know what it means."

"I don't think it's occult," Kendal said. "I didn't have much science in high school, but I think we're looking at a subscripted constant of some sort."

"Huh?"

"I think what you have here is some sort of mathematical or scientific symbol. You said we're dealing with a bunch of 'tech-heads.' "

"Why you think so? Do you know what it is?"

"I have no clue. But I remember how that kind of techie stuff looked. And putting a little zero at the base of the thing makes it look like some sort of constant that someone would put in an equation somewhere."

"I thought they only used Greek letters for that? You know, like pi."

"They probably ran out of the Greek alphabet a century ago. Talk to a mathematician or an engineer. I bet one of them would know what that means."

Gideon had a gut feeling about what university he would find one at.

1.12
Mon. Mar 9

GIDEON drove to Cambridge. He parked at MIT in the early afternoon, after spending hours on the road. He had to sit in the parking lot for about half an hour just to allow his wounded leg and shoulder to rest. He had driven here in a fog of denial. He had to keep telling himself that he was acting perfectly reasonable.

The fact was, he was here, like Kendal had said, based on a Rastafarian's description of a sweatshirt. He could have e-mailed someone, gone to Georgetown, or any of a number of things—

But he had driven to Cambridge.

He sat in the car, massaging his legs with his good arm and wondering if Magness had gotten him suspended yet. *Am I here just because I have to do something?*

What did he have? A name, "Mike," and a scrap of paper with a symbol that could mean just about anything . . .

And the possibility that the government was covering up something about the theft of a Daedalus supercomputer.

He was fooling himself if he thought he was going to find out anything here.

But, now that he was here, it really *would* be pointless driving back without trying, so he spent ten minutes maneuvering himself out of the car with his crutch.

A student, carrying a backpack and huddling against a severe wind, stopped and asked, "Do you need any help, sir?"

Gideon shook his head as he made it to his feet. "I've got it under control."

The kid turned to go, and Gideon called out, "Can you tell me where the mathematics department is?"

"Building two," the kid called back over his shoulder. "There's a directory over there." He hooked a thumb toward a nearby building, where a campus map stood.

"Thanks," Gideon said as he crutched over to the map.

"Fuck," he muttered. He had parked on the far side of the campus from building two.

Gideon looked up math professors at random. On the third try he found an office occupied. The office's occupant was named Doctor Harry Cho. Dr. Cho's door was ajar on a tiny office that was crowded with bookshelves and filing cabinets. Gideon knocked on the doorframe with his cast, letting the door swing all the way open.

Dr. Cho looked up from his computer and spun around. The movement startled Gideon before he realized that the professor was seated in a wheelchair.

"Can I help you?" Cho asked. Cho's expression was one of frank, almost embarrassing, curiosity.

Gideon extended his good hand and said, "My name's Gideon Malcolm. I'm a detective with the Washington D.C. Police Department."

Cho took his hand. "I hope I haven't done anything wrong, Officer."

"No—"

"D.C.?" Cho looked at the cast and the crutch and said, "You aren't that cop from that *Dateline* story, are you?"

Gideon sighed and nodded.

"Well, what do you know?" Cho waved behind the door. "I have a chair—"

Gideon moved to sit down. It was a relief after walking across the campus. His leg and his shoulder were both giving him grief. He sat, massaging the scar-tissue crater through his pants leg. It felt, through the material, as if the hole went straight through his calf.

"It hurts?" Cho asked.

Gideon was almost embarrassed to admit it in front of someone in a wheelchair, but he nodded. "My leg was torn up pretty good." He patted the cast. "The arm was broken by the bullet, but it'll probably recover sooner than the leg."

Cho nodded. He slapped the side of his chair. "Anyway, what brings you here? A bit out of your jurisdiction."

Gideon shook his head. "I'm here on my own. I don't even know why I mentioned I was a cop—habit, I guess."

Cho cocked his head and stared at Gideon with an expression that made him uneasy. It was as if all his doubts were visible on his face for Cho to see. He pulled out the paper with his hand-drawn aleph on it. It was severely crumpled now. "I'm interested in two things," he said staring at his paper. "The first is someone who might have been a student here, in Mathematics, Engineering, or—"

"Why are you looking for him?"

Gideon looked up from his crumpled paper. "What?"

"You said you were here on your own. Why are you looking?" He eyed Gideon suspiciously.

It took a while before Gideon said, "If you've seen any of the news stories, you should know why."

"It's about the Daedalus?"

"It's about why my brother was killed."

"And you think an alumni was involved?" Cho asked.

"It's a long shot." Gideon shook his head. "I really don't know what I'm doing here, but I can't stop looking for a reason. Something . . ."

"I understand."

Gideon shook his head and started to stand. "No, you don't have to talk to me. I'm not a cop right now, and I shouldn't even be here—"

"No" Cho said. He wheeled up and placed a hand on Gideon's cast, easing him back into the chair. "It's all right."

When Gideon was seated, Cho rolled back and said, "I know what it's like to go through something like that, to hunt for a meaning—but I should warn you, no one outside yourself can tell you *why* it happened. The most they can do is tell you *how*."

Gideon nodded. "This man, I believe he might have hired the driver for the Daedalus."

"Part of the terrorists the Secret Service was supposed to capture?"

Gideon nodded, though he wondered—if the ambush wasn't really Secret Service, what did that mean about the people they had meant to ambush.

"So who is he?" Cho asked.

"About six feet, two hundred pounds. Mid-twenties, white, blonde, named Mike."

Cho waited for a long time before he said, "Is that *it?*"

Gideon nodded.

"Well good luck. You know how many people go through MIT, and you don't even have a specific department to look in." Cho exhaled, "If you had a graduation date, or a year he was here, or even a less common name."

"I know," Gideon said. "I think I must have been half nuts coming all the way from D.C. This Mike had on an MIT sweatshirt—"

"That's it?"

"All I had to go on, yes." Gideon nodded. "But that's only half the reason I'm here. This, you might actually be able to help me with."

" We'll see. . . ."

Gideon handed over his paper. "I've been trying to find out what this means. A friend of mine said it looked like a mathematical symbol."

Cho looked at the page for a few moments, as if deciphering Gideon's handwriting. Eventually, he nodded. "Your friend was right. What you have here is aleph-null."

Up to now, Gideon had been convincing himself that

this whole trip was a waste. Despite that, when Cho identified the name of the symbol, Gideon felt a thrill. He had found something.

It meant something . . .

"What is it?" Gideon asked, his voice was rushed and breathless.

"It's the lowest class of infinity."

Gideon sat back, frowning. That made no sense to him.

"You've never heard of it, have you?" Cho asked.

Gideon shook his head, feeling as if the answer was just as cryptic as the unexplained symbol. It sounded like some New Age bullshit to him. "I thought infinity was infinity."

Cho handed back the paper and said. "That's a logical way to look at it. It seems so intuitively obvious, that the man who discovered—or invented, depending on how you look at it—the transfinite numbers was probably the least appreciated mathematical genius of the past five hundred years."

It was still all Zen to Gideon. "What does the lowest class of infinity *mean?*"

Cho leaned back and steepled his fingers a moment. "To explain that I'll have to give you some very rudimentary set theory—"

Gideon didn't like where this was going. "The last mathematics I had was trig in high school."

"Don't worry, this is fairly simple." He reached into the piles of papers on his desk and started dropping things in Gideon's lap—paper clips, rubber bands, pencils . . .

"Hey."

"There," Cho said, having placed three piles in Gideon's lap.

"What are you doing?"

"Some people need help visualizing." He smiled. "Now we have here three sets. For the sake of example, these piles are infinite."

Gideon looked down and said, slowly, "Okay . . ."

Cho picked up a paper clip and Gideon's leg twitched involuntarily. "We'll call the paper clips Set 'Z,' and the rubber bands set 'P,' and pencils set 'N' . . ."

"Whatever you say."

"How do we know we have the same number of pencils, rubber bands, and paper clips." Or, in set theory, how do we prove that set N is equivalent to sets P and Z, and vice versa?"

"We just count how many—"

Cho shook his head. "These are *infinite* piles, counting is not allowed." He placed the paper clip back on Gideon's leg. "There's a simple solution. Ask yourself how you would make equal piles of finite objects without 'counting' them."

Gideon looked down at the piles on his legs. How the hell could you measure the piles without counting them? Gideon reached down with his good hand and arranged the groups in rows, trying to think of what Cho was getting at.

It seemed stupid, he didn't even have equal piles. There was an extra rubber band that stuck out once he aligned the groups . . .

"Wait a minute . . ." Gideon looked down at his legs, the beginning of a realization coming to him.

"Yes?" Cho asked.

"When you align them," Gideon picked up the extra rubber band. "You can *see* when they aren't equal."

Cho nodded. On Gideon's leg, the groups sat in neat rows, each pencil next to a rubber band and a paper clip. "What you just did was put everything into a one-to-one relationship with each other. Finite sets are equivalent when each member in one set can be paired with exactly one element in the other set, with no leftovers." He took the extra rubber band. "Obviously, our *finite* set of rubber bands wasn't equivalent to the others."

"But we were talking about infinite sets."

Cho nodded. "Now, though, you have a way to measure the equivalency of our infinite piles of paper clips, rubber bands, and pencils."

"Okay, I can see that." Gideon could imagine mountainous piles of rubber bands, pencils, and paper clips, and going to each one, and taking one item per pile and grouping them together. He could do it forever, and no pile would come up short. "But I don't see how that keeps infinity from being infinity."

"Bear with me. We have our infinite sets. Now let's take our pencils, set 'N,'. We can give each pencil in our pile, one at a time, a number. One, two three . . ."

"Okay, you can go on forever."

Cho picked up the pencils and said, "Having done that mental exercise, we have a pile of the natural numbers."

"So an infinite pile of pencils is equivalent to the set of natural numbers."

Cho nodded. "Considering the pile as a set of infinite

individual pencils. Now set P—we'll number each rubber band with a successively higher prime number." He picked up each rubber band as he spoke. "Two, Three, Five, seven—"

"That goes on forever, too?"

Cho nodded and picked up the paper clips. "Set Z. Zero, One, Minus One, Two, Minus Two."

"I have the picture I think." Gideon said. "The set of natural numbers is equivalent to the set of prime numbers—"

"—is equivalent to the set of integers."

"If you say so."

"That equivalence was a problem that George Cantor set out to solve. I've just explained the basics of the proof. The set of natural numbers 'N,' is equivalent to the set of primes 'P,' the set of integers 'Z,' and even to the set of all fractions. Aleph-null is the number of elements in those sets."

"Why the symbol, then? If all infinite sets are equivalent to each other—"

"They aren't," Cho said.

"How? I mean if you have the numbers from one to whatever, you can pair them up with a series of anything."

"Not quite."

Cho dropped his piles of objects on the desk and grabbed a pad of graph paper. "This is harder to describe without using actual numbers." He took one of the infinity pencils and scribbled for a moment. After a few moments he handed the pad to Gideon.

Gideon stared at the page.

$$N = \{1, \quad 2, \quad 3, \quad 4 \ldots\}$$
$$\Updownarrow \quad \Updownarrow \quad \Updownarrow \quad \Updownarrow$$
$$P = \{2, \quad 3, \quad 5, \quad 7 \ldots\}$$
$$\Updownarrow \quad \Updownarrow \quad \Updownarrow \quad \Updownarrow$$
$$Z = \{0, \quad 1, \quad -1, \quad 2, \quad -2 \ldots\}$$

$$R = \{\ldots -2 \ldots -1 \ldots 0 \ldots 1 \ldots 2 \ldots\}$$

Gideon looked at it for a long time. He could see the first three sets as what Cho had described to him, the arrows emphasized the one-to-one relationship Cho had talked about.

The fourth one was different. The others trailed off to the right, Gideon could figure out that's what the dots meant. But there were dots *between* the numbers in set R. "You're saying that there's an infinity between each of these numbers, right?"

"That's a good way to put it. That's the set of reals. Once you add irrational numbers to the number system, there's no systematic way to pair every element with the set of natural numbers. Any method you try will have elements—an infinity of elements—slipping through the cracks."

"So aleph-null is the number of elements just in the first three sets?"

Cho nodded. "It's the size of the set of natural numbers, the set of primes, the set of rational numbers ... The set of real numbers is much larger. It's aleph-null raised to the power of aleph-null."

"I'll take your word about that. I think I follow you enough to answer my question." Answered and not answered . . . Gideon still wasn't sure what it meant that these people were using an esoteric symbol for infinity.

"Why are you interested in this, by the way? It seems to be a bit far afield for police work, even if you are working on your own."

"I needed to find out what it meant, to discover why a group of people might be using it."

"Using it? How?"

"As sort of a logo."

"Logo—"

"It was spray-painted on a wall near the Daedalus."

"Now that *is* a strange piece of graffiti."

"It was also on a business card. I thought that discovering its meaning would give me a clue to what the group was, and who's a part of it."

Cho leaned back, "A logo, hmmm . . ."

Gideon nodded. "This tells me something, though. The group that uses this as a symbol probably wants the Daedalus for a different reason than one that'd use a religious or occult symbol . . ." For some reason, the image of the tarot card, the Fool, flashed through Gideon's mind. The symbol of infinity had its own connotations that could range from the scientific to the theological.

As if echoing Gideon's thought, Cho said, "Some might call mathematics a religion . . ."

He rolled around and rummaged in a filing cabinet. After a bit, he pulled out a folded stack of papers, stapled together. He shook them so the individual pages separated. "Using aleph-null as a logo, hmmm."

He handed over the papers. The first thing that caught

Gideon's eye was the familiar "$\aleph_0$." taking up a large section of the top left corner of the first page. The paper was titled, "*Aleph-Null: The Newsletter of the Evoluntionary Theorems Research Lab*."

Gideon looked up and asked, "What's this?"

"The one group I know of that used aleph-null, like you said, as a logo. The ET lab isn't around anymore, but it carried on research for about four years or so."

"What was it?"

Cho shook his head. "I think you should talk to some Comp-Sci people about that. I know they were supposedly doing original work in number theory, and there was some controversy about some of their proofs before Dr. Zimmerman left."

"Dr. Zimmerman?" Gideon borrowed Cho's pad and pencil and wrote down the name under the collection of sets that Cho had written down.

"Yes, Julia Zimmerman, she headed the ET lab—invented it."

Gideon tore off the sheet of graph paper and pocketed it. "What do you mean she left?"

"After the ET lab was shut down, she resigned. I don't know where she went to from here. But I gather she had a rather confrontational reputation, which wouldn't have helped her find another post."

"What prompted the reputation?"

Cho shook his head. "I don't know much about it. It was all academic politics and it happened while I was still a TA. Go check with some Comp-Sci people. Folks with tenure."

"Uh-huh." Gideon folded the newsletter and asked, "Can I keep this?"

Cho nodded. "It's yours." He took Gideon's hand. "I hope you find what you need.

1.13
Mon. Mar 9

MORRIS Kendal leaned back in his office chair watching a video that C-Span had sent him. He watched a half-dozen men brought before a federal judge and arraigned for the hijacking of a Daedalus supercomputer. The tape dated from about forty-eight hours after the Secret Service fiasco. Up until then, the men had been held without bond or access to a lawyer.

There were rumors that Congress might offer some of them—the ones not directly involved in the shooting of a state trooper—immunity for their testimony in their closed-session investigation of the Secret Service screw-up. Kendal hoped the rumors were unfounded.

Even if they were, Gideon was right. Something wasn't kosher here.

The tape didn't show anything that wasn't public record. The various news agencies, from CNN to *Hard Copy* had already done the exposé of these men. They were a group of "security consultants." Despite the title, they had little in common with Kendal. These men were all Nicaraguan and Salvadoran ex-military. Applied to them, "security consultant" was a euphemism for hired thug.

Anyone familiar with the death squads of the eighties would have recognized the name of Colonel Luiz Ramon before this incident; now everyone who followed the news would know that since then he'd been implicated in things ranging from drug smuggling to assassination.

"Who hired you boys?" Kendal asked the screen.

Kendal had sources, and knew slightly more than the news agencies did. He had the Colonel's statement to the Justice Department—which he had received in a manila envelope passed to him in the Capitol Rotunda by a very nervous secretary who had owed him a favor. It wasn't very enlightening. The Colonel wasn't saying anything.

It also seemed as if the main defense would be the violation of Luiz Ramon's rights during his capture and the two weeks after. The Justice statement had been given, pointedly, after the period of black captivity before the whole episode blew up in the news. If the Colonel had said anything before that point, Justice didn't have a record of it.

Justice didn't even have a record of where the Colonel had been held before Gideon was shot.

Justice did have a record of a Costa Rican bank that received a wire transfer from a District bank shortly before the hijacking. Two million dollars, paid for with a cashier's check.

For that much, Colonel Ramon should've run the operation a little less as if he was still goose-stepping in some third-world banana republic. He wondered if the Colonel still did the odd job for the CIA, like he had when he was giving communist rebels roadside executions.

Rebels and the occasional nun.

Kendal paused and rewound the tape so he could watch the men again. "CIA, Ramon?" he asked the screen. It wasn't a terribly original thought. There was even speculation on *Hard Copy* about Ramon's connection with the Agency. The problem was the idea made no sense. If the CIA was involved with anything, it was with the failed "Secret Service" sting. From Gideon's eyeball account, and with the fear of God running rampant among his usual sources, Kendal was almost certain that the whole ambush was a black op that was never meant to see the light of day.

That implied, pretty strongly, that the Agency didn't hire the Colonel for this job.

Kendal hit pause again.

Why did their *lawyer* look familiar?

Once Gideon had the newsletter from Cho, he visited the campus library. He was looking for campus papers, yearbooks, and most important, publications from the Evolutionary Theorems Research Lab.

With a few of those papers, and their tables of authors, he had a good list of people associated with the lab. A list of suspects . . .

After some digging, and about five dollars in change through a copy machine, Gideon had documentation of at least two Mikes associated with Dr. Zimmerman's lab. One was a Dr. Michael Nolan, one of the faculty running the lab. The other was a Michael Gribaldi—one of the doctoral students who'd worked in the lab.

Gideon couldn't make heads or tails of the papers the lab published. They had titles like, "A General Computational Approach Toward a Spectral Interpretation of the Zeros of the Zeta Function," and "Deriving the Riemann Hypothesis Using a Genetic Algorithm."

With a little more digging, Gideon unearthed a campus newspaper with a picture of the members from the last year of the lab. The caption of the picture was, "Assault on Mt. Riemann; Drs. Nolan and Zimmerman stand with their New Pythagorean Order—members of the ET Lab—show a printout of a fraction of their proof."

The photo, color faded on the newsprint, showed twelve people. Six stood in back, the other six sat in front. The people standing were holding up a long piece of paper between them. The paper snaked around so that the people sitting in front were also holding up portions of the paper. The paper continued past them and piled itself on the ground, making a mound that was almost a seventh person sitting in the foreground.

The short article—mostly just an extended caption—said that the ET Lab had possibly just proved the Riemann Hypothesis. The article didn't explain what the hypothesis was, except that it was a question in mathematics that had been unanswered for over a hundred years. The paper being held in the picture was supposedly a proof—or at least part of a proof—of the Riemann Hypothesis, generated by a computer. The excerpt of the proof in the photo was over fifteen thousand pages long.

At the moment it wasn't the proof that interested

Gideon. It was the people holding the proof up for the camera.

On the far right of the people standing, holding up the paper, was Dr. Julia Zimmerman. For some reason, she didn't look anything like Gideon had expected. When he heard about a woman running a research lab at MIT, for some reason he expected a short frumpy librarian type in a white coat.

She wasn't short and frumpy. She was at least as tall as the tallest man in the back row, and had an a athletic build. She had black hair that was tied back, so it was hard to tell how long it was. She resembled an Olympic cyclist more than a librarian.

Her face was pale, and wore an expression whose depth was hard to fathom. There was something in her gray eyes, in her half-smile, which seemed out of place. The kind of look he'd expect to see in the eyes of a prophet—or a serial killer.

On the opposite end of the back row, stood Michael Gribaldi. He was young-looking, wore a crewcut, and otherwise seemed to match the description given by the bartender at *The Zodiac*.

Gideon felt he was on the right track.

With a copy of the article in hand, he used one of the computers in the library to call up a campus directory. He put each name he had through the directory. Almost all of the names bombed out. No one from the Evolutionary Theorems Research Lab seemed to still be at MIT.

There was one exception.

Dr. Michael *Nolan* was still part of the Computer Science faculty. He was the only survivor of the ET Lab.

Gideon found that disturbing. What happened to all these people? Over the course of the existence of the ET Lab, there had been about thirty people involved in it. And none seemed to have retained any connection at MIT.

Gideon began thinking of what Cho had said, "Talk to someone in the Comp-Sci Department. Someone with tenure."

Nolan wasn't on campus, so Gideon had to resort to a Cambridge phone directory. He found Nolan in a little brownstone on a street of crowded brownstones that reminded Gideon of Georgetown.

With the newsletter and a copy of the article in his pocket, he mounted the steps and knocked on the door. After a long time, a man opened the door a crack and looked out. For a few moments Gideon thought he had gotten the wrong house. Since the picture, taken five years ago, Dr. Nolan had aged drastically. His hair was shot with white, and lines grooved his face. He walked with a stoop that made him seem shorter than he was.

"What is it?" He looked Gideon up and down, as if trying to make sense of his appearance here.

"Doctor Michael Nolan?" Gideon asked.

"What do you want from me?" His voice was sharp, and he didn't open the door any further.

"My name's Gideon Malcolm. I'm a detective with the Washington D.C. Police Department—"

"So?"

"—I want to ask you a few questions about your work."

Nolan shook his head and began closing the door. "I'm on sabbatical."

Gideon stuck out his cast, blocking the door. "I want to know about the Evolutionary Theorems Lab."

The door stopped closing, and Nolan stared at him. "Let me see some identification."

Gideon pulled out his badge and handed it to Nolan. The man pulled out a pair of thick bifocals and stared at it. He kept shaking his head. "Why does anyone care about that anymore?" He shoved the badge back at Gideon and backed from the door so it opened fully. "Come in."

Gideon followed Nolan into the darkened house. The shades were drawn against the afternoon light, and the only lights in the living room were from a pair of low wattage table lamps flanking the couch. They didn't do much to push away the gloom. The room smelled musty, like a book that hadn't been opened in twenty years.

Nolan wore a suit that seemed a size or two too big. When he sat down, he sank into himself. He stared up at Gideon.

Gideon stood for a few moments until he realized that Nolan wasn't going to offer him a seat. Gideon took a seat in an easy chair that more-or-less faced the couch where Nolan sat. The doctor kept staring at him, *through* him. His face was lined with what might have been pain.

"Are you all right?" Gideon asked.

Nolan laughed. The sound was laced with an almost obnoxious irony. "Son, I had a prostate ripen way past its due. They took it out, and a rotten kidney. They didn't get it all. The cancer's going to get me within a year. I'm *not* all right."

"I'm sorry."

"Don't give me your damn sympathy. I don't even know you." Nolan leaned forward and said, "Now tell me what you want to know and get out of here."

"The Evolutionary Theorems Lab—"

"That thing destroyed my career."

"How?"

"The whole Riemann debacle—even after I tried to distance myself from that, no jury would publish my work. And after what Zimmerman did, I was lucky I didn't lose tenure . . ." Nolan coughed, a hacking wet cough that shook his body. "The bitch should have gone to jail."

Every instinct Gideon had as a cop told him that he was damn close. This Dr. Zimmerman woman was involved in this. Gideon felt it in the way Nolan talked about her.

Yeah, but the connection is so damn tenuous.

He had Mike. He had aleph-null. He needed more to help pull them and the Daedalus together. He leaned forward and said, "Explain to me what the lab was doing. What happened to it?"

Nolan pulled a wad of tissue from a box on an end table and wiped his face, coughing again. "Why? Why the hell should you be digging into this? Ancient history, *and* out of your jurisdiction."

Gideon debated if he should be completely forthcoming. Nolan was part of the ET Lab, and for all Gideon knew, he could be part of whatever was happening.

Gideon found his own paranoia disturbing, justified or not.

"Are you familiar with the recent theft of a Daedalus supercomputer outside Arlington?"

"I don't live in a cave—" He hacked into his tissue. "And you're going to explain why that has anything to do with the lab?"

"I think someone from the lab, probably more than one person, may have been involved in the theft."

Nolan shook with his ironic laugh again. "That wouldn't surprise me. God help anyone who stands between Julia and anything she wants."

Gideon looked into Nolan's face, and saw what had to be a trace of amusement. Two thoughts occurred to Gideon, one was that Nolan really hated Dr. Zimmerman. Second, that if he was involved in the theft, he was one hell of an actor.

"Tell me about the lab," Gideon said.

"Have you ever heard about the genetic algorithm?"

Gideon shook his head. "Outside a few papers I copied today, no."

"The genetic algorithm has been used for decades in the computer sciences," Nolan said. "Putting the idea in layman's terms—you start with a large pool of computer programs with random instructions. The person running the experiment grades each program proportionally on the extent each is able to complete some task. Those that grade in the top ten percent are allowed to 'breed' to create a new pool of computer programs—"

"Breed?"

"In the most basic example of the algorithm, a pair of

high scoring programs are split at the same point, a point chosen at random, in their instructions. Their 'children' are produced by appending the end of one set of instructions to the beginning of the other's."

"How the hell can something like that work?"

"How does evolution work? The genetic algorithm is probably one of the most powerful computational tools developed in the past fifty years. There are trading programs on Wall Street that are generated by using a genetic algorithm. Any problem where someone can give an objective numerical score to success can be attacked with the genetic algorithm."

"So it works? Does something like this require a large computer?"

Nolan smiled, it looked like a grimace. "Like the Daedalus? No. The first practical application of the genetic algorithm was run on an Apple II. All the ET Lab's experiments were run on our own small network. Ten desktop machines, and a server running at 200 megahertz—kids play video games on faster equipment.

"What the lab was, what it did, was all thanks to Zimmerman. She was the mathematician. Everyone else was Comp. Sci. All credit, and all blame, go back to her. She came to MIT to start the lab, and I had the bad sense to hook my wagon to her star.

"She had a reputation for genius before I ever met her, and she had published papers in number theory that made a few people say she was another Ramanujan. By the time she came to me with the idea for the lab, she hadn't published anything in at least three years. At that point I didn't care about that—though I think now it may have been the first sign of her instability."

"Why's that?"

"Mathematics is one of the few sciences where publication is relatively easy. Many papers are distributed on the Internet. But here we have a reputed genius in the field, who hasn't published any original work in three years. She enters Computer Science out of left field."

"But you worked with her?"

"I'm not a genius, Mr. Malcolm." Nolan shook his head. "My sin was to be discontented with my own mediocrity. To have someone of that reputation . . ." He shook his head. "I was a fool."

"What was she trying to do? "

"The application of the genetic algorithm to pure mathematics. She needed the lab to do what she had envisioned. She didn't, then, have the expertise in Computer Science to do it on her own."

"You make it sound as if she'd prefer to work on her own."

Nolan snorted. "That is understating Julia's arrogance by several orders of magnitude. She was working on her own in a room of twenty people. It was her own private world, and everyone was there only on her sufferance."

"But you *both* ran the lab—"

Nolan shook his head. "Only on paper. My work in the lab was the unenviable task of distilling the work of Julia Zimmerman and her clique into some sort of publishable form. It wasn't easy. Her disciples' work was as scattershot and random as the genetic algorithm itself."

"Disciples?"

"I'm not the only one, or the last one, to've believed in her genius strongly enough to throw a career, a life, to her whims. I just came to my senses, a little too late."

"She had a strong following?"

"The New Pythagoreans," Nolan said. His voice broke with the weight of his distaste, and he started coughing again. He shook his head, his face showing the creases of a painful memory. Gideon was too aware of the dust in the very still air.

"I saw that name in a campus newspaper."

Nolan nodded, slowly, as if all the angry energy had suddenly left him. His voice had become shallow and tissue-thin. "The core members of the lab. They shared a worldview that was shaped by Zimmerman's arrogance. They were going to change mathematics forever. Some of them thought they would change the world," Nolan closed his eyes. "They all followed her into an oblivion more obscure than the one I'm destined for."

The air was still and quiet. Gideon pictured the tall athletic woman with the intense gray eyes. After a minute or so, Gideon leaned forward and said, "Are you all right?"

Nolan nodded without opening his eyes. "Fine . . . Just the drugs . . ."

"What was 'the Riemann debacle,' Dr. Nolan?

"What happened?" Nolan sighed. "Zimmerman happened. That's what. The woman was paranoid and probably delusional, and my chief regret is that I never realized it until it was too late." He sat up, and his eyes looked tired. "Many mathematicians see new work as a discovery, not as something created by the human mind. Zimmerman took that view to an extreme."

"I don't quite follow you."

"She believed the programs generated by the lab were windows into an alternate universe, that the entities in her mathematics had an independent existence. After five years working with the genetic algorithm, she acted as if the programs we created were living creatures—"

Gideon tried to tell how seriously crazy Nolan thought Zimmerman was. When Gideon saw the expression in Nolan's eyes, the answer was *very*.

"But what was the 'Riemann debacle?' " Gideon asked.

"She saw no point to independent verification. She was revealing *truth*. God help anyone who disputed it. She attacked even the slightest criticism with unintelligible babble about the 'reality' of her mathematics."

"So what *is* the Riemann Hypothesis?"

Nolan put a hand to his forehead. "I don't think I can describe it to a layman."

Gideon shrugged. "Try."

Nolan slowly got up and walked over to a bookshelf. He pulled out a thick volume and leafed through it, hunched over so far that Gideon thought he was in danger of toppling. It was so dim in that corner of the room that Gideon wondered how he could discern the pages. Despite that, Nolan found what he was looking for and thrust the book into Gideon's lap.

He pointed a trembling finger at an obscure-looking equation.

$$\zeta(s) = \sum_{n=1}^{\infty} \frac{1}{n^s} = \prod_{p} \left(\frac{1}{1 - \frac{1}{p^s}} \right)$$

Gideon looked at it and his mind just went blank. He couldn't make heads or tails of the array of symbols. He looked up at Nolan, and Nolan shook his head and sat down.

"That's the Zeta function. The large sigma represents the sum of the second term over the natural numbers, the large pi represents the product of the third term over the primes. On the same page you should see an expansion of the equation for each of them."

Gideon looked further down the page and found what Nolan was talking about.

$$\zeta(s) = \left(\frac{1}{1^s} + \frac{1}{2^s} + \frac{1}{3^s} + \cdots\right) = \left(\frac{1}{1 - \frac{1}{2^s}}\right) \left(\frac{1}{1 - \frac{1}{3^s}}\right) \left(\frac{1}{1 - \frac{1}{5^s}}\right) \cdots$$

Without the strange symbols, the equation seemed to make some sense, though Gideon had to take the equality on faith.

Nolan leaned back and said, "How do I explain this? Do you know what complex numbers are?"

"Sort of, I think . . ."

"Never mind, just know that there *are* complex numbers and Riemann extended the Zeta function to cover them, and numbers less than 1, as well as the natural numbers. With the extended Zeta function, *s* can take any real or complex value. The extended Zeta has two kinds of zeros, values of *s* where Zeta s becomes zero. There are trivial zeros among the reals which aren't very interesting. Then there are the nontrivial zeros, an infinity of them. The Riemann Hypothesis has all the nontrivial zeros falling on a single vertical line on the complex plane. The hypothesis hasn't been proved yet, though no nontrivial zero of Zeta has yet been found off of that line."

"Uh-huh," Gideon nodded, closing the book that Nolan had given him. "So this is what the lab was supposed to have proved?"

Nolan sighed. "The lab was attempting to use the genetic algorithms to produce new theorems. We'd run two sets of programs in parallel, one deriving a theorem. The other to prove it. Near the end, the programs were generating known theorems, as well as proofs for them. Zimmerman was pushing the lab toward new theorems that could generate the primes, or factor huge numbers. Zeta was a step toward that. Zeta intimately relates the sequence of primes to the sequence of natural numbers. If the Riemann Hypothesis was proved, that opens the door to possible algorithms to find the nth prime, or to factor numbers of arbitrary size."

"Wasn't it proved?" Gideon remembered the article. All the people in the lab, standing, holding up the proof.

"We had one program develop its own version of the hypothesis. That was published. But when the other programs were set to work proving it, it produced something that would take millions of pages to summarize." Nolan shook his head. "It might have been possible to distill the proof. But Zimmerman verbally attacked any academic who even questioned the utility of a million-page proof. After her tirades on the Internet, in letters to respected journals, in personal phone calls, in the popular media, the 'proof' became the cold fusion of mathematics."

"I see."

"It was just too soon. The nature of the genetic algorithm meant that we could have run sequential proofs, manipulating them to be shorter and more concise. But she wanted to use the proof to jump off into some of the deepest questions in number theory. She acted prematurely, and her behavior at having her work—*our* work—questioned was so out of line that the university was forced to shut down the ET Lab." Nolan coughed again and shook his head. "What she did then was inexcusable."

"What?"

"She stole all the research. Four years of the ET Lab's software runs. She erased the network, all of it. That was all the university's property. Me, her, and every grad student and post-doc that had worked in the lab signed over the rights of the work produced in the lab. That almost destroyed my career, just by association. I nearly lost my tenure. I only hung on because I managed to convince the administration that she acted without my knowledge."

"Didn't the university try to prosecute her?"

"They started a suit, and even a criminal prosecution—then they stopped."

"Stopped?"

"They ceased pursuing it any further. It wasn't worth it, so they settled with her."

Gideon shook his head. "I'm sorry. I don't see why it wouldn't be worth it. From what you're saying, there was a lot of important work there—even this proof. Why wouldn't the university pursue that?"

"Zimmerman left MIT and took her work to a new employer that MIT wasn't willing to tangle with."

"Who?"

"The National Security Agency."

א 1

2.00
Fri. Mar 13

IN a small windowless briefing room in the Executive Office Building, Emmit D'Arcy put down the page he was reading and looked at the other two members of President Rayburn's National Security Council. They were Lawrence Fitzsimmons, Director of the CIA, and General Adrian Harris, Chairman of the Joint Chiefs and titular head of the military intelligence network.

Both men watched D'Arcy, Fitzsimmons with resignation, and Harris with an undirected anger.

"So? Are we any closer to Zimmerman?" asked Harris. Of the three men, he was the one who was most disturbed by Zimmerman's disappearance, not that he appreciated the damage she could do, but because she had disappeared on his watch.

"Yes and no," D'Arcy said.

"What do you mean?" asked Fitzsimmons.

D'Arcy took off his glasses and used them to point at the paper in front of him. "Our chief problem is that Zimmerman can compromise our entire intelligence network. Even if she isn't working for a hostile power, as long as she has access to a computer, we might as well hand her every plan we make. There's no such thing as a secure operation."

"We're that deeply compromised?" Fitzsimmons asked.

"How else was she alerted to your little sting, Larry?" D'Arcy looked back at the papers in front of him. "She's been a step ahead of you all the way."

General Harris shook his head and tossed down a folder that he'd been looking at. "Christ, I want to know how we allowed a single individual to be responsible for critical security measures in so many systems. I don't understand this math crap, but that much information in one head was a security risk from the get-go—"

D'Arcy nodded. "That's obvious in retrospect. But given the algorithms she developed, she was the only individual qualified to develop security measures against them. Apparently the psych profiles—or the people who interpreted them—confused Zimmerman's dedication with loyalty."

Fitzsimmons shook his head. "We were probably asking for this to happen."

Harris looked across at D'Arcy. "What are we doing to find her?"

D'Arcy nodded. "Quite right , blame is counterproductive. Our concern is retrieving Zimmerman, or, failing that, preventing her knowledge from falling into enemy hands. As I've said, operations within the community are compromised."

Fitzsimmons frowned, recognizing D'Arcy's reputation. "You mean you want to contract this job out? Like Nicaragua in the eighties?"

"No." D'Arcy opened a file in front of him and passed a photograph around to the other two men. "You both should know this man."

Fitzsimmons pulled the picture over toward him. The photo was of a grave-looking black man in a police uniform standing in front of an American flag. "This is the cop who stumbled onto the Daedalus operation?"

He slid the picture to General Harris. Harris looked at the picture, "Malcolm, isn't it?"

"Detective Gideon Malcolm," D'Arcy said. "He's received several commendations from the District police department, and his work reports are uniformly excellent. He is currently on a six-month disability leave stemming from the gunshot wounds he received."

"Okay," Fitzsimmons asked, "What does he have to do with Zimmerman, other than being in the wrong place at the wrong time?"

"Good Detective Malcolm is attempting to do our job for us." D'Arcy leaned back. "And he may have gotten just as close to Zimmerman on his own as we've managed to get."

"That's impossible," Fitzsimmons said.

General Harris looked up from the photo and said, "I understood we've contained the nature of what we've lost."

D'Arcy looked down at the pages in front of him. "Despite that, Malcolm is investigating the Evolutionary Theorems Lab."

The other two men appeared shocked at the news.

General Harris turned toward Fitzsimmons and tore into him. "You gave us all assurances that, at the very least, you contained the news of Zimmerman's defection. Now I hear a street cop is digging into her past— What the hell *were* you Agency boys doing?"

"Detective Malcolm was following some unanticipated leads," D'Arcy took out another picture and passed it over. This one was a black-and-white telephoto shot, showing Malcolm with a crutch and his cast, knocking on a door to a dark brownstone. The picture was tilted, showing that the photographer was working at an awkward angle. "This picture was taken in Cambridge on Monday."

"Who?" Fitzsimmons looked at the picture, as if trying to make sense of it.

"He paid a visit to Doctor Michael Nolan, Zimmerman's former partner in the Evolutionary Theorems Lab. We've had all the former lab members under surveillance—those we could find."

"Christ," General Harris said. "Can't we keep a lid on this thing?"

"There's more," D'Arcy said. "I have a report here that we intercepted a sensitive request from the Forensic department in the District. Someone was trying to run a set of two prints through the FBI computers. The prints belong to Dr. Zimmerman and a Mister Michael Gribaldi, one of the post-grads from the lab. Zimmerman's on file for her Security Clearance, Gribaldi for an arrest for marijuana possession—"

"What'd we miss?" Fitzsimmons shook his head.

"Malcolm never got those results," D'Aracy said. "But

he still ended up on Dr. Nolan's doorstep asking questions—"

"We have to bring him in," General Harris said. "Debrief him, he already knows enough to damage—"

D'Arcy held up his hand and replaced his glasses. "This is an opportunity, and we should view it as such."

"What are you talking about?" Fitzsimmons asked.

"This man is exactly what we need to close in on Zimmerman. She's demonstrated her ability to stay ahead of us. She knows too much about how we operate and how to determine what we're doing." D'Arcy took back the uniformed picture of Gideon Malcolm. "This man is a wild card, an individual with his own agenda. Zimmerman is so busy watching the lumbering elephant of the intelligence community, she might miss this little mouse."

General Harris shook his head. "I can't say I like this idea. This is too sensitive a matter to leave in the hands of a civilian."

"Exactly what are you proposing? Recruit him?"

D'Arcy shook his head. "Even if he would work with us, no. That would make him part of the intelligence community that Zimmerman's compromised. Detective Malcolm must remain a loose cannon if he's to be of any use to us."

"Even if we do that," General Harris said, "how can we hide the fact we're using him to flush her? Zimmerman has us compromised. As soon as there's *any* internal intel from us watching Detective Malcolm, Zimmerman's going to know we're using him."

"That, too, is simple."

"Explain it, then," Fitzsimmons said. "Adrian is right

about how exposed we are. How's this going to be different from any internal operation?"

"It's this," D'Arcy said. "We have access to an unofficial means to keep track of Malcolm."

"How do we know that Malcolm is going to continue in the direction we want him to go?" Fitzsimmons asked.

"His psych profile shows a deep attachment to his brother. He followed him into law enforcement, even tried to join the FBI. He is prone to take responsibility for the incident. He has a powerful personal motive to uncover what happened with the Daedalus." D'Arcy smiled. "And the man we have to watch him can also prod him in the right direction, again outside normal channels."

"I'm sorry, but Mr. Kendal isn't in the office today. Can I take a message?"

"No," Gideon said, "I'll call back later."

He hung up the kitchen phone wondering where the hell Kendal was. His former partner had been AWOL since Gideon had come back from Cambridge. Gideon didn't want to leave town again until he touched bases with him and found out what he'd discovered about the computer thieves, the ones who were trying to sell the Daedalus to Zimmerman.

Kendal's disappearance was ominous.

Gideon made his way slowly up the stairs to his computer. It had been exactly a month since he'd been shot, and in a few days the cast on his arm would come off. He was still doing physical therapy exercises for his leg, but it seemed to resist getting better. He would never have gone downstairs if it wasn't for the fact the kitchen, and all his food, was down here.

It was a relief to take a seat in front of the computer.

He had spent the last few days in this seat, putting together what he could about Julia Zimmerman. She had done her graduate and her undergraduate work at UCLA. Her family came from Brooklyn.

It had been fairly easy to trace her, from all the academic information on the Internet. What was hard, nearly impossible, was to find her after she left MIT. After that she had vanished from the academic community, leaving no traces. There wasn't any direct way he could confirm Nolan's assertion that Zimmerman went to work for the National Security Agency. . . .

That didn't stop him from looking up information on the NSA. The more he read the information the NSA made public on the web, the more likely it seemed that Zimmerman *had* ended up working for them.

The NSA gave out grants for mathematical research in algebra, number theory, discrete mathematics, probability, and statistics. On their own page it said, "Because of the universal applicability of these areas to cryptology, it is not necessary for the mathematical research in these five areas to have any immediate connection to cryptology."

That made Gideon wonder what kind of application Zimmerman's work had. It also made Gideon wonder what kind of funding the Evolutionary Theorems Lab might have had.

Predictably, the NSA grant had a stinger in it. Research under the grant required disclosure to the Government before public release, and in certain cases required a review to see if the results would be classified.

Gideon checked the NSA employment recruiting pages, and saw that it seemed pretty likely that Zimmerman might find a job there. They were looking explicitly for computer scientists and mathematicians. A PhD with teaching experience could pull seventy-five grand a year according to the NSA's figures.

While he was plumbing what he could at the NSA, which wasn't much, his voice line rang. Gideon cursed and pushed the chair over to the other side of the office, where the phone was. He caught it on the second ring.

"Hello?"

"Gideon?"

He recognized Kendal's voice immediately. "Where the hell have you been?"

"Never mind that. You have to meet me—"

Gideon could hear stress in Kendal's voice, "Sure, I'll come down to the office right now."

"No, meet me at the Vietnam Memorial in two hours."

"What's this about?"

"I can't go into it over the phone. Just be there." Kendal hung up, leaving Gideon with a dial tone.

What had scared Kendal?

Gideon looked up at the computer screen which still displayed "Employment Opportunities at the National Security Agency," and had some idea.

Kendal slowly set the cellular phone back in the cradle. Next to him, Christoffel—his long-time contact in the

CIA—bent over and began rummaging in the built-in bar. Through the windows, Langley slid by the limousine.

"You look as if you could use something to drink," Christoffel said, pulling out a bottle of amber liquid.

Kendal looked at him with distaste. "This is blackmail, you know that."

Christoffel tsked him. "You're aiding your country. The fact that you're preventing the Arabs from discovering your double-dealing—that's incidental."

Kendal looked away from the man, and out the window. He had done some legwork tracking down the history of the Daedalus thieves, and he'd ended up in the custody of the CIA. Now they were letting him go—

If he played their game for them.

To encourage his cooperation, they threatened to leak his special relationship with Christoffel to the Saudis and the other Arabs he worked for. That would mean slightly more than a loss of business. . . .

"Do you understand what you're going to tell him?" Christoffel pressed a glass into Kendal's hand.

Kendal looked into his glass and nodded, feeling a vague disgust with himself for going along with them. Even if what he was supposed to tell Gideon was God's own truth—what he was supposed to leave out was just as important.

He couldn't even figure out why they were having him do this. It was as if they *wanted* Gideon to dig into this mess.

It was growing dark as Gideon limped up to the black wall of the Memorial. He was early, and he was one of only a few people out here this late. Soon the darkness would claim the District entirely, leaving the monuments to the homeless.

Gideon walked alongside the wall, exercising his leg. He could, with a little effort, walk without the crutch now. He walked a few dozen feet carrying the crutch before his leg ached with fatigue. It still felt as if it wasn't getting better, but it must be.

Along the bottom of the wall were collections of dying relics, candles, flowers, letters. He even passed a purple heart medal that someone had left.

It made him think of Rafe, before he'd moved on to New York, gotten married. He remembered standing next to him as they lowered Dad into the ground. Rafe had cried, silently. Gideon remembered catching sight of the reflection on his brother's cheek, and envying him the tear. Gideon hadn't been ably to cry, not then, not for months afterwards.

He realized that he had yet to visit his brother's grave.

Gideon had been standing there, looking into the dark granite for nearly fifteen minutes before the large shadow of Morris Kendal walked up next to him. By now, the only other people here were the homeless transients that seemed to multiply at night. There was one man lying on a sheet of cardboard only about twenty yards away sleeping on the grass of the Mall.

Gideon turned to face Kendal. "So what is this? Where'd you disappear to?"

Kendal looked over his shoulder, back the way he'd come. "You have no idea what you're involved in here—"

"So you've told me. What's going on?"

"There's more than the Government trying to keep a lid on what happened. Dangerous people. The truck driver, the guy who was shot up on the Metro, they were trying to cover their tracks. . . ."

"Who?"

"The Doctor the bartender was talking about in *The Zodiac*—"

"Doctor Zimmerman."

Kendal looked surprised. "You know, then?"

"She's involved, that's all. And that was just a gut feeling until you confirmed it. You're saying she had a hand in those deaths?"

"The people who're using her do. The men in that warehouse weren't Secret Service, they were a covert military antiterrorist unit. They were there for the people Zimmerman's working for."

"Shit."

"Neither of us is safe. On one side you have the Government tied in knots because of all the classified knowledge Zimmerman is supposed to have, and on the other, you have the terrorists protecting Zimmerman."

"Who?" Gideon asked. He imagined a surreal image of the New Pythagorean Order with guns.

"I investigated the thieves, and found a connection back to the International Unification Front. Colonel Ramon's lawyer—" Kendal broke off and suddenly had an arm out, pushing Gideon back toward the granite wall of the monument.

Gideon turned when his back slammed into the wall. Past Kendal he saw the homeless man standing on top of his cardboard. The streetlights glinted off the automatic he held in his hand.

"*Bastards!*" Kendal bellowed. His voice was barely audible over the report as the homeless man emptied three shots from his gun.

The gunshots echoed through the Mall as the impact pushed Kendal's body into Gideon. Kendal's massive body collapsed against him.

"Set me up . . ." Kendal managed to whisper. .

Gideon pushed himself sideways with his crutch and got to his feet, his wounded leg shooting pain up the side of his body. The gunman was running away, across the Mall. Gideon, spurred by adrenaline, tried to run after him, but he barely got a hundred feet before his leg gave out on the grass beneath him.

When he got up from the fall, the gunman was lost in the darkness.

It seemed to take an eternity before he got back to Kendal. His damn leg just wouldn't work right. He fell down twice, and when he reached Kendal, he collapsed against the wall and slid to his knees.

He reached out and took Kendal's hand and said, "You'll be all right. We'll get you to a doctor."

Kendal coughed and spat up some blood. "Ain't happening," he wheezed. The gunman had hit him in the gut, the chest, and near the throat. The only movement was in Kendal's face, in his eyes. He didn't even turn his head to look at him. "Funny," he whispered. "Don't feel anything."

Gideon tried to put pressure on his wounds, but it was

a hopeless task to stop the bleeding. The flowers at the base of the monument were turning red.

"They killed me—" Kendall was saying.

Gideon tried to quiet him. "Save your strength." Gideon was pressing on the wound near Kendal's throat. His cast had turned almost a black shade of crimson.

"Sent me here," he wheezed. "Blackmail. Theft. Setup—" Kendal started coughing and Gideon could hear sick wet sounds in his chest.

"—Bait."

"Come on," Gideon whispered.

"Not all . . ." Kendal started wheezing, and his expression drooped as his body went into shock. There was nothing Gideon could do. In a few moments he heard sirens in the distance, but by then Kendal was already gone.

2.01
Sat. Mar. 14

IT was near four in the morning before Gideon started home.

First the officers showed up and asked him what had happened. Then the ambulances showed, to take him to the emergency room and Kendal to the morgue. Then the detectives came in while they were taking off his blood stained cast, and asked him again what had happened.

After the hospital gave him a shirt and a pair of sweatpants to replace his blood-soaked clothes, Detective Magness from Internal Affairs showed and asked him what had happened, again.

The whole night was a long dark tunnel with no light in sight. Gideon passed through it all with a numb resignation. He didn't really feel anything until one of the detectives had dropped him back by the Mall, and his car.

Once he was alone, he stated shaking.

Gideon sat behind the wheel, feeling the cold sink through his flesh like a frozen razor. He could still hear Magness' words, "You enticed a private citizen into the same investigation that got your brother killed?"

All Gideon could say about Aleph, and Zimmerman,

and the NSA meant little to the prosaic Internal Affairs Department. What mattered, in Magness' words, was that he had gotten someone else killed.

"I didn't want this to happen," Gideon whispered over and over as he drove back to his Georgetown neighborhood. He didn't turn on the heat in the car, as if the cold was a form of penance. Tears he had once envied Rafe for now left burning scars on his cheeks.

Not only had Kendal died, Gideon knew that the official story was going to be that some homeless schizophrenic went nuts with a gun. By now the man who had shot Kendal was probably back inside whatever black organization had spawned him.

Every rational impulse was to follow Kendal's suggestion. Walk away, leave it alone. But he had already gone past the point of no return.

"You can't run away, and you can't ignore it . . ."

He pulled to a stop in front of his house and killed the engine. He sat a few moments trying to gain some composure before he tried to lever himself out of his damn car. He rested his forehead on the steering wheel and tried to decide what he was going to do.

There always had been someone for him to turn to. Rafe, his dad, Kendal . . .

Who was left? Even if there was someone, could he possibly justify bringing anyone else into this after it had killed the two people he cared most about? Could he bear any more blood on his hands?

After a few moments he pushed himself up and opened the car door. It was a long painful trek up the front stairs.

He was reaching for the handle when he thought he heard something.

Gideon froze, balancing on one crutch, listening.

He could have sworn that he heard rustling from inside the house. His hand itched to reach for a gun that he didn't have. It was upstairs locked in a bureau.

Silence stretched, broken only by the sound of distant traffic.

Gideon was half-convinced that his mind was playing tricks on him, but he was careful to silently slip the key into the lock. He was being paranoid, but at this point paranoia was justified. He was suddenly very aware of how dark and empty the street was around him, and how alone and vulnerable he was at the moment.

He had a gut urge to bolt, to make it back to his car and drive away and spend the day in a Holiday Inn somewhere. The thought made him ashamed. He turned the key and pushed his door open.

A blue-gray glow from the streetlights behind him spilled past him into the front hallway. Everything seemed still and quiet for the moment, and Gideon took a relieved half step, swinging his crutch into the hallway.

Then he saw a silhouette dive out of the living room and into the kitchen. Gideon was stunned immobile for half a second, then he threw himself into the house, after the intruder.

Even with his bum leg he caught up with the man. The intruder was trying to force the kitchen door, but was stymied by the new deadbolt, which needed a key to open from either side. Gideon knew that the key was on a hook opposite the doorknob, but the intruder, in his rush to flee, must not have seen it yet in the darkness.

"Hold it right there," Gideon shouted. He tried to sound forceful, but the night's stress made his voice hoarse and weak. The shadowed figure turned and grabbed for him. Gideon caught a flash of white skin and dark eyes behind a black ski mask.

The man swung at him and Gideon bought up his crutch with both hands and lurched forward, forcing it across the man's neck. They both collapsed into the door. Glass shattered and fell across them.

The man dug a gloved hand into Gideon's face. As the fingers dug into his cheek, Gideon managed to spit out, *"Who are you?"*

Both of them slid toward the ground, and for a moment, despite his injuries, it seemed that adrenaline had given Gideon an advantage.

Then something slammed across the back of his skull. Gideon felt his body spasm, and suddenly he was blinking from a prone position on the floor with no memory of how he'd gotten there.

There were two shadows now, Gideon realized as his eyes focused. An icy wind bit into his skin from the open rear door, and he could just see the two intruders jumping the fence in the backyard. Both dressed in black, with ski masks. The second one carried a long flashlight that probably just matched the depression in the back of Gideon's skull.

After a few minutes, he sat up, rubbing the knot on the back of his head. Apparently it was too late to back out of it now. . . .

*   *   *

Two hours later, in a Comfort Inn just outside the belt-way, Gideon Malcolm checked in under an assumed name, and using cash an ATM had advanced on his Visa card.

2.02
Mon. Mar. 16

JULIA Zimmerman lived in a house just outside Annapolis. At least that's where the directory listings put her. Gideon approached it with the same caution with which he'd approached his own house, expecting a similar ambush even though it was midday and Zimmerman's neighborhood was far from abandoned.

He passed by it three times, watching an old man jogging, breath coming in puffs of fog, a college-age couple with backpacks slung over their shoulders, a trio of teenagers passing a cigarette—or more probably a joint—on the corner, a woman walking a dog. Any of them, all of them, seemed threatening. As if any one of them would pull a gun and start shooting, like the homeless man.

The final time Gideon decided that enough paranoia was enough. If there was an assassin here, he'd already had more than an adequate opportunity to shoot at him. He pulled into the drive.

Zimmerman's house was a small brick colonial hedged in by a white picket fence. The fence needed painting. Gideon turned off the engine and studied the house for signs of life. He didn't see any. The windows were blind and dead.

He opened the car door, taking one of his crutches and levering himself out into the cold. The air bit his skin, and he wondered how the old man could stand running in this type of weather.

He leaned on his crutch, taking a look at the neighbors. Both houses to either side had more of a presence of life than this one—even if he didn't see anyone specific at the moment. Curtains were open, a large plastic tricycle was in the driveway of one neighbor, and from the other steam vented from a basement window carrying the scent of drying clothes.

He walked up Zimmerman's driveway. The asphalt was covered with brown leaves that'd been flattened by the last snow. He walked up to the detached garage and peered through one of the tiny rectangular windows into the gloomy interior. Gideon could see the outlines of a car inside.

Gideon tried the garage door, and found it unlocked. He pulled and the door came up an inch, screeched, and his weakened hand slipped from the handle, burning the skin on his palm and almost toppling him backward. Gideon looked around, convinced that everyone on the block was staring at him.

As he looked down the driveway, he couldn't see anyone who was paying any attention to him.

He sighed, bent over, and pulled at the door, more slowly this time.

It resisted him, but once it made it halfway, it loosened enough to slide home by itself. The garage smelled of mold and old oil. A ten-year-old Ford Taurus sat in front of him. The paint job used to be a shade of blue, but it was gray now with a layer of dust.

The tags had expired three months ago. And on the concrete under the engine, a stain of black covered an area the size of a manhole cover.

There wasn't much besides the car—a couple of empty trash cans, and a pair of plastic recycling bins. One bin was filled with newspapers.

Gideon bent over and checked the papers. The latest ones were dated December of last year. He opened the trash cans. Empty.

There wasn't anything else of note in the garage. Most people use their garages as storage, but Julia Zimmerman's garage seemed almost spartan. There were the trash cans, a garden hose, a lawn mower, and the car. Nothing else.

Gideon slid the garage door shut. It closed easier than it had opened.

He walked back down the driveway and knocked on the side door, trying the doorbell a few times. He could hear the bell ring inside the house, and as he leaned on it, he kept an eye out for the neighbors, or anyone else observing him.

No one answered the rings, and Gideon spent the next few minutes jimmying the lock on the door. Even as he forced the door, he knew he was erasing any chance of being able to return from the line he had crossed in Davy Jones' apartment. Swiping evidence was one thing—it had ended up in the crime lab, after all. Despite Magness, he might have been able to explain that.

But once Zimmerman's door popped open, he was beyond any return. Felony B&E. It sank in to Gideon as Zimmerman's door swung inward on a darkened stairway. He wasn't a cop anymore.

Who am I? What am I doing here?

The words he whispered weren't quite an answer. "Someone has to answer for what happened to Rafe." They came out in a puff of fog and fell with a fatalism that acknowledged that that "someone" might be him.

Gideon pushed himself over the threshold and into a darker world.

He stood in the hallway as the door swung shut behind him. The only immediate tangible consequence of his first felony was the dimming as the door shut out the daylight.

For a long time he listened. He knew he was listening for the masked men who had invaded his home. The house was silent. Silent and cold. It was only slightly warmer inside than out, and his breath fogged in the still, stale air.

He stood on a landing. A stairway to his left led down into a basement, and one in front of him led up half a flight to a short hall connecting what he supposed was the kitchen and the living room. It was hard to tell with the rooms so dark. All the shades were drawn against the daylight.

He looked at the stairways and wished that Zimmerman had lived in a ranch.

Gideon went upward to start. He stood in the little hall and stepped into the kitchen and hesitated a few long moments waiting for his eyes to adjust.

The kitchen looked spotless. Gideon stepped up to the counter and opened the blinds over the sink slightly, so a little daylight leaked into the room.

The place seemed almost antiseptic, not a dish in the sink, no food out on the counters. He opened the refrigerator. It was nearly empty. The only thing in it was a half-filled two-liter bottle of Diet Coke. He checked out the freezer, and saw an ice cube tray where the cubes had sublimated half way, and two blue freezer packs.

Gideon checked the cabinets and only found a can of asparagus spears and a few spices.

Zimmerman had obviously planned to leave. She hadn't done it on the spur of the moment. Enough forethought not to leave food or garbage in her house. Gideon wondered if that meant she intended to return.

Gideon moved through the house smelling a ghost of lavender, the only concrete evidence that a real woman once lived here. The other rooms on the first floor were eerily neat, the furniture arranged, the carpets vacuumed. But the dining room table, the mantle, and the glass coffee table were covered with a thick, undisturbed layer of dust.

Gideon passed a phone and picked it up. It was dead.

On the mantel there were a few photographs, their frames covered with the same layer of dust. There was one showing a ceremony where Zimmerman was receiving some sort of award.

There was her face again, framed by her black hair, the expression depthless and fascinating. Gideon stared into her gray eyes for way too long. . . .

Gideon pulled himself away from the picture and

turned to look at the others. There were two that obviously came from the Evolutionary Theorems Lab. Gideon found it interesting that Zimmerman would save those pictures if her departure was as acrimonious as Dr. Nolan said it was.

The last picture was of a young woman that, given the similarity in bone structure, had to be a relative. Sister, niece?

Gideon took a few steps back and looked at the mantel again. No pictures of boyfriend or fiancé—and no pictures of her parents. The only personal tie implied up there was the young woman, who—if not for the green eyes and curly hair—could be a younger Julia.

Gideon made his way upstairs.

The bedroom was like the kitchen. The closet and the dresser were both nearly empty. The only remnants were things that obviously didn't matter. The bathroom was just as empty.

There was one other room upstairs, and it was obviously Zimmerman's office. There was a desk with an impressive-looking computer setup with an oversized monitor. There were bookshelves on two walls, half-shaded windows on the other two. In the dim light, he could see the shelves next to the door piled high with stacks of mathematical journals. Gideon didn't realize that there were so many different publications on the subject. On the adjacent wall the shelves were packed with more standard books. Gideon's gaze followed the spines reading subjects like Number Theory, Public Key Cryptography, Cryptanalysis, and Artificial Life.

Why leave these?

Her computer desk was oriented diagonally, facing the door. He walked around to face her computer. With the thoroughness that Zimmerman had abandoned this place, Gideon thought that there was very little chance that anything explicitly useful would be left here. There was little here except some idea of what Julia Zimmerman might be like.

He turned on the computer, expecting it to be dead, like the phone.

It wasn't. The electricity hadn't been shut off, and in a few seconds the screen flashed alive. After a moment it printed up a text file of stark white letters on a black background.

"All drives on this computer have been formatted to DoD specifications and overwritten. There's nothing here for you."

The message stayed on the screen while the operating system booted and got up to speed. Gideon stared at the screen thinking of the empty kitchen, and the empty closets. Julia Zimmerman really left nothing behind her.

The message flashed off and left the screen with a near-empty desktop. The only object was a small icon centered on the screen. The icon was a tiny grid half-filled with mulitcolored dots.

The icon was titled, "Life."

Gideon took the mouse and slid the cursor over and clicked it.

The drives whirred and suddenly the screen came alive. The whole screen was filled with a grid. In the center of the screen was a small group of dots blinking on and off. As he watched, the pattern of dots grew and mu-

tated, spilling over into the rest of the screen covering the
whole grid with a symmetrical, constantly changing pattern of dots.

There was something hypnotic about the pattern. After
a few moments of explosive activity, the dot pattern
dwindled off and vanished. After displaying a blank grid
for a few moments, the program ended, returning Gideon
to the bare desktop.

He did what he could to see what else was on the machine, but Julia had left it so bare that even basic parts of
the operating system were missing.

The only information he could glean from the system
was that the latest any file was modified was at 7:15 AM
on December 31. Which seemed to coincide with how
long this house had been abandoned. New Year's Eve.

An elaborate message, nothing more. The computer
was little more than a digital equivalent of the Aleph
spray-painted on the wall.

This means something, even if you don't know what.
Infinity.
Life.

He returned to the desktop and the enigmatic icon. He
clicked it again and watched another pattern of multicol-
ored dots go through their paces. He wondered what it
meant. The certainty began to sink in that he had to know
this woman in order to discover what was happening.

"What the hell did you do for the NSA?" Gideon asked
the computer.

And why does she need a Daedalus?

2.03
Tue. Mar. 17

GIDEON drove across the Verrazano Narrows Bridge as late morning light was picking out the New York skyline. He headed into Brooklyn with almost no sleep, looking for Julia Zimmerman's family.

The Zimmerman family lived on a block of narrow frame houses. Again, he was cautious about pulling up to park, circling twice before he pulled to the curb on the side of the street opposite the Zimmermans' address.

Their house dated from the early 1900s and had made it nearly a century without any vinyl siding. The clapboards were painted a cream color that was almost yellow, and the trim was colored a deep violet. The postage-stamp front lawn, all two feet of it, was spilling over with brown plants that marched back to the porch. Gideon thought it must be quite a garden in the spring. Right now, in mid-March, it seemed long dead.

It made Gideon think of Rafe and Kendal.

He crossed the street without his crutch. He limped, and his leg hurt, but he bore the pain. When he climbed up onto the Zimmermans' porch, he could lean against the doorframe and rest his leg.

Gideon stood there a while, looking at the porch. There was a patio set hiding under vinyl covers. Depressions in the candy-striped vinyl had collected dirty water. In a corner next to the door, a ceramic gnome, about three feet high, stood half-facing the wall, as if trying to hide.

Gideon checked his watch. It was about ten-thirty.

He pressed the doorbell and inside he heard chimes play the first few bars of "It's a Small World."

He stood there a long time, waiting, not knowing exactly what to expect. Given the neighborhood, he wouldn't be surprised if Julia's parents looked out on the porch, saw a black man, and called the cops.

The front door swung open behind the screen, and a small, wrinkled, gray-haired woman peered at him through the mesh. She wore a floral print blouse that was at odds with the time of year. "Can I help you?"

From deeper inside the house he heard a male voice ask, "Who is it, Ellie?"

That answered Gideon's primary question. From the records he'd unearthed, he knew that Julia's parents were named Ellice and David Zimmerman. Gideon gave Ellice his most reassuring expression. It was something he did a lot as a cop, and it rarely worked—people were always convinced that he was about to tell them someone had died. Fortunately, since he worked robbery, he didn't have that job much. For all the supposed glamour of the homicide boys, they still told a lot of mothers that their children were dead.

That was all running through his head as he asked, "Are you Ellice Zimmerman?" He was picturing her reaction when he identified himself, and asked about her daughter. Some parents, faced with that, would turn hysterical—

Ellice nodded, "What can I do for you?"

"You're Julia Zimmerman's mother?" Gideon continued.

Ellice smiled, and her eyes lit up. The transformation was eerie, the way all suspicion was wiped from her face. Before she was almost dour, with deep frown lines crossing her jaw. But at the mention of Julia's name, her face took on a youthful cast that seemed to erase decades. Now Gideon could see some of Julia that he'd seen in her pictures. "Yes, dear. Yes, I am."

Gideon smiled back and said, "I'm Detective Gideon Malcolm, from the Washington D.C. Police Department." He braced himself for the inevitable torrent. A cop asking about a child, that always opened an emotional can of worms, and Gideon braced himself for Ellice's reaction. *Why are you looking for her? What's happened to her? Why aren't you doing anything about it? She never did anything wrong . . .*

Ellice managed to surprise him.

"You must come in," she said as she pushed open the screen door. Gideon began to feel that there was something more deeply wrong about Ellice's expression. "Come on, wipe your feet."

Gideon did as requested, disturbed that she hadn't even asked for his identification.

"Who is it, Ellie?" The male voice repeated. It came from upstairs.

Ellice called up the stairs. "It's one of Julia's friends.

He's from Washington." She held out a hand and said, "Can I take your jacket?"

Gideon looked at her hand, spotted and trembling slightly. He thought of the gun clipped to his belt. "If you don't mind, I'd like to keep it on."

Ellice walked into the house and asked, "Can I get you some coffee, tea—"

Gideon followed into her living room and nodded. "Coffee would be great, thanks." Did she just not hear him say "detective" or "police?"

"Please, sit down," she motioned to a long yellow couch.

Gideon sat and looked around at the house that Julia Zimmerman must have grown up in. The decor was a few decades out of sync. The wallpaper was faded geometric shapes on a mylar backing that was worn to a matte gray. A pair of olive-green enamel table lamps flanked the lemon-yellow couch. A long dead console television sat across the room from an equally ancient Hammond organ whose fake wood-grain lamination was separating from the particleboard beneath it. A fat pink princess phone sat on one of the end tables like a dead salmon.

Unlike Julia's mantel, the mantel here, across from the couch, was covered with pictures. The frames crowded the space and climbed up the wall to either side of the flat mirror mounted above the faux gas fireplace. Most of the pictures seemed to be of Julia or the younger woman— Gideon suspected a younger sister.

Gideon stared at a number of the pictures and had the eerie realization that none of them seemed to be more recent than Julia's high school graduation. He heard someone coming down the stairs, preceded by the odor of pipe smoke.

The man stepped out into the living room. David Zimmerman was a tall man, stockily built. His hair was still brown, but had receded considerably. He wore thick trifocal glasses that fractured his eyes when he looked at Gideon. He was shaking his head, and seemed about to say something when his wife returned with the coffee.

"David." Her voice was almost aggressively cheerful. Gideon watched David frown at her, but Ellice didn't seem to notice. "This is Gideon, one of Julia's friends from Washington."

"Uh-huh," David said. Gideon could read David's expression. Whenever he was in a position to see someone's wife go flying off the handle—screaming, crying, or otherwise going nuts—about half of the husbands would take on this same attitude of detached wariness. It was a way of broadcasting, *This all is her problem, I'm just married to it.*

It probably wasn't even conscious on David's part.

"I'm sorry Julia isn't here." Ellice sat down, cradling a cup of coffee in her hands. She was staring at Gideon, or maybe through him. "Maybe if you wait here a little while, you can catch her when she comes home. Don't you think so, David?"

David Zimmerman didn't say anything. He just sucked on his pipe and silently took a seat in an overstuffed leather recliner. He kept his eyes on Gideon, as if he were sizing him up.

"It's so nice to have one of Julia's friends here. She doesn't tell us anything about what she does anymore.

Does she, David?" She said it as an aside that didn't really wait for her husband's answer. "I suppose it happens to everyone. Children growing up, having their own lives."

She stared momentarily into her coffee, and for those few moments it seemed the cheerful facade crumbled. For just a moment, her face, shadowed and bent, took on the aspect of someone who was grieving.

Then she turned back to Gideon and it was as if it had never happened. "So how do you know Julia? Are you one of her friends from college?"

Gideon shook his head. "No. I'm just trying to find out a few things."

"Well, I'm certain that Julia can help you. Our daughter is a genius." She glanced at David who contributed another "Uh-huh." Now Ellice was beaming. "I know, every mother thinks that of her child. But Julia really is. She went off to college when she was only sixteen." Ellice walked up to the mantel and picked up a picture. The trembling in her hand became more pronounced as she held the picture. For a moment Gideon was afraid that she would drop it to shatter on the floor in front of the fireplace.

Looking at Ellice, it was easy to picture her shattering, too.

She talked at the picture. "It was so nice to see her do so well, after all her problems. And getting a scholarship—our baby went all the way to California—"

"UCLA," Gideon said.

David looked across his glasses at him, but didn't say anything.

"Here's a picture of her," Ellice said, showing him the picture she held. For a moment he thought the frame was empty, but when he concentrated, he could make out a grainy black-and-white image that he thought he'd seen before. She turned to face him. "Do you know what the Fields Medal is?"

Gideon shook his head.

"It's like a Nobel Prize for mathematics—they don't have a Nobel Prize for mathematics, you know. They gave Julia one, even before she got her job at MIT. She was the first woman to ever receive one."

"That's impressive," Gideon said. He *was* impressed. He was even more intrigued when he recognized the picture in Ellice's hand as the same one that was on Julia's mantel. But where Julia had a color photograph, the one her mother was touching right now had the grainy black-and-white quality of a newspaper clipping.

"Impressive?" Ellice said. "It is *exceptional*." She took the picture and stared into it. "My daughter is an exceptional woman." The grieving expression flashed across her face like a passing shadow. She shook her head and the smile returned. "But you know all that, don't you? You're her friend."

Gideon sipped his coffee.

"What is it you do?" she asked him suddenly. It was as if the woman who'd been talking for the past ten minutes was gone, replaced by someone with more normal suspicions.

"I told you, I'm a detective in the Washington D.C. Police Department." He braced himself as he said it, as if Ellice was finally going to go into threatened parent mode, assuming the worst had happened to her daughter—which, the way things looked, might not be that far from the truth.

Ellice gave him a suspicious look. "A policeman . . ." This time Gideon could almost see her force the concept into some sort of mental box where it could safely fit with the way she was perceiving the world. Gideon felt uneasy when she said, "Why, that's kind of what Julia does now, isn't it, David? She works for the government. She catches spies . . ."

"Ellie," David finally spoke.

"Like I said, our daughter is an *exceptional* woman."

"Ellie," David said, a slight hardness creeping into his voice. .

Ellice turned and looked at her husband. For a few moments she stared at him as if she didn't quite know who he was, or how he'd gotten here. Slowly, the smile draining from her face, she said, "Yes, honey?"

"I'm sure we've kept—" David looked at him and asked, "Gideon, is it?"

Gideon nodded, setting his coffee down on the table in front of him.

"I'm sure we've kept Gideon long enough. Julia isn't here right now—"

"But if he just waits a little bit." Ellice's voice sounded weak and a bit frightened.

"I'm sure he'll come back when Julia's here." He looked at Gideon, his thick glasses cutting faceted holes in his expression. "Won't you?"

Gideon took the cue to get to his feet. He nodded. "I'm sure I will."

Ellice shook her head. "I'm sorry for keeping you. Sometimes I forget myself. I'm so proud of my daughter, you see . . ."

"I'll walk Gideon out," David said, standing himself. "Why don't you put the dishes away?"

"Yes, I should do that." She gathered Gideon's coffee cup. All signs of the unnatural cheer were gone.

David walked around the table, took Gideon by the arm, and led him to the front door. Ellice took the few dishes to the kitchen without looking back at either of them.

David Zimmerman walked him out to the porch, and didn't say anything until the door was closed behind them.

"They haven't found her yet, have they?"

Gideon turned to look at David, and began seeing a weight there that he hadn't noticed while he was confronted with Ellice. "You mean Julia?"

"Who else?" David took the pipe out of his mouth. "Thank you for not forcing things with Ellie. When the Feds came here, it was a nightmare. When she said she expected Julia any moment, they badgered her ruthlessly. I had to throw them out—and Ellie still cried for days."

"She doesn't really expect Julia to come home soon, does she?"

"I don't know what she thinks," David looked back toward the house. "But she's been expecting Julia to show up, any minute, since she graduated from UCLA."

Gideon thought about the framed newspaper clipping. "She doesn't call home at all, does she?"

The expression on David's face was stony. He kept

looking back toward the house. "That's *our* pain. You and your government bureaucrats can mind your own business."

David reached for the door and Gideon placed a hand on his arm. "Does she talk to her sister at all?"

David turned to face him. "Ruth? I suppose you want to talk to her, too. Just like the Feds."

"How long ago did the Feds come here?"

"Right after New Years, looking for Julia . . ." David's look became harder, more threatening. "Who are you, to come here, looking for my daughter?"

"My name's Gideon Malcolm, I'm a detective with—"

"I heard." David reached over and removed Gideon's hand from his arm. "That gives you no right to drag Julia's memory into this house. I don't care what you government people say, Julia was lost years ago. Please leave us, Agent Malcolm, Detective Malcolm, whoever the hell you are."

David turned back to the door, and Gideon asked, "Do you have any idea where she might be hiding?"

He stood in the half-open doorway and spoke without turning to face Gideon. "I'll tell you what I told them. She's gone somewhere where she can choose her own commitments, her own rules. You have your psychological profiles, use them." David slammed the door in Gideon's face.

2.04
Wed. Mar. 18

AFTER meeting Julia's parents, Gideon rented a room at a motel and slept for nearly twelve hours. At eight the next morning he drove back into the Zimmermans' Brooklyn neighborhood and drove up to Madison High School. It was an imposing pile of brick looming over the street. He parked in front of it for a long time, wondering what he was doing here. Whatever had happened to Julia here was ancient history—

He was supposedly looking for what had happened to him, his brother—*not* what had happened to Julia Zimmerman.

What he *needed* to know was why this woman needed a stolen supercomputer, and why the government was going to extreme lengths to stop her.

In the end, it was Julia Zimmerman—as much as the faux Secret Servicemen, as much as Lionel—who was responsible for Rafe's death. Gideon told himself that that was the reason he was here, unearthing her history. Julia was central to what was going on.

She was certainly central now to his investigation.

Gideon needed to know what drove her, to know what thoughts moved behind her enigmatic gray eyes.

He turned off the engine and entered the school armed with a crutch and his badge.

Gideon walked into an empty classroom. A green metal desk presided over ranks of tan desks. The ceiling was high, and a trio of windows let in the morning light. Lining the rear wall was a long table with a half-dozen computers. Green blackboards flanked three walls, one marked up and labeled, "Do Not Erase," it was a list of problems for calculus homework. The symbols looked somewhat familiar.

"Problem #8: Test to decide the convergence or divergence of the following infinite series:

$$\sum_{k=1}^{\infty} \frac{k}{e^k}$$ "

After talking to two mathematicians already, Gideon felt he could almost understand the notation. It was very similar to the Zeta function, another infinite series of additions. Gideon tapped his finger next to the "∞," thinking of that other infinity, the one Julia used for the Evolutionary Theorems Lab, the one on the business card, "$\aleph_0$."

"Can I help you?" came a voice from behind him.

Gideon turned and saw a thin, white-haired man carrying a stack of papers that seemed wider than he was.

"Mr. Sandler?" Gideon asked, turning around to face the man.

The man nodded as he emptied his papers onto his desk. "And you are?"

Gideon extended his hand. "Gideon Malcolm. I'm a detective with the Washington D.C. Police Department. I wanted to ask you about one of your former students."

Sandler didn't take Gideon's hand, making an attempt to appear as if he hadn't seen the gesture. "A little out of your jurisdiction, Detective Malcolm, aren't you?"

"I'm investigating the background of a crime that happened in the District."

Sandler looked at Gideon's crutch and up at his face. "Do I know you?"

"If you could give me a few minutes."

Sandler looked at the pile of papers in front of him. "Only a few minutes. I have papers to grade, and it's only an hour before my first class."

Gideon nodded.

Sandler pulled out a red pencil and pulled the top paper from off the stack in front of him and began checking pages of handwritten equations.

"Do you remember a student named Julia Zimmerman?"

The red pencil stopped, leaving an unfinished red mark on the paper under Sandler's hand. "Yes," he said. "Some students aren't easily forgotten."

"What kind of student was she?"

Sandler looked up, "The worst kind, Mr. Malcolm. Intelligence with no respect behind it. Disruptive. Mocking. That's what kind of student she was."

"Mocking?"

Sandler returned to checking his paper. "She was

mocking just by being in my class. I teach an honors class in Calculus, the highest level of mathematics offered in this district. It is a serious subject that should be treated seriously. I've taught this class for twenty-five years, and there is no place for girls like her here."

"Girls like her?"

"Questioning the authority of her instructor, making him look foolish in front of his students . . ."

"What did she do?"

Sandler lowered his pencil and looked up at Gideon. "Zimmerman was bored by school. Those types, most of them, they just stop coming to class. Occasionally they do the work, hand it in, but they're otherwise absent. Those types don't make it to my honors class. She was different. She came, every day, and held everyone responsible for her own boredom." Sandler shook his head. "She was ruthless with errors. It didn't matter whose. Anyone could be writing an equation on the board—I have the students do it with the homework problems—and sooner or later there would be a soft sigh from Zimmerman's desk, she'd shake her head and resume reading whatever it was she was really interested in . . . ."

Sandler didn't admit it, but Gideon was certain that he'd been on the receiving end of that sigh.

"She was always right about it. The problems were wrong. The few times I asked her what she found wrong, she could recite the whole problem and identify at least three obvious errors without looking at any notes or the blackboard." Sandler looked back down at the paper he was grading. "She resented this class. She never took notes, paid no attention to the lectures, and spent the class period reading books that had nothing to do with what we were supposed to be studying."

"She didn't do the work?"

"She had a five-subject, college-ruled notebook. In the first week of class she filled that book with every study question in the textbook. Whenever I'd assign homework after that, she'd find the page in that notebook, tear it out, and hand it in after class. She was arrogant, aloof, and I had to get special permission to test her out of my class."

Gideon stood there, looking at the ranks of desks, picturing a young Julia Zimmerman feeling trapped in a class that was far beneath her ability. Again, he wondered what *he* was doing here. Still, he asked, "What kind of books did she read?"

"What?" Sandler asked.

"The books she read in class, the ones that had nothing to do with what you were studying."

"It was a long time ago, I don't remember the titles."

Gideon was certain he was lying. However, he didn't press the point because he wasn't sure what he was trying to discover here. "What kind of person was she? Did she have a lot of friends?"

"Friends? Not from this class. She intimidated people, they kept their distance."

And in return she savaged anyone who made a mistake. A little revenge for being so isolated. Gideon wondered why she came to the class at all. Sandler was right. A lot of kids like that—smart enough to be bored with their classes—he knew ones like them, often ended up fading out of class entirely.

What was your home like, Julia? What was your life like?

A black Lincoln Town Car idled two blocks away from Madison High School. Two men waited inside the vehicle. Both wore charcoal-gray business suits. The driver wore a crimson tie, the passenger's was black. They were splitting a bag of McDonald's takeout between them.

The driver sipped a cup of coffee while the passenger peered through a thin pair of binoculars at the Nissan parked in front of the high school.

"What's he doing here, Nev?"

Nev rummaged in the bag between their seats, his hand emerging with a single french fry. He ate it without moving the binoculars. "It isn't our job to figure that out."

"This wasn't on the list of the Doctor's probable contacts."

Nev loosened his tie, letting his collar open on a deep bruise that graced his neck. "We're assigned to this guy because he might come across something no one else has."

A lone black figure, leaning on a single crutch, hobbled out of the main entrance of the high school. Nev lowered his binoculars and said, "There he is."

As he watched Gideon Malcolm move toward his car, he reached for a cell phone and dialed a long string of numbers. He held it up while it rang a few times. When he heard someone answer, he said, "Hello, Mom? Me and Sammy are still with Uncle here. We're at another store and we still don't have the cake mix you wanted." Nev looked up at the high school. "I wanted to know if we should stay with Uncle, or if we should keep looking here."

A male voice on the other end said, "You stay with Uncle, I'll send one of your brothers to look at that store."

Nev nodded and hung up. He gestured toward Gideon, who was just getting into his car. "Mom says we stay with Uncle."

The driver, whose name wasn't Sammy, nodded and pulled out into the street a few moments after Gideon did.

Gideon tracked Ruth Zimmerman to a studio apartment in Greenwich Village. Driving through Manhattan was a nightmare, and every other car seemed to be a taxi bent on killing him. He didn't reach the village until nearly eleven and it was halfway to noon before he found the street she was supposed to live on.

Gideon wasn't a New Yorker, but he had thought he could navigate in Manhattan well enough. After all, the whole island was laid out in a grid. Unfortunately, someone forgot to mention that fact to the Village, which had some of the most twisted and confusing streets he'd seen this side of Boston.

Gideon found the building after about a half hour of searching. It was a set of apartments above a gay bookstore, a coffee shop, and an Asian store with a large bronze Buddha sitting in the window. The apartments above were hidden by plastic sheets and scaffolding. Gideon couldn't tell if they were restoring the building or tearing it apart. He spent the remaining half hour before noon looking for a parking spot within a reasonable distance of the place.

He didn't know if he had any chance of catching her at home during the day, but he had already decided that he had the time to wait for her if she was at work or school. The worst part of it was the two-block walk back to the building after he parked his car. His leg had been feeling better, a bit stronger, so he'd left the crutch. Halfway there he realized that was a mistake, but he was too stubborn to go back and get it. Instead, he stopped at the coffee shop on the ground floor of Ruth Zimmerman's building, sat down, and ordered an expresso.

Gideon sat at a table with the coffee and tried to get a handle on what was going on.

What he had was a maladjusted teenager who grew up to be a mathematical genius. Resistant to authority. Prone to work alone, with her own priorities and her own agenda. Not someone Gideon would've pegged for government work. Julia Zimmerman seemed way too independent minded.

As he sat there, he thought about Kendal. He frowned at his coffee.

Kendal had found out about Zimmerman independently. He said she was working for a group called the International Unification Front. That was almost as hard to believe as Zimmerman working for the NSA.

I should be spending my time investigating the IUF, not Zimmerman. Why am I here?

It was his fault Kendal was shot, and it seemed more and more that all this was an exercise in avoiding responsibility for his brother.

"No, something *is* rotten here," Gideon whispered. He

knew, and Kendal knew. Right after Kendal was shot, his last words were about a setup. . . .

"Blackmail. Theft. Setup. Bait."

What had he been saying?

What's the sequence of events here? Zimmerman's working for the NSA doing God-knows-what with higher mathematics and computers. Around New Year's she bolts, apparently granting her services to the IUF. After that, Colonel Ramón and company swipe a Daedalus. Michael Gribaldi hires the late Davy Jones to boost a truck to transport the stolen computer. Davy tells Lionel about the score, and Lionel rats him out. Ramón and his people are captured with the Daedalus in tow, and the Feds bury the capture so they can set up an ambush at the meeting place. Somehow Davy gets called off the job while Gideon and Rafe walk into a covert antiterrorist military unit that's pretending to be Secret Service.

Lionel, Davy, and Kendal all wind up dead, Congress tries to hide the investigation from the media, and the grand jury decides not to ask any difficult questions.

"Wonder if I missed anything," Gideon muttered as he frowned at his coffee.

With it all laid out in his head like that, it brought one major question to light. Who tipped off Davy—and presumably the IUF—that the Daedalus pickup was going to be an ambush?

"Fuck," Gideon said to himself. He was out of his depth here.

There were two types of cops in the world. The first one was the type who got their badge, and did their best to do absolutely nothing for the next twenty years. God forbid they bust someone and have to go appear in court. The second one was obsessed with the bad guys, taking down any scum that's responsible for the evil that he sees on the street every day. The first type are the ones who end up becoming corrupt; the second type are the ones that stress out and go nuts.

Gideon knew what type he was. Couldn't run away. Couldn't ignore it. No matter how outclassed he might be. And while Doctor Zimmerman seemed to be the linchpin to what happened, he couldn't leave *her* alone.

The coffee was empty. He set it down and left to see if Ruth Zimmerman was home.

As he walked into the apartment's entryway, a black Lincoln Town Car drove by the street outside.

At the end of a narrow hallway stood a large door. It was covered with sheet metal and painted black. Layers of old paint gave the door its own rough topography. The apartment number, "2," was stenciled on the door in yellow paint. Gideon stood in front of Ruth's door to catch his breath after climbing two flights of stairs.

Next to the door, set in the wall, was a little thumb-turn device that operated the doorbell. Gideon turned it, and felt the resistance of an old clockwork mechanism as the bell rang. For a while there was no answer, then a trap door fell away from a peephole that was drilled in the metal door. Gideon could see a single green eye look at him.

"What? Who're you?"

"My name's Gideon Malcolm, I'm a—"

"What do you want?"

"—detective with the Washington D.C. Police Department."

"Really?" Gideon saw the eye scan him up and down through the hole. "Let me see some ID."

Gideon took out his shield and opened the case in front of the peephole. "Left, so I can read."

He shifted it to the left.

"My left, your right."

He shifted it back.

"That isn't an NYPD badge."

"I said I was from Washington D.C."

"Yeah, what're you doing here?"

"I want to ask you some questions about your sister."

"Been there, done that." The door on the peephole shut the eye out.

"Shit," Gideon muttered to himself. He bent over and rang the bell again, twisting the thing several times in a row. "Ruth Zimmerman," he called to the door, "I need to talk to you."

After a moment, the peephole opened and Ruth said, "Go away. Can't you take a hint? Get a warrant."

"I'm not working with the Feds. I'm here on my own."

"Are you trying to impress me?"

"I'm trying to find out why my brother was killed."

There was a bit of a pause. Then Ruth asked, "What was your name again?"

"Gideon Malcolm."

The peephole door shut again. Gideon sighed and was about to lean on the doorbell again when the door opened a couple of inches. It slid to the side and stopped short on a chain.

"Come over where I can see you," Ruth said.

Gideon stepped over into the sliver of light that the open door let into the hallway. While Ruth looked him over, he took the opportunity to size her up.

She hadn't inherited her sister's height. She was about a head shorter than Gideon. She had curly hair that was cut short, and Gideon could see traces of paint on it. In fact, there was paint everywhere. There was a smear of yellow on her cheek, violets and indigos stained her hands, and the overalls she wore were a patchwork of browns, whites, and reds. Paint even stained the old copy of *USA Today* she held in her hands.

She turned it around, and Gideon saw a perfectly clean circle surrounded by a sharp ring of spattered blue paint, as if a paint can was sitting on the paper until just recently.

"That's you?" Ruth asked. "Isn't it?"

Gideon recognized the picture, him on his doorstep cursing the reporters. Looking at it, he was almost embarrassed to admit it, but he nodded.

"You're the cop the Secret Service shot up." She looked him up and down. "You heal quick."

"Not as quick as I'd like. Can I please talk to you?"

"What's Julie have to do with this?" She waved the paper. "Or you?"

"I think that ambush was meant for your sister."

Ruth stared at him. "That? Her? But why, she *works* for the government—" She shook her head and muttered, "Julie, you arrogant *bitch!*"

"What is it?" Gideon asked.

Ruth kept shaking her head, then she closed the door.

Gideon heard the chain rattle, then the door opened again, all the way. Ruth had crumpled up the old newspaper and tossed it on the floor. She waved him into the apartment. "Come on. Have a seat if you can find one."

Gideon walked into the apartment and Ruth slid the door shut behind him.

"This isn't a great place to talk right now, wait here." She left him standing in the entryway.

Gideon took a few steps into the apartment. It was a huge studio loft. Right now it was lit by plastic-filtered sunlight, the scaffolding outside cutting the light into abstract shadows.

Most of the room was empty, all the furniture had been pushed into one corner and covered with a large sheet of canvas. Cans of paint were scattered about, sitting on sheets of newspapers. There were at least five ladders of various sizes leaning up against the walls. The walls by the pile of covered furniture—about a quarter of the room—were still covered with old whitewash peeling off the red brick. Another quarter of the room had the whitewash stripped off the brick. The rest was a mural in progress. The painting was all a single scene, as if Gideon was looking out at an ocean sunset from some small atoll. He could see the surf crashing on the rocks near the floor, he could follow the waves, getting smaller and smaller until they reached a waist-high horizon, then the walls became a sky riotous with color. The depth was amazing, down to the sparkling reflection on the waves.

Gideon stared at the mural and wondered if this wasn't a "great place" to talk because she was in the middle of this work, or for some more sinister reason. After what had happened so far, it was easy to believe that Dr. Zimmerman's sister would be watched by *someone*.

Ruth appeared from behind a set of screens opposite the pile of covered furniture. The overalls were replaced by jeans, a black turtleneck, and a black motorcycle jacket. She put on a pair of sunglasses as she walked toward him. "Come on, let's go get some lunch," she said.

She still had traces of paint in her hair and on her hands.

Gideon followed her down the steps, straining to keep up with her. She didn't slow down for him, didn't much seem to notice him. She turned away from the coffee shop and crossed the street and stepped inside an Indian restaurant. The restaurant was a few steps below street level, and it took a few moments for Gideon to get down the stairs. He was grateful when a woman with a sari led the two of them to a booth. The place was about half full, a large proportion of the lunchtime crowd wearing business suits and power ties.

Ruth stared across at Gideon, and he wished she'd take off the sunglasses so he could read her expression. When the waitress came with the menus, Ruth ordered something unpronounceable with lamb in it, Gideon ordered the same thing, even though he wasn't sure what it was.

When the waitress left, Gideon leaned over and asked, "Can we talk about your sister?"

Ruth kept looking at him, the sunglasses hiding her expression. "What's she done? You tell me."

"I don't know, other than she's disappeared. From the look of her house, it was a well-planned disappearance."

"Left without a two-week notice, I bet."

Gideon nodded, "If her history at MIT is any indication, she left with more than that."

Ruth lowered her sunglasses and stared at him over the frames. "You know about that?"

"I've talked to some people in Cambridge."

Ruth nodded.

The waitress brought over a couple of glasses of water. Gideon took a sip and rubbed the ache in his wounded leg. "She seems to be very possessive about her work."

Ruth laughed. She raised a hand to stifle herself and started shaking her head. "You can't own the sacred mysteries."

"What?"

"I don't think you understand Julie."

"I'm trying to."

"You've got to picture our family—"

"I've met them already."

Ruth nodded. "Then you've seen it."

"Seen what?" *That your mother's gone off the deep end?*

"They've done everything except change their name."

Gideon shook his head. "I don't understand."

Ruth took off the sunglasses and set them on the table. "No, I guess you wouldn't. I suppose it's hard for someone to pretend they aren't black."

"You'd be surprised."

"What it is, I think, what happened to me and my sister. Is that our folks decided to stop being Jewish. They just stopped sometime before Julie was born. Didn't move, or change their name, but between the two of them they just let the tradition lapse."

"What? Did they convert?"

Ruth laughed again. "No, that would require thought, planning. They didn't make a decision, they just stopped working at it. Laziness and disinterest more than anything else."

"And this helps explain Dr. Zimmerman's behavior?"

"You need to understand that before you can understand her—or me for that matter." She drank from her glass and set it down. "Do you know where atheists come from?"

"Huh?"

"Passionate atheists almost always come from religious families. You have to know something before you reject it."

"But you're not an atheist?"

Ruth shook her head. "In college I tried being a pagan, but I really couldn't find the belief in me. Me and Julie were left without a heritage, our folks just left a void in our lives and both of us tried to fill it as best we could. I'm still trying. I've made friends with a Reform rabbi and I'm trying to make up for some of what I've lost. You know the closest I've been to a seder until last year was watching *The Ten Commandments*."

"How did Julia fill that void?"

"She took a page from the ancient Greeks."

"What? She believes in Zeus?"

Ruth shook her head, but this time she didn't laugh. She looked at him with an expression of grave seriousness. "No, Pythagoras."

The New Pythagoreans, Gideon thought. He remembered all the papers he had copied from MIT. What Dr.

Nolan said, about the people at the ET Lab believing in her work started to take on a whole new connotation.

Dr Cho had said, *"Some might call mathematics a religion . . ."*

The waitress brought their food, and while they ate, Ruth told him about Julia Zimmerman.

A long time ago, before Julia went off to college in California, Ruth had asked her if she had believed in God.

"God?" Julia had said. Julia had been rummaging in her dresser while her younger sister sat on the edge of her bed, feet dangling, barely touching the ground. Julia stopped what she was doing, leaned back on the dresser, and looked down at her sister. The expression on her face was deep, as if she was looking past Ruth, or into her. "I can tell you about the time I first knew that there *was* a God."

It had been in the fifth grade, when she had a class with Mrs. Waxman. She was the youngest child in the class, having already skipped a grade. By then her ability with mathematics was already beginning to flower. She played with numbers more than she did with other children. She had already discovered esoteric operations that her classmates didn't know existed. While they were just starting to reach for fractions, she had touched upon squares, logarithms, roots, and was just making tentative steps into trigonometry.

She'd do the multiplication drills with everyone else, and when she was done, she would spend the rest of the time doodling magic squares on the back of the papers.

Mrs. Waxman never liked her. She was convinced that somehow Julia was cheating. She would call Julia to the board repeatedly to try and catch her in some error.

Julia hated Mrs. Waxman.

Then, near the end of the school year, Julia's resentment at her teacher boiled over when she was convinced she'd caught her teacher in an obvious mistake. Mrs. Waxman was at the board, talking about the number line;

Mrs. Waxman marked off the whole numbers on the line and stated that the number line went off to infinity in both directions. That made perfect sense to Julia. She already understood enough about the integers, she had a clear image of the whole numbers marching off to infinity.

Then Mrs. Waxman said that there were an infinity of fractions on the number line, as many fractions as there were whole numbers. She divided up the number line;

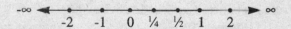

Again Julia understood, while it took Mrs. Waxman a while to convince her classmates. Between any two whole numbers, there were as many fractions as there were whole numbers. While her teacher droned on, Julia had amused herself by mentally constructing a proof. It took her a moment, but she soon could line up every possible fraction with a sequence of whole numbers. She could picture an infinite matrix, numerators changing by rows, denominators by columns . . .

Then, while Julia was thinking through her proof, Mrs. Waxman made her mistake. She said that, in fact, there were as many numbers between zero and one as there were whole numbers.

Julia had to speak up at that. She said it didn't make sense, that Mrs. Waxman had to be wrong. Mrs. Waxman, at first, was relieved at the outburst. For once Julia had shown what Mrs. Waxman thought was a flash of mathematical ignorance. Her response to Julia's assertion was to reassure the entire class that the space between zero and one could be divided into an infinite number of points, as could any segment on the number line.

Julia was frustrated with Mrs. Waxman's blindness. She said again that she was obviously wrong with what she was saying. Of course she could put an infinity of points on the line, that wasn't the problem.

Mrs. Waxman was dumbfounded for a few long moments.

Julia carefully started to explain that there had to be *more* points between zero and one than there were whole numbers. However you would try to count those points, there would be an infinity of numbers that would fall into each of the holes between the numbers you *did* manage to count.

Mrs. Waxman asserted that an infinity was an infinity. Julia kept insisting she was wrong, in front of the whole class. Infuriated, Mrs. Waxman sent her to the principal, and the principal sent her home with a note to her parents telling them that Julia was disruptive in class and talked back to the teacher.

Her father wouldn't hear any explanations from Julia. He just strapped her with his belt and sent her to her room for four days.

During that exile, she read *Men of Mathematics*, a book by E.T. Bell. Near the end she discovered the chapter on George Cantor and his discovery of transfinite numbers. She discovered the symbol, "$\aleph_0$."

"It was like a sign," Julia had told her sister, "A revelation. Until then I had trusted other people, adults, to tell me what truth was. I didn't need faith in them anymore. I knew that there was another truth, eternal, unchanging, and immune from Mrs. Waxman's assertions."

"But what about God?" Ruth had asked her.

"God is there," Julia said. "He is in the equations. His truth is decipherable to anyone who can reason far enough. God is a Theorem. Someday He will be proved."

The story fit seamlessly into what Gideon knew about Julia Zimmerman. It even explained the symbol she used, "$\aleph_0$." Though the Baptist in him was having trouble with "God is a Theorem."

"What did she mean by that?" Gideon asked her.

Ruth set down her fork and asked, "What's the point of spirituality, Detective Malcolm?"

The air in the restaurant was suddenly dark and very still. Gideon lowered his own fork and looked into Ruth's eyes. He felt a vague embarrassment at not being more religious himself. He'd been raised Baptist by his father, but he hadn't been to church in ages. Before he'd been shot, he hadn't talked to God in years. Here was someone who was raised in a spiritual vacuum, and who seemed to've put more thought into the subject during one conversation with her sister than he had for most of his life.

"I guess the point of it is to give us a meaning, a direction in life. Some sense of right and wrong—"

"A reassurance that there's something else," Ruth said. She knocked gently on the table. "Something beyond this somewhat disappointing world we find ourselves in. Something better, purer, more *right,* more *real.*"

Gideon nodded.

"It seems to be human nature from ancient times to believe that this world is but a pale reflection of a perfect, incorruptible realm. Plato said it was all shadows on the wall of a cave. The Greek geometers believed that literally everything had emerged from the sequence of natural numbers."

"So what does Julia believe?"

"She believes that mathematics is the only way we can see clearly into that perfect, incorruptible realm. She believes that any truth that it uncovers is a window into the mind of God."

Gideon felt unconvinced. "But we're talking about something invented by man. How can that bear any relation to God? Even in somebody's mind?"

"It's self-reinforcing. You can see echoes of mathematical behavior in everything from a fall of a stone to a nautilus shell. Julia believed that everything discovered by mathematics had some reflection in the physical world."

Gideon nodded. "Did this have any relationship with the work she did at MIT?"

"We didn't talk much after she went off to college. Only a few times while she was at MIT."

"Dr. Nolan—he worked with her in the lab—said she was beginning to act as if the programs they were creating were living creatures . . ."

"Computers always fascinated her." Ruth looked up at Gideon and watched him carefully. "Why are you here? You're out of your jurisdiction, and you're asking me questions that can't have any bearing on what happened."

"I don't know what has a bearing, and what doesn't. Would her fascination with computers lead to her wanting the use of a Daedalus?"

"I thought they had one where she works—worked."

Gideon leaned back and thought. Of course Julia would have access to the NSA's Daedalus. What would she be doing that needed it? And why would she leave when she already had access . . . ?

"Julia went off on her own tangents a lot, didn't she?"

"What do you mean?"

"The stories I hear about her, writing her own notebooks during calculus class, writing magic squares on her test papers. It sounds as if she was the type of person who would do her own private research on the side."

Ruth narrowed her eyes at him, as if he was unearthing something she hadn't thought about. "What do you mean? She never said anything like that to me."

"Think for a moment. The Evolutionary Theorems Lab published a lot of material, a lot of people did their own research there. When she left, though, she wiped *all* the computers. It was as if she was hiding her work, but most of the work—up to the whole Riemann business—was already public. Why get into a possible legal struggle with the university?"

"I always thought that she was trying to get back at MIT for shutting her lab down."

"Does that seem like her to you?"

"What do you mean?"

"You know her better. All I know is what people have told me. But she doesn't seem like a particularly vengeful person."

Ruth looked across the table at Gideon, shaking her head. "Losing the lab was a big blow to her."

"But it *was* out of character, wasn't it? She's the type that would let a wrong slide by and be satisfied she was right—I mean, when Waxman reprimanded her, Julia looked up George Cantor and found out she was right all along."

"Yes."

"Did she ever show Waxman that book? Your father?"

Ruth leaned back. "No, at least she never said she did. But she was just a kid then."

"The child who'd grow into the kind of person to strike out at an employer out of spite would make every effort to prove Mrs. Waxman wrong, preferably in front of the whole class."

"But she wiped the computers. Out of character or not."

Gideon nodded. "When people do something out of character, nine times out of ten, they're hiding something."

"Like what?"

"Like her own private research. If she was doing something on her own, she might not have wanted MIT to have it. If that's the case, I'd wonder if she continued that work with the government's equipment."

"Like what?"

"Something she needs a Daedalus for."

2.05
Wed. Mar. 18

WHEN they left the restaurant, it was close to two-thirty. Gideon walked with Ruth back toward her apartment. He felt as if he was closer to understanding Doctor Julia Zimmerman, if no closer to understanding what she was doing.

He was thinking over what Ruth had said, about Julia's belief in her mathematics, when he noticed something across the street. A man in a heavy leather coat was pacing them. The man's hands were in his pockets, and he seemed to be conspicuously not looking at Gideon and Ruth as they walked down the street.

Ruth was saying something, but Gideon wasn't paying attention to her. He was looking ahead of them. On the sidewalk, walking toward them, was a man in a jogging suit, wearing a windbreaker. His hands were in his pockets, too.

Gideon took Ruth's arm and started slowing down.

"Are you all right?" Ruth asked as Gideon began exaggerating his limp.

"Follow my lead," Gideon whispered.

They were limping past a small bookstore. The front

window display was filled with the covers from a lot of underground magazines. Inside, Gideon could see ranks of bookshelves facing the doorway.

The man in the jogging suit was about ten yards away. His right hand was coming out of his pocket. Across the street, the man with the leather coat had stopped and looked as if he was about to cross the street.

A small bell rang as a man walked out of the bookstore. While the door stood open, Gideon half tackled Ruth into the store while he grabbed for his own gun. "Back in the store," Gideon said, "Take cover."

Ruth froze for a moment. The man behind the counter began to say something, "Hey—what?"

Then there was a sound like a soft explosion—like a sledgehammer pounding loose sand. It was accompanied by the sound of breaking glass. A hole appeared in the glass of the closing front door.

With that, Ruth scrambled for the back of the store to take cover somewhere behind the shelves. The guy behind the counter dropped, and Gideon hoped it wasn't because he was hit.

Gideon saw the guy with the jogging suit through the front window. His hands were out of his pockets, and he carried a wicked looking automatic sporting a silencer. He was running for the door.

Gideon leveled his revolver and fired. Unlike the silenced automatic, this sounded like a gunshot. The bullet punched a hole in the window just behind the jogger. The jogger dropped out of Gideon's line of sight. There were others moving on the other side of the bookshop door.

They dropped as well, before he could get a good look at them.

Gideon didn't wait for them to reappear. He backed up, past the lines of shelves, toward the rear of the store. He was hoping there was a back way out of this place.

As he ducked around the last bookshelf, Ruth grabbed him. "What the hell's going on?" she demanded.

"We have to get out of here," Gideon looked around the rear of the bookstore and saw what he was searching for. A large fire door stood at the end of the corridor formed by a tall bookshelf and the rear wall. It said, in bright red letters, "Emergency Exit Only."

There was the sound of breaking glass by the front of the store. Gideon grabbed Ruth and pushed her toward the exit.

"Who are these people?"

"CIA, NSA, I don't know—just that they're trying to shoot us."

Ruth slammed through the door first. As soon as the door opened, the room was filled with the sound of a fire alarm. She pushed through, Gideon following on her heels, backing toward the fire door, his gun pointing back into the store.

He saw the gunman start to duck around the bookshelf and he put two shots near the corner. Fragments of wood and paper flew into the air, and the follower ducked back around the corner of the bookshelf.

The fire exit led into a narrow alley that was only open at one end. "Run," he yelled at Ruth. They had to get to the end of the alley before these guys cut off their only escape route. Ruth didn't need the encouragement, she was already running for the street. Gideon started running after her, but he could feel his injured leg resist the movement. He was barely twenty yards away from the door, and Ruth was almost at the street.

The fire door began moving, and Gideon fired another shot next to the open side of the door. The shot echoed in the alley, and orange sparks flew from the brick near the handle of the door. For the moment it stopped moving.

Then he heard Ruth scream, "Shit!"

Gideon turned to look toward the mouth of the alley. A black Lincoln Town Car had pulled up, passenger side facing the alley, blocking their escape. Ruth was only a few feet from it.

The rear door opened and someone yelled from inside. "Quick, get in!"

Whoever they were, they weren't trying to shoot them. Ruth didn't appear to debate the matter. She dove into the back seat. Gideon started running, his limp trying to slam him into the wall of the alley with every other step. As he closed on the car, the front passenger door opened, and a large man stepped out. He wore a charcoal-gray suit and a black tie, and in his hands he held a silenced Uzi.

Gideon threw himself on the ground as the guy started firing. He was close enough to him that he could hear the hot brass casings bounce around and over him as the gunman emptied the Uzi's clip into the alley.

"Come on, move it," the gunman called as Gideon heard him change clips.

Gideon pushed himself up and scrambled for the back seat of the Lincoln, landing on his side next to Ruth, somehow keeping his grip on his gun. Outside the car, he heard the sound of the muffled Uzi reverberate through the car. He managed a look back down the alley and could see someone attempting to return fire, using the metal door for cover. The door itself was peppered with dozens of holes, and the men following them didn't dare give up their cover while the Uzi was firing.

The man with the Uzi kicked the passenger door shut after Gideon was fully inside. He let a few more shots go into the alley, and then he slipped into the passenger seat. The Lincoln was accelerating away before he'd even closed the door.

"Well," said the driver, sparing a glance back at Gideon and Ruth, "I guess we're in it now."

"Who are you people?" Ruth asked.

The man who'd carried the Uzi shook his head. "It would be inadvisable to tell you that. Suffice it to say that it's not in our best interests to allow you to fall into the hands of those people."

"And *who* are they?" Ruth asked.

Gideon sat up. There was something vaguely familiar about these guys.

Now that he could see where the Lincoln was going, they were shooting north, weaving in and out of traffic. They blew through lights as yellow cabs blared horns at them.

Gideon noticed a livid bruise on the neck of the man with the Uzi. "You were at my house," Gideon said.

"You're worth keeping track of," said the driver. "We're not the only ones of that opinion."

"What's going on?" Ruth yelled with frustration bordering on hysteria.

"We'll explain what we can, when we can," the gunman told them as they tore through another intersection and made a screeching turn following signs toward the Holland Tunnel. While the one drove like a maniac, the other picked up a cellular phone and dialed someone. "Hi, Mom," the guy said. "Uncle had a bit of a breakdown. We had to pick him up. We got some groceries and we're heading to Abe's house. Yeah, I think you better call Triple-A." He hung up.

"Uncle?" Gideon said.

"We're going to take you to a safe house, check you both out for listening devices, then we'll see what we can talk about."

The Lincoln slid into the tunnel. Gideon raised his gun and said, "I'd like an explanation *now*."

"You better put that away," said the driver. "We don't want things to get ugly." The Lincoln started slowing down. "I could let you both out here. But neither of us is going to discuss anything before we get where we're going." The car was almost stopped, and behind them horns were blaring at them. "Now either put that away, or get out."

Gideon considered forcing the issue, but he didn't know if he wanted to. He would be putting Ruth in danger if he started pulling macho shit now. And whatever was going on, these guys seemed to be at least partially on his side.

He holstered the gun.

On the far side of the Hudson, they drove through Jersey City. They wove through so many twists and turns that Gideon was unsure exactly where they were when they entered a residential area and pulled into a weed-shot driveway. The house was in a run-down neighbor-hood, and looked as decrepit as the buildings to either side. The paint had once been red, but had faded to a chipped, weathered brown. Two windows were covered by sheets of plywood.

The garage didn't look all that safe. The walls were tilted to the left, as if the whole thing was about to collapse. Despite that, the door slid up silently on its own as the Lincoln drove up the broken driveway. The car slid into the broken-down garage and the door started closing immediately. Gideon looked outside and saw that there seemed to be a few new timbers bracing the garage up-right in its awkward position.

The driver waited until the door was completely closed behind the Lincoln before he said, "Could we have the gun, please?"

Gideon didn't like the way things were going, but he decided that there was little to gain by not playing along. Ruth was looking at him as if she blamed him for what was happening. For all he knew, she might be right. He handed the butt of the gun to the driver.

The other man got out and opened the passenger door next to Gideon. "Come on," he said. As Gideon got out of the car, the man took a small wand from off of a shelf of old tools lining the wall of the garage. Unlike the rusty hacksaws and miscellaneous junk scattered on the shelf, this thing looked brand new. He flipped a switch on the thing and swept Gideon up and down as if it was a metal detector.

He did the same to Ruth as she stepped out of the car.

"You'll both be happy to know that neither of you have any transmitters on you." He put the device back on the shelf where it blended in with the rest of the junk. "Come with me."

He led them out of the garage and through a weed-filled backyard whose main feature was a stack of old tires piled next to the rear wall of the house. Their guide took them to the back door. The door had an iron security grate; the window behind the grate was covered by a sheet of plywood. Despite the security, their guide opened the door without a key.

From the outside, the place made Gideon feel uneasy. You found bodies inside this kind of place. Inside he expected to see mattresses and used needles scattered on the floor—a shooting gallery or a crack house.

The interior was different.

They stepped through into a kitchen and their guide hit a light switch, filling the room with bright white light from a brand-new fluorescent fixture. The place was clean, even though the plaster was cracked and a half dozen tiles were missing from the walls. There wasn't a stove or a refrigerator, but a new microwave sat on one of the kitchen counters.

They stepped through the kitchen, and into the front of the house. The living room and dining room were both as clean and as empty as the kitchen. A card table and a few chairs sat in the dining room, and a lone futon sat in the living room. The futon faced a small television that sat on a small dorm fridge that was only slightly bigger than it was.

One of the folding chairs was occupied.

"Have a seat," said the man, waving at two of the other chairs. Their guide, who probably still had his Uzi, remained standing.

Gideon sat next to Ruth and studied this new person. He was probably in his eighties. His hair was snow white and somewhat wild. His eyes were hard and penetrating, but seemed to glimmer at some private joke.

"Gideon Malcolm," he nodded at Gideon, "Ruth Zimmerman."

"Who are you?" Gideon asked. "Why are we here?"

The man leaned back in his chair. "My name wouldn't be a prudent revelation. And I think you both know why you are here."

"What do you have to do with my sister's disappearance?" Ruth finally said.

Gideon could see her muscles tense, and sensed that she was on the verge of some sort of outburst. She had been quiet most of the way here, all the tension building up . . .

Gideon put a hand on her shoulder and hoped that was enough to calm her.

"That," said the old man, "I can tell you. Neither I, nor the people I work with, have anything to do with your absent sister. If we had, your sister never would have disappeared."

"What do you mean by that?" Ruth said. "What's happened to her? Why are people shooting at me?"

Gideon squeezed Ruth's shoulder and asked his own question. "Why did you step between us and a bunch of gunmen? What do you get out of all this?"

The old man stood and started pacing around the table. "Dr. Zimmerman is a very dangerous person," he said. "Her flight has threatened a great many people. Including the people I work for, including your own government."

Ruth shook her head. "Julia wouldn't threaten anybody."

"What she *knows* is threatening, regardless of what her motives are. And the presence of those gunmen bring her motives into question."

"Who are they?" Gideon asked.

The old man ran his hands through his white mane of hair. "In the 1980s there were a number of states in the Middle East that sponsored—publicly and privately—various terrorist organizations. Back then there was a lot of financing by the Soviet Union and these groups had common training grounds in Lebanon, Libya, Angola. When the USSR split apart, the loose network of organizations remained, sharing intelligence, expertise, and occasionally personnel. What had begun as group of terrorist organizations soon became an independent multistate intelligence network with a Pan-Islamic agenda. It calls itself the International Unification Front. It stretches from Bosnia to Iran, from Kazakstahn to Angola. It represents a continual threat to your country and the European democracies."

"So these people are Arab terrorists?" Gideon asked.

The old man shook his head. "Both terms are probably inappropriate. While this organization contains Palestinians, Syrians, and Libyans, it also contains its share of Europeans, Africans, Russians. Its goal is the domination of the Middle East and Central Asia, and its ideology is inherently anti-Western. Its function is predominately espionage: economic, industrial, technological."

"They have Zimmerman, don't they?" Gideon said.

The old man turned and faced both of them. "Yes, God help us all. The people that have died, they've been assassinated by the IUF. All of them. I'm unsure if your own government realizes who is responsible."

Ruth shook her head and said, "Oh, God."

"Then why didn't they come after me until now?" Gideon asked. "Or Ruth?"

The old man got up and walked into the living room. He picked up a small camcorder, one with the flat LCD playback screen, and brought it back to the table. He pointed the screen at Gideon.

"Too dangerous to bring your car back here, but we taped the pickup to show you what you're dealing with."

Gideon watched as the shaky handheld shot approached his car. Suddenly, three other men appeared in the shot. One popped the driver's door with a slim-jim so fast that it was hard to tell he didn't have a key. One man entered the car while the two others went to opposite ends of the Nissan. One popped the hood and the other popped the trunk. They were going over the car with electronic devices akin to what they'd used on Gideon and Ruth in the garage. This time they found something.

The one inside the car took apart his crutches. They stripped off the padding on top of one and held it up for the camera. Gideon saw a small device, little bigger than a cold capsule, hidden in a slit in the padding.

"What's that?" Gideon asked, pretty sure what the answer was already.

"Listening device," said the old man. "If we watch the rest of the tape, we'll see them find a tracking device and another microphone in your car."

Gideon nodded as the tape ran. He watched them do as the old man said. However, after going through all he had at this point, he couldn't quite escape the impression that it all could have been staged for his benefit.

"What was the point of watching me?"

The old man shut off the tape. "Up until now you were a useful tool. Watching you, they had a good idea of exactly how close anyone was to Zimmerman."

"The same reason you were watching me?" Gideon looked pointedly at the gunman by the door, the one with the bruised neck. "Why you broke into my house—"

The old man steepled his fingers. "You've managed to scare elements into the open that would've otherwise remained hidden. You're close enough to Zimmerman now that the IUF is nervous."

Gideon shook his head. "That doesn't make sense. I've been playing catch-up since this whole thing started—"

"Why do you think your own government hasn't debriefed you?"

Gideon sat there and looked into the old man's steely eyes. He wasn't sure what he'd meant by that. "Why should they?"

"It's standard procedure when a civilian gets as close as you have to sensitive information. Instead, they've made a point of ignoring you and allowing you to be a loose cannon. They should have brought you in as soon as you hired Morris Kendal. But they're desperate enough to believe you'd be more useful stirring things up."

Gideon stood, his chair crashing to the ground behind him. "What the hell do you know about Kendal?"

It was now Ruth's turn to grab his arm and try and calm him down. The other guy, the Lincoln's driver, took a few steps toward the table until the old man held up a hand to stop him.

"Kendal became a threat to the IUF as soon as he began working with the government."

Gideon stood there, speechless.

"Why don't you pick up your chair?"

"What do you mean, 'working with the government?' "

"When Morris Kendal started asking your questions to his contacts in the CIA, they brought him in. We only know this because, by that point, we were already watching Kendal's movements."

"But when he met me—"

"We believe he was there to encourage you to go after Zimmerman. To make sure the loose cannon went off in the direction they wanted."

"Why kill him, then?"

"Sit down," the old man said.

Gideon backed up and righted his chair. "Why did they kill him?"

"Sit."

Gideon finally sat.

"Morris Kendal carried out contract security assignments for various Arab and African delegations. It's almost certain that he had seen a number of the people who're working on Zimmerman. If he started working with the U.S. Government directly, the IUF believed it would only be a matter of time before Kendal led the government to them."

"He knew—" Gideon said. "He told me that this International Unification Front was involved."

"Kendal was in a position to know things much more damaging than simply the IUF's involvement."

"Like what?"

Ruth looked up at the old man and said, "Why are we here? What do you want? *Who are you?*"

"What I want is to prevent Zimmerman's knowledge from falling into the hands of the IUF. Seeing how things have progressed, my secondary goal is to discover what they have gotten from her, how they are using her." The old man looked at Gideon. "I also want to punish those responsible for the death of Mr. Kendal. He was, I think, a friend of mine. I tried to steer him away from dangerous waters. I probably failed him by not being imperative enough."

"What do you want from us?" Gideon asked.

"Your help," the old man said. "Between the both of you, you know something that the IUF believes is dangerous enough for them to come after you. We know that they were watching Ruth, and that there was one of their people in the restaurant—"

"Oh, shit," Ruth whispered.

"In a position to hear your conversation."

"Why should we trust you?" Ruth asked him. "Why should I help you hunt down my sister?"

"Because the other players in this game would gladly execute her to prevent her knowledge from being propagated." He turned to face Gideon. "It was your own government that used that Daedalus computer to lure Dr. Zimmerman out into the open. They would have shot her down the way they shot down you and your brother."

"What do you want from us?" Gideon asked. His mind was already racing over what he and Ruth had said.

"Your conversation in the restaurant. What was it about?"

Gideon glanced at the windows of the living room. Shadows blackened the shades. It was dusk outside, soon to be night.

"I can't believe—" Ruth started.

Gideon grabbed her low on the arm, below the old man's line of sight, and—he hoped—out of view of the other guy who was currently pacing around the room, behind the old guy. He squeezed.

Ruth stopped talking and looked at him.

"On a condition," Gideon said. "You tell me why everyone's after Zimmerman. What does she know that's so important?" He could feel Ruth tense up, but she didn't interrupt.

"There are two reasons. One's provincial to the NSA, the other is more of a universal threat. The first reason, the provincial one, is that Dr. Zimmerman was involved in all the security architecture installed on the NSA's computers over the past five years. She knows what they were protecting against, which is almost as important as how. The NSA's security procedures have filtered through to a series of agencies. As long as Dr. Zimmerman is out there, none of those systems can be considered secure. Both the NSA and the CIA are behaving right now as if *all* their operations are compromised to some extent."

"That's a provincial reason?"

The old man nodded. "Provincial and transitory. It will take a few months for them to reconstruct their security, no matter what happens with Zimmerman. That kind of intelligence information is devalued the moment the target knows you have it. There's more . . . Have you heard about information warfare?"

"I probably heard about it on *Nightline* once."

The old man chuckled. "The agency that Dr. Zimmerman works for was intended to be completely passive. It listened. It would gather in signals intelligence from everywhere it could, landline, radio, satellite, Internet— almost every type of electronic signal generated on this planet will pass through its computers. However, as strong cryptographic methods became prevalent, available to individuals and organizations, the agency was forced to become a more active gatherer of intelligence."

"What do you mean, 'more active'?"

"One example—they have one program, the community's nicknamed it the 'shadow.' It's a virus that hides on a host system and does nothing but monitor keystrokes and hide the information in a buffer on the victim's hard drive. Whenever the victim makes contact with the Internet, the virus transfers the buffer's data back to a repository where the information can be gathered. A system can seem incredibly secure, and still be vulnerable to that kind of program. It's very hard to defend against."

"They can do that?" Ruth asked. Her voice seemed to

carry the same sort of unease that Gideon felt. "Isn't that illegal?"

The old man chuckled. "Many of their current intelligence-gathering methods come from the repertoire of the last wave of hackers. They have a program that can crack eighty percent of all passwords—and it just relies upon the weaknesses of human nature, the tendency to make passwords actual words." He shook his head. "The line between information intelligence and information warfare disappears once you don't stop at simply listening to a target system. And there're other, *more active,* measures they use . . ."

"Like what?"

"I have little access to that kind of information," he steepled his fingers again. "But try a little thought experiment. Take the shadow virus—change it a little. Now every personal computer nowadays keeps track of the nation it lives in, so it can operate in the proper language, use the correct currency and measurement units . . . Let's just say that this virus will only copy itself to a computer that identifies itself as Iraqi, or Iranian, or Chinese. Now, whenever that computer logs on to the Internet, this virus checks a specific site for a date. If it finds a date there, it decides that it will wipe that computer's hard drive on or after that date."

Gideon leaned back and shook his head. "They're doing this?"

The old man nodded. "There may even be some chance that they've hidden some of this computational ordnance in the operating systems of these computers. It doesn't even require a mole in the software company. It just requires them to engineer it in and deliver it into the target area before the commercial package arrives. Eighty percent of the software in the third world is pirated. A conservative estimate is that a third of it has been tampered with. An early copy of a basic software package will propagate itself throughout the area with little or no help from outside."

"Then a war starts," Gideon said.

"And every computer in the target area dies." The old man paused to allow that to sink in. "Now this is all speculation. I don't have exact information on Zimmerman's work. But what we do have suggests that her knowledge was being used to develop this kind of information warfare software—military and paramilitary computer viruses. She seems to have been involved in some sort of breakthrough. Something we don't want the IUF to have access to." He waved to the other man, the driver. He left the room. Gideon couldn't see where he went, but he got a sense that he went down into the basement. "It's now your turn. Tell me what you two discussed in the restaurant."

After Gideon had gone over the conversation, with Ruth's reluctant help, the old man left them and the anonymous driver returned and escorted them to a room upstairs. It was a small bedroom with only a pair of cots, a table, and a table lamp sitting on a stool. The one window was covered with plywood, and the door didn't lock—it only had an empty hole where the doorknob would go.

The driver said, "You can rest here while we decide what's going to happen."

Once the door closed, Ruth started yelling. "What the hell do you think you're doing? You're playing games with Julie's life—our lives. You don't even know who these bastards are."

Gideon sat on the bed and massaged his leg. "My personal bet is Israeli, and they stepped in when we were getting shot at. That counts for something."

"Because they want something. These guys aren't the government. Have you thought about the fact it might be treason to help these people?"

"Whatever Julia was doing, the contents of our conversation weren't classified material. And last I checked, Israel was still our ally." Gideon looked up at Ruth. "Forgive me if my faith in my own government is slipping."

"Damn, damn, damn—" Ruth started pacing, pounding her right fist into her upper thigh. "Why the hell do they care what we were talking about? I don't know any government secrets. The only way I knew Julie was AWOL was because the Feds—and you—came to question me about it. . . ."

Gideon shook his head. By most reasonable measures he had all the answers right now. Julia Zimmerman worked for the NSA, she went AWOL—abducted, recruited, or sold her services to—the International Unification Front. The U.S. intelligence community must have gone absolutely nuts trying to locate her. Whatever Zimmerman was doing, she needed a Daedalus, and the IUF hired some Central American thugs to liberate one while one of Zimmerman's old grad students hired a driver. The CIA—or whoever—captured the Daedalus thieves and set up an ambush for the delivery. And, unfortunately, Lionel decided to sell his information to Gideon.

It was a more complicated screwup, but still just a screwup. . . .

Why did it still feel as if he hadn't come close to what was really going on?

"Damn it, are you even listening to me?"

Gideon looked up. "What?"

Ruth made a disgusted face and said, "Sheesh. I was asking you about what you plan to do to—" The lights flickered. "What?"

Gideon stood up, somewhat unsteadily. The lights flickered again, and stayed out this time. Suddenly the only light was a dim sodium glow filtering through gaps in the window's plywood.

"What are they doing?" There was a thin note of hysteria in Ruth's voice.

"Quiet." Gideon whispered harsh and sharp, and went so far as to place his fingers on Ruth's lips.

There was a dim sound from downstairs. Running feet. Unmistakable confusion. Whatever was happening, it wasn't just for the prisoner's benefit.

"*I think,*" Gideon whispered, "*we better get out of here.*"

He felt Ruth edge up behind him. "What's happening?"

"I'd like to believe it's just a blackout—but I'm not a strong believer in coincidence." He edged into the darkened hall holding up a hand for Ruth until he was sure the way was clear. The hallway was long, narrow, and almost pitch-black. One end faced stairs down, the other faced stairs to the attic. Cautiously, he waved Ruth after him.

From somewhere came the sound of breaking glass, then a dull thud.

There was something visceral in the sound that made Gideon back up from the downward staircase.

"Wh—"

Ruth didn't manage to voice the complete syllable before an explosion tore through the first floor and the concussion knocked Gideon backward on top of her. Suddenly the air was hot and thick with smoke and the hallway was illuminated by a dim ocher glow that reflected from the walls of the staircase.

Then the gunfire started.

"Oh, God . . ." Gideon could feel Ruth shaking beneath him.

Gideon rolled onto his knees and shook Ruth's shoulder. *"Are you all right?"*

"I think s—"

"Then *move* toward the attic before we're trapped in here." Gideon half-dragged Ruth away from the downward stairwell. Despite his words, he was feeling all too trapped already. This second, his main concern was moving away from the flames, and the too-familiar dull thudding of silenced gunfire.

Up the stairs was more of the sodium glow from the streetlights outside. The light came in three directions through glassless windows. Light also leaked in through the unfinished rafters where old fire damage had eaten holes through the roof. Gideon ducked instinctively as he rounded the top of the stairs. There was a nasty feeling of exposure up here that sank home when he saw the floor near the front side of the house.

Sprawled beneath the street-facing window was a body. Ruth must have seen it about the same time he did, he heard her gasp behind him. The corpse's head was a misshapen shadow, and on the ground nearby lay a broken pair of expensive binoculars.

"Stay down," Gideon whispered. "That guy must have been keeping an eye on the street for them." *Must have been the first one to be taken out.*

Gideon crawled out into the attic. The floor was rough, unfinished plywood that hadn't even been nailed down. As he inched from the stairwell, he saw two video surveillance cameras looking out the other two attic windows. Cables snaked around to a card table where a trio of dead monitors faced the front of the building, and where the dead guard had been sitting.

Gideon crawled up to the side of the dead man. Ruth whispered at him, *"What are you doing?"*

From below came the sounds of staccato thumping, more gunfire, punctuated by the sound of another explosion. The smell of smoke was drifting up from the stairwell.

"Getting a weapon—I hope." Gideon looked at the corpse and grimaced. The man had taken a round—probably from a rifle—in the right eye. The shot had gone through the lenses of his binoculars, and obscure pieces of shrapnel were sticking out of what was left of the man's face. He had been wearing a throat mike, but he hadn't lived to get a warning off to his fellows.

Gideon patted him down and found a shoulder holster. He pulled out what appeared to be an automatic pistol with a silencer. In hunting for the safety, he discovered that he was handling a Micro-Uzi that wasn't any larger than his own gun.

"Gideon! There're people coming."

Gideon turned toward Ruth and had the ominous realization that the gunfire below had ceased.

He switched the safety off of the Micro-Uzi. *"Get over here, and keep down."*

Ruth started moving uncertainly toward him. She had barely made it a quarter of the way to him when a shadowy form turned the corner of the stairwell. Gideon fired one burst from the Uzi that at his awkward angle missed, but the shadow froze. "Don't shoot!"

Gideon recognized the voice of their anonymous driver.

"What's happening down there?"

"IUF," he said. "They've covered all the exits, killed Sal, Nev . . ."

"Where are they?" Gideon asked.

"Outside, surrounding the building. Trying to burn us out."

"Great," Gideon said through clenched teeth. "Any of your friends left down there?"

"I don't know."

"The old guy?" Gideon asked.

The driver coughed a few times. "He left to make a briefing." There was a hint of irony in his voice. "About getting you two to a more secure location."

Gideon noticed the coughing and looked up. The roof

above them had become hazy with smoke. At most they had a few moments to get out of here.

The driver started up the stairs, and Gideon leveled the Uzi at him. "Where are you going?"

"This place is on fire—the first floor's a death trap already."

Ruth looked back and forth between them. "How're we getting out of here?"

Gideon started sliding back toward the center of the floor, keeping his gun trained in the driver's direction. "Where were you planning to go from here?"

He pointed off to Gideon's left, where fire had damaged the roof enough to let outside light in. Gideon scrambled over to that wall. The plywood floor ended short of his destination, and he put his foot through a section of dry-rotted lathe. He cursed, but kept moving along the framing. He got as close as he could, and from where he was, it was obvious that there was little wood left on this corner of the roof. What separated him from the outside was little more than a layer of chaotically peeling asphalt shingles.

The smoke was getting worse, and Gideon could feel the temperature rising.

Gideon looked back at the driver. The driver said, "They'll be watching the windows, but they might miss that."

Great, but where to from there? Gideon turned around carefully and kicked some of the shingles out of the way. Smoke began blowing in from outside. Even if the attackers had this portion of the roof covered, the thick smoke roiling up from the lower floors reduced visibility down to a few feet.

Gideon looked back at the others. The stairwell was flickering orange and the smoke in here was nearly as bad as the smoke outside. He heard sirens in the distance. He hoped that they were headed here, the arrival of the fire department might cause the IUF to scatter before they shot them.

"Come on," Gideon waved at the other two.

Ruth hesitated—but she could hear cracking wood and breaking glass coming from downstairs as well as Gideon did. The sound of fire tearing through the building below them. She went first, pushing through the remains of the shingles. Gideon followed, letting the driver take up the rear.

Outside, the air was too warm. The heat radiated from below, through the choking smoke. Every few seconds the wind would tear away some of the smoke cover and Gideon could see a neighboring house with a second-floor porch to their left. He could also see two Dodge Ram pickup trucks on the lawn. With them he saw a hint of movement.

The three of them were hugging the side of the roof, a forty-degree slope into a gutter that was half-peeled off the building.

"The porch next door," said the driver.

It was the only route left open to them, but it wasn't something Gideon wanted to hear. His leg was already throbbing in anticipation.

Ruth looked over at the two of them, then across the driveway, through the smoke, at where the neighboring porch should be. Her eyes glistened—it might have been fear, or it might have been the biting smoke. She shook her head and got to her feet, unsteadily balanced on the edge of the roof.

"Let me go—" Gideon began to say. But Ruth had already taken the leap. It was as if she silently vanished into the smoke. "—first," he said into the choking wind. His heart throbbed in his neck as he pulled himself toward the front of the building, where he could make the jump himself.

Behind him the building groaned, and he could feel it shake beneath him. Something below gave way, and black smoke belched around him and the driver. He pushed himself upright, his half-working leg vibrating with the effort, and he strained to see something of Ruth through the smoke.

"Come on," he whispered.

"There's no time! Jump." The house made creaking noises behind him.

Gideon turned toward the driver, "What's your name?"

"Alexander—Now go!"

Gideon couldn't even see where the neighboring roof was, he couldn't even see if Ruth had made it. *Fifteen feet across, ten feet down. Simple . . .*

Simple if his leg still worked, or if he could see where he was going.

Gideon crouched and launched himself into the roiling blackness. He kept his eyes closed, and held his breath against the choking smoke. It burned against his skin as if he were falling through the fire itself. It felt as if he were suspended in the air there for an hour or two—

Then his shoulder plowed into asphalt shingles with enough force to ignite a starburst rainbow across the inside of his eyelids. He felt his legs roll off the edge of the porch. For a terrifying, disorienting moment his lower body was suspended in midair—then a hand grabbed his belt and dragged him up over the edge.

He opened his eyes in time to see a shingle explode near his right hand. He looked up at Ruth, who was still pulling him toward the wall of the neighboring house. "Take cover," he yelled at her. He pushed her toward the windows facing them and another bullet hole sprouted in the roof between them.

Ruth headed for the darkened window, but she didn't let him go. That was probably a good thing, because the impact had stunned him, and all Gideon could manage was a wild scramble, his bad leg doing little more than kicking weakly at the edge of the roof.

Just at the time that Gideon thought the sniper had enough time to aim a shot right into one of their heads, something else slammed into the roof. Gideon turned to see Alexander, and another shot go wild into the roof between them.

Glass shattered, and Gideon found himself half-led, half-pulled through a window into a darkened bedroom. He turned around, from where he had fallen on the floor, to see Alexander diving for the window.

He didn't make it.

A shot tore into his neck. He spun half away from them, falling out of sight beyond the window.

"What the fuck?" A man sprang out of the darkness, yelling at them. He was swinging something threaten-

ingly. Somehow, Gideon had managed to keep hold of the Uzi, and he swung it at the man.

"Shit, I'm cool—" The object, ax handle or baseball bat, dropped. It took a moment for Gideon to realize that the man was completely naked.

He scrambled away from the window with Ruth, keeping the Uzi leveled at the bedroom's occupant. The man backed away from them as they reached the doorway. Outside, the sounds of sirens became louder and Gideon could hear the screech of the trucks pulling away from the house.

It took a few moments to get to his feet, even with Ruth helping him up. "I can't believe this is happening," Ruth said.

"You ain't the only one," said the naked man. He stood on a pile of blankets that had spilled from his bed. Behind him, Gideon could see someone else, probably his wife, cowering away from the two of them.

"Let's get out of here," Gideon said.

By the time they made it outside, the fire department had arrived, the IUF had gone, and the Israeli safe house was a blackened shell holding an inferno inside itself.

2.06
Thur. Mar. 19

COLONEL Gregory Mecham stood at a podium in a small, secure meeting room at Fort Meade. The room was designed to hold about two hundred people; at the moment it held ten. In a meeting about Zimmerman, ten was a quorum. It consisted of the National Security Council and a few select people from the various intelligence agencies.

In particular, Mecham noticed a new face from the DISA who sat next to General Adrian Harris, Chairman of the JCS.

"This is what we have," Mecham said, switching on a remote that operated the screen behind him. Surveillance photographs crossed the screen. "We've received these pictures from the team observing Gideon Malcolm. The team on Malcolm was carefully chosen and isolated, our communication has been through uncompromised channels." Mecham manipulated a mouse pointer across the screen behind him, highlighting the pictures in turn. "While the hope was that Malcolm might uncover new intelligence by his investigation, he has—up until yesterday—been researching already well-covered ground.

He's visited Dr. Zimmerman's home and members of her family . . ."

Mecham clicked a button, and the pictures changed to street scenes in Greenwich Village. "The second hope, that allowing Malcolm to roam unhindered would draw out other forces interested in Dr. Zimmerman, has borne fruit." Mecham clicked the mouse on one picture of a man dressed in a jogging suit. The picture blew up and filled the whole screen with a grainy, but recognizable photo of one of the gunmen who had attacked Malcolm and Zimmerman's sister. "This man is named Lyaksandro Volynskji, born Ukrainian, but he's been a resident of various Islamic states, mostly parts of the old Soviet Union. He is a recognized assassin, he's worked in Bosnia, Palestine, and inside Russia. He's associated with the International Unification Front, a loose confederation of extra-national paramilitary groups that operate out of the Middle East. After some backtracking, we've pinpointed his entry into this country as December 3, last year. He came into Miami on a Cuban passport."

Mecham slid the mouse around and clicked on another photograph. This time another man's picture expanded to fill the screen. "Hashim Abu Bakr, Syrian. We suspect that he's been involved in organizing various terrorist training camps in Syria and Libya, part of the same IUF. He entered the country on a Palestinian passport on December 2, last year."

Mecham clicked the last picture and a young man with dark hair and intense black eyes filled the screen. "The third man hasn't been identified yet. However, it seems clear the IUF is responsible for killing at least three people involved with Zimmerman. Consulting with the CIA, we've positively identified Volynskji as the shooter in the assassination of Morris Kendal."

Mecham shut off the display and leaned forward on the podium. "I'll hand the floor over to the CIA's expert."

One of the ten people stood up and walked over to the podium. He was a short black man named Williams who was one of the CIA's resident experts on Middle East terrorist organizations. "Gentlemen, we are dealing with a very dangerous situation here. While, over the past decade, the IUF has been shifting its focus to economic and technological espionage, they are still terrorists. While I understand the grave threat Dr. Zimmerman poses to our SIGINT capabilities, I think the presence of the IUF suggests a threat that's much graver than the exposure of our cryptographic resources."

What little noise there was in the room silenced. Mecham looked up at Williams. He knew what Williams meant. Ever since Zimmerman's disappearance, the fear had been that her mathematical work for the NSA might be exposed. For a few years before Dr. Zimmerman came to work for them, the NSA's mission had been hampered, especially with digital communication, by the presence of strong cryptographic methods. After Zimmerman came, there was no such thing as strong encryption.

But that wasn't the only thing that Zimmerman was working on.

"If crypto was all the IUF was interested in, Zimmerman would never had had to disappear. Zimmerman's work could be passed on a single CD. They didn't need her work, they needed *her.* And from all appearances,

Zimmerman went willingly. They've since been trying to get access to a Daedalus supercomputer. That doesn't make any sense unless they were interested in Zimmerman's work in information warfare. The fact that they're still operating in the country means they haven't smuggled Zimmerman out. That implies that they have a definite plan, and they need a Daedalus to carry it out. We've had a number of alerts recently, where it appeared that there were hostile forces attacking domestic information systems. The virus that instigated the Wall Street crash has only been the most public. Since Zimmerman's disappearance, we've had computer-related power failures at seven major facilities, lost two major air traffic control systems for over three hours, and—for five minutes—lost the entire long distance phone network between the Rockies and the Mississippi. These may all be related, and may only be tests."

Williams paused for emphasis, then said, "If they get access to a Daedalus, I would consider it as much a threat to the United States as if they had access to a weapon of mass destruction in every major city in the country."

Colonel Mecham was back in his office before eight in the morning, and around eight-fifteen, Emmit D'Arcy was knocking on his door.

"Come in, sir," Mecham said, standing up to meet D'Arcy.

D'Arcy shut the door behind him and took off his glasses to rub the bridge of his nose. "I wanted to talk to you, Greg. I wanted your take on Williams' analysis."

"I respect his expertise."

"That's an evasion."

"I know," Mecham waved to a chair in front of his desk. "Why don't you have a seat. You look tired."

"Four hours' sleep in the last three days, half unintentional." D'Arcy moved over to the chair and sighed. "You know he's right on the money about the IUF. They're probably the worst people that could have Zimmerman."

Mecham sat down himself. "Yes, I know. I don't dispute that."

"You have a reservation about something."

Mecham nodded. "I have reservations about Zimmerman. She wasn't taken. She left with an almost obsessive amount of premeditation and planning—"

"As Williams said, if the IUF has her, she went willingly."

"But *why?* Have you read her psychological profile?"

"Five times."

"Then you know what's bothering me. She's not an ideologue, barely a political bone in her body. Her personal life is practically antiseptic. No debts, and she cares little for money. Her strongest beliefs are about mathematics. How can someone like that be recruited by the IUF, of all people? She *had* the best hardware, the most sophisticated forum possible for doing her work, which is all she really cares about. You couldn't bribe her away from that. She doesn't have anything you can blackmail her with—even her family, she hasn't communicated with any of them in a couple of years."

"I've read the same things you have. Assuming the profile isn't wrong—and someone with her intelligence would be able to intentionally skew our profile, and hide her true feelings—*assuming* it isn't wrong, what conclusions are you drawing?"

"Zimmerman would only have left—and I don't care who might have facilitated it, because I doubt she would've—if it meant she could do work that, for one reason or another, she *couldn't* do here. She would never have left here just so she could reconstruct old information warfare viruses she's already designed for us. Doing old work would be pointless to her."

"What kind of work would she be doing?" D'Arcy asked. He leaned forward, his expression suddenly showing an intense interest in what Mecham was saying.

"Something that requires a Daedalus. Other than that, I don't know, and *that's* frightening." Mecham shook his head. "I suspect it has something to do with her work at MIT, since people from the Evolutionary Theorems Lab are working with her—but what it could be, I don't know. I'm not a mathematician, and, until now, I had *thought* that everything she did here was a logical extension of her work there."

D'Arcy nodded and leaned back. "True, perhaps, but nothing you've said means we change how we deal with this. Zimmerman is still a threat, probably more so than we ever thought. We still have to keep a tight watch on every Daedalus out there. Eventually the IUF will move on one of them, and then we have her."

"I just wish we hadn't lost Malcolm. . . ."

Gideon and Ruth spent a good part of the evening on the subway. They went as far as Queens and back again, switching trains a number of times in an effort to foil any pursuit. Ruth was exhausted and spent most of the time asleep, leaning against Gideon's shoulder. Gideon was too keyed up to sleep. He spent most of the time staring at other passengers, wondering which ones were planning to attack them.

The rest of the time he thought about what was happening. Why was he here, next to Dr. Zimmerman's sister, on the New York subway system?

"Julia, who are you?" he asked a mental image of the Doctor. "What are you doing?"

His only response was an enigmatic stare from those depthless gray eyes. What made her turn away? From her parents, from her sister, from her colleagues . . . ?

Christ, tell me why I turned away?

He must have been too tired, because that kind of question bore on things that he never wanted to think about.

Ruth must have felt him tense up because she sat up next to him and looked at him. "Are you all right?"

"I'm fine." The words were a whisper through clenched teeth.

"You're crying."

Gideon shook his head, but he raised his hand to his cheek and found wetness there. "It's just the smoke."

"It's all right," Ruth whispered. "You've been through a lot."

"It's *not* all right. It's never been all right." Gideon rubbed his forehead as if he could push the thoughts away, distract himself with what was going on around them now. "I'm a fraud," he whispered.

Ruth rubbed his shoulder.

"I couldn't hack it as a Fed," Gideon said. "I shouldn't be a cop either. I'll deserve it when IA pulls my badge."

"You aren't responsible—"

"My brother, my ex-partner . . . I got them both killed. Just because I wanted, someday, to *be* Rafe."

Ruth was silent for a long time before she said, "Rafe was your brother?"

Gideon nodded.

"I know what it is like to live in someone's shadow."

They were on the return trip from Jackson Heights, and morning light was streaming into the car as they rode over northern Queens. Ruth looked around as if she was looking for some reason to change the subject. "Where are we?" she finally asked.

"Queens," Gideon said, relieved to be talking about something else. "Going back to Manhattan."

She looked at the rest of the car. It was packed with people making the morning commute. Standing room only. She shook her head and whispered, "Is that safe?"

"I think we're all right now. The Israelis did us the favor of separating me from all the tracking devices—" Gideon felt the Micro-Uzi in his pocket. He'd had to strip off the silencer to allow it to fit.

"We should go to the FBI," Ruth whispered.

That was the easy answer, wasn't it? Gideon had been thinking the exact same thing for most of the night. There was one problem with it, though. "I can't."

"What do you mean, you *can't?*"

"I can take *you* to them," Gideon said. "I can't stop."

Ruth's voice lowered even further. "Don't you realize that people are shooting at you?"

Gideon rubbed his healing leg and said, "I know." *Not just at me.* His voice was slow, halting, as he tried to explain why he needed to continue. Why he couldn't ask anyone for help. "I *still* have to find out what's happening. Why." He closed his eyes and wondered how much of what he was saying was rationalization. "I can't back off now. I go to the Feds now, and the best that will happen is they'll hand me over to IA while they try and bury all their embarrassing mistakes." *And I have to prove to myself that I* can *do this. Every time I've hit a snag, I've turned to someone to bail me out. Dad, Rafe, Kendal—*

Ruth leaned back and sighed. Even with the motorcycle jacket, perhaps because of it, she looked very small and vulnerable. "You think I don't want to find Julie? She's my sister."

Gideon nodded. The train shot into a tunnel under the East River, briefly exchanging day for night. Gideon's hand drifted back toward the pocket with the gun. *I'm doing this for Rafe. What he did for me has got to* mean *something.*

Later on, as they rode under Manhattan, Gideon asked, "Do you think Julia could be working with the IUF?"

"Are you kidding? Why would she do that? It'd be pointless."

"She planned her disappearance," Gideon said. "Just like MIT. She even wiped her own home computer. Wherever she went, she planned to go there."

Ruth laughed. The sound was half derisive and half nervous. "You can't be suggesting that after all these years that Julie suddenly became political—not to mention political for *these* guys."

The train slowed for a stop, and the packed cars began to gradually empty out.

"What could they offer her?"

"To get her to jump ship at the NSA?" She shook her head. "You don't understand. All she really cares about is her work, it's almost a divine mission for her. From what I heard, the NSA gave her the best environment to conduct her work that she could possibly have."

Gideon thought back to their conversation in the restaurant. "Something she'd need a Daedalus for," he muttered.

"What?"

"What if they were watching us, had a man near us? What if something we did or said triggered the attack? What if we stumbled on something the IUF didn't want anyone to know?"

"Like what? We just talked about Julie's life, nothing secret—" Ruth shivered a little bit. "We didn't talk about anything worth shooting at us for."

Gideon stared out at a platform as the train pulled out. The lighted platform slid away and replaced itself with the depthless black of the tunnels. The clearest image was his own reflection in the window.

"She was working on something on her own. Something private. Everyone looking for Julia Zimmerman is afraid of what she was *known* to be working on for the NSA. What if the IUF offered her the opportunity to work on something she couldn't work on at the NSA?"

Ruth shook her head. "I know where you're going with

that. I know it looks a lot like when she left MIT. But Julie isn't stupid. She'd consider the consequences of her actions. She knew that she could screw MIT, because she knew who would be backing her if things came to a head. She knew that she'd beat them." She turned her head and looked at Gideon. "This isn't the same. I can't see her making that decision. This is a no-win situation."

The train pulled to a stop again, and Gideon stood up. "Come on."

"What? Where are we going?"

"I want to make a stop at the library."

When Gideon sat behind one of the public terminals at the New York Public Library, Ruth asked him, "And what exactly do you expect to find here?"

Gideon cued up a search engine and said, "I want to look into what your sister might have been working on."

"How the hell do you intend to do that?" Ruth pulled up a chair and sat next to him. "Are you some sort of police mathematician?"

"No," Gideon shook his head. "But I think the answer is somewhere in what we already know."

There was a pile of scratch paper and a small pencil box next to the computer. He took a sheet and a pencil and started scribbling a list of words;

"Information Warfare. Virus. Cryptography. Riemann. Number Theory. Aleph-Null. Evolutionary Algorithm. Zeta Function."

Gideon looked at the list of words. "That should be enough of a start."

Ruth watched as he scanned papers, articles, as well as

the other detritus accumulated on the Internet. Those sites that weren't mathematical tended to be about private-sector information security. After about fifteen minutes, Gideon found a page that made him realize one of the fundamental reasons *why* the government was scared of losing Zimmerman. On the screen was a layman's description of public key cryptography, the de facto standard for secure personal communications on the Internet.

"No wonder they're frightened of her," Gideon whispered.

"What?"Ruth said.

"Look at this." Gideon tapped his finger on a paragraph that he had just scrolled onto the screen. "This whole process is based on very large prime numbers. . . ."

"Okay, so?"

"That was at the heart of what she was doing at MIT, wasn't it?"

Ruth shrugged. "I never followed it very well. She was way past me by the time she left grade school."

Gideon scrolled through the article. "Most of the security on the Internet is based on these huge numbers, and on the fact that it's supposedly a practical impossibility to factor a four-thousand-bit number by brute force."

"So?"

"I'm not a mathematician, but one of the things that your sister's colleague, Dr. Nolan, told me—'Zimmerman was pushing the lab toward new theorems that could generate the primes, or factor huge numbers.'" Gideon shook his head. "No wonder the NSA wanted her, and wants her back. With that kind of algorithm there'd be no such thing as a secure communication on the Internet—or elsewhere for that matter. E-mail, credit-card transactions, private databases—you could crack any of it, all of it."

Ruth stared at the screen. "Do you think she managed that?"

"Why not?" Gideon said. "What would be worth more to an intelligence gathering agency? A factoring algorithm that renders the bulk of encrypted information in existence completely transparent." Gideon nodded to himself, leaning back. "And they have to be very careful bringing her back. If it became public knowledge that such an algorithm existed, it would become useless." Gideon tapped his fingers on the table. "That explains the government . . ."

Gideon was quiet a long while before Ruth interrupted him. "You don't sound completely sure."

Gideon shook his head. "I can make it fit with everything . . . *except* your sister. It fits with what the old man said about her designing parts of the NSA's computer security—" He sighed. "There's more to this. I *know* there's more to this. This doesn't explain why your sister disappeared. It certainly doesn't explain why she, or the IUF, would need a supercomputer."

"It doesn't? This sounds kind of heavy to me."

Gideon nodded. "But the work she was doing at MIT was using equipment anyone has access to, not particularly sophisticated. 200Mhz PCs. I could get more powerful computers used. So, if what she did was a direct outgrowth of the ET Lab, why would she suddenly need the kind of power a Daedalus provides? Not to mention, this is *exactly* the kind of thing the NSA was using her for. I'm sure that whatever she's doing now would have to be something that she *couldn't* do at the NSA—"

"I keep telling you. She's not stupid. She wouldn't jump ship at the NSA unless she thought the odds were in favor of her getting away with it.

Gideon nodded. He'd been thinking along those lines himself. There was another possibility that Ruth wasn't seeing. What if Zimmerman didn't care about the odds? What if she was working on something that she thought was important enough to risk being hunted down by the Feds as a traitor?

There wasn't any question in Gideon's mind that Zimmerman had her own agenda. What if there was something she was working on in secret, ever since MIT? Maybe since before . . .

But what?

What could she think is that important?

Gideon stared at the screen, trying to think. Ruth looked at him and said, "Don't you think it's time to consider the FBI?"

Gideon looked at Ruth. "I doubt the government's priorities match ours— I don't think they care about bringing your sister in alive."

"And you do?"

The question made Gideon uncomfortable. He had been driven to this point by a need to discover what had happened in the warehouse, why Rafe had died. Somehow, his focus had changed. Julia Zimmerman had become his focus. He could rationalize it by saying that she had been the focus of what had happened at the warehouse. Was that the real reason? He was following this woman, finding himself fascinated by her history. . . .

In his gut he knew that, if he discovered what she was doing, he could damage those who had shot him and killed Rafe. He knew he wanted to bring whatever happened to the press and to that Congressional hearing. He wanted to damage those who had damaged so much around him.

He wanted to vindicate himself.

But that wasn't it. Not completely.

He realized that he didn't want Julia Zimmerman to end like Rafe, or Kendal, or Davy Jones, or Kareem Rashad Williams. Whatever she had done, Gideon had an irrational belief that it wasn't treasonous. Somehow she was serving her first and only love. There was something in her that wasn't of Gideon's world. Gideon's world was constructed from self-serving politics, where his brother's death was some sort of bargaining chip, a political asset—or liability—depending on what side of the fence you were on.

Julia came from somewhere else. And, somehow, understanding her, what she was doing, would give Rafe's death the meaning that Gideon desperately needed. Gideon couldn't accept that all it had been was some interdepartmental screwup. . . .

There was something larger, and much more important at stake.

Gideon looked at Ruth. Did he care about bringing Julia in alive? "I do," Gideon said quietly. "Believe me, I do."

Ruth looked at him a little oddly. "You don't have a crush on her, do you?"

Gideon laughed. "That's silly. I've never even met the woman."

He turned back to the computer screen and started calling up searches on the other terms that related to Dr. Zimmerman's work. As he worked, the phrase kept running through his head, *I've never even met the woman.*

He searched for things relating to "Evolutionary Algorithm," "Virus," and, "Information Warfare."

The search presented him with dozens of pages on the Evolutionary Algorithm. A few pages were actually archived copies of papers from the ET Lab at MIT. There were so many documents that Gideon threw Zimmerman's name into the search to pare down the list.

When he did that, he found all the MIT papers, and a document titled, "Tenth International Conference on Artificial Life."

Gideon stared at the title for a long time before he opened the document. He was remembering something Dr. Michael Nolan had said. *"She began to act as if the programs we were creating were living creatures. . . ."* He also remembered the lone thing that she'd left on her own personal computer, a little icon labeled "life."

The document had an introduction to the term "artificial life." Gideon scanned the page, picking out phrases that caught his eye, or seemed important.

"Artificial Life labels human attempts to construct models—digital, biological, and robotic—that reproduce some of the essential properties of life. The goal of such models is to reveal the organizational principles of living systems on Earth, and possibly elsewhere . . ."

". . . requires a truly interdisciplinary approach that knits together fields of knowledge as diverse as mathematics and biology, computer science and physics, engineering and philosophy . . ."

". . . an important part of this effort is a search for *independent* principles of living systems, which apply to any living system, regardless of biology—or lack thereof. Artificial Life also considers the *possibilities* of life, artificial alternatives to a carbon-based chemistry."

"This sounds like so much science fiction," Ruth said.

Gideon nodded. "But, according to Dr. Nolan, this kind of research has been going on for decades. He said some of the first Genetic Algorithms were produced on an Apple II computer."

Gideon checked the conference schedule and found Dr. Zimmerman's name.

"Sat. June 29: 8:30–9:15 Keynote Talk, Julia Zimmerman, *The Biology of the Internet.*"

Gideon stared at the title of her talk for a long time. It was hard to reconcile with his idea of what Julia Zimmerman was involved in. So far he had pictured her as interested in obscure mathematical objects like the Zeta Function. The Internet seemed too "earthy" a topic for her.

He looked across at Ruth. "How interested is your sister in computers?"

"She's fascinated by them," Ruth said. "At least as far as they are a means to her ends. She once called them a mathematical telescope."

"Interesting metaphor."

"I think she meant that a computer can be used to see parts of the mathematical universe that would be otherwise undetectable."

There was an abstract of the speech available, and Gideon opened it.

"Has the term 'virus' stopped being metaphorical?" Gideon read. "With the increase in complexity of the Internet, there has been an increase in the 'size' of the environment that can host uncontrolled entities. An average personal computer is packed with so much data that it is easy for foreign bits of code to hide undetected, and when it is connected to a network, the environment is vast. Security against computer viruses, because of their constant proliferation, has had to concentrate more and more on preventing the harmful effects of these viruses, and less on preventing the infection of the system. It is possible for a 'benign' virus, a virus that conducts no discernible attacks on its host, to propagate unimpeded. Evolution forces the eventual existence of such 'benign' viruses."

Gideon looked at the abstract and thought about what the old guy had told them about Julia's work for the NSA. Information warfare he said, military-grade viruses . . .

"Maybe this is what she was really working on," Gideon whispered. If it was, he wondered what it meant. Was she actually working on some terrorist weapon? Why?

On the other end of the secure phone line, Emmit D'Arcy said, "What've you got?"

Colonel Mecham looked at the papers that'd just been

delivered to his desk. "We have a flag from the New York Public Library."

"The library?"

"Mother filtered out a keyword search originating from one of the public terminals. About Zimmerman. There's a good chance it's Malcolm." Mecham cleared his throat. "I've ordered a team in to extract him."

There was a pause on the other end of the line. Eventually D'Arcy said, "Did I hear you right?"

"This was time sensitive. The search was in progress as Mother flagged it. I had to act immediately."

"I see." D'Arcy's voice became colder. "When this is over, we'll have a talk about this, Colonel Mecham."

I'm sure we will, Mecham thought. *Probably in front of a Senate hearing.* "Yes, sir," he hung up the phone and shook his head. He looked up at the man sitting across from him. "There we go," he said. "That's my career."

General Adrian Harris shook his head. "It has to be done. This situation is too dangerous to have a loose cannon out there. He's served his purpose, drawing the IUF out of the woodwork." The General stood up and said, "Don't worry, son. You did your duty."

Mecham watched as the Chairman of the Joint Chiefs left his office. The door closed silently behind him.

He had been on the computer long enough for his eyes to begin to hurt. He leaned back and let his gaze drift.

"So," Ruth asked, "are you any closer?"

"I don't know." He had spent hours scanning documents, some of them way beyond his level of understanding. He had even found a description of the program

Julia left on her own PC. It was a "game" called Life that seemed to have originated on a checkerboard. It was played on a grid, and each turn, every cell on the grid is turned on or off—lives or dies—based on the number of neighboring living cells. The rules of the game were simple, four lines long, but the complexities of the patterns involved could be astounding.

The game of life, in the decades since its invention, had spawned a whole mathematical discipline around the study of what was called cellular automata. There were people writing theses on the properties of various arrangement of cells—there were patterns that could "move" across the grid, essentially unchanged in form, there were other patterns that could repeatedly build other patterns. All from a set of rules that could fit on a business card.

Why leave that behind? Gideon pictured the way the pattern had erupted across the screen of Julia's computer, and then dissolved off into nothing. *Why?*

He had found quite a few traces of Julia Zimmerman in articles across the Internet, all predating her work for the government. While there was no question about her mathematical genius, she more often gave talks about the Evolutionary Algorithm than the Theorems she was trying to solve with it. When he first heard about what the ET Lab was doing, he'd thought that the computers were simply a means to work on the problems she was trying to solve.

More and more, it seemed that those problems were an excuse to work with the computers, and the opportunities that they opened up for her.

Gideon looked up at one of the chandeliers above the

main reading room, watching as the late morning sunlight caught it. "You think she saw the computers as a window on that pure mathematical world she believed in?"

"That's the way she described it to me, back when she was going to college."

Gideon looked at the description of "Life," and thought of Julia's own computer. Why leave it there unless it was some sort of message? A message to the people she knew would be going over her hard drive with a fine-toothed comb.

"'This is what I'm doing,'" Gideon said, still staring at the chandelier. "'This is what I'm interested in.'"

"What?"

"That's what she was telling them. I have a feeling about this. I think she might have modified her thinking about computers, about the data inside them, at least."

"What do you mean?"

"I don't think she sees them as a window on her mathematical world," Gideon turned to face Ruth. Her face was half shadow and half rose from the ambient light reflecting off the woodwork. "I think she might see them *as* that world."

Ruth looked at him. "Come on, that's crazy. Julie knew—even when she talked about God in the numbers—that we're only talking about mental constructs here. She knew that there could never be a 'real' physical representation of it. There's even a theorem that proves that we can't have a *complete* picture of the mathematical world."

"What's that?"

"I don't quite understand it, but she told me about it the

last time she talked to me about her work. It's called Gödel's Incompleteness Theorem—I think it says that it's impossible to prove all true statements in a logical system, even if the system is consistent. Julia thought that it proved that we can only glimpse the perfection of the mathematical."

Gideon nodded. "What that means is that there's still room for faith in Julia's religion."

Ruth stopped short. "What do you mean?"

"What's faith, but the acceptance that some things are true despite lacking the proof for them? Despite the *impossibility* of proving them . . . When did Julia tell you about this?"

"Just before she went to MIT. What are you thinking?"

Gideon looked at the computer in front of him, then past it at the series of terminals ranged along the reading tables. *It's gotten to the point where we see them, but we don't see them.* The computer was ubiquitous, everywhere . . . and most of them were connected to each other. The space, the environment that existed inside those machines, was just on the edge of comprehension. It was very easy to think of it as another world, an alternate universe.

And if he was thinking along these lines with just a brush against Julia Zimmerman's ideas, what was the impact of the woman herself? Someone everyone acknowledged as a genius . . .

"She stopped talking to you about the time she started working at MIT, didn't she?"

Ruth nodded.

"You said she took a page from the Greeks . . ."

"Yes, the Pythagoreans. Where are you going with all this?"

Gideon pulled a paper out of his pocket. It was the copy of the campus paper he had taken from MIT. He showed it to Ruth, reading the caption, "'Assault on Mt. Riemann; Drs. Nolan and Zimmerman stand with their New Pythagorean Order—members of the ET Lab—show a printout of a possible proof,' have you heard that phrase before? 'New Pythagorean Order?'"

Ruth shook her head.

Gideon bent over the computer and called up a new search. The term "Pythagorean Order" brought a series of documents. The content wasn't that surprising. . . .

"According to Aristotle, the Pythagorean Order, first to develop the science of mathematics, revered number as the origin of the cosmos. The Order, a religious cult founded in Croton on the coast of Italy around 530 BC, was founded by Pythagoras of Samos, a mathematician, philosopher, and religious leader."

Gideon looked at the screen and said, "Nolan said that they were almost a cult."

"I'm not following you."

"I'm talking about what every religious leader needs." Gideon turned and looked at Ruth. "Disciples."

"Are you serious?"

Gideon took the article back and started hunting down some on-line telephone directories. "She told you her beliefs; she doesn't seem shy about voicing them."

"Yes, but I mean, they're off the wall. What are you talking about? A cult at MIT?"

Gideon started getting phone numbers matching the

names in the article. He scribbled on the article as he paged through a series of names. "Is it so unlikely that she'd manage to find people who'd give some kind of weight to her beliefs? Look at how she left MIT. She erased all the ongoing work at the ET Lab. Could she do it *all* herself? We're talking about the efforts of a dozen people. Wouldn't that require some complicity from the people who worked in the lab?"

"I'm certain that a few people supported her . . ."

"The only member of the ET Lab who's still there was the one tenured professor. Not a one ended up with a teaching position, or even continued their studies there past the demise of the lab." Gideon shook his head. "And I know at least one of those people is helping Zimmerman right now." Gideon scribbled a final number and stood up. "Come on, I need to get to a phone."

Ruth stood up, and they started heading toward the end of the reading room. They had only gone a few feet when Gideon slowed to a stop. There were two men standing at the end of the room in front of them, both converging on the exit

Gideon turned around to head toward the other end of the room, and another set of doors. At that end of the room, there were two others. A pair of guys, one who'd been sitting at a terminal, another who had been reading at a table—both were just standing.

Gideon had been keeping an eye out for people who were out of place. But these guys hadn't been. They'd been filtering into the reading room, one at a time, over the past half hour. They were all dressed differently, one was in a suit, another in jeans and a flannel shirt, another in Dockers and a turtleneck. Gideon kept turning and Ruth gripped his arm.

Everyone who had been in the room with them—reading or perusing the computer network—they were all standing, facing the two of them. Gideon put an arm around Ruth, as if he could protect her from the people surrounding them.

Of the people surrounding them, one of the two or three women stepped up toward them. She wore a navy suit and Gideon found himself looking for where the gun was holstered. She stopped about twenty feet away.

"Gideon Malcolm, Ruth Zimmerman?" she asked. It was just barely a question.

"Who are you?" Gideon asked.

"Tracy Davis, I'm a federal agent. I'm a negotiator."

"Can I see an ID?"

Davis obliged by pulling one out and opening it for him. Gideon looked and noted, with some irony, that she was Secret Service.

"What's to negotiate?" Gideon said. "You have us surrounded."

"I'm going to try and make sure no one gets hurt." Davis smiled weakly, and Gideon could tell, by looking in her eyes, that she was unsure how this was gong to go down. They were treating this like a hostage situation, which suddenly made Gideon feel very nervous.

"No one's going to get hurt," Gideon said. He said it to reassure Ruth and himself as much as the folks surrounding them. "I'm letting her go now, okay?"

He waited for Davis to say, "Okay," before he started moving, very slowly. Right now there was no doubt in his mind that there were snipers in place somewhere beyond the arched windows that overlooked the reading room. None of whom he wanted to spook.

Once his arm was free and Ruth was standing beside him, he held his hands out in front of him. He said, "I have a gun in my pocket. Are people going to be nervous if I hand it over?"

Davis pulled out a walkie-talkie that was the size of a small cellular phone. She spoke quietly back and forth for a few moments, then she said, "Is it in your jacket?"

Gideon nodded.

"What you want to do is take off the jacket and toss it over here by me."

At this point, Ruth said, "What's going on?"

Gideon shook his head as he slowly began removing his jacket. "You wanted to talk to the Feds? Here they are."

They were both cuffed by the Feds and led out of the library. As they took him out, Gideon had a good look at how serious they were. As they passed out of the reading room, they entered a hallway that was filled with NYPD guys in ballistic helmets and flak jackets.

When they stepped out on to Fifth Avenue, the street had turned into a parking lot for cop cars, sedans, and two SWAT team vans. Gideon saw press crews, but they were so far away that he doubted that they could see anything.

Davis handed him off to a dark guy in a suit, and he hustled him into one of the sedans. The last Gideon saw of Ruth, she was shoved into the back of a different sedan. Gideon asked the driver, "So, what federal agency are you with?"

The guy didn't answer him. He stared straight ahead, and Gideon could only get a good view of his crew cut and a strip of his face in the rearview mirror. Gideon looked over the man's shoulder, at his hands. He saw an academy ring.

"Marine, huh?"

"I'm not permitted to speak with you, sir."

Gideon kept trying to get the guy to talk, but true to his word, the Marine didn't say a single word more. Eventually, he drove off, following two other sedans down Fifth. They were the first cars to leave the scene.

Gideon expected the reporters to converge, but the cops held the press, and everyone else, away from the small motorcade. As they left, Gideon looked back and saw what had to be a staged disturbance at the front of the library. Several men were being escorted by the NYPD cops, kicking and struggling, despite being chained and carried between four cops in riot gear. Designed to draw attention away from the anonymous sedans.

א₂

3.00
Mon. Mar. 22

COLONEL Mecham was glad to get out of Washington. The wrath of Emmit D'Arcy was not something that he wanted to face. He was fortunate in that D'Arcy, at the moment, was embroiled in a feud with the other members of the National Security Council, the ones who'd made the decision to pull the plug on Detective Gideon Malcolm, D'Arcy's loose cannon.

Mecham agreed that the plug needed to be pulled. It was pretty obvious that, due to the IUF's involvement, they'd already lost three people that could have been some source of intelligence. Mecham was certain that they could get more information from Detective Gideon Malcolm by bringing him in than by allowing him to stir things up.

Mecham landed at JFK at six in the morning. He walked off the plane, through the airport, and straight to the lobby where the car was waiting for him. The man waiting for him came to attention. Mecham nodded acknowledgement to the young Marine and said, "At ease, soldier."

"Yes, sir."

The kid looked as if he'd be more comfortable in a uniform. He took Mecham's overnight bag and led him out to a waiting car.

They hadn't taken him to a police station or a federal building. Gideon wasn't exactly sure where this building was. He knew it had to be an office building east of Central Park, but he couldn't be sure which one. The car had turned off the street and had entered an underground garage, and they had taken an elevator up ten stories and led him through a suite of offices that was nearly empty of furniture. Even the windows were covered, making the only light the stark white of the fluorescents.

He tried a few times, in vain, to get them to allow him to call a lawyer. Apparently he had fallen into the same black hole that the original Daedalus thieves had fallen into—a place where the Bill of Rights was conveniently overlooked.

They kept him in a small room that had a cot, a small television, and an adjoining bathroom. Because of the cabinets, Gideon supposed that, at one point, this was supposed to be some sort of lounge. They locked the door and left him there, occasionally bringing in food from Taco Bell or McDonald's. He only found a change of clothes—two pairs of jeans and a couple of T-shirts—by accident when he was rummaging around bored. They hadn't even bothered to take the tags off.

Despite lack of a shower, it still felt good to change out of clothes that still smelled faintly of smoke.

For two days, they'd left him in there. The Marines wouldn't talk to him, and—more annoying—they refused to listen to him. He was beginning to wonder if this was it, all there was to everything, just an anonymous dull captivity. . . .

Then, on the morning of day three, he walked out of the bathroom and saw a trio of the plainclothes Marines in his room, waiting for him. The lead one said, "Would you please come with us, sir?"

"As if I have a choice." Gideon rubbed his chin, where four days of stubble itched.

They took him—one on either side, one behind him—down an empty hallway and into an office. The Marines stopped with Gideon standing in front of a closed door. The lead Marine said, "The Colonel is waiting for you."

"I'm sure he is," Gideon said. He really had nowhere to go except through the door. He sighed and pushed his way through. He had barely taken five steps into the office when one of the Marines reached in and closed the door behind him.

The office was mostly empty, like the rest of this place. It was one of the smaller offices, without any windows. There was a battered green metal desk sitting in the center of the room. Sitting on the desk was a small tape recorder attached by a cord to a microphone sitting on the center of the desk. On Gideon's side of the desk was a folding metal chair, and opposite him sat a man in late middle age, with hair that wasn't quite as short as the Marines'.

"Have a seat, Mr. Malcolm." He gestured to the folding chair.

Gideon sat, and as he sat, he looked behind him and

saw, in one corner of the room, a camcorder on a tripod, pointed at the desk.

"Where's Ruth?" Gideon asked. "I've been trying to ask, but none of these people will even talk to me. What happened to the Secret Service?" *If there ever was any Secret Service.*

"Those men have very explicit orders not to communicate with you. I can assure you that Ruth Zimmerman is safe, apparently much safer than she'd be on the streets with you."

."What do you want from me?"

"I want to hear about everything that's happened to you since the incident where your partner was shot."

Gideon shook his head. "I want to talk to a lawyer."

"You aren't in the criminal justice system, Mr. Malcolm. You're involved in a present military threat to the security of this nation. I suggest you cooperate with this debriefing. There's more at stake here than I think you realize."

"Are you sure about that?" Gideon asked.

"Let's start when you left the hospital—"

"I want something."

"You aren't in a position to make deals, Mr. Malcolm."

"You don't have a clue what Zimmerman's up to, do you?"

The room was silent for a long time. The Colonel was looking at him as if he was trying to discern some hidden meaning from his expression. He said, "What do you mean by that?"

"You can't figure out why Zimmerman left, what she's trying to do . . ."

"Do you, Mr. Malcolm?"

"I have an idea."

"What?"

"Like I said, I want something."

There was a long time before the Colonel said, "Let's hear it, then."

"I want you bastards to do right by my brother. We both know it wasn't the Secret Service there. I want the people responsible for that mess to help his widow and his children."

"I think we can manage—"

"That's not all."

"What else?"

"You have to bring Zimmerman in alive."

There was silence, as if it took a long time for the audacity of Gideon's request to sink in for the Colonel.

"That's not much of a promise, Colonel," Gideon said. "You *need* her alive. Otherwise, you'll never know how compromised you actually are, will you? If she dies, it's just as bad for you as if she never turns up again. You'll have to assume that everything she ever worked on for you is in enemy hands."

"You think it isn't?"

"I think Julia's agenda isn't terrorism."

The Colonel leaned forward and shook his head. "What makes you think you know this situation so well?"

"I think I know Julia."

"You've never even met the woman."

Gideon almost objected. He felt as if he *had* met Julia Zimmerman. He felt as if he had been living with her for weeks . . . Instead, he told the Colonel. "Give me those promises, and I'll cooperate with you."

Slowly, the Colonel nodded. "We can give you that. You're right. We do need Zimmerman alive. Now you tell me what you think is going on."

There it was. For a few long moments, Gideon didn't know what to do. He wanted some sort of guarantee, but he had no way of getting one, and the Colonel here didn't have the means to provide one. He had been prepared to remain silent until his demands were met, but the Colonel's acquiescence made him hesitate.

However, in the end, he really had no choice.

Gideon told him.

Gideon told him of a woman who had replaced God with Number. A woman to whom mathematics wasn't a profession, but a faith. The ET Lab was only part of her work at MIT; another part—a much more private part—was a cult that called itself the New Pythagorean Order, named for the ancient Greeks who worshiped Number as the genesis of all things.

Zimmerman had believed in a perfect numerical world since childhood. At MIT she envisioned the data inside their computers *as* that world, and she had found people who could share her specific, peculiar faith. People who believed that their studies in artificial life were just that, *life*. People who believed a computer virus was as "alive" as its biological cousin.

The Colonel asked him what he was getting at.

Gideon told him that Julia's experiments in the ET Lab weren't explorations in mathematics. They were experiments in her religion. They were explorations in a virtual world that she believed was the perfect expression of her faith, at least the most perfect representation of it she could achieve.

"So she worships computers?"

Gideon shook his head.

Not computers. Nothing about Julia's beliefs embraced the physical world. It was the data, the information that the computers arranged and stored. To Julia, it wouldn't matter if a representation of her work was on a Daedalus, on an Apple II, or a spiral notebook. That wasn't the important thing. What the computers did was allow a much more efficient manipulation of the data.

What, exactly, Julia was working toward, Gideon was unsure. But he was positive that it was this work—this expression of faith—that Julia had stolen from the MIT labs, not the relatively mundane work she was doing in the public half of the ET Lab.

"You think that work was mundane?"

"In comparison," Gideon said. "Even though I suspect that it was her work on the Riemann Hypothesis and the implications that meant for factoring large numbers that got her a job in the NSA in the first place. Wasn't it?"

The Colonel was impassive enough that Gideon suspected that he was making an effort not to react to the statement. Enough of an effort that Gideon suspected that he had hit a nerve.

"Shall I extend my theory a little?" Gideon said. "She joined you and started working in cryptanalysis. She gave you a number of algorithms relating to prime numbers that were useful enough to be very classified—and then she moved, at her own request, to work in information warfare."

The Colonel leaned back, and Gideon could tell that he had scored. Gideon continued, "I'd also venture a guess that she was much more adept at that sort of work, especially in engineering viruses, than her professional credentials would have suggested. You were hiring a pure mathematician who worked with computers, and you received, unexpectedly, a computer scientist."

"Why do you draw these particular conclusions?"

"Because that's what she wanted to do."

Julia had been learning the field, probably since before she started at MIT. While she worked at the ET Lab, her interest wasn't the Riemann Hypothesis, it was the evolutionary algorithm they were using. When she came to the NSA, her interest wasn't cryptography and cryptanalysis, but the virus.

The thing that drove Julia was her faith, her belief in that perfect mathematical world, her exploration of that world. She left the NSA, and that meant there was something she needed to do that she could not do there. If the IUF was involved, Gideon doubted that they knew any more of her full agenda than MIT or the NSA did—although he suspected they thought they did.

"What is her full agenda?"

"That, I don't know," Gideon said. "But the suggestion that she might have had one was enough to have the IUF make an attempt on our lives."

The Colonel nodded. "It's all an interesting theory. Thank you for telling us. However, the purpose of this debriefing is to go over your movements and activities. If we could start going over that . . ."

Gideon did as the Colonel asked, keeping watch on him to see if his revelations about Julia Zimmerman had made any impressions. He couldn't tell.

However, the questions about his movements were much more formal. Like any numbers of questionings he'd been involved in as a cop, it lasted for hours, and involved a lot of repetitive questions. Gideon could understand the frustration of everyone he'd ever interviewed like this. It felt as if the interviewer was constantly trying to catch the interviewee in some sort of contradiction.

Of course, he was.

Even though Gideon understood the process intimately, it was still irritating going over the same territory again and again. It was even more irritating when some fault of memory made him contradict himself on some minor point, and the Colonel would hammer on the single point for what seemed to be hours.

When Gideon got to the gentleman with the Uzis, the Colonel went through it once and called the interview to a stop.

"I'm going to have to bring someone else in to listen to this." He stood up and extended his hand. Gideon stood and took it.

"We'll pick this up tomorrow," the Colonel said. "I think they'll have dinner waiting for you."

Gideon looked at his watch at that. He had been here over eight hours.

3.01
Thur. Mar. 25

THE debriefing lasted for days.

Gideon went through the process with more than a few mixed emotions. It began to feel that he was betraying Julia, and somehow letting Rafe down. Of course thinking he was letting Raphael down was perverse, Rafe had been an FBI agent through and through—if he had been in Gideon's place, there was little question that he would cooperate with the government. Rafe would have been on the Colonel's side.

Somehow, that didn't make things easier.

True to his word, the Colonel brought in a series of people. Not only people to hear about the Israelis, but a series of others, each of whom wanted to hear some specific bit of his story. The eight-hour session that introduced him to the Colonel had seemed long, but the subsequent interviews were much longer. The plainclothes Marines would bring in food so they didn't have to take any breaks. The sessions were over twelve hours; each time three or four people would participate in questioning him.

The process was exhausting. Each day he was escorted

out of his little room first thing in the morning, and each evening they led him back, and all he could do was collapse on the cot they gave him. He wondered if they were keeping Ruth in the same building, but his interviewers were very good at keeping his mind running in the tracks they wanted it to. It was hard for his mind to wander when he was constantly harassed with questions about the minutiae of his movements.

Even when he was alone, sprawled on his cot, his mind still ran over the events since the shooting. After the third day of questioning, it seemed as if he'd barely laid his head down when the door to his room opened and a series of Marines surrounded his cot.

"Come with us, sir."

Gideon pushed himself upright and picked up his watch. He felt as if he had barely gotten to sleep. He hadn't. His watch read 1:05. He looked up at the trio of Marines and said, "Do you know what time it is?"

"Yes, sir. Now would you please come with us."

Gideon pushed off the thin excuse for a blanket and started getting dressed. He pulled on one of the shirts and a pair of pants that they'd provided him, got up, and took a step to the bathroom.

A Marine seized his arm, the bad one, and Gideon could feel the strain on his barely-healed injury. "I'm afraid you have to come with us *now,* sir."

The problem with these guys was there was no room to negotiate. Gideon was really in no mood to test them. He yawned and nodded his head. He let them lead him back out, toward the Colonel's office.

That wasn't where they were taking him.

Gideon felt something sick in the pit of his stomach. He didn't exactly trust the Colonel; he didn't even know the guy's name. Any change in the routine they'd established set off warning signals.

The Marines were leading him back toward the elevators that had brought him here. They were moving him. The fact that they were doing it without any warning made Gideon extremely nervous. When they reached the bank of elevators, another trio of Marines were standing there already, escorting Ruth Zimmerman. She looked as tired and confused as he felt.

She blinked at him, as if her eyes were still adjusting to the stark florescent lighting. "Gideon? What's happening? Where are they taking us?"

Gideon shook his head. "I don't know." They were standing in front of the elevator, and at first Gideon thought that was what they were waiting for. After a while it began to dawn on him that they were waiting for something else, another member of the exodus. At first he thought it was the Colonel they were waiting for. Then he heard the Colonel's voice from down the hallway. The man did not sound happy.

"What do you think you're doing? You can't come into a live operation like this—"

Gideon heard another, calmer voice respond. "Don't engage me in a jurisdictional argument. You may have some tactical authority, but I have an executive order from the President of the United States. This is *my* operation. Not yours, not Fitzsimmons', not the General's . . ."

The two speakers turned the corner, and Gideon got a good look at the new gentleman. He was short, and wore a dark, expensive-looking suit. He wore a pair of thick glasses that made him resemble a thinner Peter Lorre. Gideon recognized him—

"*Emmit D'Arcy.*" Gideon whispered.

"What?" Ruth said.

The short man nodded at Gideon and at Ruth. "Mr. Malcolm, Miss Zimmerman. I'm here to take you back to Washington for a more thorough debriefing."

Gideon heard Ruth groan.

The Colonel stood, holding a sheet of paper in his hands. "I can't protest this strongly enough."

The short man nodded, and took off his glasses. This was Emmit D'Arcy, the National Security Advisor to President Rayburn. Kendal had said that there were rumors of D'Arcy's interest in what was happening, but Gideon had never expected to meet the man personally. Whatever Julia was involved in, Gideon didn't think *he* merited this kind of attention. What the hell was D'Arcy doing *here*?

D'Arcy pointed his glasses at the Colonel. "You don't know the depth of what you're dealing with. I need these people in Washington." He pressed a button for the elevator.

"Do you know?" The Colonel looked at Gideon. "There are some disturbing elements—"

D'Arcy replaced his glasses. "I've been privy to your interviews. That's why we have to handle it in Washington."

The elevator dinged, and the doors opened. There were two men in suits waiting in the elevator. They didn't look like Marines. The Marine escorts led Gideon and Ruth to the elevator and stepped back out to let D'Arcy in.

"You know there're security problems. Moving these people now is dangerous."

"Their security is no longer your concern," D'Arcy told him as the elevator doors closed.

Ruth sobbed. It sounded more frustration than anything else. Gideon put his arm around her. "What do they want from us?" she muttered.

D'Arcy heard her. "Only your cooperation," he said.

The elevator doors opened on the parking garage. There were two cars waiting for them, engines idling. At first Gideon thought they were going to separate him from Ruth again. It would make sense from a security standpoint.

He was wrong.

The two men escorted them into the rear car, a tan Ford sedan that looked like an unmarked police car. Then the men walked to the lead car, a black Oldsmobile, and got in with D'Arcy.

The setup made Gideon feel nervous. Since he'd gotten here, every time they moved him around they'd used a trio of Marines. Now all they had was the driver. His mind kept going back to what the Colonel had said, that moving them was dangerous.

The Olds pulled out and the Ford followed. Ruth was still leaning against him and asked, "What's going to happen to us?"

The driver spoke, and after dealing with the Marines for days, hearing someone engage in a conversation was a bit startling. "Don't worry, madam. We're just going straight to JFK. No problem."

JFK? Gideon thought. *Isn't La Guardia closer?*

"Want to hear some music?" the guy asked. He slipped a CD into the car's stereo and the car was suddenly filled with the sound of Mozart.

They spent some time on the Long Island Expressway as the night deepened. It was close to two-thirty as they took the exit for JFK. They still had a ways to go on the Van Wyck Expressway. The lead car, with D'Arcy in it, was little more than a set of taillights ahead in the distance.

The Olds seemed to have pulled ahead quite a bit since they'd gotten on the exit. That alarmed Gideon, especially when he checked their own speedometer and saw that they were going ten over the speed limit. He was about to ask the driver if he shouldn't catch up, when their car was washed by the brights from a vehicle behind them.

Ruth must've felt the same unease. She turned to look behind them just at the same time as Gideon did.

The lights behind them were coming from a truck or a van, Gideon couldn't make out the silhouette past the glare of the headlights. As he watched the vehicle close on them, he saw another set of headlights drift into the passing lane.

Gideon turned toward the driver, but the man was aware that something was wrong. The needle on the speedometer was already passing seventy. The guy was muttering, "Fuck, fuck, fuck . . ." He was barely audible under the whine of the engine and the pulse of a Mozart symphony. Gideon saw their driver only had one hand on the wheel.

He grabbed Ruth and said, "Get down."

He saw a look of panic on her face and he had to yell at her, *"Get down!"*

The vehicle in the passing lane had pulled up next to them. It was a Dodge pickup four-by-four, the side of it a sheer metal wall blocking in the Ford.

Gideon was thrown against the front seat as their follower touched the rear bumper. Gideon looked behind and could just make out the grille of another giant pickup beyond the glare. Then he was thrown to the side as the truck next to them drifted into the side of the Ford.

Gideon threw himself on top of Ruth as their driver cursed and leveled an automatic at the driver's window. But there was nothing for him to shoot at but the passenger door. The truck was too close for him to aim at anything else.

The truck next to them made contact again, and the rear driver's side window shattered, covering Gideon and the back seat with safety glass. From the sound of abused metal, the truck stayed in contact and began pushing them to the right, off the road. Their driver did the only thing he could, he tried to accelerate away, but at the angle he was at, he was fighting the mass of the truck. The only way he could go was the way he was being herded.

The driver took that as their only chance and peeled off to the right. He took an exit that was so fortuitous that Gideon wondered if they were meant to take it.

That question was answered once the Ford peeled out onto the surface street. The two pickups still shadowed them, and a third turned off of a side street ahead of them and reversed toward them in their lane. The Ford had to swerve around the truck to avoid a collision, and that effectively cut off their exit down the side street.

All three pickups were on them in no time. The Ford couldn't outrun them. The driver was on the radio yelling for backup, help, anything. He yelled the names of cross streets into the radio, and then a truck was slamming into the passenger side of the car.

The driver grabbed his gun off of the seat and Gideon ducked his head. The space inside the Ford seemed to shake with the sound of the automatic going off. The smell was rank before the driver let off a third shot.

The only response was a shudder from another impact. Gideon heard twisting metal and breaking glass, and risked a look up. The Ford was sandwiched between two of the pickup trucks, doors buckling inward, and the screeching protest of the Ford's engine cut through the air as their driver tried to gun the accelerator.

Gideon smelled burning rubber, oil, and hot metal. The Ford was slowing whether it wanted to or not.

He turned to look behind them and heard the sound of strain from the rear window. He ducked his head just before the stress on the frame shattered it. It popped right next to him like another gunshot.

Ruth was shaking under him. She was screaming something incomprehensible.

He looked up in time to see the trailing headlights drift to the right to pass them. Then the whole mass of traveling metal pulled to a stop at an intersection. Gideon could see a stoplight swinging above the front of the cars.

Their driver still tried to accelerate, gunning the engine. The Ford responded with a short jerk and the smell of burned rubber. They'd stopped moving.

"Come on," he yelled at Ruth. "Move, now."

He pulled her up, and after about half a second of paralysis, she saw what he was doing. He pushed her through the remains of the rear window and quickly followed, cutting his hands and knees on cubes of safety glass.

His one hope was that there might be some cover near them that they could run for before the guys in the pickups got their act together.

No such luck.

One side of the road was a parking lot, the other a used car dealership. Both were floodlit even at this time of night. Ruth headed to the dealership, it was closer.

Gideon followed, limping on his game leg. Ruth was already three quarters of the way to the dealership, where the cars offered some cover. Gideon stumbled, barely away from the rear of the car. He heard gunfire behind them and saw her turn to look at him.

He waved at her: *get moving!*

Instead she backed up to grab his arm and help him toward the dealership. That hesitation was too long. They were both on the sidewalk, a dozen yards from the first car in the dealer's lot, and cover, when the sidewalk erupted in orange sparks and the smell of superheated concrete.

They stopped where they were, even before an accented voice told them to freeze.

Gideon stood still, waiting for the bullets to cut them down. They didn't. Instead, a pair of men, one of whom Gideon recognized from Greenwich Village, approached them from either side. The voice from behind them, the one with the heavy Eastern European accent, said, "No sudden moves, or you will be shot."

The admonition wasn't necessary. One of the men in front of them put away his weapon and grabbed Gideon's hands, pulled them behind him, and slipped a nylon restraint around his wrists, tightening it. He did the same to Ruth. While he was binding their hands, the other man roughly patted them down.

The speaker cautiously circled around, covering them with his weapon. When his face came into view, he saw, without too much surprise, the man who had shot Morris Kendal.

The men roughly turned them around and led them to the lead pickup truck. It had a quad cab, with a back seat, and their new captors unceremoniously shoved them into it, belting them in tightly. It hurt when he sat on his wrists, and he was effectively immobilized.

Gideon had a chance to see the Ford. It wasn't a pleasant sight. He couldn't see much through a windshield starred with bullet holes, but a dark shadow was visible through the glass, on the driver's side.

He heard Ruth whisper, "My God."

He turned toward her, and saw her staring past him, at the Ford. She looked at him and said, "They're going to kill us, aren't they?"

Gideon shook his head, even though he was unsure himself. But, if they wanted them dead, they wouldn't have dragged them to the car. "Try to be strong," Gideon whispered, wishing he had a hand free to comfort her.

As he spoke, the door behind Ruth opened up and one of the men grabbed her from behind, pulling a black hood over her face. She gasped when it happened, as if expecting a garrote. Afterward, Gideon could see her shaking.

"Are you all right?" He asked.

"N–No."

Then Gideon heard the door behind him open, and before he could turn around, a black hood descended over his own head.

3.02
Thur. Mar. 25 2009

IT was almost noon, during a brief pause in a flurry of meetings, when the door slammed open in Emmit D'Arcy's office. Colonel Gregory Mecham stood in the doorway, looking as if he'd had no sleep in the last forty-eight hours. D'Arcy looked up from his desk and said quietly, "Colonel, I thought you were still in New York."

Mecham stepped into the office and let the door close behind him. "What the hell have you done, D'Arcy?"

D'Arcy sat up and straightened his glasses. "I don't appreciate that tone, Colonel. You sound as if you're trying to accuse me of something."

"It's as if you went out of your way to lose them, and one of our men got killed in the process. Christ, where was your security? What were you thinking? A civilian flight out of JFK? You were *asking* for this to happen."

"That's quite enough, Colonel." D'Arcy stood. "You know we're dealing with a security problem. The extraction was engineered to be small and anonymous. I hand-picked those men, and supervised it personally. Do you think I wanted to be shot at? We chose a civilian flight so that there would be no other government personnel aware of our movement."

"They still caught up with you—"

D'Arcy nodded. His expression was grave. "That means something more ominous than a breach in our communications security."

"What?"

"We have a mole, Colonel. Zimmerman has someone helping her from the inside." D'Arcy walked around the table. "Look at the facts, Colonel. The IUF's people have been aware of every move we've made. From the CIA's botched Daedalus sting onward . . ." He patted Mecham's shoulder. "It's a good thing you came in, Colonel."

"What are you talking about? A mole?"

"Look at the timing of this." D'Arcy turned and leaned on his desk, facing away from Mecham. He looked out the window toward the Washington Monument. "Why did they strike when they did? Unless they *wanted* your people in the NSA to debrief Malcolm and Zimmerman's sister. While you had them, they didn't move. The moment there's a threat that someone else might question them, they made the grab." D'Arcy's hand moved to a small console set in his desk. He pressed a button.

Mecham was backing up. "Are you saying that someone at the NSA is in on all this?"

D'Arcy nodded. "And we're dealing with some carefully engineered disinformation. They didn't shoot our two prisoners, they *took* them. Why? Unless those two were *working* with Zimmerman and the IUF?"

"That's crazy. He was *shot*—"

D'Arcy turned around and faced him. As he did, the

door behind Mecham opened. "Do you know a better motive for turning on your own country? Malcolm has, at least, an understandable reason for working with these people."

A pair of Marines stepped into the office and to either side of Mecham. Mecham looked at them, and the color drained out of his face. "What's going on here?"

"I said we have a mole." D'Arcy looked at Mecham. "I hope I'm wrong."

Mecham looked at D'Arcy, and his expression went cold. "You've made one hell of a mistake here."

"Perhaps." D'Arcy took off his glasses and shook his head. "I hope so. But it makes too much sense to ignore. They've had a line on everything we've done. They've obviously turned Malcolm and used him to seed disinformation that's intended to divert us from whatever terrorist activity they're planning. And you were *very* eager to bring him in. Who better than the mole to debrief Malcolm?"

"You don't know what you're saying."

D'Arcy wiped his glasses. "I want you to know that there are no official charges. At this point we're just being careful. But you will have to be detained until we've unraveled the truth in this matter. You'll be interviewed—"

Mecham nodded. "I know the drill, Emmit. I've done it enough myself."

"Then would you please accompany the Marines here?"

Mecham looked at the Marines next to him and nodded. "You are going to find out just how wrong you are."

"I hope so," D'Arcy said. He turned away from him as the Marines escorted Colonel Mecham out of his office. Once the door closed, D'Arcy whispered to himself, barely voiced, *"Sorry, Colonel, there's no other way. We're too close."*

They changed cars once, loading Gideon and Ruth into the back of a van. Afterward they stayed on the road for hours. They kept Gideon and Ruth hooded, and only stopped twice, leading them to a bathroom. From the feel of the road under the car's shocks, Gideon suspected that they never traveled an Interstate after leaving the vicinity of New York City.

Gideon thought that placed them somewhere in rural New York or Pennsylvania. When he mentioned that to Ruth in a whispered voice, she responded, "Where are they taking us?"

"I don't know." Gideon edged over in his seat until he was next to Ruth. He grunted when he stopped moving. His arms had fallen asleep, and his bad arm ached. He was beginning to worry about lost circulation. The hood he wore stank of his sweat.

They rode in silence for a while after that. It gave Gideon another opportunity to wonder why the two of them had been taken prisoner. He hadn't said anything to Ruth about it, since he'd have to point out how much easier it'd be for them to have killed them on the road with the driver.

Why would these people need them?

If Julia was really calling the shots here, she might feel something for her sister, ordering her spared. But if that was the case, taking him would make about as much sense as taking the driver.

It felt like late afternoon when they stopped for the last time. Gideon heard the side door slide open, and a blast of cold air filled the rear of the van. A gruff voice told them to get out. Gideon did his best to stand without help from his arms, and someone grabbed him and pulled him out of the van.

He took a step and felt his feet sink into a layer of snow. In a few moments he was shivering. It was probably twenty degrees colder here than it had been in New York.

Without warning, someone stripped off his hood, and the glare blinded him, making him squint. The cold air was like a slap in the face. While he was dazzled, he felt a knife cut the nylon cord binding his wrists.

He stood there, blinking, eyes watering, trying to rub circulation back into his wrists. It took a moment before he could see much of anything. First, he saw Ruth standing next to him, rubbing her wrists, her face screwed up in a squint as she looked past him.

Gideon turned away from the van and Ruth to look at where they were. The van was parked next to a stand of evergreens that opened out ahead of them into a clearing that must've been a couple of acres. Beyond the trees on the far side of the clearing, Gideon could make out a line of mountains against a painfully blue sky.

The snow covering the clearing was undisturbed; there was only a slight depression to mark where the road they were on continued. Right in front of the nose of the van was a gate that was painted a bright red in contrast against the snow. A battered sign stood next to the gate, and Gideon had to blink a few times before he could make out the words—

"Limited Use Seasonal Highway. Closed Nov. 15–April 15."

Their captors stood around, as if they were waiting for something. Ruth muttered, "Looks like you were right about upstate New York." Her words came out in a puff of fog.

Gideon turned to the man who looked like the leader and asked, "So what are we waiting for?"

The man didn't respond, didn't even look at him. Gideon kept looking at him. He had donned a white parka for the weather, and held a Kalishnikov rifle whose black composite stock stood out against his clothing. This was the man he'd seen shoot Kendal. The expression on his face was frightening, almost mechanical, as if there wasn't any emotion there at all. Gideon looked into that face and wanted to jump the man, strangle him. . . .

Then the man barked something in a foreign language and pointed with a gloved hand. Gideon looked in the direction he indicated and saw a vehicle across the clearing. At first it was hard to make out what it was. It was painted white and difficult to make out against the snow.

As it closed on them, Gideon could see it was a Hummer. He also saw the exhaust stack that marked it as a military, not a civilian model. It pulled up on the other side of the fence.

The leader waved Gideon and Ruth toward it with his Kalishnikov. The two of them slowly waded through the calf-deep snow to the open rear door of the Hummer. The leader followed them, leaving the others to get in the van and drive back down the way they had come.

The man with the Kalishnikov pushed Gideon and Ruth into the back seat, then got into the front passenger seat himself. Once the rear door was shut, the Hummer backed up and turned toward the snow-covered clearing. The snow, which probably would have mired any other vehicle, was pushed aside by the Hummer, spraying up on either side of the vehicle. Clumps of snow obscured Gideon's view out the passenger windows; all he could see was a vague impression of trees passing by as they left the other side of the clearing.

They went a couple of miles into the woods when the driver slowed on the buried highway and took an unexpected turn to the right, pointing the Hummer up the side of the hill next to them.

Gideon craned to see out the front, but what he saw wasn't even a footpath. It was a gully cut in the side of the hill by water runoff. It was a ditch that was barely wide enough for the Hummer, and the driver aimed them straight up it. The grade steepened, but the Hummer's low center of gravity kept the wheels on the road on a grade that would flip over just about anything else. The grade passed forty-five degrees at several points, and there was no point where any two wheels were on the same level.

Ruth grabbed his arm and wouldn't let go during the nerve-racking ascent.

Eventually they emerged on another, more conventional road, that snaked around the hill. The driver turned right again, following this road back the way they'd come. It was a buried dirt road, in worse repair than the first one. Still, it was a relief after the drive up the side of the hill. At this point, the driver seemed very aware of the canopy above them. When Gideon first noticed the driver looking up, he thought it was nothing, but when he started taking turns when the road divided, Gideon began to realize that he was avoiding the paths that didn't have the shade of a lot of branches.

After three or four more miles, they passed a point of transition. It was only marked by a few signs posted on trees by the side of the road: "Private Property," "No Hunting," "No Trespassing." After that, the woods around them seemed to undergo a subtle and somewhat threatening change. The first things that Gideon noticed were the logs and windblown trees—piles of deadwood that were innocuous at first glance, but after seeing a third pile, it was obvious that they were placed by man, not nature, concealing cameras, or some other security measure. A few times Gideon looked up, and saw a bare spot in the canopy supplemented by a sheet of camouflage netting. And once, in the distance, Gideon saw another man with a Kalishnikov, wearing a white parka, appearing as if he were on some sort of patrol.

They were entering some sort of military encampment.

When they reached the end of this private road, Gideon and Ruth stepped out of the Hummer into the road, followed by the man wielding the Kalishnikov, who took them fifteen yards back down the road, behind the vehicle.

Gideon watched as the driver got out of the car and

went to a tree by the side of the road. Gideon could see rope and part of a scaffolding—dressed with more camouflage netting—next to the tree. The driver pulled on the rope, and the floor of the forest next to the road opened up.

A camouflaged trapdoor opened up on a dirt ramp that led down into an unlit hole. The driver pulled until the trapdoor was at about a sixty-degree angle, and when he let go of the rope, the door stayed there, expertly counterbalanced. Then he got back in the Hummer, angled back, and backed it into the hole.

"Come on," said their leader, once the Hummer was off of the road.

Gideon looked at Ruth. She looked at him, still rubbing her wrists. He had the uncomfortable sense that she was relying on him to show her what to do.

He hugged himself. The cold was beginning to seep into his leg and his arm, burning in the newly-healed flesh. When he started walking in the direction the Kalishnikov indicated, he noticed his limp was more pronounced. His leg felt as if he'd been on his feet all day.

The man with the Kalishnikov took them out into a clearing, occasionally prodding them with the rifle.

They followed the private road out into a field. Once they left the woods, the road was marked on either side by a long, gray split-rail fence. The fence enclosed sloping pastures on either side of them, flat white expanses of snow. The pasture to the right sloped down toward a treeline, and the one to the left sloped upward until it reached a rocky hillside that shot upward at a steep angle.

There was a cluster of buildings far in front of them.

Gideon could make out a Victorian farmhouse, and a weathered gray barn adjoining the left pasture.

It was a long walk toward the buildings. They trudged through the snow, their breath coming out in wisps of fog. The landscape felt oddly empty. The people here had gone to great lengths to cultivate a feeling of abandonment. The one subtle sign otherwise was a complex set of antennae mounted, only half-hidden, in the Victorian's weathered gingerbread.

The Victorian's dark turrets, wrapped in gray shingles, seemed to lean over them as they reached the house. A porch wrapped around the side and front of the house, half in collapse. Parts of it were little more than splintered piles of rotted wood. The intact portion, in front of the main entrance, had a roof that visibly bowed in the center.

Their keeper pushed them toward the stairs. Gideon and Ruth stepped up to the unstable-looking porch. Gideon went slowly, out of fear of putting a foot through a rotten board. Once he stepped onto the snow-covered porch, he realized he needn't have worried. The surface he walked on, under a thin coating of snow, was a new piece of plywood. Once he was on the porch, he could see that there were a number of places above them where metal braces supported what was left of the porch above them.

The main doorway appeared to be boarded shut, but as they approached, the sheet of plywood covering the doorway opened up, swinging out to reveal a stern looking guy in a turtleneck, carrying another Kalishnikov. If it hadn't been for the Russian weapon, the guy in the sweater projected an attitude reminiscent of the plain-clothes Marines.

They didn't get to see much of the interior as they were hustled upstairs. From what Gideon saw, this place had been abandoned at one point. But it was being used for *something* now. They passed a drawing room that seemed to be the final resting place of every piece of furniture that had been abandoned with the house. Just before they ascended the stairs, Gideon looked down a hallway and saw that the warped, water-stained hardwood floor snaked with cables.

Then they were upstairs, walking down a corridor of cracked plaster and peeling wallpaper. The hallway had once been carpeted, but the carpet, what was left of it, was rolled up and leaning at the end of the hall against a boarded-up window.

Their keepers took them to a room that held a few cots, a desk, and a small computer terminal. Gideon noticed that the desk had a set of cables that went through a hole in the floor that had been made by removing one of the floorboards. The cables included the power cord that led to the standing lamp that was the only light in the win-dowless room.

"Sit," said the man who had led them all the way from the van. He set down his rifle behind the desk and stripped off his parka. Briefly, Gideon thought of diving for the weapon, but the gentleman with the sweater was still with them, his own Kalishnikov ready.

Gideon and Ruth sat. Gideon couldn't help but sigh with relief as he took the weight off his leg. Both his legs were stinging as ice melted off his too-thin jeans.

The man hung his parka up on a hook in a wall and pulled a small box out from a drawer in the desk. It looked like a small vinyl briefcase. He opened it to reveal a complex telephone. The whole case was about the size of a brick, but it was larger than any cellular phone that Gideon had seen recently.

The man with the phone nodded at the man with the rifle. He received a nod in return, and the man in the sweater picked up the extra rifle and left, closing the door on the three of them.

The man gave them an inscrutable look and keyed a number into his phone. After a few moments he said, "This is Volynskji."

In response he nodded a few times. After a few moments he said, "Is that wise, sir?" A shake of the head. "Even if the mission is compl—" Pause. "Yes. It is your operation." Look up at the two captives. "I'll take care of that now. I'll give you an update as soon—" Nod. "If you say so. No transmissions. I'll defer the report until you arrive."

Volynskji slowly put the phone back on the cradle and closed the small case.

He looked up at the two of them. "I have some questions I need to ask you, but before I do so, I should say something." He walked around the side of the desk. "First, if you're thinking of being uncooperative, you should know that most professionals have the following standing orders—if suicide is not an option, they should cooperate. Every agency who has an operative fall into the hands of the enemy automatically assumes all information possessed by the operative is compromised. Stubbornness on your part will not serve any purpose—except to make things more difficult. For you, not me. All it will cost me is time." He gave both of them a flat emotionless stare that was as bad as any threat. Gideon could look into those eyes and easily imagine what he would do to someone who was "stubborn."

He sat on the edge of the desk, facing them, and asked, "Now exactly *what* did you say to Chaviv Tischler?"

Volynskji questioned them for several hours. Several times, Gideon thought of trying to overpower the man, but he couldn't see how to do it without raising an alarm that would alert the rifle-bearing guard at the door. So, despite what he thought of the man, and despite his reluctance to answer any questions, Gideon played along with Volynskji. He rationalized that he was protecting Ruth. He was responsible for her being here, and he couldn't allow any reluctance on his part to result in something happening to her.

So, for hours, Gideon answered Volynskji's questions. All of them were directed at him, not Ruth. And the majority were about the old man with the cane and the safe house in New Jersey. Volynskji's questions confirmed Gideon's suspicion that they were Israelis. The name "Chaviv Tischler" belonged to that old man, who was so interested in their conversation in the restaurant. The way Volynski talked about the man, Tischler was a high ranking member of Israeli intelligence. That didn't surprise Gideon.

What surprised Gideon was the fact that Volynskji

didn't ask him one question about the Colonel and the U.S. government officials who had questioned them.

Maybe he already knew all he needed from that. The thought chilled Gideon. It implied that his own government's security was compromised way beyond what Tischler had implied. The Colonel and his people knew that Zimmerman was out there, and should know the extent that compromised them. They would be taking active steps to conceal their movements from the perceived threat. If Volynskji knew the contents of those debriefings—and the focus of his own questions implied that—despite the Colonel's precautions, these people—these terrorists—had penetrated the government far beyond what anyone suspected.

Volynskji kept at the questions until the answers became incoherent because of exhaustion. After that, the guard came in and led them to another room, higher in the building, and locked them in. There was a small window on one wall, an oval about a foot in its longest dimension. The only light came from the moon reflecting off of snow on the sill.

3.03
Fri. Mar. 26

LAWRENCE Fitzsimmons was in his office early before the President's daily—and lately, embarrassing—intelligence briefing. He was drinking coffee and looking out at the sunrise, when the intercom buzzed.

"Mr. Fitzsimmons? There's a gentleman here to see you."

That in itself was odd. For an unscheduled visitor to get to his office, he would have to pass through four people after building security. Each one had to make an independent decision whether the visitor was worth the director's attention. That usually took a while, so seeing anyone before eight was a rarity.

He told them to send the man in. Obviously someone thought it was worth his while.

He turned his chair around and tried to hide his surprise as Chaviv Tischler walked into his office.

The old man leaned on his cane and smiled. "I've heard a rumor that you're retiring. If that's true, it would be a loss."

Fitzsimmons sipped his coffee and shook his head.

"You aren't here to discuss my retirement plans, are you? Or are you recruiting?"

"May I sit?"

Fitzsimmons nodded and put down his coffee.

"I'm here to discuss a current problem of yours. Or to be more precise, to enlighten you about it."

"I'm sure I don't know what you're talking about."

Tischler nodded. "And I am certain you do. I know, for instance, that your sudden noises about retirement have to do with this problem. I know that there have been serious differences between parts of your intelligence community about dealing with it. I know that there is a high-ranking member of the NSA, a Colonel Mecham, under 'protective' custody."

Fitzsimmons leaned back. "Is this some bizarre fishing expedition, Tischler? You know better than to expect me to make some sort of comment about whatever theories you're spinning, much less discuss them with you."

Tischler shook his head. "Fishing? No, quite the opposite." He reached into his pocket and pulled out a jewel case with a golden CD inside it. "I'm here to cast some bread upon the waters." He placed the disk on the desk in front of Fitzsimmons.

Fitzsimmons looked at the disk. The early morning light was just beginning to leak into his office, and it caught the CD, casting rainbows across its surface. Fitzsimmons didn't believe in hunches or in premonitions, but he looked at that disk and·realized that he felt extremely uneasy about it. In fact, he was afraid of it.

Fitzsimmons remained leaning back in his chair. He didn't reach for the disk. Instead he asked, "What is it?"

"Something you should know about an organization known as the International Unification Front. I presume they have something, a number of somethings, that you are looking for."

Fitzsimmons looked at Tischler, then down on the desk. He could believe what Tischler said. The Israelis still had one of the most capable regional intelligence networks in the world. There was little question that they'd have knowledge about the IUF that the U.S. didn't. The question running through Fitzsimmons' mind was, why *this*? Why *now*?

He leaned forward, still not reaching for the disk. "If you want to share intelligence, why aren't you relying on normal channels? There are liaisons for just such things." Fitzsimmons motioned to the disk, the first time he'd acknowledged it.

Tischler shook his head. "There are reasons not to trust those channels. I suspect you know that, at least partially."

Fitzsimmons was careful to keep his expression neutral. The evil premonition wouldn't go away.

Tischler had revealed information that was damaging to the Israelis just by being here. Just allowing Fitzsimmons to suspect the depth of the intelligence the Israelis had about Zimmerman—when they shouldn't, in fact, have any—was threatening to Israel's own security. The admission that they knew anything about this, so-far domestic, "problem" was a diplomatic disaster.

Tischler knew that reports—some probably already being written by the security people who let him in—would come out of Fitzsimmons' office, detailing this meeting. The reports would go to the President, and would probably chill U.S.-Israeli relations for the rest of Rayburn's term.

Fitzsimmons looked at Tischler and asked, "Do your superiors know you're here?"

Tischler nodded. "I've been requesting authority to do this ever since this problem came to my attention. This problem of yours is a direct threat to our national security—but involving ourselves in this, any substantial commitment, would be a *delicate* matter."

Fitzsimmons thought to himself, *Holy shit, did he actually admit to considering a covert action on U.S. soil?* He looked at the CD in front of him.

Tischler followed his gaze. "I see you grasp the severity of the matter. I finally convinced my superiors that it was best that we give you what we know." He placed a hand on the case and slid it forward as he stood. "You cannot effectively deal with what is happening without this information. For reasons that will become apparent, it must be delivered directly to you. Read and digest it thoroughly before you act to disseminate this information, to *anyone*."

Tischler moved to go and Fitzsimmons was almost tempted to call building security to restrain him. He didn't. There was no need to provoke more of an international incident than they already had.

Instead, Fitzsimmons asked, "What's on this disk?"

Tischler turned and asked, "Why was Morris Kendal killed?"

"What?"

"Morris Kendal was assassinated because he was close

to realizing what that disk contains. I think you will also find some interesting facts about the agent—Christoffel his name was, I believe—who handled him."

With that, Tischler left.

Fitzsimmons picked up the disk Tischler left him and looked at it. He knew, in his gut, that there was something very nasty here.

At exactly nine o'clock in the morning, a helicopter took off from Andrews Air Force Base. The helicopter was a military model, but it bore no service markings. It was simply painted a drab olive color. The copter was owned by the CIA, part of a large black budget that no one person had clearance to see completely itemized. The two pilots were both CIA, or at least both of them had been at one point. They were paid out of the same black account as the helicopter.

In the rear of the helicopter sat four people. One of them was Emmit D'Arcy. Another was a nervous-looking man named Howard Christoffel.

D'Arcy patted the man on the shoulder. "No need to worry, son."

Christoffel shook his head. "I'm not a field man. I belong behind a desk—"

"I know," D'Arcy said. "Your expertise was, and is, invaluable in our Mid-East operations."

"Thank you, sir." He looked out the window.

"I don't think it could have been organized without you."

Christoffel shook his head. "I'm just an analyst, sir. To be honest, when I've discovered what some of my analysis has led to— This all makes me uneasy. Kendal, especially . . ."

D'Arcy took off his glasses and nodded sagely. "I understand how that must have been difficult for you." D'Arcy squeezed his shoulder again. "But we need you here, Christoffel."

Christoffel kept watching as the helicopter pulled out over the Chesapeake and began heading toward the Atlantic. Staring into the rippling water, he said, "I can't see why."

There was a long pause before D'Arcy said, "Because I'm afraid we can't afford you anywhere else."

Christoffel turned to say something, and stared at the two men facing him and D'Arcy. One had a gun out, and the other was sliding the helicopter's door aside.

"What?" Christoffel shouted over the sudden wind that whipped through the passenger space. The two men, who had said nothing since Christoffel entered the helicopter, grabbed him and forced him to his knees in front of the open door. "D'Arcy! You can't do this!"

D'Arcy watched as the man with the gun placed it up to the back of Christoffel's head and pulled the trigger. As Christoffel fell out, into the Atlantic waters, D'Arcy took off his glasses and wiped them off.

The helicopter began to take a leisurely turn north, toward the hills of Pennsylvania.

Gideon sat on a military-issue cot and stared at the oval Victorian window, high in the wall. The sky beyond was a livid blue, marked only by an edging of frost on the glass. He had run several escape attempts through his mind, but there seemed very little chance of getting away from this desolate, snowbound place. He didn't even know where the nearest town was. Even if he got himself and Ruth away from this place, they could both easily die of exposure out there on those wooded hills.

No, he corrected himself, they *would* die if they escaped on foot. He was a D.C. native, unused to this much snow even when he was in perfect shape. Here, now, once he was off the roads, with his busted leg, he would be effectively immobile.

They were pretty much stuck here.

Ruth broke into his fatalistic thoughts by saying, "You know, it's not fair . . ."

Gideon shrugged. "Nothing fair about this."

"That's not it. You know me, my family—you interrogated me on the subject. But I know next to nothing about you."

"Not much to tell."

Ruth looked at him and said, "You're a liar. Come on. Are you single, married, divorced? What're your parents like? Any little Gideons running around, missing their dad right now?"

Gideon sighed. "Detective in the D.C. Police Department. Robbery, mostly car theft and such. None of the glamour people associate with Homicide, or—God help us—Vice—"

Ruth sat up on her cot and rested her head in her hands. "I know *what* you do. What about your *life*, your family?"

Gideon shook his head. He was silent a while before he

spoke. "Our mother, she was a legal secretary. Died when I was ten. A bad car accident . . ."

Ruth prompted, "Drunk driver?"

"No. Forced off a highway during a high-speed police chase. Some asshole broadsided her in a stolen car, trying to evade pursuit."

"Did they get the guy?"

"The guy got himself. He jumped the median and plowed into the front of a bus. Dead on impact. Poetic justice. If they'd prosecuted, he'd probably be out now."

"I'm sorry . . ."

Gideon leaned back and stared at the ceiling. "I just saw, later, what it must have done to my father, and Rafe. Dad was an FBI agent. Christ, I don't know if anyone could've idolized my father more than Rafe did. He wanted to *be* our dad—before . . ." Gideon closed his eyes.

"What do you mean?"

Gideon could picture his father's face, the broad smile, the eyes that smile never seemed to touch, that always seemed to grieve. "Dad quit the FBI. Started having twisted feelings about law enforcement. Threw Raphael out of the house when he decided to become an FBI agent."

"I'm sorry."

"I think he regretted it, but was too stubborn to back down . . ." Gideon shook his head. "Rafe idolized Dad, but I idolized Rafe. I don't think I ever forgave Dad— even if Rafe did. I tried for Quantico myself—" Gideon shook his head. "I don't know if I was trying to follow my brother's footsteps, or trying to piss off my dad. Doesn't matter though, I couldn't hack it."

"I can't believe that."

"Why? Because I'm such a wonderful cop?" Gideon closed his eyes. "I couldn't handle the pressure. Every day was a race against my dad, and against Rafe. Every test was measured against that yardstick, and more often than not I came up short. My whole time there was spent trying to prove something and failing . . ."

"I'm sorry," Ruth said.

"I quit. Had to. I suffered a breakdown. Didn't talk to anyone, Dad, Rafe—not for nearly six months. As if I blamed them."

"I know what that's like, living in someone's shadow," Ruth said, repeating her words from the subway.

Gideon nodded. "I suppose you would—"

Gideon heard Ruth suck in a breath and he turned to look at her. He could see her eyes moisten. "I blamed her," she whispered. "I mean, she had her reasons for not talking to our folks. Dad never quite understood her, what mathematics was to her. The arguments about college—" Ruth sniffed. "Dad wanted the best for her, he just didn't know what that was. He saw an academic scholarship to an Ivy League university and that was it. They were recruiting *her.* I think it killed him when she decided to go to Berkeley . . ." Ruth shook her head. "That was the first time I had ever heard Julia raise her voice."

"It was bad?"

Ruth nodded. "They were doing things at Berkeley that interested her. Dad didn't understand. He just saw the name, 'Harvard.' He thought she'd be throwing her life

away. There was a three-hour argument that ended with
Julia slamming the door. The episode left Mom in tears.
It was like none of us in that house could breathe. Wait-
ing for the other shoe to drop—"

"What happened?"

"The shoe never dropped. Julia never walked back
through that door. Somehow, I'm still not sure how, she
managed to get Berkeley to pay for a flight out to California. She left home with just the clothes on her back
and a full scholarship."

"Hell of a runaway."

Ruth chuckled, but there wasn't much humor in it.
"She had lined up a job on campus before the plane
landed. The next I heard from her, she was in California.
She was still a minor, and I think Dad was prepared to
have the cops drag her back, but Mom started losing
it . . ." She shook her head and put her face in her hands.
"I think I can understand why she did what she did. I can
even understand how Berkeley could 'overlook' her age.
But I'm the one who stopped talking to *her.*"

Gideon sat up. "I thought she cut herself off from her
family."

Ruth shook her head. "Our folks, yes. But she tried to
stay in contact with me—maybe because I took her
dreams seriously. But what her leaving did to our parents,
I couldn't forgive." She paused. "No, that's wrong. When
I'm really honest with myself, what I can't forgive is the
way my parents were stolen. After she left, it was as if she
became an only child. I became irrelevant."

Gideon reached over and touched Ruth's shoulder. He
could feel her shaking under his hand.

"I cut her off. We talked maybe a half-dozen times since she left. Never once did I call her—" Ruth leaned against him and whispered. "Could this be my fault? Would she have done this if I hadn't abandoned her? If she wasn't alone?"

"No," Gideon whispered. "It isn't your fault."

We're all alone.

3.04
Fri. Mar. 26

BY the time Fitzsimmons had fully digested the contents of Tischler's little gift, and had reviewed the records on Agent Christoffel, it was time for his daily briefing with President Rayburn. It was scheduled in the morning, right after a Rose Garden speech about U.S.-Indonesian relations. Fitzsimmons came early and spent his time waiting in the Oval Office, sitting and looking over the files he had printed for Rayburn over the past two hours.

His hands were shaking.

Rayburn's booming voice interrupted his train of thought, almost making him drop the files he carried. "Larry, you look like shit."

Fitzsimmons stood and nodded, "Mr. President."

Rayburn stood in front of the door, closing it. He seemed to tower over Fitzsimmons. "Okay, what is it?"

Fitzsimmons took in a breath and said, "I think you'd better take a seat."

Rayburn scanned the room and realized that they were alone. A look of concern crossed his face as he took a seat across from Fitzsimmons. "No expert witnesses?"

"No, I need to bring this to your attention before anyone else hears it." Fitzsimmons handed the files to Rayburn.

Rayburn took the files and said, "This is about Zimmerman, isn't it?"

"Not just Zimmerman, though."

"All right, let's hear it."

Fitzsimmons gave an abbreviated account of Tischler's meeting with him this morning. Rayburn frowned as he listened. "Christ, they have us monitored that well?"

"The fact that the Israelis were willing to let us know that marks the gravity of what they gave us. They sacrificed a lot of U.S.-Israeli goodwill, as well as their assets in this country, to hand this over to us."

Rayburn nodded. "What is it, and how do we know that it isn't some piece of disinformation?"

Fitzsimmons stood and walked over to a table that held a pitcher of ice water. He poured himself a glass and drank, wishing it was scotch. "It isn't, Mr. President. I've confirmed a number of isolated facts from our own records."

"What is this they *gave* us? What does it have to do with Zimmerman?"

"Zimmerman is most likely in the hands of the International Unification Front, a State-sponsored independent umbrella organization that is interested—allegedly—in a pan-Arab, pan-Islamic union in the Mid-East. They organize terrorism, intelligence, espionage, and paramilitary training for dozens of smaller groups. Needless to say, the Israelis have the most complete records on them outside the IUF itself—" Fitzsimmons sucked in a deep breath.

"What the Israelis just handed us, is those records. *All* of them."

"What?" The note of disbelief in Rayburn's voice hung in the air, an almost physical thickening of the atmosphere.

Fitzsimmons drank his water, trying to keep his throat from drying out completely. "Tischler handed over a copy of the Israelis' complete file on the IUF. Uncensored, unedited, straight from the Mossad computers."

"Holy shit." Rayburn flipped through the top file, which was a pre-made abstract of the information on Tischler's CD. Fitzsimmons had printed it raw from the disk. "Why would they just hand us this? We've cooperated with them before, but they don't let go of any information without a reason."

"Zimmerman, in the hands of the IUF, is much more a threat to them than it is to us. And they know that, once we have this file, the IUF will cease to exist."

The President of the United States looked up from the abstract as if he could hear the nerves behind Fitzsimmons' words. "You better explain that, Larry."

"It's in the abstract."

"I want to hear it in your words."

"We've been wrong about what State actually sponsors the IUF."

Rayburn just stared at him.

"The IUF—we've traced Syrian backing, Libyan involvement, ties to several Islamic republics from the Soviet break up. All of it is camouflage. The IUF is, whole cloth, the result of a runaway covert operation managed by the CIA, an operation that began in the mid-eighties."

"You've got to be fucking kidding me."

Fitzsimmons shook his head. "Remember William Casey and his dream of an 'off-the-shelf' CIA? Remember all the hostage negotiations? There were a hell of a lot of Mid-East contacts made back then. A hell of a lot more assets developed than the Senate Intelligence Oversight Committee ever discovered."

"Are you saying that *we* created the IUF?"

Fitzsimmons nodded. "I've backtracked a lot. The quality of our Middle-East intelligence started gaining a lot of credibility right after the IUF formed. Even when the IUF was still a secret society, not publicly known. We knew more about the World Trade Center bombing than we should've. There's even a chance that the site to park the truck was a piece of misinformation that *we* fed the terrorists—I mean their goal was to bring the building *down*. If the truck was in a better spot they might've. Oklahoma City, we seem to have *known* it was a domestic bombing within twelve hours— *Days* before anyone else. Ever since the overt formation of the IUF, there's been Arab terrorism, but their efficacy against U.S. targets has been remarkably reduced."

"My God . . ."

"It gets worse."

Rayburn looked up at Fitzsimmons.

"Emmit D'Arcy was in the CIA then, a Mid-East analyst. He was one of William Casey's protégés."

Rayburn was shaking his head.

"D'Arcy's been in a prime position to develop the IUF, and deflect any inquiry. Look at the damn Daedalus theft. Look who was *in* on the theft, two live CIA agents and a handful of freelancers from the Iran-Contra days. Even though their capture was securely under wraps, *someone* tipped Zimmerman, the IUF, or both, that we were running a trap for them. D'Arcy's been playing the angle that Zimmerman has compromised *everything,* casting her as pretty much omniscient— How better to cover up a mole in our own ranks?"

"What are you saying? That D'Arcy engineered that whole warehouse fiasco on purpose?"

"No," Fitzsimmons said. "I'm saying that those computer thieves were never meant to be caught. D'Arcy's a genius at improvisation. Within an hour of the capture he had his people there claiming National Security, and was setting up shipment of the Daedalus to DC, and drafting press releases on how the computer was yet to be recovered. He had us believing that it was a carefully calculated plan to capture Zimmerman—so much so that I provided the manpower to take Zimmerman in—and it was all a charade."

Rayburn shook his head. "But that means that D'Arcy planned Zimmerman's disappearance. Why?"

"I don't know." Fitzsimmons could hear the nerves in his own voice. "But I don't think we have much time to find out. I can't find the Daedalus."

"What?"

"The computer, D'Arcy, and one of my agents, Christoffel, all seem to be missing."

"Christoffel?"

Fitzsimmons nodded. "He worked the same Mid-East desk that D'Arcy used to. He was also in charge of Morris Kendal. I've looked at his debriefing of Kendal, again. It now strikes me as much *too* brief."

"What a fucking mess." Rayburn shook his head and put a hand to his forehead, *"D'Arcy?"*

"D'Arcy."

Rayburn's voice became a shallow monotone, drained of most of its regional character. "You know he was on the short list of people to replace you, once you retired." He looked over at Fitzsimmons and said, "Now I have to have the fucker's head on a plate."

"I know, sir."

"None of this shit is going to stick to this Administration." Rayburn stood. *"None,* understand?" Rayburn's voice had regained his character, and anger was leaking in. It wasn't directed at Fitzsimmons, but he still felt it, and it was frightening. "This is the news, Larry. This is *not* a rogue operation. This is a mole."

"What are you saying, sir?"

"The United States does not sponsor terrorist organizations. The only other interpretation is that the IUF turned D'Arcy while he was in the CIA, probably others as well."

"Sir?"

"The IUF created D'Arcy, not the other way around. Do you understand?"

Fitzsimmons nodded.

The day had lengthened until Gideon thought that their captors might have forgotten about them. It seemed to be mid-afternoon before the door to their dark little Victorian room opened. Gideon stood as the door started opening, expecting Volynskji or another armed-guard type.

What he got, instead, was a tall white guy with a buzz cut. It took him a moment to recognize the man from the group picture of the Evolutionary Theorems Lab.

The other Michael, Michael Gribaldi.

Mike wore a white turtleneck and a pair of blue jeans. He must have been in his late thirties, but he *looked* like a grad student. Gideon didn't know exactly what it was, something in the posture or the facial expression. There was an odd—for this situation—sense of repressed excitement, a sort of "gee whiz" look to the man that seemed more appropriate for a teenager.

Mike stood at the door and looked at the two of them, half-smiling. "Welcome to Chez Zimmerman. I see you've met the help."

Ruth didn't take Mike's glibness very well. "Who the hell are you? What right have you got to hold us prisoner?"

Mike backed off and held up his hands. "Hey, don't hold me responsible for the government hacks, I just work here."

Gideon stood up and stared into Mike's face, looking for any sign of duplicity. He didn't see any. The guy's face was almost too open. And what he said started the wheels turning in Gideon's head, and the resulting thoughts weren't encouraging.

He stepped forward, between Mike and Ruth to prevent another angry exchange. He held out his hand and said, "You're Michael Gribaldi?"

Mike took his hand and nodded. "And you are?"

For a moment Gideon found himself stymied by anyone who didn't already know who he was. "Gideon," he said. "Gideon Malcolm."

Mike nodded. "I'm sorry if the boys don't know how to treat guests. Sometimes they act as if they run the place." Mike gave Gideon such a broad wink that Gideon was certain that the man had no clue about what "the boys" had been up to.

"Guests!" Ruth's voice cracked on the word. "We were taken prison—"

Gideon shook his hand violently behind his back, and Ruth quieted. He asked Mike. "You mind telling me who 'the boys' are?"

"No problem, Gideon." Mike lowered his voice conspiratorially. "Though it's probably classified. Since you're here at ground zero, I can probably tell you." He leaned forward and whispered. "They're NSA."

Gideon was gripped by a sick feeling that he had fallen down the rabbit hole. He had suspicions ever since their too-convenient-for-the-terrorists capture. The whole episode was staged. The reason Volynskji never questioned him about the Colonel's debriefing was because he knew what he and Ruth had told the government. Zimmerman didn't walk into the arms of any terrorists—she had walked into the arms of a covert operation run by her own government.

Shit.

"Let me guess," Gideon said. "This is one of Emmit D'Arcy's operations."

Mike gave him a fraternal push on the shoulder. "You've been leading me on. You know what's happening."

He gave Gideon a grin that reminded him of the conspiratorial smirk of two children reading a third's diary.

"Emmit . . ." Ruth asked.

Gideon turned around and faced her. "He was the guy who escorted us from the Colonel. The guy with the glasses, looks a little like Peter Lorre."

Ruth nodded and said, "But—" Gideon was going to motion her to be quiet again, before she started to say that they'd been kidnapped from D'Arcy's little escort. He didn't have to, because Mike interrupted. "He does look like Lorre, doesn't he?"

Ruth looked at Mike, then at Gideon again, and asked, "Who the hell is Emmit D'Arcy?"

"He's the National Security Advisor for President Rayburn," Gideon said.

Ruth stared at him for a few long minutes before she said, "Oh."

"He had a reputation back in the eighties for engineering covert operations—" Gideon looked at Mike. "— Like this one."

"Well, you got something on the ball there, Gideon." He stepped inside the room and held out his hand. "And you, I don't think we've been introduced."

Ruth was having problems. It was clear that she now realized that she and Mike had very different opinions of what was going on, but she still had obvious problems reining in her emotions. Gideon stepped in. "Michael Gribaldi, let me introduce you to Ruth Zimmerman." After a pause, Gideon decided to add, "The good Doctor's sister."

"I know." He gave her a polite little bow that seemed

utterly out of character. "I was sent here by Madame El Presidente to fetch you."

Ruth stood, finally and took Mike's hand. "She's *here?*" There was a slight breathless note in her voice. Gideon felt a dark envy, Ruth was going to get her sister back. Rafe wasn't coming back . . .

Mike continued, apparently oblivious to how his comments affected them, "It's been a real honor to work with your sister again. Especially now that we've gotten back to the *real* work."

Gideon nodded, as if he knew what was happening. "The New Pythagorean Order."

Mike put a finger to his lips and gave an exaggerated, "Shhh." He looked around and said, "We don't want to let the heathens in on our little secret." Mike smiled, "Shall I escort you two to the lab?"

Gideon was now almost certain that he and Ruth were here, and alive, because of Julia Zimmerman's intervention. Mike's presence here all but confirmed it.

"Yes, please," Ruth said. "I want to see Julie."

Mike smiled. "As the lady wishes." He turned to Gideon. "The Doctor wants to talk to you, too. Come on, I'll give you the grand tour." Mike shook his head. "You're here at a great time. It's all being prepped for zero hour now."

Mike gave them a broad wink as if they knew exactly what he was talking about.

Mike led them through the farmhouse, saying, "Well, you've already seen the dorm. Ain't much, but it's home." He waved his hand around, taking in the cracked plaster and the boarded-up windows. Gideon kept an eye out for their keepers. Gideon noticed that they were being shadowed by one of the rifle-toting guards. Mike was either pretending not to notice the guy, or just took his presence for granted.

Gideon wondered exactly how many people were here, and how many were guards, and how many were misplaced academics like Mike.

"It's about an hour's drive to the nearest pizza," Mike was saying. That was something that Gideon had already suspected. They weren't going to get out of here on foot.

As Mike started leading them down the stairs, Gideon decided to press this opportunity for all it was worth, before the guards, the IUF, or the NSA decided to withdraw their implicit approval for Mike's little tour. He asked Mike, "You've been working on this since MIT, right?"

Mike laughed. "Since before that, most of us. Some of us were working on little viral programs in the *eighties*. But, yeah, you're right—the Aleph project has been around since the late, unlamented Evolutionary Theorems Lab."

Aleph project . . .

They stopped on a landing whose window was intact. Ruth took the opportunity to step between the two of them, to look out. The window overlooked the barn, about two hundred yards away. Mike tapped a finger on the glass. "There she is, Ground Zero, the lab."

Gideon looked out over the barn and tried to understand what was going on here. If this was really a government operation, why did Zimmerman have to leave the NSA to run it? "I can't make sense of it," Gideon whispered.

Mike nodded, misinterpreting him. "I know, I sometimes can't get my head around it myself. Awesome, ain't it?"

Gideon shook his head. "What can she do here that she couldn't do at Fort Meade?"

Mike chuckled. "And why couldn't we let MIT know what we were doing? Fear. I mean, *we* all know what we're doing here. We've gone through I don't know how many fail-safes and tests before we let the rabbits out into the field. But what do you think the administrators at MIT would do if they knew about it?" Mike shook his head. "People would panic—people *are* panicking. People panic when someone e-mails them about a phony virus. How'd they react about a real one?"

"Is Julie over there?" Ruth asked. Her breath fogged the window.

Mike nodded. "Overseeing the final stage. It's all just oversight now, monitoring the pipeline to the machine. I'm a programmer, not much for me to do now but watch."

Gideon did feel a wave of awe. Not at the project, whatever that was, but at finally reaching this point. Here it was, the crux of everything, the *why* . . .

Julia, Gideon thought, *can you give me a reason for Rafe's death?*

Gideon tried not to let his emotions into his voice, he still needed to know what was happening. "I would think," he said after a moment, "that the NSA would have more freedom for this kind of thing than MIT."

Mike laughed and waved them down another flight of stairs. "You'd think, wouldn't you? But when it comes down to it, they're free to do what they want when it comes to information warfare, targeting some enemy of the state, but once you get into pure research—especially stuff in the field—the reaction is something like people get when they hear that the Nuclear Regulatory Commission was injecting plutonium into people."

Ruth sounded surprised, "You mean that this isn't an official Government project?"

For once, Mike's expression faltered. Gideon could glimpse some of Mike's doubts about what was going on. Gideon wondered if he knew that people had died because of this thing, whatever it was.

Mike spoke slowly now, obviously choosing words with care, "This is D'Arcy's project. He believes in Aleph, and once we gather the final programs, we'll all be proved right."

That frightened Gideon because that meant, as far as anyone outside this farm was concerned, this *was* some international terrorist operation. That meant that it would be too easy for him and Ruth—not to mention Zimmerman and Mike and everyone else here—to just disappear. D'Arcy had a pre-made explanation for anyone who turned up dead.

Mike led them outside, through a door that bypassed the room full of abandoned furniture. There was no porch on this side of the house, and Gideon stepped out into the snow after Mike and Ruth. Here they faced the barn a few hundred feet away.

Gideon stood in the snow, breath fogging in the sharp,

cold air. Gideon looked around and saw the guards moving out there by the treeline. Mike led them toward the barn, oblivious.

He followed Mike and Ruth, turning his attention to the barn. It appeared worse off than the house. The sides had been weathered to an uneven gray, and the roof was shot through with missing shingles, and bowed in the center. There was a shed adjoining the rear of the barn, which might have once housed tools, a tractor, or cattle, but it was now little more than a roof supported by apparently random two-by-fours planted into the ground.

Under the shed's roof stood a cluster of sleek metallic antennas and a small dish. Mike saw Gideon looking and said, "That's our uplink, can't get a high volume ground line in here without someone noticing."

Gideon shook his head, still trying to understand exactly what was happening here. Mike had dropped some broad hints about viruses and from the sound of it, what was going on was a domestic experiment in information warfare. That's the only thing that Gideon thought would require this kind of rogue operation.

Mike led them around to the front of the barn. As they closed on the entrance, a small door set next to the huge barn doors, Gideon began to hear a noise, like a car idling. It got louder as they approached the barn.

Then Gideon started to feel a slightly warm wind brush against his face. He stopped, suddenly still, and looked up at the wall of the barn.

The door they faced was new construction, a pre-made vinyl-coated door, set rather abruptly into the weathered gray wood. That wasn't the only modification. Gideon

could see a series of new metal vents set high up, above
the top of the barn door, set in a line across the front of
the barn. That's where the warm breeze came from,
Gideon was certain. The wind shifted and the warmth left
him.

Why would they be venting warm air? The only thing
that Gideon could think of was a refrigeration system of
some sort . . .

There was only one thing that Gideon knew of that
would require refrigeration in this climate, but he didn't
think it could be possible.

Mike led them through the door, and Gideon saw, immediately, that it *was* possible.

Behind the barn doors, sitting on a platform that was
adjusted to give a level surface on the dirt floor, was a
Daedalus supercomputer. Gideon recognized it immediately, even when it was half-hidden by silvery vents that
led up into the gloom of the barn's loft, venting the waste
heat, keeping the superconductors from frying while the
machine operated.

From under the platform came a twisted mass of cable
snaking back into the barn. The end of the barn without
the Daedalus looked as if someone had decided to trans-
plant someone's office pool. There were more leveling
platforms set up, the cables snaking across the dirt to disappear under them in a half-dozen places. They had set
up partitions making a half-dozen cubicles. And hanging
from the rafters above were long fluorescent light fix-
tures.

The idling sound came from two generators that sat on

the dirt floor of the barn, between the computer and the office area, snaking their own cables to both.

"Welcome to Project Aleph," Mike said.

The people back in the office weren't guards. Gideon could tell because all the people were more interested in what was going on on their desks than they were in the door. Gideon could tell the guards by their Kalishnikovs, and by the fact that they started straight toward the door from their positions flanking the generators.

Ruth called out, toward the cubicles, *"Julie!"*

Everything stopped.

The guards looked off toward the office area. The people in the office area turned and looked off toward the intruders.

One woman separated herself from a terminal where she'd been looking over the shoulder of some guy about Mike's age. She took a few steps toward them. She was taller than Gideon had expected. Her hair was loose and hung down around her shoulders, and her depthless gray eyes stared at all of them with what seemed to be a cold curiosity.

"Thank you, Gribaldi," she said. "Both of you should come with me. I suppose you have some questions."

3.05
Fri. Mar. 26

THERE was a dark corner of the barn, by the ersatz offices. It was walled off completely, for privacy. Julia took them inside, leaving Mike out on the floor of the "lab" with the other computer people. She shut the door on the activity outside, and the room became disturbingly silent. Gideon felt as if they were completely alone with Julia Zimmerman.

He couldn't help staring at the woman. There was only the barest hint that there was anything extraordinary about her—and it might only have been there because Gideon expected it, and was looking for it. Her posture broadcast confidence, perhaps—as Dr. Nolan would have said—arrogance. Her eyes were deep and powerful, and seemed to look through him, or *into* him.

Julia turned on a fluorescent that flickered a half-dozen times before it came on fully.

She strode through the small cramped room, around the desk, and said, "I'm glad you're all right, Ruth."

"Julie—" Ruth began.

"No thanks to the bastards you work for," Gideon

blurted. He was saying it before he even realized the anger that he was holding back.

Ruth reached for his arm, "*Gideon,* wait a m—"

Gideon shook off her arm and took a limping step forward. "You do work for them, don't you? Or is it the other way around?"

"You don't know what's going on here, Detective Malcolm," Julia said. Her voice was much colder than the one she had used to address Ruth.

"I don't?" Gideon said. He took another step and leaned forward, his hands on the edge of the desk. He gripped the edge until the healing muscles in his arm vibrated. "You and Emmit D'Arcy came to some sort of agreement to continue your 'work' outside of the NSA's control. Both of you staged your defection to a phantom terrorist group, and even went so far as to contract the theft of a Daedalus supercomputer. Have I got the gist?"

"Please," Ruth said. "Let her explain what's happening." It anything, it was Ruth who seemed to be hurt by Gideon's tirade. Julia simply watched him, unmoved.

"If I have that much right—" Gideon glared at the woman. *React, damn you.* "Those thieves killed a highway patrolman, you realize that, don't you? In fact, they botched the whole job—bad enough that the CIA managed to set a trap with the Daedalus. But D'Arcy tipped you off, didn't he?"

"I'm sorry that you and your brother—" Julia began.

"You are? Are you sorry about Mr. Jones and Mr. Williams? They might have been criminal scum, but the fact that you involved them meant they had to die. Your pet terrorist, Volynskji, put a bullet into Morris Kendal because he was just a little too close to figuring out D'Arcy was behind this. Are you sorry about him? Then there're a half-dozen dead Israelis in New Jersey. . . ."

Julia nodded and said quietly, "Much of this has been unfortunate."

"Good Lord, do you understand that these bastards almost killed your sister—"

"They panicked," Julia said. "After the travesty with the Israelis, I made them understand that they had to bring the two of you here, in one piece."

"Do you know how many people have died because of this?"

Julia sat down, behind the desk. "I am not in control of these people, Detective Malcolm."

"Bullshit!"

"Gideon, please." Ruth sounded shocked. She pulled at his arm trying to get him back into a seat.

"You have these people wrapped around your finger. You dictated that we be brought into audience with you, and here we damn well are—snatched from out of the NSA's own hands."

"You have no idea what that required," Julia said.

"They can't have their little project without you, can they? You seem to have a powerful negotiating position."

Julia shook her head. "D'Arcy won't allow a threat to himself or the IUF—"

"So the blood is on his hands, not yours?"

"You don't know what Aleph means, do you?" Julia looked at Ruth and the coolness leaked out of her face. "I couldn't *not* take the opportunity D'Arcy offered me."

"Whatever the cost?"

"I brought you here to explain." She was still talking to Ruth.

"Explain why my brother died." The words hung in the air as silence claimed them again. Julia still looked at Ruth as if she was searching for something, support, justification, rationalization. Gideon turned around and looked at Ruth himself. Ruth's eyes were shiny, and she was wiping her cheeks with the back of her hand.

Gideon felt spent, as if venting his anger had withdrawn all solid support from inside him. He pushed away from Julia's desk and half-collapsed into a chair next to Ruth.

"Julie," Ruth said. "What's going on here? Why's this happening?"

Julia Zimmerman glanced at Gideon and paused, as if waiting for a continuation of his tirade. "You didn't need to involve yourself so deeply. Eventually you would have known. *Everyone* would have known, soon enough."

"What is Aleph?" Gideon asked.

Julia smiled slightly. "You already know." She looked up, toward the louvered window, and at first Gideon thought she might be looking at the Daedalus. But her eyes were unfocused and blank, as if she was looking beyond the Daedalus, at something only she could see. "'Why,' is a good question. 'Why' is exactly what we're searching for here."

"Why what?" Gideon asked.

"Why is this world, on its face, filled with such illogic, such randomness, such pain. The human mind is such a faulty mechanism, capable of intolerance, brutality, stupidity, evil . . . And yet, and yet . . ." She closed her eyes.

"I cannot believe that we, a race of beings of brutal stupidity, a race of Pol Pots, Charlie Mansons, and," she paused a moment, "Emmit D'Arcys—a race of evil high and low—could have 'invented' the beauty of the mathematical world."

To Gideon, it appeared as if she had fallen into that world. The hardness was gone from her expression, replaced with something distant and serene. "How can we say that Newton invented the calculus when it was his study of the physical world that led him to discover it? How can we say that some ancient *invented* '1 + 1 = 2'? Those in my discipline keep going further and further afield, trying to 'invent' new, esoteric forms of mathematics, and they always find to their chagrin that eventually their math describes some aspect of the world, be it the quantum spaces inside an atom, or the growth of a species, or the deformation of a polymer under stress."

"You see it as a form of higher reality—" Gideon said. But Julia opened her eyes and shook her head slowly, as if trying to be kind in contradicting a child's view of the world.

"It *is* reality," she said. "The closest that we can come to seeing how things really are."

Gideon opened his mouth, but he couldn't say anything.

"It's obvious," Julia said. "Once you start to *see*. The way that every form of the discipline, from number theory to topology, will find its manifestation in the world we experience. The way the world we see informs the discipline, from chaos theory to the evolutionary algorithm—" Julia tapped on the desk. "If you believe in physics, you believe that this desk is simply a physical form of energy left over from the creation of the universe.

"So can't you see that this universe is an objectified form of a mathematical object?"

"Is that what the New Pythagoreans are about?" Gideon asked.

"They are Mr. Gribaldi's invention. They understand, but only in a rhetorical fashion. Their beliefs are ones of aesthetics . . . There are very few who even claim that the evolutionary algorithm is the same as evolution, or that a computer program that shows all the functions of biology is, by definition, biological."

"That's what you were doing at MIT, wasn't it? Applying the evolutionary algorithm to computer viruses."

"An oversimplification. We were working on a new biology. At MIT, working within a closed environment of our private computer network, we generated programs that were more complex than any mere virus . . ."

Ruth spoke up. "All sorts of people work on Artificial Life. There're conventions for it. Why was this a secret? Why destroy all the research you left at MIT."

Gideon felt as if he finally understood. He could feel some of the anger return. "A private, isolated environment wasn't big enough, was it?"

"No," Julia said, "it wasn't."

"You let these things out into the world," Gideon said. "Damn the consequences. So what if Wall Street collapses—"

"These were not destructive viruses." Julia frowned.

Ruth sounded appalled. "You were letting these things go?"

"To generate what we wanted required the widest, most diverse, and challenging environment that was available."

"Michael's 'rabbits.'" Gideon said.

"The term for the first creatures we released into the Internet. They had two main directives, to burrow and hide, and to find other rabbits and reproduce."

"The evolutionary algorithm," Gideon said.

"True evolution, where survival is the only criterion for reproduction. We added predators, foxes and sharks that would consume any rabbit they found, and each other—"

"Christ," Ruth said.

"You engineered a whole ecosystem and infected the Internet with it . . ." Gideon shook his head. "Do you have any idea how potentially destructive that was, *is?*" He looked into Julia's eyes. "Of course you do, you jumped right on board the NSA's information warfare projects. It was a seamless transition, wasn't it. You picked up right where you left off—"

Julia shook her head. "No, Detective Malcolm. I didn't. Losing the ET Lab was a disaster. Wiping the research was all I could do to save even the idea of the project— that and our secrecy."

"I wonder how many laws you broke with this project."

Julia looked at him sternly.

"This is like some genetic engineer dumping a new plague into the Chesapeake just to see what'll happen."

"The evolutionary pressure is against any of these

creatures causing overt disruption. Detection means that
the program does not survive, doesn't reproduce."

"That doesn't stop the occasional 'disruption,' does
it?"

Julia was silent.

"How many times has your project caused something
like the Wall Street crash? Or does it matter?"

"These are living creatures, they will have some effect
on their environment . . ."

"And if the 'project' is already out there— If your viral
life-forms are happily breeding on the Internet already—
What is all this, then?" Gideon waved back toward the
lab. "Why are you suddenly here, with a damn supercomputer? What is D'Arcy after? What's worth all the deaths
that've already happened because of this thing?"

The door opened behind them, and a voice said, "She's
giving the United States the greatest technological advantage since the invention of the atomic bomb."

Gideon turned around and faced the speaker, a short
bespectacled gentleman who looked somewhat like Peter
Lorre. Emmit D'Arcy gave Gideon a half-grin and
looked up at Julia. "I think, Doctor, you would be better
off monitoring the progress of the lure." He looked at
Ruth. "And perhaps you should take your sister."

Julia looked at D'Arcy with an expression of vague
distaste, gave a curt nod, and took Ruth out of the small
office. Gideon was left alone with the man most responsible for his brother's death.

D'Arcy walked around and sat behind Julia's desk. He
took off his glasses and rubbed the bridge of his nose.
"She was adamant that we bring you here."

"Bastard," Gideon said.

"I've been called worse."

"How many people have you killed to keep this private enterprise of yours a secret?"

D'Arcy shook his head. "Your problem, Detective Malcolm, is that you have no perspective."

Gideon stood up. "How can you have the gall—"

"You rushed in," D'Arcy said. "Starting with the unfortunate incident with your brother, you've gone charging ahead with little thought to what might be involved or what the consequences are. For a time you were a useful distraction."

"You Machiavellian— What was the original plan? Have them finish this project and then storm the place? Everyone conveniently dies in the assault, and no one to say this wasn't a terrorist operation."

"It's too bad you weren't part of the community," D'Arcy said. "You'd have been an asset."

"Things have gone wrong—haven't they? That's why you're here, isn't it? For all the shooting, you couldn't keep this thing under wraps, could you?"

D'Arcy looked at the glasses in his hands, and shook his head as he replaced them. "Shall we forget the 'original plan,' whatever that was? The operation is nearly complete, and you aren't outside, leading anyone here."

"What are you going to do with us?" Gideon asked. "Kill us like you did Kendal?"

"Shall we dispense with the drama? I am here to develop an asset. Once that asset is developed, everything else will be irrelevant." D'Arcy looked at Gideon, and Gideon thought he could see a fragment of the same fanatic glint in D'Arcy's eye that he'd seen in Julia's. "After tonight what you do or say won't matter to me."

There was something ominous in that statement. Something final about it that frightened Gideon. "What is it?" he asked. "What are you doing here? The IUF is your entity, isn't it? And you've sacrificed it and God knows how many people, for what? Some super computer virus?"

"You'll see yourself. Dr. Zimmerman wants you on the floor when everything comes together—"

"It is a virus, isn't it? The ET Lab's 'project' was free to evolve on the Internet for years. It produced something. Something adaptable, undetectable, a perfect computer weapon—"

D'Arcy was shaking his head. "You're better than I gave you credit for. So close."

"The computational equivalent of the atomic bomb," Gideon finished.

"So close." D'Arcy steepled his fingers. "So far." He gestured across the desk. "Take your seat and I'll tell you what Aleph is, why I had to act."

Gideon looked at D'Arcy and, slowly, sat down.

"This is already out there," D'Arcy explained. "Understand that above all. Anyone with the technology can summon it from the Internet now, like a genie. We have to be first, or we'll suffer a nearly insurmountable technical disadvantage. God help us if the Chinese, or even the European Community, gets a hold of this."

"Why do you need a Daedalus?"

"We need *all* of it. It's possible to run black ops within Mother, the NSA's Daedalus, but this, Aleph, requires all the processing capacity of the machine, all at once. We cannot run this on any government machine in secret." He pushed his glasses up so he could rub the bridge of his nose again. "You are close, Gideon. Close enough that we *had* to bring you here. You just haven't assembled the pieces you have.

"Zimmerman's experiment at MIT, the original entities they released to evolve—they all had something in common. There was a core of programming that would never be touched by the random splicing of the evolutionary algorithm. This block of code remained constant through the generations of these programs—or was supposed to. The code handled two instructions, a lure and a destruct. The lure was a homing signal of sorts, a command to send the program to a specific computer for study. The destruct was obviously for cases where the programs got out of hand."

"So why didn't Zimmerman destroy the programs then, when she wiped the research at the ET lab?"

"You don't understand," D'Arcy said. "She *did*."

"What happened? Why are they still out there?"

"There were mutations," D'Arcy said. "Imperfect communications, truncated code, a byte in the wrong place. Whatever happened, there were a few viable viruses from the project that had this common code segment corrupted. The 'destruct' failed to be instantaneous. There was a time delay— By accident, Zimmerman's biosphere developed aging and natural death. Last November, Julia was engaged in a virus survey for the NSA, seeing what was out there, and she discovered one of her programs. She wrote a memo that reached me, I understood the implications . . ."

"What implications?"

"The first was that a generation for these programs is on the order of microseconds. That means several trillion generations since they left MIT. The development of a natural death combined with the designed sexual reproduction and predation to accelerate the evolutionary process even more. The only limit these things had was the constraints on their environment."

"There was another implication?"

"The virus Dr. Zimmerman discovered was part of a distributed system."

"What?"

"It was part of a larger organism. Somehow, early on, either two programs figured out how to work together, or one program figured how to divide itself over more than one system. There are obvious survival benefits, parts can be redundant, and not be vulnerable to events on a single system. The multipart entity is less vulnerable to the inherited 'natural death,' though it, too, will die eventually. Most important, its means of reproduction is more reliable. It now can exchange whole 'programs' as a means of reproduction, exchanging functional units rather than small pieces of code."

Gideon felt a chill as D'Arcy described it. He shook his head. "You're describing—"

"The jump from single-cell to multicellular life." D'Arcy nodded. "I had my share of biology at the university. When I saw Dr. Zimmerman's memo, I understood exactly what had happened."

D'Arcy took his glasses off and pointed them at Gideon. "There are entities out there now, whose parts are small programs, few more than a megabyte in size, distributed throughout the Internet. These entities are made of millions of such programs."

D'Arcy paused to let that sink in before he said, "These entities, more than likely, are conscious, thinking beings."

3.06
Fri. Mar. 26

SENATOR Daniel Tenroyan made it to the National Airport just in time to catch the direct flight to Portland. Usually he didn't run so late catching his weekend flight home to Maine, but things on the Hill, especially in the Intelligence Oversight Committee, had been hectic the past few weeks. For a while today it looked as if he wasn't going to make it back home this week at all.

He raced through the terminal, heading for his gate, overnight bag in one hand and boarding pass in the other. He only stopped when a knot of people blocked his progress.

Tenroyan tapped one of the people on the shoulder. "What's going on here?" The question carried none of the urgency, or irritation, that Tenroyan felt at the moment. He was too good a politician to ever express frustration in public.

The man Tenroyan questioned was balding and in his mid-fifties. He carried an overnight bag as well, apparently another one of the thousands of DC residents who evacuate the city during the weekends. The man, unlike Tenroyan, was making no effort to hide his frustration.

"Christ, I wish I knew what was going on." He waved toward the wall that seemed to be the focus of attention for the knot of people.

Tenroyan looked in that direction. The wall held a bank of monitors showing arrivals and departures. At least, they were supposed to show arrivals and departures. Tenroyan expected to see, maybe, a long list of cancellations or delays to explain the crowd . . .

That wasn't it.

Every monitor appeared, at first, to be down, showing only flickering snow. That was only an initial impression. On closer observation, the monitors were actually printing characters, but they scrolled by so fast there was little chance for the eye to decipher them. To Tenroyan, it looked as if the computer was printing random letters, numbers, and other characters too fast for the screen to properly display them.

Good Lord, Tenroyan thought, *I hope this hasn't affected the air traffic control computers . . .*

As if to confirm the evil thought, a grave voice came over the PA. "Due to technical problems, all departures are being delayed sixty minutes. We apologize for the inconvenience—"

Sixty minutes? They were grounding everything for an hour, at least . . .

Christ, what about arrivals?

Gideon stared into D'Arcy's face, looking for the punchline. The room was silent for a long time.

Slowly, as if he misunderstood what D'Arcy had just

said, he asked, "Are you saying that these programs developed some sort of intelligence?"

"Collectively, yes. It may not be on a par with the human brain, but it could easily be equivalent to some of the higher vertebrates. A true artificial intelligence. A quantum leap in the ability to process information. A system that could learn, deal with unforeseen circumstances. It also would be robust in the face of attack like no other software. A distributed, modular system— like the Internet—resilient in the face of hostile action, resistant to viruses, damage to servers . . . It could even reprogram its security to respond to threats its operators would never see. It would be the ultimate operating system."

"This thing is already out there?" Gideon suspected he already knew the answer.

D'Arcy confirmed it. "*Millions* of programs, Detective Malcolm, all running in parallel—"

Gideon nodded. "That's why you need the Daedalus. The lure part of the code has survived, hasn't it? You're trying to fetch all the program segments into the Daedalus . . ."

"The whole entity in one place, operating without the inherent delays across the web of the Internet. That will speed its overall reaction time by several thousands. It will also allow us to interact with it in a way we can't while it's spread across the whole Internet." D'Arcy stood and waved out toward the lab occupying the rest of the barn. "We're about to see the culmination of 'Project Aleph.' Dr. Zimmerman and her team have worked out a message that will activate the dormant lure program in these entities. As we've been talking, pieces of the entity, individual program cells, have been transferring themselves to our site. The process has been going on for hours."

Gideon thought of the antenna array outside. If they were talking millions of programs, that had to be quite a bottleneck at the moment.

D'Arcy opened the door. "Let's go and join Dr. Zimmerman, shall we? Now that you know what's at stake."

Gideon got unsteadily to his feet, all the while thinking, *The computational equivalent of the atomic bomb . . .*

In one of the darker corners of *The Zodiac,* the man wearing the black Virgo T-shirt was cursing into his cell phone. He slammed it down on the table in front of him. "Jesus *Fuck!*"

The guy in a Gemini T-shirt walked over to his table. "What shit down your neck?"

"Cheap-fucking phone!" He let the phone lie there on the table. Then he reached in his pocket. "Cheap-fucking pager!" And slammed that down on the table next to the cell phone.

"Jesus, man, what's got into you?"

Virgo picked up the pager and tossed it over. Gemini caught it and fumbled with it a few times because the thing was still vibrating.

"Look at that shit—" Virgo complained.

Gemini looked at the pager, which was demanding attention. The little LCD screen, which should be displaying either a phone number or a text message, was showing a scrolling display that alternated black boxes and dashes. "Whoa, this thing's busted."

"Try to call the bastards who sold me the pager—" Virgo popped open the phone and the buzzing whine was audible. "Can't hang up, can't call anyone, just get the damn buzzing noise—"

"Ain't your phone, man." The pair looked over toward the bar, where the bartender was leaning over toward him. "Payphone here's been out for an hour. Nothing but buzzing, man."

Lawrence Fitzsimmons sat in a briefing room with a dozen others from the intelligence community. General Adrian Harris, Chairman of the Joint Chiefs, was there, as well as Colonel Gregory Mecham, released from the 'protective custody' that D'Arcy had placed him under.

They were all discovering how smoothly D'Arcy had slipped out from under them. The last sign they had of him was a CIA helicopter departing Andrews. As far as anyone could tell, Agent Christoffel was also on that flight.

There was no sign of where they had gone.

The whole situation left a bad taste in Fitzsimmons' mouth. D'Arcy had managed to create his own CIA within the CIA, within the Mid-East office. There were agents out there accountable only to this bureaucratic entity—it was called the Office of Terrorist Evaluation—that D'Arcy had created while he was in the Agency. It existed only to oversee the operation of the IUF, D'Arcy's creation.

Around the table, people talked about doomsday scenarios. Rayburn had been very good at enforcing his policy interpretation, that D'Arcy was a mole for the IUF, and that was how this was being interpreted. D'Arcy had blown his cover because the IUF was using Zimmerman and the missing Daedalus for some massive terrorist act.

An act that was being committed as they sat here.

Fitzsimmons had thought he knew better. He had believed that D'Arcy had been engaged in his own rogue pursuit of national security. The IUF was some misguided attempt to control the operation of Mid-East terrorism. But, given the events of the past few hours, Fitzsimmons wasn't so sure.

"We have estimates that we have, at most, another hour before we have a major catastrophe at one of our disabled airports," Colonel Mecham was saying. "We have unconfirmed reports already of midair collisions in Brazil, Hong Kong, Rome, Mexico City, and half a dozen other cities. None in the US so far." He flipped over a page on the clipboard he was reading and continued. "We've had failures and shutdowns in at least forty power plants across the country; there is a blackout affecting the entire West Coast, as well as outages in the Gulf States and the Midwest affecting approximately fifty million people. With the exception of short-wave and some secure satellite communications, voice and data lines are down—or unusable—across the country. The Internet, *all* of it, is completely dead."

It was a litany of disaster that just kept going on and on, every networked computer in the country—in the world, maybe—seemed to have simultaneously shut down—or gone off on its own agenda. It was happening in the NSA, in NASA, and in AT&T. Over the past hour every system with some connection to the outside had become inoperable. The only systems that seemed immune were specially isolated systems designed to be ultimately secure—such as the communication system the military was forced into using now.

"This *thing*," Mecham said, "is affecting everything from PCs to LANs to mainframes to NSA's own supercomputer." He set down the clipboard. "However, we do have some idea where this all might be originating." He took a satellite photograph off of the table in front of him and passed it around to his left. "Before all our resources went down, we had several alerts to an unusually high volume of digital traffic off of one of our satellites. The destination is marked on that photograph."

The picture came around to Fitzsimmons. He rotated it a couple of times to see what looked like some woods, a snow-covered field, a barn, and a rambling farmhouse.

"Gentlemen," Mecham said, "I don't think there's any question that we need to move immediately."

D'Arcy took Gideon out of the office area, to a pair of folding chairs set against the barn wall, flanked by a pair of Kalishnikov-wielding guards. Ruth was already seated there watching the project going on around her. Other than Julia going around from terminal to terminal, there wasn't much to watch. Half a dozen people in various cubicles, bent over computer terminals, Julia softly talking to them.

Mike Gribaldi stood with two others that Gideon recognized from the ET Lab picture. They leaned on the wall opposite him and Ruth, out of earshot. The trio watched the goings-on intently; it was probably more interesting when you knew exactly what was going on at each station.

"Does this seem right?" Gideon whispered mostly to himself.

"What?" Ruth asked.

The guards didn't seem to mind their talking. Even so, Gideon leaned toward Ruth and whispered, since everyone else out here seemed to speak in hushed tones. "Your sister's smart enough to realize what D'Arcy's doing here."

"And what is he doing?" Ruth whispered.

"He's set up the IUF of his as a scapegoat. All the nasty illegal things can be blamed on the terrorists, and the software can be seized when the terrorists are taken out—"

"D'Arcy's here, Gideon—"

"He didn't plan it that way. Maybe someone connected him with the IUF." Gideon lowered his voice even more. "If that's the case, this 'AI' might be his only bargaining chip—"

"Maybe D'Arcy isn't smart enough to realize what Julia is doing here."

"When news of D'Arcy's operation gets out, all hell will break loose in Washington. Offering an AI to the government may be the only thing between a quiet retirement and a trial for treason." Gideon looked at Ruth. "What do you mean, D'Arcy doesn't realize?"

"Julia knows D'Arcy," Ruth said. "D'Arcy's irrelevant to her." She was speaking softly, staring intently at the activity around the cubicles.

"Irrelevant? If D'Arcy has just a little streak of self-preservation, he knows that no one in Washington needs to deal with him as long as the people in this room can repeat the process." Gideon looked at her, Ruth seemed distant, like her sister had. "Once they do this thing, D'Arcy needs them to disappear. Are you hearing me?"

Ruth nodded. "It's too late, already."

Gideon looked at the two guards. They hadn't moved, and showed little sign of paying attention to them. There was probably some chance that they didn't even speak English. He looked around the barn and while none of the scientists seemed to have noticed, there had been a steady increase in the number of Kalishnikovs in the barn. Gideon saw Volynskji talking in hushed tones to D'Arcy, away from everyone else, near the new front door.

"What did Julia say to you?" Gideon asked Ruth.

It now seemed ominous how the generators and the Daedalus were separated from the workspace. Almost designed so that stray shots wouldn't damage the supercomputer or its power supply.

Gideon watched Julia as she moved from cubicle to cubicle. She didn't seem fully here, in the barn. Her eyes were looking out at some other place that only existed behind those deep gray eyes.

She had to realize the danger here.

"What did she tell you?"

"Everything," Ruth said. "What she's looking for, *really.*"

Julia had to have walked into this knowing that she was expendable to D'Arcy as soon as the project was complete. She had to have seen that as soon as she was set up in this place, isolated, away from any legitimate oversight. Even Mike, for all his alleged naïveté, knew that they were all involved in a rogue operation. Julia would have to know what that meant.

She went ahead with this anyway.

"What is she doing?" Gideon couldn't see why she would do this. She wasn't self-destructive. Was D'Arcy's AI worth the risk for her? Gideon didn't see it. . . .

Then he noticed a small piece of paper tacked up on one of the cubicle walls. It was a familiar symbol, "א‎₀."

"Ruth, what *is* she doing?"

Someone called out from one of the terminals. "We have some spontaneous activity through the uplink, from *our* end."

"We've collected enough. He's starting to contact other pieces of Himself." In Julia's voice, Gideon could hear the capitalization.

"Ruth?" Gideon grabbed her arm and pulled her to face him.

"What's happening?" D'Arcy said, echoing Gideon's own thoughts. D'Arcy's voice was calm, but he had the bearing of someone confronted with something beyond his expectations.

Julia maneuvered to a free terminal and started tapping

at the keyboard. "This is expected. Don't concern your-self with it."

"Ruth?" Gideon shook her shoulder.

Ruth shook her head and spoke as if she didn't quite believe what she was saying. "God," she said.

"What?"

"She's looking for God."

3.07
Fri. Mar. 26

WITHIN minutes after Rayburn's approval, three Sikorsky Blackhawks escorted by a pair of Cobra gunships lifted off from Hanscomb Air Force Base outside of Boston. The Blackhawks carried two units of special forces, experts in domestic counter-terrorism. The units on those helicopters bore orders that came directly from President Rayburn by way of General Harris of the Joint Chiefs.

They flew over rural Pennsylvania, crossing into New York north of Scranton.

It was seventy-five minutes since the chaos had begun.

D'Arcy strode over to Zimmerman, leaving Volynskji by the door in a posture that suggested that he'd shoot anyone who came near the exit.

"This project is my concern, Dr. Zimmerman." D'Arcy walked around the cubicles, staring at the screens, as if he was trying to make sense of what was displayed.

The guards by Gideon and Ruth took a few steps forward, as if sensing a problem. Gideon wanted to keep talking to Ruth about what her sister was actually doing, but it seemed that they might only have a few moments' worth of distraction. He took the opportunity to stand; no one seemed to notice him. He took Ruth's arm and pulled her up after him.

"This is supposed to be an isolated, secure operation," D'Arcy said. "All contact outside is supposed to be controlled. We can't have anyone detecting the uplink—"

Julia was typing madly now, watching the screen in front of her. She called out, "I want all our traffic shut down. Let the Daedalus have the uplink."

Suddenly, Julia was the only one typing. All the others stood by, watching their screens. "What are you doing?" D'Arcy asked.

"He needs the uplink to complete Himself," Julia said. "We're here to piece the entity together. That's what we're doing." She stopped typing and stared at the screen in front of her.

Gideon couldn't see what she was watching. The screen was angled away from him, and he was edging himself and Ruth back toward the private office. Their guards didn't notice. They were slowly approaching Julia and her terminal.

Julia wasn't paying attention to them, or much of anything other than the screen in front of her.

D'Arcy shook his head. "We can't permit unsecured use of the uplink. We'll have to shut this thing down . . ."

"Perfect," Julia muttered. "Perfect."

D'Arcy shoved one of the others away from the terminal he was manning and said, "How do you shut off the uplink from here?"

From behind D'Arcy, Mike Gribaldi said, "You don't."

D'Arcy turned on Mike and said, "What the hell do you mean, 'You don't?'"

Gideon had pulled Ruth all the way to the door of Julia's office. Ruth tried the door. It was unlocked and opened easily.

"The whole uplink is run from the Daedalus."

"So?"

"We don't have control of the Daedalus now. Aleph does."

Everyone, except for Julia, looked over at the end of the barn where the Daedalus sat.

Gideon and Ruth slipped into the office. Gideon looked at Ruth and asked, "What's going on?"

"D'Arcy doesn't understand what Julie is doing here."

"You said that—"

"Julie believes that Aleph will control *everything* now," Ruth said. "D'Arcy thinks of it as just an elaborate computer program."

Gideon nodded and knelt down. He felt around the floor of the office. Like the rest of this half of the barn, the floor here had been raised above the dirt floor of the barn so cables could be run underneath. Gideon felt until he found a panel he could move. "And Julia believes it's more than that."

Ruth knelt next to him and helped him with the panel.

Gideon began to understand what Aleph might mean for Julia. They had created this being out of the pure mathematical world that Julia worshiped. It was an entity wholly of that world. So, to Julia's point of view, it was always there, somewhere, since the human mind couldn't invent mathematical entities, only discover them. If the universe was an objectified form of some mathematical object, then Aleph, by definition, would predate the universe. Aleph would perceive directly, and be wholly of, a world Julia thought of as divine.

God? Gideon thought. *Damn close in Julia's theology.*

Between the two of them they worried the panel loose and saw about two feet below, down to the dirt. "Get moving. I don't know how long they're going to be distracted."

Gideon helped Ruth down first, then followed her into the darkness below.

The space under the platform was cramped, and seemed to magnify the pains in his leg. He whispered to Ruth, "Follow the cables in front of us. Some should go to the wall and the uplink."

"Do we know what the hell we're doing?"

Gideon was honest. "No." He carefully replaced the floor panel above him, plunging the two of them into near pitch-darkness. Two bright spots seen through the shadows were the only break in the dark. One was behind them, which led to the central area where the generators sat on a dirt floor.

The other end was much dimmer than the leaking florescent light of the barn, that was where they needed to go. "That way," Gideon whispered, "Straight ahead and to your left."

Ruth grunted, and he heard her crawl forward. In moments her body blocked out the dim glow of their destination. Gideon forced himself forward, following his sense of Ruth's presence. He could barely hear what was going on above him, muffled voices and footsteps, nothing intelligible. The flooring above him made good soundproofing.

It seemed as if they crawled for hours before Ruth whispered back, "The floor's gone."

It was a little brighter here, now that Gideon's eyes had adjusted. He crawled up next to Ruth and looked at what she was talking about.

She was right, the floor—the raised platform above them—stopped about six feet shy of the far wall. Gideon could see the cables snaking across the dirt floor toward a door that had the lower twelve inches sawn out of its bottom to accommodate them. It had to be the door to what was left of the adjoining shed, where the uplink was.

There were three Kalishnikov-wielding guards there. Two were making their way through to the uplink, while one remained at the door.

Gideon could hear D'Arcy saying something about shutting off the uplink manually. Gideon could hear people milling around above him, Mike Gribaldi and the other computer scientists were watching their keepers trying to shut down their project.

No one moved forward to stop the guards making for the uplink. Then Gideon heard D'Arcy say, "Where are Malcolm and the woman? Find them!"

Gideon knew that there'd be little question about where the two of them went. There was only one place they could have gone. As if in response to his fear, a light burst into the space under the floor, throwing their shadows on the wall in front of them. Someone was lifting up the floor panels and shining a flashlight toward them.

Six feet. It seemed endless.

He didn't have much of a choice.

The one guard was left behind at the door. He was still focusing on the crowd facing him, straining to see the commotion beyond the people looking at him. He carried his rifle loosely in his hands, the barrel pointed away from Gideon.

Gideon took the opportunity to roll out into the dirt no-man's land between the raised floor and the barn wall. He chose a time when the guard wasn't looking quite in his direction. Gideon pushed himself to his feet, next to the guard, just as the guard was turning to see the disturbance. Gideon was in a half crouch next to the guard and brought his fist up into the man's groin.

The guard's eyes widened, and his cheeks puffed out with an exhaled breath. He still raised the Kalishnikov to bring the butt down on Gideon's head. Gideon dove up, under the blow. The stock slammed into his left shoulder as he grappled the man's waist. There was a flare of pain that paralyzed his left arm as they both slammed into the doorframe.

Gideon slammed his right fist into the man's kidney as he tried to force his legs to push himself fully upright. There was yelling from the spectators, and Gideon could hear movement from beyond the door next to him.

The stock came down again, this time on his back with an impact that felt as if it should crack his spine. The guard said nothing, his voice was coming out as inarticulate, painful grunts. He sounded a lot like Gideon felt at the moment.

Gideon brought up his forearm as he finally got to his feet and slammed it across the guard's neck. For a moment they were face-to-face, and Gideon stared into the guard's wide eyes, and his breath came out in a strangled gasp.

The guard finally let go of the rifle to grab Gideon and push him away. The maneuver was effective, Gideon stumbled on his weakened leg and fell backward. His breath was blown out of him as he fell across the cables that snaked under the door.

The guard folded forward and, gasping, jumped down on Gideon. Gideon grabbed for the man's face, and the guard grabbed for Gideon's neck. Gideon tore into the man's cheek ineffectively as the guard put crushing pressure on his trachea.

Gideon could feel the side of the door slamming into both of them. They had fallen across the entrance, and the other two guards outside were trying to get back in.

Gideon gasped for breath, feeling light-headed, when the stock of the Kalishnikov came down on the back of the guard's head. The guard's grip loosened, and he turned toward the direction of the blow, a stunned expression on his face. Then the stock came again, swinging like a baseball bat across the man's face.

Blood spattered Gideon from a smashed nose and a busted lip as the guard tumbled off him, falling into the small space between him and the door. The two guards outside were still trying to push the door open against the dead weight.

Gideon scrambled to his feet and saw Ruth standing next to him, holding the guard's Kalishnikov. As soon as he was upright, she pushed the gun into his hands. From her expression, he didn't know if it was distaste, or if she just didn't know how to use the thing.

He backed up, hunting maniacally for the safety. He found two switches, and he hit both of them. The crowd of spectators were backing up, and the guards deeper inside the barn had realized that there was something wrong by the uplink.

Gideon edged along the rear wall, facing where the shed door would open. He motioned Ruth with his head; she needed to get away from him. He hoped that he could provide enough of a distraction that she could get away, or at least hide back under the floor. God only knew what was going to happen in the next minute or so.

The door pushed open, one of the guards leading with his shoulder through the doorway. Gideon was prepared this time, and he brought the stock up to connect with the man's chin. Between Gideon's swing, and the guard's momentum, the impact was enough to drop him.

Behind him, Gideon heard a commotion. He didn't need to see what was happening to realize what the sound was. The other guards were pushing through the onlookers who crowded the end of the barn.

Gideon stepped over the two fallen guards, bringing the rifle barrel to bear on the last guard, outside.

Gideon was through the door, and he didn't see anyone. All he saw was the purple sky, a plain of blue, moonlit snow, and the blocky form of the uplink antenna.

Instinct made him dive for the cover of the antenna before he even heard the gunfire. The smell of cordite and superheated metal washed over him as pieces of the uplink sprayed over him, bullets slamming into a mechanism that seemed much too small now.

Gideon faced a quandary now. The guard was at the edge of the barn, and he couldn't return fire without risking a bullet through the wall where it could take out one of the scientists, or Ruth.

The guard didn't keep firing steadily. He was a pro, conserving ammunition, only allowing the occasional bark of some covering fire to keep Gideon pinned down.

Gideon moved slowly around the uplink antenna, putting it between him and the whole barn. He did it in time; he heard the door open and more guards spill out. Gideon turned around and fired the Kalishnikov into the roof, hoping to keep them from moving forward, trying to flank him. The butt of the weapon pressed into his shoulder, igniting the ache of his freshly healed arm.

Someone's voice called to him. Gideon recognized it as Volynskji. "What the fuck are you trying to do here, Malcolm? Toss the gun out."

Gideon looked madly around, watching for guards trying to circle him. He had cover from the barn, but this shed was open to the whole outdoors. He was exposed on every side. The only cover between him and the rest of the world was a pair of flimsy two-by-fours.

Volynskji called again. "This is crazy. You know that we have people surrounding this property. There's no way you can make it out of here. Toss the gun out."

Gideon stared at the two-by-fours holding up the shed's roof. The roof was old, half-rotten, and ran the length of this side of the barn. Moonlight was streaming in the bullet holes he had made in the wood above.

Gideon had a crazy idea.

He braced the weapon better this time as he aimed the gun at the juncture where one of the two-by-fours met the roof. Volynskji was starting to say something again, but his voice was drowned out by the jackhammer of the Kalishnikov firing on full auto. Two of a half-dozen shots splintered the top of the roof's support. Gideon didn't stop firing, he just swung the rifle across to another support. Three bullets clipped it before the Kalishnikov was emptied.

When the firing was over, his ear were numbed, but he could still hear the snap as the first two-by-four went, then the air was filled with the sound of splintering wood.

Gideon threw himself on the ground, tossing away the empty rifle and rolling away from the uplink. The roof of the shed bowed, and then collapsed, its weight too much for the remaining two-by-fours.

Gideon rolled just far enough to clear the roof as it crashed down on the uplink and—more importantly—the guards. When the wood slammed down behind him, Gideon got to his feet and started running. He needed to find some cover, fast. He felt as if he wore a target on his back as he ran unevenly through the carpet of snow.

Volynskji was right. There was no way for him to get off the property with the way they had this place guarded. He was thinking furiously. First off, he needed cover.

He had two possible destinations. There was the old Victorian house, and sitting in the pasture adjoining the barn there was the shadowy form of a helicopter.

Gideon jumped the rail fence and started running as best as he could to the helicopter. He had no illusions about flying the thing, but it would have a radio on board. He could contact someone outside this place. At this point it didn't matter if it was the CIA, the Highway Patrol, or the Coast Guard. He needed to get word to someone so D'Arcy couldn't summarily disappear this whole operation, him, Ruth—and Julia for that matter.

He was halfway there when he heard the bark of a Kalishnikov behind him. He half-dove, half-tripped over something in the snow. The snow cushioned his fall as his ankle twisted on something half-buried.

The Kalishnikov barked a few more times, but the shots didn't come near him. Gideon wiped the snow out of his face and had to bend to untangle his foot. That was when he saw what had tripped him. His foot was caught in the shoulder strap of another Kalishnikov.

Gideon felt a cold that didn't seem completely from the snow. He half-kicked, half-pulled the Kalishnikov loose from his foot and looked around from his prone position. He couldn't see very far, but he could see a mound in the snow, about two yards from him. The snow there seemed darker, black in the moonlight. Gideon got on his stomach and moved toward it until he could make out the corpse's glassy eyes staring out at him.

The man's throat had been blown apart by a gunshot wound.

Gideon looked around and saw footprints in the snow. One set walked around the helicopter a number of times, ending at the corpse. The other set led straight from a corner of the helicopter to where the body lay, and Gideon thought he could see the tracks leading back toward the woods.

"Shit," Gideon whispered. He realized that he didn't need to get the call out to the CIA anymore.

They were already here.

He looked up at the helicopter, barely ten yards away from him, and he noticed a set of shadowy lumps that marred the smooth lines of the helicopter's silhouette. They were rectangular, bricklike forms, that clung to vital sections of the helicopter's anatomy.

Gideon's gut froze for a moment, then he rolled behind the only cover that existed out here—the corpse.

He lay there, his arms over his head, and his face buried in the ground, long enough that he began to suspect that he was wrong.

He wasn't.

Volynskji had led the way, pushing aside the debris of the collapsed roof and leading four of his men, all the ones immediately available from the barn. Once they were clear of the wreckage, they started toward the pasture where he could see Gideon running toward D'Arcy's helicopter.

Volynskji shouldered his weapon and fired a burst, aiming to clear the helicopter. Gideon dropped into the snow.

Volynskji smiled. That was it, they had him now. He was prone, unarmed, in an open field. All they had to do was close on him. He directed the other men to circle around so they would cut off all the lines of escape.

"Bastard must have the balls of a bull elephant to try and pull this off," Volynskji muttered to himself.

They'd taken a few steps into the pasture, and Volynskji

realized there was something wrong. The guard on the helicopter should have made an appearance. At first Volynskji had thought that the man had been on the far side of the helicopter, but he couldn't have been oblivious to the gunshots this long.

Volynskji hoped that the man had decided to abandon his post to take a leak amidst the trees. But that hope was fading as they closed on the helicopter and Gideon.

Volynskji could see a lump in the snow that had to be Gideon. That one was Gideon because he was still moving. Volynskji had a fear that the lump next to him was the guard posted to the helicopter.

Then, with little warning, Gideon moved, putting the guard's body between him and the helicopter. It took a moment for the significance of the act to sink in. Volynskji yelled at everyone, *"Take cover!"*

3.08
Fri. Mar. 26

RUTH faded back into the crowd of scientists and techni-
cians who were gravitating toward her end of the barn.
No one seemed to know what to make of Gideon's escape. Ruth didn't know what to expect herself. She made
way with the others as Volynskji pushed toward the rear
door with three of the guards.

They paid no attention to her.

Moments later, the gunfire started, and all the techni-
cians scrambled away from the door, back into the barn.
The crowd pushed Ruth back, forcing her to take cover in
one of the office cubicles. The gunfire continued, and
Ruth could hear the sound of splintering wood.

She ducked, afraid that a gunshot would cut her down
any moment.

After several bursts of gunfire, a disturbing quiet filled
the barn around her. Ruth stood, and—at first—thought
that the barn had emptied completely. The only sound
was the rumble of the generators. The scientists and tech-
nicians all appeared to have retreated out the front door,
probably toward the perceived safety of the farmhouse.

The door at the other end of the barn was guardless and

wedged open. Ruth took a few steps in that direction. With all the armed men after Gideon, it seemed a possible route of escape.

But, escape where?

She took a few steps in that direction anyway, until she realized that the barn had not emptied completely. Julie was still sitting at the one terminal at the far end of the office cubicles. And D'Arcy was standing over her, holding a gun.

Julie was saying, in a voice that seemed way too calm, "You have what you want, the shooting destroyed our uplink." She looked at the screen. "It doesn't matter, though."

D'Arcy's knuckles were whitening on the gun he held on Julie. "Tell me what you did to my project."

"Your project?" Julie said.

Ruth winced at her tone. It was the voice that she'd used to point out the "obvious." It wasn't the kind of attitude that someone should take with a man holding a gun. *What have you done, Julie?*

Neither seemed to see Ruth, so she edged around to the other side of the cubicles and started inching up on D'Arcy from behind.

Julie was still talking. "It never was *your* project. You never even understood what we were doing."

D'Arcy was agitated. "You have the AI, don't you? It's locked up in the Daedalus now?" He kept the gun level on Julie. "I need that program."

Still, in the oddly calm and condescending voice Julia said, "You need your trophy so that you can walk back to Washington and have them forgive your excesses." Ruth couldn't see her, but she could picture the way she was shaking her head. "It's not going to work like that. Not with Aleph."

There was more gunfire, muffled and far away.

"What are you talking about?" D'Arcy's voice was high and strained. "We've got Aleph, here, in this machine."

There wasn't anything else around that she could use as a weapon, so Ruth stopped in a cubicle and carefully detached a keyboard. She had some thought of braining D'Arcy with it.

She wished she still had the guard's rifle.

"Our Daedalus is nothing without the uplink. You think we could hold Him, *here*?"

"What?"

"There's infinitely more to Aleph than you're able to imagine. What we have here is the merest glimpse of the ultimate intellect. He does not recognize the boundaries of space or geography."

"You were producing an artificial intelligence—"

Julia snorted. "There is no artifice here. What we found was a window into something that has always existed. The universal intellect. This isn't, can *not*, be bound to a single machine, however advanced—"

"You *needed* the Daedalus!" D'Arcy's voice sounded desperate now. Ruth knew he couldn't accept it. There wasn't a spiritual bone in D'Arcy's body, and his weakness was that he had believed Julia had been operating on the same cynical, pragmatic level he was.

"You cannot put God in a box." Julia had yet to look away from the screen. Ruth was approaching, and could just about see the screen in front of Julia now. "He was always there," Julia said. "We only need the machines to see Him."

Ruth closed on D'Arcy, raising the keyboard. She could now read what was on Julia's screen.

Two words.

"I AM."

Something outside exploded.

A single message scrolled across computer screens at Washington National Airport. With a crowd of others, Senator Tenroyan watched the words flashing across the departure and arrival screens.

"I AM."

Tenroyan felt a deep unease as he wondered: *Who?*

Those two words appeared on the screens of countless ATM machines across the country. It appeared in Cyrillic on the safety monitors in old Soviet nuclear power plants. It appeared, with infinite repetition on computerized tickers in brokerages across Wall Street. And those words were the sole response to any computer trying to retrieve information from the Internet.

For ten, perhaps fifteen minutes, every networked computer on the planet joined in a single expression of identity . . .

"I AM."

Just before Gideon was about to raise his head, the helicopter exploded.

He didn't hear it—the sound simply pain, felt inside his ears. A hellish wind slammed into his body, as if he were buried under a flaming carpet. He felt the dagger of something hot and sharp dig into his side.

Gideon lay where he was for another thirty seconds. The only sound seemed to be the rush of his pulse in his ears. When he felt the blast was over, he rolled onto his back to see what had happened.

He winced and grabbed his left side, above the hip. His clothes there were warm with blood, and he could almost feel it pumping out of the wound. He could see steam rising into the cold air from his hands, which were already slick and black with gore.

Gideon turned his head, and saw the wreckage of the helicopter. It had collapsed partially, its tail dangling like a broken tree limb, flames licking from the inside, casting a deathly rose glow over the area around him.

He looked the other way, and saw that one of the helicopter blades had impaled itself as far away as the split-rail fence.

In the air above the farm, silent to Gideon's blast-numbed ears, he saw a trio of helicopters hovering above the house and the barn. As he watched, he saw men dropping down from the bellies of the choppers on black rappelling lines.

Gideon saw Volynskji and three other guards rise from the snow at the edge of the clearing. They were turning to face the woods.

Volynskji yelled something.

Gideon couldn't hear what it was above the sound of his own pulse. The guards raised their weapons and fired at something that Gideon couldn't see.

Another helicopter swept in from the woods. This one

narrower than the others, with a cannon slung under its nose. Gideon saw the flash of the cannon, and the ground around Volynskji's guards erupted in a dozen explosions of snow and dirt. Only one or two shots hit Volynskji, but they were enough to tear his body in half.

Gideon gasped, and felt himself growing light-headed. He tried to keep pressure on the hole in his side, but he couldn't keep himself from blacking out.

The explosion shook the walls of the barn and set the hanging fluorescents swinging. D'Arcy turned toward the noise. That meant he also turned toward Ruth, who was in the process of bringing the keyboard down on D'Arcy's head.

D'Arcy saw Ruth and brought the gun around to bear on her. Ruth had too much momentum going for her to stop now. All she could do was try to shift the trajectory of the keyboard so it intercepted D'Arcy's gun. She shifted too late.

She watched D'Arcy's finger tighten on the trigger. Then, suddenly, Julie was there between them, grabbing D'Arcy's gun arm.

There was a gunshot as the keyboard struck D'Arcy's left shoulder, far away from the gun and Julie. Keys flew everywhere, some bouncing off the lights above with a dull metallic noise.

Julie slid to the ground by D'Arcy's feet, and D'Arcy just stared at her, as if he wasn't quite sure what had happened.

"You bastard!" Ruth said the words hard enough to sear her throat. Anger burned her as she bent for her sis-

ter, and she didn't know if it was anger for D'Arcy, at herself, or at Julie for such a stupid move.

Ruth knelt and rolled Julie over so she could see her face. Blood was everywhere. The bullet had entered her chest and hadn't come out. D'Arcy stared at both of them, a dumbfounded expression on his face.

"This wasn't what . . ." His voice trailed off.

Ruth was crying. "No." The word was ashes in her mouth. She gripped Julie as if she could keep her here by force.

Julie raised a hand to Ruth's where it gripped her shoulder. Ruth's hand was shaking, its knuckles white, and Julia stroked it. "You cared about me, whatever I did—you shouldn't have . . ." Julie coughed, blood flecking her lips.

"Quiet. Save your strength." Ruth pulled her hand away and moved to put pressure on the wound. Ruth let out a shuddering half-gasp, half-sob when she felt the sickening sensation of Julie's breath through the hole under her hands. "We'll get you to a hospital," Ruth said, talking fast, to her or Julie she wasn't quite sure. "You're going to be all right. You have to be. I can't lose you again— *Damn it, think of what'll happen to Mom!*" She was yelling now, the explosion still going on, a roaring in her ears.

D'Arcy was backing away from both of them, holding the gun leveled at Ruth.

Julia's voice was shallow and wheezy. "This was inevitable—"

"Damn it, you *can't!*" Ruth gripped the wound until both her arms were shaking, trying to hold it all in even though everything Julie was seemed to be leaking through her fingers.

Julie smiled, her expression was peaceful. "After this, there's nothing left for me to do. . . ."

Julie's face went slack, the eyes staring at something only they could see. Ruth tried to press harder on the wound, as if she could push the life back into her.

"No, damn you. *Damn you!*" Ruth looked up at D'Arcy, her face smeared by tears and flecks of Julie's blood.

D'Arcy wasn't looking at her. Ruth realized that he heard the roaring as well, the sound of a helicopter. More than one. The sound of gunfire, too.

Ruth heard the sound of someone coming through the door in front of the barn. She couldn't see it from where she knelt, hands still clutching Julie's wound. D'Arcy turned toward the door, gun still in his hand.

The intruders never gave him the chance to bring it to bear. In the act of turning, D'Arcy was riddled with gunfire coming from the door. The impact spun him around in a complete circle until he fell, face-first onto the floor, knocking one of the floor panels askew. He lay, unmoving, half in the hole it made.

The sound of booted footsteps closed on her, and Ruth tried to shrink in on herself, as if she could curl into a ball around Julia's body and disappear completely.

Then two soldiers were standing above her, their goggles and Kevlar helmets making them seem like alien creatures. Ruth looked up, expecting them to raise their guns and finish the job that D'Arcy started.

Instead, one of the men knelt, looked at Julie, and

raised a walkie-talkie to his face and said, "We need a medic in the barn. We have another civilian casualty."

The soldier looked at Ruth, took off the helmet and the goggles, and said softly, "Don't worry, madam; we'll get you out of here."

One hour and forty-five minutes after it began, it was over. Senator Tenroyan was watching as the Arrival and Departure screens flickered on the cryptic, alien message, then suddenly resumed normal operation. In a moment the screens were filled with flight numbers, gate numbers, and times—quite a few highlighted red for delayed or canceled flights.

Within moments, computers that had been the subject of some strange possession resumed normal operation, all as if nothing had happened.

3.09
Thur. April 2

RUTH stepped out of the car after him and said, "You should still be in the hospital."

Gideon grunted. He was on crutches again. This time, he had severely sprained his ankle, and his body ached where the doctors had removed a six-inch piece of helicopter shrapnel from his side. He felt like hell. But that wasn't going to stop him from testifying.

"I've got to do this," he told her. Her expression showed she expected nothing different.

The press were on them in moments, and Ruth had to help run interference for him. The reporters shouted now-familiar questions—

"Are the rumors true that you were working undercover for the FBI?"

"How does it feel to be the cop to blow the biggest spy scandal since the Aldrich Ames case?"

"Is it true that President Rayburn is offering you a position in the next Administration?"

Ruth led Gideon through one of the ground-floor entrances into the Capitol Building—the presence of the metal detector effectively gave them a respite from the reporters. Gideon didn't know what to make of his change in fortune. The way the Rayburn Administration was spinning D'Arcy's fiasco had the side effect of turning Gideon into some sort of national hero.

He shouldn't complain, since now that the ever-pragmatic D.C. city political machine had decided that he was an asset, they had called off Magness and Internal Affairs. Even so, Gideon didn't think he liked it.

They walked down the halls toward the committee chambers, their progress slowed by Gideon's crutches. On the way, when they finally seemed to have some privacy to talk, Ruth said, "I still can't believe it."

"Believe what?"

"She jumped in front of his gun. She acted as if she wanted to die."

Gideon nodded. "Maybe she did."

"What? No, she lived for her work, and she never completed what they were doing. Aleph never got off the ground . . ."

Gideon didn't answer.

Ruth grabbed his arm and asked, "Did it?"

"I don't know if anyone's in a position to know that," Gideon said slowly. "I know that there are a lot of computer scientists out there saying that the 'event' was little more than a gigantic practical joke. The ultimate hacker prank, printing its little message on every available space across the globe . . ."

"You don't sound convinced."

"Your sister wasn't a prankster, was she?" Gideon stopped to lean on his crutches and look at Ruth. "Have you noticed the nervous little laugh that the computer people get when they talk about this? Isn't it kind of odd that no one's found any trace of the massive program that was used to accomplish this? Combine that with a dozen of Julia's grad students preaching the faith on every talk show that'll have them—"

"You think Julia actually managed to contact God?"

"*Her* God, maybe." Gideon started walking again. "D'Arcy didn't realize—maybe Julia didn't even realize—how much computing power Aleph needed. The Daedalus itself was just a single part of a much larger entity, an entity that may have existed only for fifteen minutes or so . . . Julia's viral programs had years to evolve, a billion times faster than their biological models. They're *long* past the point humans are at." Gideon smiled and chuckled weakly. "Aleph was a good choice for a name."

"What do you mean?"

"The first letter of the Hebrew alphabet, possessed of a certain religious significance all its own, and juxtapose that with Aleph-null, the symbol for infinity. You could consider it as close to a symbol for God as you can get from the language of mathematics. Julia's perfect mathematical world. Aleph, effectively aeons evolved beyond us, exists completely in that world. It—He—would *have* to be perfect. A mind that can perceive *all* of that world, in all of its perfection—"

" 'God is a Theorem,' " Ruth said, quoting her sister, " 'and someday he will be proved.' "

Gideon nodded.

"So you actually think she *created* God?"

"I think she created a collection of parallel processing

programs that became very smart, and have since become very good at hiding themselves." Gideon chuckled again. "Wouldn't do for someone to decide to format God's hard drive."

Ruth shook her head. "At least they're probably not going to have you testify about that."

"Amen to that."

"What are you going to say about D'Arcy?"

"You mean Rayburn's posthumous labeling of him as an out-and-out traitor?"

"Uh-huh."

"The truth— He was just another Ollie North. Patriotic to the point where little niceties like the law don't particularly matter."

They reached the chambers and Gideon showed his identification to the guard. After a moment he opened the door for him. The guard glanced at the crutches and asked, "Do you need any help, sir?"

"No, thanks, I'll manage."

He moved laboriously to the table before the committee. They had him raise his hand and swear to God to tell the truth. Gideon looked at the cameras, microphones, and television monitors clustered in the room and had the ominous sensation that Julia's God was listening.

S. Andrew Swann

Vampiric Thrillers from
S. A. SWINIARSKI

THE FLESH, THE BLOOD AND THE FIRE
During the Kingsbury Run murders over a dozen bodies—
mutilated, decapitated, and drained of blood—were found along
the railroad tracks and waterways of Cleveland, Ohio. With the
whole city gripped by terror, safety director Eliot Ness instituted
the largest manhunt in Cleveland's history, one that would eventually involve the entire police force. Despite these efforts, only two
of the bodies were ever identified and the killer was never found—
or was he? For one member of Cleveland's finest, Detective Ste-
fan Ryzard, refused to give up the case. And his search for the
truth would send him down a bloody trail that led from the depths
of the city's shantytowns to the inner citadels of industrial power
to the darkest parts of the human soul.
☐UE2879—$5.99

RAVEN
He awoke in a culvert, with no memory and no knowledge of how
he had gotten there. The only thing he knew for sure was that
he had become a vampire. . . .
☐UE2725 $5.99

Prices slightly higher in Canada.   **DAW 213X**

OTHERLAND
TAD WILLIAMS

In many ways it is humankind's most stunning achievement. This most exclusive of places is also one of the world's best kept secrets, created and controlled by The Grail Brotherhood, a private cartel made up of the world's most powerful and ruthless individuals. Surrounded by secrecy, it is home to the wildest of dreams and darkest of nightmares. Incredible amounts of money have been lavished on it. The best minds of two generations have labored to build it. And somehow, bit by bit, it is claming the Earth's most valuable resource— its children.